YOU DON'T KNOW ME

SARA FOSTER

Legend Press Ltd, 51 Gower Street, London, WC1E 6HJ
info@legendpress.co.uk | www.legendpress.co.uk

First printed in Australia in 2019 by Simon & Schuster (Australia) Pty
Limited, Suite 19A, Level 1, Building C, 450 Miller Street, Cammeray,
NSW 2062 | www.simonandschuster.com.au

Print ISBN 978-1-78955-9-774
Ebook ISBN 978-1-78955-9-767
Set in Times. Printing Managed by Jellyfish Solutions Ltd
Cover design by Rose Cooper | www.rosecooper.com

SARA FOSTER is the bestselling author of six psychological suspense novels. Born and raised in the UK, Sara worked for a time in the HarperCollins fiction department in London, before going freelance as an editor.

Sara's novel *The Hidden Hours* was shortlisted for a Davitt Award in 2018 and was No. 56 in Better Reading's Top 100 books for 2017. It is currently being developed for television by CJZ and will be published by Legend Press in 2020.

Sara lives with her husband and young daughters in Perth, Western Australia. She is a Doctoral candidate at Curtin University, studying Young Adult dystopian fiction.

Visit Sara
www.sarafoster.com.au
Follow her
@SaraJFoster

For Matt
whose gift is
to know me
and to love me
as I am

Prologue

'Lizzie?'

The search parties move through the forest shortly after dawn, flashes of neon jackets among the trees, the slumbering air stirring towards an early morning chill. They call her name again and again, then wait, hoping for something in return. But the only response is the agitated shrieks of parrots and the occasional rustle of panicked creatures in the undergrowth.

Again their voices echo.

'Lizzie?'

'Lizzie?'

'Lizzie?'

Nearby on the main road, close to the spot she was last seen almost thirty hours ago, more police and emergency workers poke about in the bushland. Rumours are already flying and it's hard to pluck the facts from them, but some snippets recur. She'd argued with her boyfriend at a party. He'd gone home without her. She'd followed him and they'd had another fight on his doorstep, around midnight. Then she ran off into the wet, cold night.

There was one possible sighting of her, reported only hours ago, after the first evening appeal for witnesses. Lizzie had been walking along the road near the place they now searched, hunched over in the rain, skirting the national park as she headed in the direction of home. But she'd never arrived. No one had seen her since.

Day after day they keep searching, calling out Lizzie's name, never hearing an answer. Birds and possums repeatedly pull apart the roadside posters that beg for information with the lure of a ten thousand dollar reward. The bouquets of flowers left at the nearest layby become raggedy, colonised by ants, ravaged by the wind, stems and petals peeling away from the bunch one after another, each finding their own nooks in which to settle, wilt and wither.

The weeks turn to months, and by the time the year clicks over into 2007, most people have returned to their lives. Only a few stooped figures are left to cover the same ground again and again, their futile hope the one thing keeping them sane. Yet, eventually, they too relinquish the search. The future will not indulge stragglers, it gathers them in and charges on.

The forest resettles, the searchers now spectres of another time, just like the missing girl herself. And yet, on that very first day, if anyone had known, they could have walked into the undergrowth to a ragged bloodwood tree, dug a fingernail into the peeling bark, and plucked out a single red strand of Lizzie Burdett's hair.

1

Twelve years later

The morning is hot and humid, but the instant he sees her, Noah goes cold. She is standing on the deck of a packed river taxi in a bright, flowing dress, facing away from him as she stares out across the murky water of the Chao Phraya River.

His breath catches and his heart stills, the next belated beat slamming hard against his ribs. There's an orange flag on the roof of the ferry, and Noah realises it's the boat he's been waiting for, but he's stuck behind the crowds on the jetty. Undeterred, he begins pushing past people, suddenly desperate to get on board. He leaps from the wooden platform only seconds before the vessel leaves the dock, earning himself a stern rebuke in rapid Thai from the wiry man gathering the mooring ropes, whose glowing cigarette is tucked temporarily behind his ear.

Noah mumbles an apology over his shoulder, looking for a spot by the railing, moving closer to the woman. The shock of her resonates, shaking him harder than the rocking boat as it begins to negotiate the heavy river traffic. Her long red hair has brought Lizzie to life again, letting him briefly imagine he has found her, thousands of kilometres from home. Then his senses kick in. This woman's face has a different shape:

her eyes more oval than almond, her lips fuller and her skin freckled.

Nevertheless, his heart is still pounding.

Twelve years ago, Noah had thought that Lizzie Burdett was the most glorious thing to ever happen to his family, but she'd proved to be a wrecking ball. She had been in their lives for six short months, and then, without warning, she wasn't – at least not in the same way. Her face still smiled out from the missing person posters, and sometimes made it onto the evening news. Her name was whispered along school corridors on a continual loop, or so it seemed to Noah, because he was the boyfriend's younger brother and therefore immediately connected to Lizzie's disappearance. Since then, Lizzie had become the nightmare Noah couldn't fully explain to anyone, and the pull of his memories has intensified lately, now her name is in the news again.

He turns his attention back to the woman on the boat. Her hands lightly grip the rail, as her gaze falls on the semi-clothed kids playing at the edge of the muddy riverbank. He'd guess she's a few years younger than him – early to mid-twenties, maybe – but there's a rare air of self-containment about her. Even when passengers jostle her, they capture her attention for only a moment before she settles back into daydreamy stillness, as though she nurtures a secret that's hers alone. The din of hectic conversations coalesce into a background hum as Noah studies her, drawn to her poise, curious as to where her mind might be travelling. But then, as though sensing his gaze, she turns.

There is no chance to pretend to look elsewhere. He stills. She stares. Then her lips curve into a small smile, and there's a flash of curiosity in her eyes. It only lasts a second before she turns away, and Noah lets out a slow breath.

She is stunning.

He forces himself to focus elsewhere – anywhere. He studies a seated row of shaven-headed monks cloistered in mustard robes, and eavesdrops on the bickering Canadian couple behind him, allowing himself the occasional sidelong glance at the mysterious redhead. She is looking across the river now, and his gaze follows hers to the golden temple stupas that gleam in sharp contrast to dirty white office blocks. Then the boat knocks against the pier of Tha Tien, his stop, and he turns away, still reeling, pressing into the swaying throng to get onto the boardwalk.

Once on land, he moves to one side to study the map in his guidebook. When he looks up and begins to walk in what he hopes is the right direction, the woman is there again, striding confidently some distance ahead of him. He's buoyed by the idea they might be heading to the same place, but only has a brief moment to admire the shape of her, the swing of her hips, before he loses sight of her at the entrance to Wat Pho as the crowds deepen.

He joins the back of one of the lines for tickets. The queue edges forward, and he waits patiently, until a polite voice interrupts.

'Excuse me, mister, what's your name?'

He turns to find a young Thai man with a wispy moustache beaming at him. 'Noah.'

'I am David,' the man says with a small bow of the head. 'I am guide at this temple, I can show you best places, very private tour just for you. I will tell you about history of temple, reclining Buddha, symbols of Buddhism...'

'That's okay, I'm not—'

'Only two hundred baht, includes entrance, very cheap, special tour for you. You want massage too? Massage three hundred baht. Pay at the end. Come with me.'

David propels him by the elbow, hustling past the queue for the entrance, answering in hurried Thai as people complain. They are waved on after a brief exchange at the ticket desk.

'Reclining Buddha first,' David beckons Noah forward, 'this way, this way.'

Noah follows him across the flagstone courtyard, weaving between tourists as he tries to focus on David's monologue.

Once inside the long, intricately decorated room, David begins to point out scenes from the *Ramakien*.

But Noah isn't listening, because there is the redhead again, walking slowly beside the reclining golden Buddha, her hand trailing along the wooden railing that separates the statue from the masses. As the aroma of incense hits him in a heady, perfumed wave, he's gripped by a compulsion to speak to her. The feeling is ill-formed and potentially disastrous, and yet he finds himself taking a few steps forward, trying to decide on an opening line. He's almost reached her when David taps him on the shoulder, beginning a well-rehearsed speech about the 108 auspicious signs of Buddhism inlaid into the mother of pearl on the Buddha's feet. The woman turns, startled by the sound of David's voice so close, and meets Noah's eye again. She arches one eyebrow and her smile broadens. He grins back like an idiot, but before he can speak there is a meaty hand on his forearm and an iPhone shoved into his face.

'Hey, buddy,' says a man with a strident drawl, 'can you take a picture of me and my wife?'

'Sure,' Noah replies, taking the phone. He has to wait while they fuss about where to stand, determined to get the best view of the Buddha in the background. But by the time he hands the phone back, the woman has disappeared again.

He hurries outside, barely registering the resurgence of warm air, dismayed to discover he can't see her anywhere. David appears beside him. 'Now I will show you Bodhi tree that is descended from the very tree under which Buddha sat to attain enlightenment.'

Noah quickly finds his wallet. 'Here,' he says, handing over two hundred baht. 'I have to go now, but thank you.' And he strides away before David can reply.

The trickle of tourists in the temple complex is rapidly becoming a stream. Noah gets lost among them for a while, his mind adrift from his surroundings, until he realises he's heading for the exit gates. Not yet ready to leave, he turns abruptly, and crashes straight into the person behind him.

His reflexes are quick, but he's too late. The impact sends an expensive-looking camera crashing to the ground, lens first, with a sickening crunch.

Horrified, he squats down to pick up the broken pieces, aware of another person doing the same. As he looks up to apologise, he sees it's *her*.

Their eyes lock, and he puts a hand to the ground to steady himself. Her face is just centimetres from his, her cheeks rising in colour. Those green eyes with their tiny golden flecks are mesmerising – but now they are the colour of questions, the shape of dismay. *Oh god, what has he done?*

Noah's face burns. 'Here, let me help you. I'm really sorry.'

She stands up and he does the same. A few witnesses to the incident have slowed to watch them.

'It's okay. I should look where I'm going.' Her voice is quiet and soulful, but she glances away as she speaks.

'No, it was my fault,' he insists. 'I should replace it for you.'

'You don't have to do that. It's an expensive lens.'

'Is it insured?'

Her expression is his answer.

'Then I should fix it.'

She seems to consider him. The pause stretches.

He tries again. 'If you let me take the lens, I promise I'll get it replaced for you today. I can bring it to your hotel, if you like, or you can come to mine?'

She shakes her head. 'I don't live in a hotel. I could come to yours, though – if you're really sure... I mean, I know it was just an accident...'

'It's all right, leave it with me.' He smiles in encouragement. 'Can you meet me tonight at the Royal Orchid? It's right on the river – do you know it? About eight o'clock?'

She nods, and then her face finally breaks into a radiant smile. 'All right then. Thank you! You were on the river taxi, weren't you?'

Noah's heart soars. 'I was.' He holds out his hand. 'So can I take the lens?'

'Okay – well, if you're sure.' She turns her attention to unscrewing the lens from the camera body, and hands it over. As their fingers touch, a rush of heat surges through Noah.

'Thank you,' she says again, as she tucks the body of the camera into her bag. 'I'm Alice, by the way.'

'Noah.' He straightens, offers his hand, and she takes it. Once again, he is ambushed by a fierce heat that threatens to reach his face and embarrass him. 'Nice to meet you, Alice. See you later.'

He turns away and heads out of the gates without looking back, marching up to the first tuk tuk driver he sees. 'I need to find a camera shop.' He points at the lens in his hand in case the man doesn't speak English. The driver gives a thumbs-up, gesturing for Noah to climb inside. As the little vehicle edges into the traffic Noah clutches the damaged equipment tightly, trying not to notice that his hands are shaking.

A few hours later, as the setting sun burns its fiery gold onto buildings and river, Noah turns away from the expansive view and stares at himself in the mirror. He's decided to dress up, in the hopes he can persuade Alice to have dinner with him. He can't stop thinking about her, and each time he remembers her face, so close to his own, his body responds, wanting more.

He solemnly regards his own dark, troubled eyes. *Are you sure about this, Noah?*

No, he isn't. The timing sucks. Perhaps the less he overthinks this, the better. He showers quickly, and as he pulls on his jeans he catches sight of the silvery scar that runs down the top of his right thigh, ending in a point like an icicle. He dares to wonder if Alice will ever see it – and how he will explain it if she does. Will he fob her off with a biking accident, as he had done with other lovers? Or will he admit it's a permanent reminder of his recklessness? That he can never look at it without thinking of another girl, whose face still haunts him.

He knows he's getting way ahead of himself. First things first: he needs to hope she turns up. If she doesn't, it's going to be tough to find a woman called Alice with long, red hair, who resides somewhere other than a hotel in Bangkok. Because that's all he knows about her.

He heads for the lobby at ten to eight, palms sweating, the bag containing the prized lens dangling from his fingers. As he counts down to the hour, he convinces himself she won't come, but she walks in right on time, dressed so differently that he almost doesn't recognise her: lips ruby red, her hair pulled back in a loose braid. A fitted black shirt and cropped jeans skim her curves all the way down to a pair of sequinned sandals with low heels. As she glances around, searching for him, he's unbalanced again by the overpowering pull of her.

As soon as she sees him, her face lights up, and her eyes drift to the bag in his hands. 'I can't believe you did this for me,' she says as he offers it to her.

'It's no problem.' He fleetingly thinks of the rapid increase on his credit card that afternoon. Every cent was worth it to see her looking at him like this.

He hesitates, but Alice is beginning to glance around. He has to speak now, or he might never get another chance.

'Do you – are you doing anything tonight?' Shit, he can barely get the words out. He's a stuttering fool. 'Would you like to grab some dinner?'

She looks uneasy. 'Actually, I have plans –'

He makes sure his smile stays firm, but inwardly he resigns himself, bracing for rejection.

'– Although... I don't think my friends would mind if I brought you with me. Do you want to come to a house party?'

'Okay.' He tries his best to sound nonchalant, even though he would have dressed up in a tutu and gone ballet dancing if it meant more time with her.

'It's not too far to walk – are you ready now?'

He smiles. 'Sure – let's go.'

He's a step behind her as they exit the grand lobby of the Royal Orchid and set off along the busy night streets of Bangkok, among the throngs of people that meander between steaming food stalls and the haphazard lights of restaurants. Stray cats with docked tails doze on the boxes and mats beside shopfronts, and cockroaches skitter along the pavement beneath stalls selling fried insects. Smells come in alternating waves of barbecued meat and raw sewage. Alice isn't distracted by any of this, and he notices her confident sense of direction.

'Do you live here?' he ventures. 'You don't seem like you're on holiday.'

'Yes, I teach English,' she replies, eyes on the road as they hurry across it and into a narrow alley, skirting around motorcyclists and pedestrians. A few stray dogs hide along the recesses of the walls, diving out to collect food scraps discarded by the street vendors. Noah quickens his pace to keep up.

'Really? Have you been here long?'

'It's a six-month stint. I'm halfway through. So what about you? Are you here with anyone?'

'No – I was meant to be coming with my mate, Jez, but he broke his leg the day before our flight. I went up north for a week, to Chiang Mai and Chiang Rai, saw the hill tribes, then got the train to Ayutthaya and Kanchanaburi. I've only been in Bangkok for a couple of days, so I'm still finding my way around.'

'Are you missing your friend?'

'Yeah, a bit, but I'm used to it now. It's been good having time on my own.'

He stops short of mentioning his other reasons for coming. In truth, he'd been about to cancel the holiday, when he'd received news that his brother was about to make his first visit home in eleven years. Whenever Noah thought of Tom, he thought of Lizzie, and the world darkened. So the prospect of being on another continent, thereby avoiding a run-in, had been irresistible.

Alice interrupts his thoughts. 'So whereabouts in Oz are you from?'

'Sydney – the Northern Beaches. And you?'

'A little place on the Central Coast.'

His spirits lift as he realises their homes are only a few hours apart. As their arms brush against one another, the feeling intensifies. He's aware of people watching them: the admiring glances thrown Alice's way, the envious looks at Noah. He briefly imagines them as a couple; thinks of holding her hand, pulling her close. Feels a charge of excitement. Tells himself to get a grip.

The conversation falters. Discomfort hovers in the silence.

Noah is searching desperately for something interesting to say, when a soccer ball comes flying towards them out of nowhere, heading straight for Alice. He moves in front of her at the last moment, but too late to catch it, so it smacks into his shoulder. Alice almost trips over him, clutching his arm to stop herself from falling.

'Bloody hell,' she says, 'I didn't see that at all. Are you okay?'

'Fine.' He rubs at the sore spot, laughing it off.

She doesn't let go of his arm. Her touch burns through his shirt, and without thinking, he stops laughing, putting his hand over hers.

'Sorry, mister!' A worried Thai boy comes running over, hands held aloft.

The moment breaks.

Alice blinks, and steps back.

Noah grabs the ball and kicks it, inserting himself into the soccer game so he can pretend this is the reason his heart's racing. Soon he's laughing again, caught up in the joy of messing around with a ball. He hasn't played properly for years. Why hasn't he, when he loves this game?

He shrugs off the uneasy question. Luckily, he still knows

a few fancy tricks and manages to show most of them off in about ninety seconds, much to the delight of the kids. And of course he knows Alice is watching too.

Afterwards he waves at the boys then walks back over to Alice, beaming.

'Impressive!' She raises an eyebrow, smiling back at him. 'You play football at home?'

'I used to,' Noah says, rubbing his chest as he catches his breath.

'Come on then.' She gestures in front of them. 'It's this way.'

Noah follows, but the word *home* has triggered a chain of unsettling thoughts. He's trapped by a flash of another smiling face, lips thinner, eyes narrower, but disconcertingly similar in other ways. He pushes the image away, trying to force his mind back to the present.

He's grown good at denial.

At letting certain secrets smoulder.

But something about Alice is setting everything alight.

2

What are you doing*, Alice?*

Alice has been asking herself the same question over and over since she'd invited Noah along. It goes entirely against the vow she'd made about coming to Thailand: No distractions or complications. It is supposed to be essential alone time, to heal her wounds and find her own direction. And yet, here she is, with this tall, tanned stranger, whose deep, gentle voice is setting off a whole chorus of excitement inside her. Whose body occasionally brushes against hers as they walk, leaving behind patches of tingling, lingering warmth.

And the way he looks at her. As though he knows her. Really *knows*. Right from the first time she saw him, on the boat, when she had found herself smiling back, thinking that they must have already met somewhere, because of the solid recognition in his eyes.

It's unnerving. But exciting, too. *Calm down*, she chides herself as they near their destination. It's no use. Her mind races and her breaths come short and shallow. She wishes she'd thought of something else for them to do, because she suddenly wants him all to herself, to find out more about him. But it's too late now, they're almost there.

She sees Noah's curiosity growing as they arrive at a gated double-storey house in one of the little Thai laneways known as *sois*. Music is already blaring. 'Have you ever been to a

Thai house party?' she asks, and Noah shakes his head just before Niran's sixteen-year-old daughter Hom and her friends come rushing out, talking rapidly in high-pitched melody, grabbing them and pulling them inside.

These Fridays have become the highlights of Alice's week. Niran invites all the expat teachers at the language academy, but so far no one else has taken up the offer. They're missing out, because Niran's wife Bussaba always cooks up a storm in the kitchen and lays on a feast for family and friends. There are piled-up platters of pad thai and colourful curries of meat and fish beside bowls of steaming, gleaming white rice. The food smells divine and tastes even better.

Alice has shown up for the past four weeks, and each time she enjoys herself a little more, although she suspects her long red hair is a bigger hit than she is. She has lost count of the number of Thai women and men who have run their fingers through it, exclaimed at it, made jokes about it. She tries not to tense at their touch, sensing they mean well. She doesn't often understand because her Thai is still basic, but some comments are obviously bawdy in tone. Yet, for all the teasing, their kindness is a living thing that weaves its way around her. For a few hours, she can pretend she is part of their family while relaxing in the anonymity the language barrier provides. It is so nice to feel accepted on face value. No one knows anything about her or the devastation she's fled from. Here she is just the English teacher, and no one needs to know any more than that.

Niran hurries to them, dressed in the open-necked shirt and chinos he always wears for work. 'Welcome, Alice!'

'Thanks, Niran. I've brought a friend – I hope that's okay. This is Noah.'

'Of course, welcome Noah—'

'Alice!' Niran's thirteen-year-old daughter, Kulap, interrupts, greeting them with a traditional *wai*, hands clasped together in a little bow. 'What did you bring this week?'

Alice laughs. 'Hi, Kulap.' She turns to Noah. 'I bring

something every week to add to the meal.' She pulls her backpack from her shoulder and takes out a small Tupperware box. 'Lamingtons,' she announces, handing the box over.

Niran and Kulap open the box and chatter excitedly when they see the coconut-covered pieces of cake. 'It looks – delicious!' Niran beams. 'Bussaba will be happy to see these.'

Alice turns to Noah. 'I brought Vegemite scrolls last week. It'll have to be pavlova next time. I'm running out of things to make.'

Noah laughs. 'Anzac biscuits?'

'Done that one.' She grins. 'Might have to be a parmi soon!'

Minutes later, they are seated opposite one another at a little table in the corner of a modest lounge, where a dozen seats of all shapes and sizes are crammed in a circle. Everyone pushes in tightly together so that their arms press against one another as they begin their meal.

As the conversation continues unceasingly all around them, Alice can't help but keep glancing at Noah. He is so tall and bulky that he has to hunch over to eat, and Bussaba keeps reloading his plate before he can finish, a mischievous glint to her eye. He compliments Bussaba on the food, and she nods and giggles, even though Alice suspects Bussaba's grasp of English is as bad as Noah's Thai. Now and again, he catches Alice's eye, and she can see he is enjoying himself. She holds his gaze, trying to stay calm, although each one of his glances sends hot sparks shooting through her and she has to take regular cooling sips of water. Again, that needling voice: *Why have you brought him here?* These months in Thailand are a vital step towards something, and even though she isn't sure what that is, she knows what she hadn't planned, and that's to meet a tall, good-looking man who reminds her of the pull of home.

Once the food is packed away, Niran and Bussaba's teenage children and their friends take turns finding music on the television, while they dance and joke around, giggling and flirting. Someone turns more lights off, and a cheap portable disco ball strobes away in one corner. As soon as the older generation disappear, Hom selects some tinny trance music and shimmies up to Noah. He begins to dance with her, his rhythm and enthusiasm making up for his obvious awkwardness at dancing with a girl half his size. Alice claps along, unexpectedly envious as Noah twirls Hom around. As though he can sense her thoughts, Noah glances across. His smile is broad but his gaze is intense. Conspiratorial.

Alice feels herself flush.

Then the song changes to some kind of Thai pop. Hom turns back to her friends and a lanky teenager lifts her onto his shoulders. Hom laughs and touches the ceiling as they bob up and down.

Noah heads straight for Alice and holds out his hand, smiling. She takes it. He pulls her close, wrapping his arms around her. They sway to imagined music, out of time with the pace of the blaring song. He is looking at her so intently that she can hardly breathe. At every point their bodies touch, heat pulses between them, building, intensifying, scorching. It's almost too much to bear, and Alice has a few seconds of discomfort in the low light. Her rational inner voice fights for control. *You are safe here*, it reminds her. *There's nothing to fear.*

She fends off the anxiety, not wanting to let go of Noah. She can't remember the last time she'd felt so comfortable in someone's arms. A high-pitched voice briefly grabs their attention. Bussaba is pushing through the group, annoyed, gesturing to the boy to let Hom down.

Noah turns back to Alice. Refocuses and pulls her closer. All her desires are reflected in his eyes. She can't believe this is happening so fast.

He leans towards her.

She tilts her head up to his.

But before their lips meet, Alice is knocked sideways. She falls hard, the back of her head ricocheting off something sharp and unforgiving with a cold crack.

The surroundings go hazy. For a moment she slips back in time, sees herself shocked and frightened in the semi-dark of her old lounge room. Has the briefest flash of a cruel, sneering face.

She refocuses to find Noah crouching over her, stroking her cheek. 'Alice? Alice?' His face is a brief zoetrope of alarm in the strobe light, but then the main lights come back on, and she winces.

'What happened?' Her hand moves to the back of her head. To her alarm, there's a lump, and it feels wet.

'Hom and her friend.' Noah grimaces. 'They fell onto you as he was trying to put her down.'

'I'm sorry. I'm sorry.' Hom crouches beside them, her eyes full of tears. 'You need an ambulance?'

'No, no,' Alice says, struggling to sit up. 'It's not that bad. Can someone just take me home?' A semicircle of worried people are forming around them. 'What does it look like?' she whispers to Noah.

He moves behind her and gently pushes her hand out of the way. 'It's swollen and there's a small cut, but nothing more. It was a nasty knock, though.' Noah strokes her arm briefly, then turns to Bussaba. 'Do you have a cloth and some ice?'

Niran translates quickly, his words terse and urgent. Bussaba rushes away, returning seconds later with a lace-edged linen cloth, tiny flower bursts sewn all over it.

'Oh no, not that,' Alice says, but Bussaba waves her concern away.

'S'okay, s'okay.'

Hom appears with a handful of ice and they wrap it inside the cloth and hand it to Alice.

Noah leans closer. 'Hold it on the wound. Don't worry, I'll get you home.'

'No, I can grab a taxi.' She tries to get up, but immediately sways, her vision filled with sparking swirls.

'Whoa there.' Noah catches her. 'Don't rush it.'

She sits back down again, listening to Noah asking Niran

about taxis, vaguely aware of a solemn discussion between a small group of men. She wants to insist she'll be okay, but her head is pounding. She tries to keep holding the ice against the wound but it hurts so much that she has to keep taking it away and tentatively putting it back again.

Noah briefly joins the conversation, then returns. 'They're going to take you in one of their cars. I'll come with you and make sure you're okay.'

She baulks for a moment, but registers only kindness in his concerned expression. 'Thanks,' she answers quietly.

'All right then.' He helps her to her feet. She tries to smile at all the worried faces, but it doesn't seem to have any effect.

There is already a car at the front of Niran's house. A man Alice vaguely recognises is behind the wheel. The destination has to be relayed through three people before the driver appears to understand where they are going, and as she slides into her seat, Alice prays he doesn't get mixed up. She just wants to get back to her apartment and lie down.

Noah climbs in beside her and they set off. Alice's head throbs and she's grateful Noah doesn't try to talk. Halfway through the journey she realises she is leaning against him, as though they are an old married couple with no boundaries left to cross. She is unsettled by the way her body yearns towards his, even as her head explodes with questions and warnings that gnaw at her alongside the sharper biting pain of her bruised skull.

When the car stops, Noah gets out first and comes around to her side to help. As she stands up a wave of queasiness overcomes her and she barely has time to turn away from him before she vomits on the pavement. The driver disappears in haste, leaving them alone in the middle of the night, standing next to a colourful splatter of Bussaba's half-digested food.

'Come on,' Noah says. 'Let me help you inside.'

Time goes strange for Alice. One moment they are on the pavement and the next they are in front of her door. She has no memory of telling Noah how to find her apartment, or of them getting there. A flash of panic makes her clutch at the doorjamb.

Noah takes hold of her arm. 'It's okay, I've got you. Is your key in your bag?'

'Yes.'

'Can I?'

She nods and leans on the door, trying to steady herself as he rifles through her bag for keys. She feels far away, like she is watching a movie scene and they are actors struggling to recall what happens next. As he opens the door another wave of nausea hits her, taking everything as it recedes, except the desire to lie down.

'Thanks,' she says, once they are inside. 'I think I just need to sleep now...'

Noah moves towards her then hesitates. 'You might be concussed.' His concern is clear. 'I don't like leaving you.'

She takes a few more steps towards her bedroom. 'Don't worry, I'll be okay.'

'Are you working tomorrow?'

'No, the school isn't open on Saturdays.'

'I'll come back then, to check on you.' He reaches out and gently touches her shoulder. 'You can call me at the hotel if you need to. Please. Ask for Noah Carruso.'

Alice closes her eyes at his touch, for longer than she means to. When she opens them again, all that remains are the ghosts of his fingertips, as the front door closes behind him. She stumbles towards her bed, not bothering to undress. Thankful she's alone now, and home safely. Yet her head keeps on throbbing, in a refrain she can't silence. The echo of his name.

3

Noah wakes mid-morning, still wearing his clothes from the previous night. Below his window, Bangkok is alive, cyclists and vendors and pedestrians and animals and riverboats all moving in a chaotic whirl.

But Noah is closed off from it all.

After last night, he'd thought – hoped – he might dream of Alice, but it was Lizzie who came to him. As soon as he woke, he forced the vision of her away, trying to remember every detail of Alice instead: the slimness of her wrists as she'd held her arms in the air and shimmied her hips; the smattering of freckles across her nose; the fullness of her lips; the shimmering light reflected in her green eyes. But whenever he closed his eyes, Lizzie intruded again: tears streaming down her cheeks; her hair wet from the rain. In the stark light of a new day, there's nowhere to hide from her. She makes him feel ashamed.

He jumps up to use the bathroom, and when he comes out again sees he has a text from his mum. His heart quickens as he opens it.

Call me.

She'd promised she wouldn't contact him again unless it was an emergency. Shit. Seconds later, he's listening to her phone ring.

When his mother answers, he can hear the quaver in her

voice. He imagines her at the other end of the line, her short platinum hair coiffured into neat waves, and one of those sumptuous multicoloured jellabiyas – the Egyptian garments she favoured as house wear – encasing her ample form.

'Hey, Mum, you okay?'

'Oh, thank god, Noah. I know I promised to leave you alone, but the inquest has been confirmed and I thought you'd want to know...'

Noah is lost for words. Phone tucked against his ear, he moves across to the window, staring at the synchronised weave of traffic and pedestrians. Ten floors down, lives clash and disconnect. Fates reformulate in an instant.

He rolls his shoulders. 'When?'

'In four weeks.'

'And what about Tom?'

'He's already been to see the lawyers. He'll be back for the inquest.'

Neither of them speaks for a moment. Then Noah says, 'Okay, then,' and releases a long breath.

He's glad she can't see him. He doesn't want to be inspected right now, in that silent way she has. With the look that makes an apology fly to his lips, even when he isn't sure what he's sorry for.

'The vultures are already circling,' his mother adds, and now her words are snipped and her tone is harder. Darker.

He doesn't have to ask what she means. An assortment of journalists have plagued their family over the years, turning up at both their old house and the new one, visiting the restaurant, somehow getting hold of their phone numbers and harassing them. They really want Noah's older brother, Tom, but any of them will do, and these stealth attacks leave the family gasping. The journos must think that if they squeeze hard enough, apply different pressure points, one of the family will eventually choke up some vital piece of information. Instead, it sends his mother to bed with another migraine, and his dad towards the wine cellar.

Noah doesn't want to think about any of this. 'Is everything okay at the restaurant?' he asks instead.

'Ah well, hang on, your father wants to talk to you.'

Noah immediately regrets the question. He braces himself.

There's a short pause, then a brusque voice says, 'The Marston invoices are missing, Noah.'

Noah stifles a sigh. 'They're not missing, Dad. They're already paid. I told you, I left everything organised – I ordered as much as I could ahead of time. Sophie is double-checking the bookings. There shouldn't be much extra to do.'

'You know there's always a last-minute rush with a wedding.' Raf pauses to clear his throat loudly. 'So when are you back?'

The question takes Noah by surprise. He's left itineraries at home and at the restaurant. He swallows down his first defensive reply, decides to stick to the question and avoid more antagonism. 'Two full days left here, then I'm home.'

'Okay. I'll get your mother again.'

'No, don't, there's someone at my door,' he fibs. 'Tell her I'll call her later. See you soon, Dad.' And he hangs up before Raf can say more.

He wishes he were still out of mobile range. There had been a few glorious days at the beginning of the holiday when he'd realised he was too remote to get reception. Five whole days without calls, emails, Facebook, Insta. To begin with he'd been twitchy, but then he began to look up more, look around. He had conversations with strangers, read a book he picked up from a café shelf, napped on journeys, and tuned in to small details: the geckos that flitted behind the light fittings every night; the patterns on the tablecloths at dinner; the gold teeth of his tour guides. He forgot to worry or hurry, until somewhere near Ayutthaya, when his phone began to work again, and there were seven texts from his dad, all related to the restaurant. All questions that could have waited until he got home. He had debated: should he respond and lose the sumptuous holiday feeling he'd spent all those days cultivating, or ignore his dad and feel like an arsehole? Since each of those seven short pings had already destroyed his newfound sense of freedom, he did what he always did: sighed, and replied.

He lies back on the bed, trying to absorb all that his mother had said. He should have asked more about how they were coping with the news. The inquest had been mooted for years, but now it was finally happening.

Which meant everyone would be talking about Lizzie Burdett.

How is he going to handle it, once he gets back home? Because it's still painful to recall himself at fifteen years old, with an excruciating crush and a permanent erection over his brother's girlfriend. Lizzie had been glorious: confident and sassy and the answer to everything a teenage boy was looking for. She wore a series of very short shorts paired with very low tops, and every inch of her was perfect. What's more, she'd been kind too. She never talked down to him. If she saw Noah doing his homework or jobs around the house, she stopped and helped. And she'd made a big difference to Tom's attitude towards Noah – which was a welcome relief, because Tom had spent most of his childhood tormenting his brother. For years there had been insects in his bed or stale food in his lunchbox or any number of other unpleasant surprises. And that was on top of the near daily physical assaults: bangs to the head, jabs to the stomach, unexpected punches that left him doubled up and writhing. He'd grown to anticipate it, and take steps to avoid it. Until Lizzie came along, and the daily torture began to subside.

Lizzie and Tom had seemed happy together. Noah hadn't known there were any problems until that final night, the last time he'd seen Lizzie alive. He'd been the only witness to Lizzie's anguish and his brother's vicious fury. And he was one of the first to feel the panic hours later, when Lizzie couldn't be found.

Even now, he still can't bear to relive it privately, never

mind talk about it. He dreads the thought of being subpoenaed. Surely no one would expect him to remember every little detail, twelve years after Lizzie vanished, when he'd been only a teenager at the time.

And yet, he does. That night is etched on his brain, and it doesn't matter whether he is in Thailand or Australia, he can't get away from it. Peter Bowles, the family lawyer, isn't sure he'll even be called as a witness – but what if he is? What if he's compelled to tell the court everything he knows?

Should he lie? In front of Lizzie's parents and her sisters? His own parents? Tom? Or should he tell the truth, and blow his world apart?

At the mere thought of testifying, Lizzie's deep brown eyes and gentle, knowing smile are back to haunt him again.

Noah jumps off the bed. Damn those eyes. Damn that smile. Today he needs to keep moving – to stay one step ahead of her, or else the panic will creep in again. Luckily he knows exactly what he wants to do.

By midday, Noah is wandering the aisles of a large supermarket. He selects an array of antipasto-style items, unsure of the local delicacies, hoping he's picked at least something that Alice might like.

He regrets leaving her looking so vulnerable, that horrible lump at the base of her skull. He should have insisted they go to hospital, but at her apartment they were strangers again, and she was entitled to make that choice.

As he waits in line to pay, he recalls the pivotal moments of the previous night. He'd been desperate to pull Alice closer as they danced, and the dreamy expression on her face had fuelled his confidence. One moment her focus was on him... the next, she was on the ground, and his chance had gone. Adrenalin courses through him as he replays the accident. If his senses had shifted from desire to danger a second sooner, he might have got her out of the way in time.

But today there's a chance to make amends. Back on the street, for a horrible moment he thinks he's forgotten where she lives. Then he remembers he'd tapped it into his phone as they left the party, in case he needed to remind the driver. He jumps into a taxi, legs jittering impatiently as they set off. He should write her a note, he decides, just in case she's gone out. He manages, through a series of hand gestures while they edge along in traffic, to get the taxi driver to lend him a pen. He finds a receipt in his wallet and writes on the back of it: *Hope you are feeling better today. Noah (Royal Orchid Hotel, Room 1014)*

As the taxi draws up to her building, he spots a dog licking the uneven footpath. Grimacing, he gets out and pays the driver, then finds the buzzer for number 12, presses it nervously, and waits.

And waits.

It's uncomfortable standing in the relentless afternoon sun, his palms sweating as he grips the plastic bag of food. He looks up at the window he thinks is hers. Is that a shadow there, or is he imagining it? He presses the buzzer again, but already it feels futile.

Sure enough, nothing happens.

She is probably fine, hanging out with her friends, telling them the story of the goofy guy she'd spent the previous night with; how a bang on the head had saved her from an awkward rejection. But on the other hand... he doesn't like to think of her lying there in trouble, with no one to help. He wishes he'd insisted on the hospital, just to be sure.

He tries the gate, but it's firmly locked. There's nothing more he can do for now, so he leaves the bag hanging on a railing, wondering how long it will take for the dog to pull it down and make himself a meal. He walks away, disturbed by the thought they might be over before they'd even begun.

It was bad timing anyway, says the ghost at his shoulder, dogging his footsteps. He tries not to listen. He's not ready to give up just yet.

4

Alice turns away from the window. She hadn't wanted to leave Noah standing outside like that – it felt rude and ungrateful – but she needs more time to think. Last night, the connection between them had been irresistible, overriding every rational thought, but today she's trying to reorient herself. His care and concern is lovely, but it's so sudden and overwhelming. *You're not ready for this*, she reminds herself sternly. *No complications, remember?*

She waits ten minutes, until she's sure he's gone, then retrieves the food. The bag is filled with thoughtful things – a small baguette, cheese, olives – and she finds the note, thoughts skittering as she reads it.

Call him, her heart urges. *He saw you safely home last night when you were hurt and afraid. Not to mention the new camera lens. Now, look at all this food. The least he deserves is a thank you.*

She spends the remainder of the day and night trying to distract herself. She studies her Thai phrasebook. She checks her lesson plans. She reads a few articles on a photography website, and watches late night comedians on YouTube. All of this does little other than extend her procrastination, because when she wakes the next morning, feeling much better, she immediately wants to thank him for his kindness.

As she grabs her phone and searches for the number of

the Royal Orchid, she begins to panic. If he's checked out already, that's it – there's no way of finding him. Why didn't she call yesterday?

Her worries end seconds later, when she's connected to his room.

'Hello?'

He sounds sleepy. Perhaps nine is too early for someone on holiday. He was probably out partying last night. He'll have forgotten her already.

'Hi, it's Alice – from Friday night.' She paces the room as she talks.

'Oh – *oh* – hi, Alice. Hi!'

He sounds glad to hear from her. That's good.

She hears rustling, and imagines him sitting up in bed. Possibly naked. *Oh my god, Alice, control yourself*, she thinks. But she's smiling.

'Thanks for looking after me,' she continues quickly, 'and for the food yesterday. I... look, would you like to meet for dinner later? So I can thank you properly?'

'Yeah, absolutely. I'd love that. You got somewhere in mind?'

'I know a good place. I could come to your hotel again and meet you there? Would eight-ish be okay?'

'Eight is great,' Noah replies. 'So are you feeling better? Is your head okay? I've been worried about you.'

His words send a rush of colour to her cheeks. 'I'm heaps better, thanks,' she says, even though her head is still pretty tender. 'I'll see you tonight then.'

'Okay.' He pauses, then his voice deepens as he adds, 'I'm really looking forward to it.'

He's not leaving much space for misinterpretation. The frisson between them hangs in the air.

'Okay, see you later,' Alice trills, before she hangs up. Her face is hot; she feels giddy. And now there's a long, empty day to endure. Why had she suggested they meet so late?

At least it gives her a little more time to shake off her

throbbing headache. She makes herself coffee and toast, takes them back to bed and reads for a while, then falls into an uneasy slumber.

She wakes to her head thumping, and a tremendous weight pressing on her chest, pinning her to the bed. Coming to, she flings her arms out to fend off her attacker.

Her eyes fly open. Her room is bright with the daylight. Empty. Benign.

He is dead now. He is dead. You are safe. He cannot hurt you.

And yet, that's not true. To begin with, the memory had been a parasite; and despite all her efforts to recover, she can't quite get rid of it. Even in her Thai bedroom, thousands of miles from her childhood home, years away from the night it had happened, she can still be unexpectedly accosted by the smell of his stale breath and alcohol, and feel the graze of stubble across her cheek. A voice in her ear still whispers obscenities.

Anger flashes through her. She won't risk sleep again.

Once she's had a coffee, she turns her thoughts to meeting Noah. She runs through a series of outfit changes, finally settling on an all-in-one white playsuit with a flower motif running across the bodice. She pairs it with casual sandals, and as she surveys herself in the mirror she is pleased. She has brought very little from home, picking up bold printed clothing in the markets in Bangkok, and it has helped her to feel like a different person. *And yet,* she chides herself now, *you know you're not ready for this.*

When she enters the hotel, Noah is in almost exactly the same spot as two days before, but this time his hands are in his jeans pockets, and his face lights up as he sees her. He's so tall he stands out in the busy lobby. Or perhaps it's his solid, comfortable presence, or that beautiful olive skin against his pale blue T-shirt. She'd forgotten just how alluring that easy smile of his is, too.

He doesn't take his eyes off her as she walks towards him, and a delicious thrill runs through her. The pull of him is electrifying, unknown but irresistible. She suspects that even if she tries to run, invisible hands will grasp her shoulders and turn her around to face him again.

Noah comes towards her, leaning in to kiss her cheek. 'Hi, Alice. You're looking heaps better. In fact –' he steps back and gestures to her outfit, '– you look amazing.'

Her cheek is still warm where his lips have just been. 'Thanks. My head's still a bit sore, but I'm getting there. You've been so kind, looking after me and bringing me all that food. Thank you.'

There is a beat of silence and another charge of fierce energy flashes between them. They are standing way too close to one another for the strangers they still are.

'I was really glad you called.'

Noah's voice is so low and full of meaning that Alice shivers. *He feels this too – the pull.*

'Shall we go?' she asks, before he can say more. As they start walking, she adds, 'I know a great place with beautiful food. It's not too fancy, but it tastes amazing. I came across it by accident and I've been looking for a reason to go back. It's not far. So, how has your day been?'

'It was good. I went over to Chatuchak Market and wandered around the stalls there.'

'It's great, isn't it – although there's way too much temptation. If I wasn't trying to save up, I could easily go crazy buying stuff. They have these amazing lamps carved from coconut shells, have you seen those?'

'Yes.' He laughs. 'I nearly bought one for my mum.'

'Really? We must have similar taste.'

'Yeah, I reckon we do.'

They stop talking. The silence is recharged with the same fierce energy that always seems to dance around them.

'Here we are.' Alice leads Noah into a small building. She sees his gaze running over the ornate wooden panelling and soft lighting that illuminates frescoes of the Buddha along each wall. They are shown to a table and handed menus, and Alice studies Noah discreetly as he reads. His sleeves are rolled up so she can see his solid forearms. *Christ, even his forearms are sexy.*

The waitress hovers to take their orders, and once she has gone, Alice asks, 'Are you always so tanned?'

Noah contemplates his arms. 'I spend quite a bit of my spare time at the beach. And I'm part Italian. Dad's from Naples – he moved over to Australia as a boy. Mum's a second-generation Aussie, her parents were Poms. What about your folks? Where are you from?'

How she hates these questions. She hopes he doesn't see her stiffen. 'I've got English ancestry, can't you tell?' Alice answers. 'Pale skin, red hair, where else? But I've lived in Australia for most of my life.'

Thankfully, their beers appear, disrupting their conversation. 'So what do you do at the beach?' Alice asks after a sip of Singha. 'Do you surf?'

'I used to – not so much lately, though. Until about six months ago I had a rescue dog, Pepper – he was blind in one eye. When he was younger I'd leave him playing in the waves while I was out on my board, but then his vision in his good eye got worse, so we'd walk on the beach instead. Since he's been gone, I've hardly got back into the water. Work's been so busy I haven't had time. I'll have to make it a priority when I get home.'

'And when are you heading back?' She holds her breath.

'In about thirty-six hours.'

That's so soon. She tries not to make her disappointment obvious. All at once, there's an urgency to get to know him.

'So what do you do for work? No – let me guess. Professional footballer?'

He laughs. 'You noticed my skills the other night, did you? I wish – but sadly not. Any other guesses?'

'Hmm, paramedic? Personal shopper? Or –' She grins.

'Maybe a knight in shining armour, rescuing ladies with head injuries and getting them safely home?'

He chuckles. 'Okay, my job is going to sound really boring now. The truth is –' his hands drum-roll briefly on the tabletop, '– I'm a restaurant manager.'

'Wow – that's not boring at all! Does it mean you can cook?'

'Yes, but I also *love* it when other people cook for me.'

As though summoned, a young waiter brings out their meals, and goes off to get them more beer.

'This looks great,' Noah says, briefly contemplating his glossy dish of red curry before he digs in. 'So you just came across this place?'

'Yeah. I don't go out much. TESL doesn't pay well, and I'm working all day at the language school. There's lesson prep to do in the evenings, but sometimes at the weekend I explore. I just finished a part-time photography course at Photography School Asia. That's why I went to Wat Po the other day – to practise a few things I'd learned.'

'Until I broke your lens?'

'Yes.' She laughs. 'Until that. We kept bumping into each other that day, didn't we? You know, when I first saw you on the boat, I thought perhaps we'd met somewhere before. You looked as though you recognised me.'

A shadow crosses his face. 'To be honest, I did think you were someone else. Just for a moment.'

She waits for him to expand, but he doesn't. The mood has taken an unexpected turn, and Alice baulks, unsure how to recover.

Then Noah appears to shake off whatever is bothering him, and flashes her another easy smile, white teeth highlighted against his tanned skin. 'So I only have one full day left,' he says. 'What would you recommend I do?'

An answer flashes into her mind, and she hopes he doesn't notice her face flush. *Get a grip, Alice*. She stops eating, beginning to pick at the label on her beer bottle.

'Well, I'm afraid my favourite place in Thailand is a few hours from here.'

'Not possible in a day then?'

'No – but I've heard the floating markets are amazing and they're much closer. Have you been?'

Noah shakes his head as he brings another forkful of food to his mouth. 'I haven't, but I've seen the tours advertised everywhere.'

'There's one called Amphawa that continues into the night – I've been meaning to go there.'

'Sounds great. Don't know whether it would be much fun on my own though. Might have to find someone to come with me.'

She feels another flutter of excitement as he catches her eye.

As they eat, Alice describes her days at the language school, and Noah tells Alice about his travels. Every time he looks at her, his smile stirs her senses. The warm food tastes richer than ever, and she lingers over the different textures on her tongue. The beer bottle is cold on her fingertips and smooth against her lips. Each brief lull in conversation is full of suggestion.

The waiter hovers and whips their plates away as soon as they have finished, returning immediately with the dessert menu.

Noah picks it up and studies it. 'Do you want anything?'

'I'm a bit too full at the moment.' She keeps her answer light and careful.

'Me too.' He puts the piece of card back on the table. 'So what should we do now?'

Their eyes meet, and she is convinced he can read her mind. Her cheeks flush hot with anticipation. 'Well, I wasn't a very good host at my place the other night,' she begins.

'Understandable when you were bleeding from the head.' He keeps his gaze steady, intent on hers. His look sets her whole body aflame.

'I have ice cream.'

'Sounds perfect.'

'Okay then.'

They get to their feet. Glances averted now; a tacit agreement between them. All rational protest is overruled by desire. She craves him, and nothing else will do.

Once on the footpath, they hail a cab. As soon as they are inside, Noah takes Alice's hand, leans over and says in a low whisper, 'You really do look stunning tonight.'

His breath tickles her neck. The ache inside her deepens. Her pulse drums fast in her ears. Their bodies are pressed together, the backs of Alice's thighs sticking to the cheap leather seats. She is counting down every second of the journey.

They pull up at the apartment. By the time Alice gets out, Noah is already paying the driver. She keys in the code for the main gate and he is close behind her up the steps to the first floor. She leads him inside and turns around to see that his expression is a mirror of hers.

He closes the door, leans forward and his lips touch hers. A few seconds of softness, a kindling.

Then the flame ignites.

Her hands are inside his shirt, running over his smooth, hot skin, finding every muscle taut. She feels his heart throbbing at her touch. He pulls her top off, then his fingers slide beneath the lace cups of her bra, his thumbs teasing her nipples as wild longing drums through her. His warm lips run along her collarbone and flutter across the curve of her breasts and their breaths shorten in sync. She pushes her hands inside his shorts, stroking him till he gasps, and they slide to the floor, exploring and tasting every part of one another.

For the next few hours there is only this.

Alice is totally lost, and finally found.

5

Noah wakes bathed in sunlight, to find Alice sleeping on her stomach next to him, naked, the sheet at her waist. He can't resist reaching out and running his hand lightly over the contours of her back. In response, she opens her eyes and smiles.

It seems crazy that a few days ago they had woken unaware of each other's existence. He pulls her against him, his body aching to feel the smooth satin of her skin.

As he buries his face in her neck she murmurs, 'What time is it?' and leans across him to see the clock. 'Argh, it's seven already, I have to get up and shower. I can't be late for work.'

'I can help you shower. Let's go.'

He gets out of bed and stretches, loving the daylight streaming in through the windows so that they can see each other naked, watching her eyes running over the whole of him. He's grateful he put in those extra hours at the hotel gym.

'Jeez, what happened to your leg, Noah?'

He looks at the trail of silvery skin. There's a brief chain of memories: scorching pain, flashing lights, his mother's horrified face. He fights them off. 'I had a bad fall when I was a kid. It's a long story – for another time. We have more important things to do right now.'

He holds out a hand, and she laughs as she takes it. He lifts her so that her legs are around his waist, her breasts pressed

40

against his chest and his hands beneath her bottom, already caressing her as he carries her into the bathroom. They are half giggling, half gasping as they struggle to turn the taps on and are rinsed in a deluge of cold water. Noah's mouth moves into the curve of her neck, his tongue flickers over her nipples and downwards as she softens and arches against him. He's hungry for every taste of her. Doesn't want this to end.

He walks her to the bus stop. 'Can I cook you dinner tonight?'

'You don't want to go to the market?'

'You know,' he says with a wink, 'I think I'd rather spend more time alone with you.'

She laughs. 'Of course. I'll be back at six.' She kisses him and joins the push and shove of commuters pressing onto the minibus.

'I'll meet you at your place then,' he calls after her.

She waves and flashes him one of those glorious smiles.

As the bus moves off, Noah has a fleeting rush of foreboding. He should be escorting her to work, keeping her safe, because this is surely too good to be true.

He shakes off his worries, and plucks his phone from his pocket, looking for markets with fresh produce. The place he finds turns out to have piles of veg and so many pre-cooked dishes that he can't help but begin sampling them. A few hours and an assortment of curries later, he finally reaches his hotel room, a plastic bag in each hand.

As he takes a shower, he hears his phone ping. He's still drying himself as he reaches for it, expecting to find something else from his mum, but it's a message from Jez.

How's the holiday, you lucky bastard! Give me a buzz sometime when you're not too hungover.

Noah finishes dressing then returns the call. Jez picks up almost immediately. 'Hey Noah, how's *our* holiday going?'

'It's good – I won't rub it in, though. How's the leg?'

'Bloody painful. So what have you been doing? No – don't

tell me, I'll get too jealous.' He snorts. 'On second thoughts, maybe I shouldn't be such a selfish bastard. Go on, what have you been up to?'

Alice immediately comes to mind. Noah hesitates, then says, 'I met someone.'

'Seriously? A Thai girl?'

'No, she's Australian, would you believe. I literally bumped into her and broke her camera. Had it fixed for her, then we went out to dinner. Things progressed from there.'

Jez snorts with laughter. 'Only you could get a girl by smashing her stuff.'

'It wasn't the best start, but I think she's forgiven me.' His mind flashes back to the previous night and he grins. 'So are you okay? Has something happened?'

There's a small hesitation on the end of the line. 'Yeah, kind of. I presume you already heard about the inquest?'

Noah's shoulders tighten. 'I have.'

'Your folks all right?'

Only his childhood buddy Jez would think to ask that. They'd been close friends since kindy, in and out of each other's houses constantly as they grew up. Jez had first-hand experience of the creeping tensions and heavy silences that had gradually engulfed the Carruso home. 'Not sure. Won't know properly until I get home.'

'Well, look, there's some shit-stirring going on here... Do you remember Rachel Lawrence?'

Noah grimaces. Of course he remembers. When he'd last bumped into her he'd recognised her from school – she was the year below him and had played the flute in the school band. He hadn't realised she was now a journalist, and one who took invasion of privacy to a new level – who had flirted all night in the hopes he would take her home to snoop through the family's belongings.

Jez had saved him that night; he knew Rachel had once worked with his brother Ellis at the *Coastal Times*. Turned out she was doing her own investigative piece on Lizzie's disappearance, and was particularly interested in Tom Carruso. So much so that she would cosy up to Tom's brother with not a worry about humiliating him.

'Yes,' Noah says, 'I remember Rachel.'

'Thought you would. Well, she's started an unsolved crimes podcast and her first season is about Lizzie. She's putting out an episode a week in the run-up to the inquest. The first one has already dropped. She's not pulling any punches with Tom, I'm afraid, but then she seems to be trying to do a number on everyone – Josh, Miles, and whatever stuff she can find to support other theories too. It's pretty sensationalist, but everyone's listening to it.'

Noah feels sick. The media, the speculation – this is what he dreads. Blow the embers of suspicion at anyone for long enough and you'll start a fire.

'So you've listened to it?'

'I have.' Jez sounds a bit guilty. 'I thought you might want to as well, before you get back. The news is spreading fast around Belhaven – by the time you're home I think most of the locals will have tuned in.'

'Fuck.'

'Yep.'

There is solidarity in the silence. Jez has witnessed Noah's struggles over the years, and while no one knows all Noah's secrets, Jez knows the most. In their teens he'd watched Noah lust after Lizzie for months, never ridiculing him, understanding the misery because of his own unrequited love for Beatrice Dalton, one of Ellis's best friends. Jez had been lucky, though, because Ellis was a lot kinder than Tom, and pretended not to notice.

'There's another thing,' Jez adds, snapping Noah back to the present.

Noah groans. 'Go on, what else?'

'Tom's on the podcast.'

What the hell? Noah's fingers tighten on the handset. He must have misheard. 'Tom?'

'Sounds like she's interviewed him for episode two.'

'*Interviewed* him?'

'Yeah.'

It doesn't make sense. Tom never voluntarily talked about Lizzie. He'd been consistent since day one. He said nothing to his family, and only spoke to the police when he had to. He'd hidden from the journalists who had turned up at school and at the restaurant for a while after Lizzie vanished.

'And what does Rachel say?'

'She has an awful lot to say.' Jez's voice is grim. 'I think it's probably better if you listen for yourself.'

As soon as they have said goodbye, Noah goes straight to the podcast app on his phone and searches for Rachel Lawrence. The series comes up immediately: *The Disappearance of Lizzie Burdett*. As the first episode downloads, he stares at the little blurb next to the thumbnail: a tiny picture of Lizzie. He breathes steadily to induce the familiar layer of numbness, the only way to block out the churning magma of anger and distress inside him. As soon as the podcast has downloaded, he presses play. The very first voice he hears is unmistakably his brother's.

'I did not kill Lizzie Burdett.'

Noah shudders. This stark sentence is followed by a stream of thrillerish music, the kind usually found on those tabloid current affairs shows that thrive on tragedy. He hadn't been sure what to expect, but it wasn't this – a slick, professional piece of drama.

'It was like she just vanished into thin air. It has never made any sense.' This from a softly spoken woman, the emotion clear in her voice. *It must be Sylvie Burdett*, Noah realises with a pang. Lizzie's mum.

The music slices in again, a few heavy drum beats before a cymbal slashes across them.

'All we want is answers – and justice.' That's Miles Burdett, Lizzie's dad. *'Someone out there knows what happened to our beautiful daughter. It keeps me awake every single night.'*

The music abruptly changes to a more reflective piece, all harp strings and violins. It fades into the background but doesn't disappear as Rachel Lawrence begins to narrate. Noah's teeth clench as he hears that familiar, deep, confident voice and recalls how she had almost duped him.

'*I'm Rachel Lawrence, investigative journalist and author of* The Woman in the Woods. *And this is the unsettling story of a popular young girl who disappeared from the Northern Beaches suburb of Belhaven one winter's night in 2006, and was never seen again. This –*' a pregnant pause '*– is* The Disappearance of Lizzie Burdett.'

The music moves up a notch, and another voice – male – says, 'The Disappearance of Lizzie Burdett *is brought to you by Tyson's, financial services you can trust.*'

Noah has to smile at that. It's a bizarre sponsor, until you realise that Tyson's belongs to Beverley and Duncan Lawrence, Rachel's parents.

He's assailed by a wave of nausea, and hastily switches it off, unsure if he can bear listening to any more. *Why have all these people agreed to speak to Rachel? Are they desperate for answers? Absolution? Or do they trust her because she belongs to the community – she's 'one of them'?*

That one sentence from his long-lost brother has pitched him towards fury. Twelve years on, and Tom is still protesting his innocence. He wouldn't have expected anything less, but only Noah had lived with Tom Carruso for sixteen long years. Only Noah knows just how good a liar his brother really is.

6

The burnished hues of sunset are already spreading across the sky as Alice approaches her flat. Noah is outside, waiting. He sets down the bags of food and pulls her into his arms.

'Hello there,' he says, his mouth millimetres from hers.

'Hi,' she replies, pulling him into a kiss.

When they break apart, Noah says softly, 'I missed you.'

His voice, his touch, everything about him makes Alice melt. *This is too much, too fast*, she tells herself. It doesn't matter. She cannot stop.

An hour later, the table is set with bamboo placemats and chopsticks she has never seen before, and the smell of pad thai is making her mouth water. Noah is adding handfuls of herbs into the pan, tasting the sauce now and again, listening to her talk. He seems subdued this evening.

Alice tries to make him laugh with stories of her students and little snippets of Thai life: a day of food poisoning from eating a cucumber carved into a flower; wearing white during Songkran, being doused with water by enthusiastic locals and ending up with a see-through wet T-shirt. The constant requests for selfies, which she attributes to her red hair. Noah nods and laughs along in all the right places, but something has changed.

'Wow,' she says with extra enthusiasm, trying to bring him out of his fug as she takes a seat. 'This looks amazing.'

He brings the pan over to ladle food into her bowl. 'I hope it tastes as good.' Once finished serving, he turns and grabs a bottle of wine, opens it and pours them each a glass. 'So how was your day?' he asks as he takes the chair opposite.

'No, no, no,' she answers. 'I've talked enough – it's your turn! First tell me about this food. Can all restaurant managers cook like this or are you secretly a Michelin-starred chef?'

'Okay, I admit it – my parents own the restaurant. I've been in kitchens all my life. You can't help but learn some of the tricks of the trade when you're around it all the time.'

Alice tries the food, and her eyes widen. 'This is incredible!'

He smiles but doesn't say anything.

Something's wrong. She can't contain herself any longer. 'Are you all right, Noah? You don't seem yourself tonight.' It's a strange thing to say considering the short time they've been together, but this definitely isn't the same easygoing man she has known so far.

Noah sets the serving spoon down, its steel glinting in the lamplight. 'I'm not sure. I spoke to my mum earlier. There's a lot going on at home right now.'

Alice waits, but he doesn't elaborate. *Don't ask – let him tell you in his own time.* She takes a casual mouthful of rice.

He sighs. 'Shit. Okay, I'll try to explain – bear with me, because I need to start from the beginning.' He takes a deep breath. 'Twelve years ago, my brother's girlfriend disappeared. They had a fight on our doorstep, which I witnessed, then Lizzie ran off into the night. Tom chased after her, but he came back alone. A couple of guys thought they saw her on the road a short distance from our house, about ten minutes later, but after that no one ever saw her again. Now there's an inquest coming up in a few weeks, and I might have to give evidence to the coroner.'

Alice stops eating. 'Bloody hell, Noah!'

Noah picks up his chopsticks and begins pushing his food around his bowl. 'My brother Tom has already been called as a witness. I haven't seen him for eleven years – he moved away soon after Lizzie vanished. We weren't close, and I haven't missed him much, but now he's coming home.' Noah shrugs. 'So this holiday is the calm before the storm.'

A thousand thoughts run through Alice's mind. 'That's... Noah, that's terrible – your brother's girlfriend just *disappeared*?'

'Into thin air – or so it seemed at the time. She and Tom were together for six months. She was still in high school. Then she wasn't – she was just gone.'

'And no one has any idea what happened?'

'No one knows anything for sure.' He hesitates. 'But we all have our theories.'

A shudder runs through Alice. 'And what are your theories?'

Noah sets down his chopsticks and takes a long swig of his wine. 'Most people think something bad happened. No one who knew Lizzie believes she'd deliberately disappear like that – and there was no evidence she'd planned to run away. But there were rumours about Tom.'

Alice frowns. 'People thought your *brother* did something to her?'

'Yes – especially once they heard about the fight. A lot of the locals kept their distance from us afterwards. We had graffiti on our front door, the restaurant windows were smashed, and there was a scene at the restaurant, when some of the Burdetts' friends got aggressive and wouldn't pay their bill. It was horrible. Mum was always crying, and Dad completely withdrew. He worked day and night just to keep the business alive.' Noah stares into the distance as he talks. 'Since then, things have slowly settled down, but nothing's ever been the same. And now, with the inquest... I have no idea what's coming next. I just learned there's a podcast – a journalist doing her own investigation. God knows what that'll mean for us. My parents are already stressed to the max... and nowadays they seem to expect me to drop everything and solve all their problems.' He grimaces, then stops and gives her an apologetic look. 'Sorry, I'm really dragging the night down.'

'No. I'm glad you told me.'

'Really?'

'Really.' Alice reaches across and briefly strokes his hand.

He smiles gratefully and they finish their food. She stands up to clear the plates away.

'I can do that later,' he says, and gets up too, collecting the dishes from her, setting them down. He takes hold of her hand and pulls her towards her bedroom. 'We've talked about enough serious stuff for one night. And I've been thinking about you all day.' His eyes are fixed on hers, every part of him present now.

'Is that right?' she teases. *God, that look of his is irresistible.*

'Every. Single. Minute.' He stops where he is, and doesn't take his eyes off her as he undoes the buttons at the front of her blouse, pulling it open, inch by inch. His touch sets her whole body trembling; her skin is on fire. Slowly he takes off all her clothes, lifts her up and carries her across to the bed. He doesn't let her touch him until his hands have finished exploring her, while she writhes and clutches at his hair.

As they lie there, the mood slowly shifts to a subdued kind of tenderness. Alice snuggles against Noah and listens to his heartbeat, trying to stay in the moment. Wondering if this is all they will have.

'Are you okay?' Noah asks, kissing her forehead.

'You're leaving tomorrow.' Her words are sombre. 'We've only just met, and this... it feels like the start and the end at the same time.'

She looks up to see her own maelstrom of feelings reflected in his face.

He shakes his head. 'I'm not going home tomorrow. Not anymore.'

'What?' She props herself up to see him better. 'What do you mean?'

'I know it's only been a few days,' Noah begins slowly, as

though trying to measure his words, 'but it's like I've known you forever. You haven't had much chance to tell me about your life yet, but I want to know everything, because I think this – that *we* – might be the kind of thing that doesn't happen very often. Do you... do you think so too?'

His open face is aflame in the soft light, eyes searching hers. She longs to let him in completely, despite her fears. *Could I really trust him so soon?* She imagines telling him everything – tries to picture his reaction, but she can't. Not yet.

There is still a tiny part of her that wants to pull away, to protect herself, but this moment is too pivotal for doubt, and her answer comes quick and quiet. 'Yes. This is all happening so fast, but yes, I feel the same.'

'Then I'll change my flight in the morning. I want to stay for as long as I can, but I really have to be back for work next Friday. There's a big wedding reception at the restaurant and my parents won't manage it without me. And after that there's the inquest.' He kisses her forehead. 'But I don't want to leave you until I have to. Is that okay? Can we spend a few more days together and find out what happens next?'

'Are you sure your family can spare you right now?'

'Probably not,' he says, pulling a face, 'no doubt they'll give me grief for it. But this isn't about them, is it? It's about us.'

She is hot with excitement. *This is really happening. He's staying. For me.* 'Okay then, if you're sure.'

'I'm sure.' He gathers her into his arms.

Soon after they fall silent, the dishes in the sink forgotten. Alice pretends to be asleep, her body nestled against his, but her mind is buzzing. She'd so happily agreed to him staying that his words are only just registering. He wants to get to know her, but that will mean trusting him with secrets and reopening doors to places she doesn't want to go.

There are goosebumps on her arms. How much dare she say? Will he understand when she tells him why she left Australia – and why she doesn't want to go back?

7

Once Alice has gone to work the next morning, leaving the apartment keys on her bedside table, Noah drifts back into a doze. The light sleep brings uneasy dreams – Alice on his knee, her face turned away from him, her hair wet, as though she's just come in from the rain. Then she turns towards him, and it's not Alice at all, but Lizzie, her eyes pleading for help.

He wakes with a start and lies still, watching the flimsy white curtains wafting in the light breeze coming from the overhead fan. The daylight encourages him back to the present, but even as he tries to shake off the nightmare, he can't banish it completely. He doesn't want Alice and Lizzie entangled in his mind. It's bloody unhealthy. Perhaps it's happening because he's still pushing his memories away, when soon he'll have no choice but to confront them.

It's time to stop burying his head in the sand. With the inquest looming, there's no point in avoiding Rachel Lawrence's podcast forever. Since everyone back home will be listening to it, he might as well see what she's saying.

He gets up to find his earbuds and looks around Alice's studio flat. It's cramped but modern, the bedroom, living room and kitchenette all in one area, and a little bathroom with both a shower and an old-fashioned bath to one side. He remembers Alice saying she has lived here for three months, but there are fewer personal belongings visible here than in his hotel room.

There is one book on the sofa with the dark jacket and bold fonts of a thriller, the cover depicting a bridge in twilight. The colours of the room are neutral, both here and in the bedroom. A few items of clothing are scattered on the floor from last night, but that's about it. There's hardly anything that tells him more about her.

He finds his earbuds, makes a coffee, heads back to bed, and searches for the podcast again.

When he presses play, he goes back to the beginning and re-listens to the dramatic introduction. He braces himself as Rachel Lawrence continues her narration and begins to outline the facts.

'The suburb of Belhaven backs on to the beautiful Garigal National Park. It's leafy and secluded, a quiet place where you won't see much happening on the streets, except for the locals walking their dogs or jogging with their headphones on. And yet, this area hasn't felt the same since the night of the thirtieth of June, 2006, when a seventeen-year-old girl called Elizabeth Burdett – known to her loved ones as Lizzie – disappeared while walking home from her boyfriend's house late at night.'

Noah is trying to reconcile this unemotional recounting of these events with his own distraught patchwork of memories when Rachel's tone softens.

'I remember Lizzie's disappearance well. I attended the same school as Lizzie, although I didn't know her personally because she was four years older than me. However, I only began looking at the particulars of this case once I was a cadet reporter with the Coastal News. *As the years have gone by, it's been a story that has stayed with me more than most. As you'll hear, Lizzie Burdett's disappearance is a true mystery. There are a number of suspects who may have caused her to come to harm, but their involvement is based on little evidence and a lot of conjecture. It seems that if you were a male in Lizzie's life at the time she disappeared, you will remain under suspicion for that reason alone.'*

The faces of those suspects appear in Noah's mind. There's

Tom, of course. And Lizzie's father Miles, a formerly affable man with a solid career as a doctor and an obvious deep affection for his daughters. Noah can still remember Miles collecting Lizzie, always greeting her with a warm embrace, sometimes stopping for a coffee and a chat with Noah's parents, his booming laugh carrying through the house.

By all accounts, the Burdetts hadn't just endured Lizzie's disappearance, but a succession of cruel and unsubstantiated rumours about Miles and Sylvie's marriage and speculation about the darker side of their family life. Any misstep, any overheard argument or tension, had been breathlessly recounted in school corridors and shop doorways, until Lizzie's two younger sisters had stopped coming to school, sent elsewhere to finish their studies, dropping from Noah's radar altogether. There had been no baritone laughter in the Carruso house anymore, and Noah suspected the Burdett house was just as quiet.

'*Lizzie was well liked at school,*' Rachel Lawrence continues. '*She had begun dating Tom Carruso – a boy in her year, and also very popular – in January 2006, about six months prior to her disappearance. And in March of the same year, her best friend Gemma Mackleford started dating Tom's best friend, Josh Arnold. Gemma remembers that time as very happy, at least to begin with.*'

Gemma's gentle voice cuts in unexpectedly. '*We were just having so much fun.*'

Christ, Noah thinks, *is there anyone who hasn't been interviewed for this program?* He twists the wires of the earbuds tighter and tighter around his fingers as he listens.

'*Tom was the guy at school that everyone wanted to date, because he was super hot,*' Gemma continues. '*But if I'm honest, I always felt that was the main reason Lizzie liked him. They didn't seem to have much in common, but he was exciting. After a while they began to argue quite a bit. Tom would snipe at her and Lizzie would bite back, but after he'd gone she would sometimes get tearful.*'

Noah is caught on the phrase 'the guy at school that

everyone wanted to date'. Yep, he still remembers how crushing, how unfathomable, that had been for him: the negative comparisons, the cruel jokes he overheard. For a time, the Carruso brothers' nicknames were Brawny and Scrawny. Tom had found it funny. Noah, not so much.

He's drifted again, and Rachel is still narrating. He tries to focus.

'So now we have a pretty good picture of Lizzie's circumstances. However, it seems that in the weeks before Lizzie vanished, she had grown closer and closer to Josh.'

Noah sits up straight, captivated. Rachel really had done her homework, hadn't she? He'd heard the rumours, of course, but this was going to be interesting.

'About six weeks before Lizzie disappeared –' it's Gemma's voice again, *'– we all went away for the weekend. Lizzie and Josh were giving off a strange vibe. I'm not sure anything had happened – Josh later said it hadn't – but they must have had some kind of moment together. I remember feeling so nervous all weekend. Tom was angry, possessive and brooding. I think everyone knew that something was about to happen.'*

'You can already see,' Rachel chips in, *'why Josh and Tom are going to be two of the main players in this story.'*

Noah pauses the podcast, thinking back. He'd witnessed plenty of times when Tom's group of friends had hung out together. The Carruso house had been one of their regular haunts. Had he ever seen Lizzie and Josh flirting? He didn't think so, but perhaps his jealousy towards his brother had blinded him to anything else.

He presses play again, and Rachel continues. *'On the last evening that Lizzie was seen alive, all her friends, including Gemma, Tom and Josh, went to a house party at the home of their friend Beatrice Dalton. That night, there were plenty of witnesses who saw Tom storming out of the party, followed by Lizzie a few minutes later. Tom's house was only five minutes away from Beatrice's on foot – he went home, and Lizzie went after him. There they had another fight on the doorstep. Tired and emotional, Lizzie is believed to have set off home – a half-hour walk that skirted the edge of the Garigal National Park. She was last seen ten minutes from Tom's house, hurrying along the pavement, her head down, at about a quarter past eleven. The witnesses – two middle-aged men – said they thought she looked upset but were worried they would scare her if they stopped. Sadly, it would be the very last sighting of Lizzie Burdett. She didn't arrive home, and hasn't been seen since.'*

Rachel leaves a good few seconds of silence here. Noah waits, his heart drumming in his ears.

'In Tom's statement,' Rachel continues, *'he says the reason he stormed off was that he had found Lizzie and Josh together in an upstairs room, and Josh's arm was around Lizzie. However, Josh made a statement too: he said he had been comforting Lizzie, but nothing happened, and Tom had overreacted. Whatever went on, the two men have not spoken to each other since.'*

'I'll never get over it,' a new voice chimes in.

Noah exhales long and hard. He hasn't heard that gravelly drawl for twelve years, but it's unmistakably Josh.

'It's changed me forever,' Josh declares solemnly.

'That's next time on The Disappearance of Lizzie Burdett,*'* Rachel adds, *'when I talk to Tom and Josh.'*

A burst of dramatic music concludes the episode. Noah's fingertips have gone numb. He quickly unwinds the thin earbud wires from around them, seeing deep red marks where they have cut grooves into his skin.

Rachel is a good narrator, he has to give her that. So many questions are roaring in his ears. Then he clocks the time on his phone and remembers the airline office shuts at lunchtime, in exactly ninety minutes. Shit. He needs to get dressed and sort out his flight.

An hour later, Noah is exiting the airline office, having agreed to an exorbitant fee in order to change his travel plans. He messages Alice to let her know the good news, and tells her he'll have dinner ready for her tonight. Then he sends his mum a text, promising to be home by the end of the following week so he can help with the Bensons' wedding reception. His parents will likely be livid, but what can they do? Noah might be part of the family, but he's a grown man, working on his own terms.

Still, he knows he'll be subjected to the usual emotional blackmail. He isn't sure which is harder: his mother's overt disappointment, or his father's simmering silences. At least his mother might be quicker to forgive him if a girl is involved. A few of her friends were grandparents now, and Cathy has hinted at her own ambitions on more than one occasion.

Noah checks his phone regularly during the afternoon, bracing himself each time, but by the time Alice gets back from work, there has been no reply. He's distracted by her shining face as she announces she has managed to wangle a couple of days off.

'We have the next five days together and I already have a plan. In the morning, we need to pack.'

'Why, where are we going?'

'You'll see. Did you get all your stuff from the hotel?'

'I did.' He indicates his suitcase. They had agreed there was no point in him extending his hotel booking when he wasn't going to be there, so all his belongings are now at her place. It's like he's moved in after less than a week, which sounds ridiculous in his head. He can just imagine how his friends and family would react if he put anything online. But then he looks at Alice, and it all makes total sense, and it's everything else that's off-kilter.

'It smells amazing in here.' She gestures towards the little stove. 'What is it this evening?'

'Green curry,' he replies, stirring the contents of the wok. 'I saw what you liked at Niran's house, so I was fairly confident with this one!'

She sits down at the table. 'How was your day? Have you told your parents you'll be away for a bit longer?'

Noah ladles the food into bowls. 'Yeah, I sent them a message, although I shouldn't imagine it's gone down well. Dad's a control freak – he doesn't like change – and Mum is used to me being at her beck and call, either at the restaurant or whenever she needs help with Dad.'

Alice frowns. 'What kind of help does your mum need with your dad?'

'Dad had an accident, a couple of years after Tom left. The restaurant was on the brink of bankruptcy, so he decided he'd save some money and make a simple roof repair himself. He fell and broke his back.'

Alice gasps. 'Seriously? Noah, your family has had some terrible luck.'

'We have, haven't we.' Noah laughs but there's little humour in it. 'Dad's not completely paralysed – he can walk a little but it exhausts him, so most of the time he uses a wheelchair. He needs a fair amount of help. Mum does what she can, but she finds him pretty demanding.'

'That sounds really tough.'

Noah nods. 'He hasn't adjusted very well. He was a professional Aussie Rules player for a while when he was in his twenties, and he always prided himself on being strong and active.' He has a brief flash of running across a field, chasing his father and brother, back in his dad's heyday as a footy star. For a while they'd spent all their weekends outside: his dad was as good with a soccer ball as he was with the footy. But then his parents got busy. And once his father got injured, sport became something for school only, not to be mentioned at home.

Alice doesn't respond, but her expression grows solemn. 'What are you thinking?' he asks.

'I feel bad for encouraging you to stay – I didn't realise.'

'Listen.' He sits opposite her. 'I still live at home, so I can help them. I manage the restaurant, so I can help them. In fact, I have organised most of my life around them. And we're not poor – we're bloody fortunate, and we can employ carers if needs be. I've been letting it drift for a long time, way longer than I should have really, just because there was no reason to change anything. But now... well, now there's a reason.' He smiles at her.

To his surprise, Alice grimaces. 'Shit, Noah, your mum probably hates me already,' she says, massaging her temples with her fingertips.

Noah bursts out laughing. 'What? Of course she doesn't.'

'You do know that most mums hate their sons' girlfriends, don't you? Well, a lot of them do. And that's without this added expectation in your life.'

'So are you my girlfriend now?' he teases.

She narrows her eyes at him. 'Hmm, I don't know. Maybe... if you play your cards right.'

He leans over and kisses her. 'I'll do my best.' He sits back, sips his water. 'I don't think Mum seriously expects me to live with them forever.' *Although she seems very settled with the current arrangements.* He frowns at the thought, which is coupled with a rush of irritation. He's had the impression for a while that he serves as a useful buffer for his parents, who seem to get on best when they're dealing with the practicalities of the restaurant. 'I think we've all got a bit complacent. What about your Mum? Does she miss you?'

Alice takes a moment to compose her thoughts, then says, 'My mum died when I was a baby. She was found at a notorious suicide spot. I don't have any memories of her, but my dad never really got over it. It's shaped our lives. He had to bring me up alone. And of course it made him... overprotective.'

Noah gapes at her. Their connection has been so intense, and so intimate, that it's a shock to realise just how much he doesn't yet know. 'Christ, here I am going on about my problems. I'm sorry, Alice.'

She pushes her half-full bowl away. 'Don't worry, it was a long time ago. Like I said, I don't even remember her. However, in a roundabout way she did teach me that life is short, and nothing lasts forever. That's why we have to grab at whatever happiness we can.' She gets up and comes to sit on his knee, straddling him, her hands on his back underneath his T-shirt, fingers tracing up and down his spine. He instantly responds, pulling her close, his lips trailing along her collarbone as he breathes her in. 'So why don't we forget all our troubles for a while,' she murmurs, leaning in to kiss him, 'and remind ourselves how good it feels to be alive.'

8

Alice is already packing by the time Noah wakes up.

'Good morning,' he says, his voice groggy with sleep. 'So when do I find out where we're going?'

Before she can reply, he leans over and grabs her wrists, pulling her on top of him, burying his face into the sweeping curve of her shoulder and kissing her neck.

She laughs, pushing him away. 'Come on, we have a bus to catch. I'm taking you to a place called Khao Yai – one of the best national parks in the country. Think pristine rainforest with waterfalls, elephants and monkeys.' She narrows her eyes at him. 'Are you ready for a few days of adventure?'

He raises an eyebrow, his eyes shining with excitement. 'Bring it on.'

In spite of Alice's enthusiasm, the three-hour trip to Khao Yai is a minibus ride from hell. Their driver seems determined to set a personal best, whatever the cost to frayed nerves or human life. They find it funny to begin with, high on the thought of escaping the city, but a few hours of adrenalin leaves them clutching each other, grateful to finally reach the guest house.

'This place is incredible, Alice!' Noah says once they are in their room. He goes to the window and stares at the ornate landscaped gardens. 'When you said we were going to a national park I was expecting bamboo huts or canvas tents, not this.' His eyes begin to follow a mosquito around the room and he claps at it. 'Although we have a few unwelcome roommates,' he adds as he plucks the squashed insect from his palm.

'It's great, isn't it – although I didn't bring you here for the room service. Tomorrow, I have a spectacular surprise for you.' She can hardly contain her excitement. 'However, right now, you need to put on long sleeves and trousers and spray yourself head to toe with repellent. Your little squashed friend has a lot of buddies wanting revenge, and I've booked us a sunset trip to see elephants.'

'Really?' Noah's eyes light up. 'If elephants are the warm-up activity, I can't wait to find out what the main event is!'

The guide from the hotel meets them an hour later, and they climb into the back of an open Jeep. The vehicle rattles down the rough road and they cling to the rails, laughing and kissing and hanging on to each other. Eventually there is a shout from the front and they peer eagerly out of the sides of the truck, hearing sharp cracks from the undergrowth. An elephant is half-hidden in the forest, stripping branches from one of the trees. The Jeep drives on and then pulls up so they can watch. They try to fix their gaze on the spot where the elephant had been, when it appears on the road, followed by another, and another, until five elephants amble along the bitumen, shoulder to shoulder, a wobbling wall of grey. The two largest swing their trunks occasionally to nuzzle at a youngster in the centre, while those on the outside veer in and out of the treeline, stripping branches at random. Cars come up behind them, stop abruptly and begin to reverse.

Alice frames the scene with her shiny new lens. Once she's taken a few shots, she jumps down from the vehicle without a thought, wanting to get closer.

'Alice!'

She knows Noah is calling her but she's too intent on

the photograph. Through the viewfinder she sees the largest elephant come to a halt. It's looking straight at her.

'Fuck, Alice, get back in the Jeep!'

Alice takes the camera away from her face and stares into the eyes of the old matriarch. *What does she see when she looks at me?*

The answer is obvious seconds later, when the matriarch lets out a bellow of rage and begins to run towards her.

The guide shouts, but before Alice can react, Noah is there, dragging her back into the vehicle. The driver floors the accelerator and Noah pulls her onto a seat, holding her tight as they brace themselves against the sudden burst of speed. The elephant is still charging, ears spread wide in seething indignation, its face getting closer and closer. Then, as suddenly as it began, it gives up the chase, and turns back to the group.

'You must stay in the car, miss!' the guide insists, breathlessly brushing his floppy fringe from his face.

'I'm sorry.'

Noah is staring at her. 'Can I just state for the record, I do not fancy death by elephant.'

She realises she's shaking. 'Fair enough. Neither do I.'

He hugs her close, kissing her hair. 'I can see why you were mesmerised, though. It was unbelievable, being so close to an animal like that.'

She relaxes against him, grateful he's broken the tension and that he instinctively understands how she'd felt. The Jeep speeds up as it grows dark, stopping momentarily as a huge python takes its time crossing the road, at one stage so long that its body stretches right from one side of the single-lane track to the other. Once on grass rather than bitumen, the creature does a gear shift and makes a lightning-fast getaway.

'This place is amazing.' Noah's face is alive with excitement. 'Thank you for bringing me here.'

'I thought you might like it,' she replies, snuggling into his arms.

'I love it, Alice. Every day with you feels like... I'm not even sure how to describe it. The best word I can think of is freedom.' He kisses her neck. 'Thank you.'

She smiles, drinking in his delight. The creases in his forehead have lessened, and he's right in this moment with her. She cannot wait for tomorrow.

Back at the hotel, the manager ushers them to the restaurant. They eat quickly, like they have an unspoken agreement to hurry. Once in their room, they are naked in moments. Alice has never had sex like this before, with someone fully invested in her pleasure. Noah doesn't just look at her with lust but with reverence too. Every time is so different – never the same place or tempo, and she wants him more and more. And between the sex there's the easygoing way they speak to one another – teasing, laughing, limbs bare and tangled – no self-consciousness at all.

They fall asleep together, and Alice wakes to find it is already growing light outside. She checks the time and lets Noah sleep for a while longer, before nudging him awake.

'Come on,' she says, stroking his hair back from his forehead and kissing him. 'It's time for the main event.'

They breakfast in haste and head out to a waiting vehicle.

Noah's gaze falls on the ropes and life jackets in the back of the truck and he stops short. 'This looks serious,' he says with a nervous smile.

Before Alice can reply, a man leaps out of the vehicle and comes towards them, collecting their bags. 'Welcome back, Alice!'

'Thanks, Anu. This is my friend Noah.'

Anu gestures to their clasped hands. 'Looks like a very good friend.'

She beams. 'He is.'

Anu turns his attention to Noah. 'Nice to meet you, Noah. Are you looking forward to today?'

'Er, I don't actually know what we're doing.' Noah's brow

furrows as he gives Alice a look that says, *What on earth are you getting me into?*

'Aha! A secret! Well, we will have great fun.' Anu gestures to the car. 'You are strong, yes? No problem for you.'

Once they are in the car, Noah leans close to Alice. 'What is no problem for me?' he whispers.

She chuckles. 'You'll see.'

Ten minutes later they pull up at what looks like a large farm shed, with the words 'Adventure Centre' painted on a large strip of wood that's been fixed above the door. Anu comes around to help them out.

'Today, Mr Noah, Alice is taking you abseiling and kayaking,' he announces merrily. 'But first, you practise. Come.'

'Oh my god, Alice, what are you doing to me?' Noah cries, smiling and patting his chest as though his heart is palpitating. He turns away, but not before she's seen his jovial expression falter.

He's nervous. She hadn't expected that. But his joking reassures her. She wants him to love this as much as she does.

As soon as they are inside the building, Anu scurries around kitting Noah up with a wetsuit, helmet and life jacket, then shows him the different techniques they'll be using on a small indoor wall.

'Hey, why am I the only one practising this?' Noah calls from halfway down the wall as Alice emerges from the changing rooms in her wetsuit. His tone is cheerful but she can see the tension knotting his arms. His grip on the rope is much tighter than it needs to be.

'Alice doesn't need practice,' Anu calls from the top of the wall. 'You'll see.'

Noah frowns, but can't ask any more because Anu is still busy issuing instructions.

Thirty minutes later they are all back in the car, squashed in the front with Anu so he can point out wildlife along the way. There's no more time to talk.

When they reach the jungle trail, Alice watches Anu throw the heavy ropes over his shoulder like they are light skeins of wool. Even with their wetsuits rolled to the waist, it's uncomfortable walking. 'It's not too far,' she reassures Noah, who has gone quiet.

'And here we are,' Anu announces proudly as they emerge from the track. 'But first, we must go up.'

There is no hiding what they are doing any longer. Another group are abseiling on one side of a seventy-metre waterfall, clinging to the ropes amid the fierce, relentless spray. Alice gets a buzz at the mere sight of it, but in front of her, Noah comes to a complete halt. She waits for him to move again, but he seems rooted to the ground.

'Noah? Are you okay?'

'Oh, Alice.' He turns to her, fear looming large in his eyes. 'That looks really high!'

'Don't worry,' she says, patting his arm, 'you'll be secured to the ropes, and you did great in the training room. You don't have to do it if you don't want to, but I promise you'll love it. It's an incredible feeling.'

He doesn't reply, but turns to follow Anu again.

She watches him nervously. *Please let me be right about this*.

They climb in single file up the uneven rocky path. By the time they get to the top, the other groups have gone, and Anu begins securing their ropes to nearby trees. Alice cannot miss the sheen of sweat on Noah's forehead, in contrast to the paleness of his face. He looks like he might vomit at any moment.

'Are you sure you're going to be okay?' she ventures nervously. 'You really don't have to.'

'Sure. I mean, I'll give it a go... I'm just not that great with heights.'

She squeezes his hand. 'Look, why don't I go first, and I'll be waiting for you at the bottom, okay? Nothing can go wrong, I promise. You're secured to the ropes. Even if you let go, you'd just dangle there.'

'Alice,' Anu calls. 'Come on, let's do this, the other groups will be coming soon.'

'Watch me,' she says, going across to the rope. 'Just clip yourself on, and Anu will check it. Then take it slowly.' She steps into the rushing water and it surges around her legs, sucking her into the flow. 'And when you get to the edge –' she steps backwards, '– you lean back like this... and go...'

She lets the rope out and moves straight into the powerful deluge of the falls. Water hammers over her, leaving her gasping, the power of it making her want to scream and laugh at the same time. There is nothing like this. She loves these moments with no time to think or imagine, only to focus on the next foothold. She lets herself down as slowly as she can, savouring every second. Once at the bottom, she unclips, and waits for Noah.

It's a long time before Noah appears over the top of the waterfall. 'Go, Noah!' she shouts at the sight of him, watching him lean back and begin to let himself down into the rushing water.

He's actually doing it! Perhaps her plan will work after all. She hopes he's loving it as much as she does.

He gets a couple of metres below the lip of the rock, and she waits for him to draw closer, but nothing happens. He appears to be stuck.

'Noah, what's going on?' she calls, but he doesn't answer.

Heart pounding, she strides through the cold pool of water until she reaches the rock beside the waterfall and begins to climb. The slick, dark stone is treacherous, but her fingers and feet are assured in their grip. She is apprehensive – *what the hell has happened?* – but some of the adrenalin coursing through her is excitement too. It has been a long time since she's done something as risky as this. She's missed the feeling.

Noah hasn't moved. *Please don't let me find him uncon-scious.* As she draws level with him, she's thankful to see that his eyes are open. His chin is tucked into his chest as he breathes heavily.

'Noah?' she yells, trying to get his attention over the roar of the water.

He startles. 'What the hell are you doing, Alice?' he cries as he realises she's clinging on to the rock face. 'Are you insane?'

She flinches. This was a bad idea. 'Quite possibly, but you are hanging in the middle of a waterfall right now, and Anu will be getting worried up there. Let yourself down.'

'I've gone blank... I can't think...'

Shit, I've pushed him too far. 'You can't fall, Noah – you're completely safe, Anu is belaying you. Just feed the rope, like he showed you. You can do it.'

At last, Noah begins to move down. Alice stays in position until his feet touch the water, then continues her climb to the top.

She finds Anu still clutching on to the rope. 'What happened?' he asks, unfazed by her reappearance.

'He froze,' she replies, clipping herself back on to the line. 'He's okay now though.'

The waterfall thunders ominously in her ears as she lets herself back down. It doesn't feel refreshing anymore.

She unclips herself then turns to find Noah staring at her with his arms folded, his body visibly trembling.

'So you're actually Spiderwoman then?' He gestures to the rocks.

They stare at one another for a long moment, then Noah's face breaks into a huge grin.

'That is the craziest thing I have ever done – or seen.' He shakes his head. 'That was insane! I was just hanging there, forgetting everything, and then you appear out of nowhere and it looks like you're just holding on by your fingertips. Shit, Alice, what else should I know about you?'

Relieved, she echoes his laughter, but his words jolt her. *There is so much more, Noah. So much more.*

But now is not the time.

They spend another hour kayaking, and to Alice's relief,

Noah completely recovers, joking with Anu as they go. They have their photo taken with a green pit viper dozing in a branch above their heads, and glimpse clusters of small monkeys surveying them from the trees. When they are back in the Jeep, finally in dry clothes, Noah puts his arm around Alice and kisses her.

'Thanks for an awesome day.'

She hadn't been aware of the tension in her body until his words break it. 'Do you mean that? I was terrified I'd forced you into an ordeal.'

'It was an ordeal! But it was worth it. To be there, to feel the power of the falls – to do something I never thought I'd be able to do. And then to spend time on the water, with everything we saw. It was amazing.'

'She is an excellent climber, yes?' Anu chips in.

'Yes! I thought I was hallucinating when I saw you halfway up the rock wall, Alice. Where did you learn to do that?'

'Back in Australia – the coast and the mountains – it was a way to let off steam, to escape the world for a while. It makes me feel... invincible is the best word I can think of.'

'I can see why. Damn, Alice, you are incredible. Crazy, but incredible.'

She tries to bask in the compliment, but it's hard, because she remembers the person she was when she started climbing. How can she tell him about that desperate girl who hardly cared if she lived or died? Or the fear that she is cursed, and if disaster can't reach her, it will snatch those closest to her instead.

She can't. Not yet.

She needs to change topic. 'Have you always been scared of heights?'

He looks away. 'Not always,' he answers. The mood changes and she wishes she hadn't asked.

There's so much about Noah that feels right, but it only makes these moments more disconcerting. How long before the need to know each other means excavating the deepest, darkest corners of their lives? She isn't ready for that, and neither is Noah, by the looks of it.

She tries to push away the panic at the thought of losing all they've just found together. But a small, insistent voice repeats its warning.

You know you can't avoid the truth forever.

9

Back at the hotel, they fall quiet. As they undress, Noah is unsettled. They seem lost for words, and although it's probably just exhaustion, it's still disconcerting.

He climbs into bed, and Alice gets in beside him, snuggling close, her warm fingers idly tracing a path from his chest down to his stomach. He puts his hand over hers, gently stilling the movement. He can't erase the vision of her halfway up that rock, so comfortable, a creature of the forest. Until then, everything about her had seemed so safe, yet that moment had been anything but. His heart beats faster at the memories.

'So how many times have you been here abseiling with Anu?'

'Two before today.'

'And you used to come alone?'

'Yes, I came alone.' She props herself up so she can look at him. 'Believe it or not, when I came to Thailand, the plan was to spend time on my own.'

Noah keeps his gaze level with hers. 'Believe it or not, I came with the same idea.' He laughs and pulls her close. 'So tell me about your climbing. I've never seen anyone do that. I still have no idea how you can hang on to those wet rocks.'

'I've had a lot of practice,' she answers, her voice muffled against his skin. She kisses him and he waits, hoping she'll say more.

'I fell in love with it at university. It came along at the perfect time in my life and was the best form of escape.'

'But aren't you frightened, without any safety gear? I was terrified just watching you.'

'Well, I don't do that as a rule. I'm quite good at it – and I went through a bit of a reckless phase and did it quite a lot – but a good friend of mine got worried and took me to task. I saw the sense in what he was saying, so I stopped and went back to the ropes and harnesses... but I felt a bit desperate today when I saw you just hanging there, and my instinct took over.'

Noah tries to ignore the mention of a 'he' – a male in her life he knows nothing about. A friend, she said, but didn't elaborate. He wants to ask more but it might look like jealousy – because he *is* bloody jealous.

He doesn't want to think about that. He rolls Alice onto her back, coming to rest on top of her. 'So you're saying it was my fault for being a wuss – you had to risk life and limb to save me.'

She laughs. 'Well, you could look at it that way.' Her curious eyes are close to his. 'Is there a reason you're so scared of heights?'

He lets go of her, and moves back to his side of the bed, staring up at the swirling fan, absently rubbing the scar on his right thigh. He remembers how he'd felt earlier, going over the edge, struggling to lean into the water while enduring the agonising flashbacks he knew would come: the nightmare of falling, the crippling pain in his leg.

'Noah?' Alice moves closer, her expression concerned. 'I didn't mean to upset you. Don't answer that if you don't want to.'

'It's okay,' he says, as she lays her head on his chest again. 'I fell off a balcony when I was a kid. Ever since, I've been a bit of a sook when it comes to heights.' He doesn't elaborate, because how can he tell her about the worst moment of his life: the terror of those flightless seconds; the anticipation of bones splintering on landing. That 'fall' wasn't exactly the right word for what had happened.

Lizzie had been there that day. He can still remember the alarm on her face, as she'd mouthed the word 'don't'. If only he'd listened. But when it came to Lizzie, he'd always made the wrong decisions.

He looks down, lost in regrets, and for a split-second it's not Alice's red hair fanning out across his bare chest, but Lizzie's. He reacts without thought, pushing her roughly away, swinging his legs over the side of the bed.

There's a beat of silence.

'Noah... are you okay?'

He can hear the uncertainty in her voice. Fuck, what's wrong with him?

Don't screw this up.

He bows his head. 'It's just some crap memories. Not your fault at all.'

Alice strokes his back. 'I'd never have arranged it if I'd known. I thought you'd love it.'

He doesn't want her feeling guilty. 'I did love it.'

She gives him a soft, sad smile, doubt written across her face. 'You don't have to say that.'

He strokes her hair. 'Listen, it's about time I got out of my comfort zone. I meant what I said yesterday about you helping me feel free. I don't want to let my fears stop me from trying new things. In fact –' he laughs, '– I promise that when you come back to Australia, I'll take you to the Blue Mountains and you might even persuade me to try another climb. My family have a little place there. Have you been?'

'Yes.' She brightens. 'It was one of my regular daytrips. Maybe I climbed past your house! I don't know about Australia, though – we should go somewhere more exotic. Greece, maybe. There's a climbing festival on Kalymnos that I'd love to go to.'

'Hmm, on second thoughts perhaps I'll just drink raki and watch.'

'Well –' she grabs his hand and pulls him towards her, '– I promise no more heights for a while. There are plenty of other ways we can get our kicks.'

She kisses him, and in a few seconds he has forgotten everything but the feel of his body against hers.

They've had no phone signal during their time at the national park, and Noah's battery has slowly died. He only remembers to plug his phone in as they are about to fall asleep, and as soon as there's enough charge, the screen lights up as the phone begins pinging.

Alice watches curiously as Noah rubs his eyes while scrolling through the messages.

I thought you were only going to Thailand for a couple of weeks?

Your father is furious with you, Noah.

Why aren't you answering now? You're scaring me, Noah. It's the last thing I need. At least let me know you're not in hospital somewhere.

If I don't hear from you within 12 hours I'm going to call the consulate.

He shows Alice the phone. 'Alice, meet my mum. Mum – Alice.'

'This is intense. You've only been out of touch for a day or so, right?'

'Yes. Oh, I don't know. Mum reads too much shit online – it fuels her paranoia. And I've upset them by changing my plans. I knew they wouldn't go easy on me.'

'Is your dad really furious with you then?'

Noah grimaces. 'Probably. Nowadays Dad is just pissed off with life. He hates the daily struggle, and I can't blame him, really. Even the simplest tasks are difficult and take forever. After his accident, he had to relearn how to go to the toilet, how to dress himself, basically pretty much everything we take for granted. He used to get through a lot every day, but now he's clumsy and absent-minded, and when things frustrate him he loses his temper easily. He didn't want me to have a holiday – he said I was being selfish and we had a huge argument about it – but I wouldn't back down because I knew I needed a break.' *And I also wanted to keep right away from Tom*, he thinks, but doesn't add that out loud.

He switches his phone off and sets it on the table. 'To be honest, I wish he'd retire and let me get on with running the restaurant, but he insists on being involved. Still, I guess it keeps him busy and stops him drinking too much, which tends to happen if he sits around with nothing to do.'

Alice makes a sympathetic face and nods at the phone. 'So are you going to reply?'

'I don't know yet. I might end up pissing Mum off even more, especially if I tell her what a brilliant time I'm having.'

'You're making me pretty nervous about meeting your mum!'

He laughs. 'Don't be, she fusses a lot, but she'll love you.' Then he registers what Alice said. 'So when are you planning to meet my mum?'

She looks surprised. 'I have no idea. I said that without thinking.'

'So there's no chance you'll come back with me?'

Alice is quiet for a while, then she says softly, 'I can't.'

'You can't... because of your contract?'

'Among other things.'

'So you really don't know when you'll be back in Australia?'

'No.' She sighs. 'Can we not talk about this – it's depressing. I just want to enjoy what we're doing right now.'

'Sure,' he replies quietly, but the doubts are creeping in. How can this ever be long-term if Alice's plans lie overseas? He's not in this for a holiday fling. He wants so much more.

She seems to read his mind. 'We're living in a beautiful bubble, aren't we?' she says sadly. 'But it can't last much longer.'

Noah doesn't reply.

They lie there for a while before he realises she has drifted off to sleep.

He props himself up on his elbow to watch her. Here and now it's his other life that seems unreal, and this is the place he belongs. If only they could stay here forever. He reaches out and touches a lock of her beautiful red hair, twisting it gently between his fingers. It must be almost the same colour as Lizzie's was, he thinks idly. Then he closes his eyes so that Lizzie's ghost can't creep in between him and a future he hasn't dared dream of for years.

When he has steadied himself, he opens his eyes, leans forward and kisses Alice lightly on the forehead. She doesn't stir. He wishes she would. He wants her reassurance that they'll work this out. That they'll figure out how to be together.

But he won't wake her. Instead, he lies down and stares up into the darkness, the minutes ticking by as he goes over everything again. Why are the highs with Alice interspersed with such a nagging sense of worry? He'd abseil down every bloody waterfall in Thailand if it would guarantee their happiness, but that's not it. There's something between them that's beyond his control. He can't name it yet, but he senses it lurking, casting those swift-falling shadows across Alice's face.

What if, no matter what he tries to keep them together, it isn't enough?

He pulls Alice into his arms as she sleeps, offering prayers to gods he has never believed in, so that he'll never have to let her go. The deep scar on his leg tingles, as though even now it hasn't quite healed. It feels like a warning, but he cannot decipher it yet.

10

Five days left. They waste the first on the journey back to the city, a stop-start affair that takes twice as long as it should, thanks to endless road repairs, leaving them frazzled and fighting exhaustion. The weekend is a lazy haze of food, sex and sleep.

Then Alice has to go back to work. She finds it unbearable, dreaming of Noah and counting down the clock while listening to her Thai students practising their faltering English. Last week she had cared about getting every detail right for them. This week she can hardly concentrate on what they are saying, and has to keep asking them to repeat themselves, to an increasing chorus of background murmurs as they sense something amiss. Her distraction worsens as each day goes by, until she's counting minutes rather than hours.

On each of their final, precious afternoons, Noah waits for her outside the school. They give up their intimate dinners at Alice's place and instead try to cram in all the experiences the city can offer them, as though each memory might cement them together a little more. They visit temples at sunset, and find an entire shopping mall made to look like a London street. Noah chats to locals in faltering Thai and they chuckle at his efforts, while Alice photographs the street cooking. They eat on the move: rice dishes wrapped in paper, and barbecued sweetcorn. Noah is more adventurous and tries an assortment of insects: roasted scorpions and cockroaches encased in banana leaves. For dessert they share dragon fruits, bright pink on the outside but pure white within, polka-dotted with black seeds and deliciously sweet.

On their last night together Noah tells Alice he has a surprise for her. He meets her on the steps of the language school, wearing navy jeans, dark red shoes and a patterned white shirt that gleams against his tanned skin. When he sees her he sweeps her into a long kiss that sets a group of nearby students giggling. Alice glances across and one gives her a thumbs-up.

They hail a cab, but as the car speeds them out of the city, an unspoken tension begins to build. Once this evening is over, Noah will have to go.

It's growing dark by the time the taxi stops. Noah climbs out and holds the door open for Alice. 'We're looking for the *khlongs*,' he says once she's standing next to him. 'They're like canals. It'll be this way, I think.' He gestures at a pathway between a dozen brightly lit market stalls. They politely deter the gaggle of persistent sellers, cutting through the melee of bartering. As the first *khlong* comes into sight, Alice sees that the water is almost hidden from view by narrow boats piled full of wares, mostly fruit and vegetables. Some vendors are cooking on little stoves perched precariously inside their boats. Each little vessel is lit by lanterns, while dozens of lights dangle from lines of wires along the sides of the canals.

'You remembered!' she says, thinking back to their first night alone at the restaurant when she'd told him about the floating markets. She stops to take in the scene. 'Wow, this is incredible.'

Noah doesn't hear her. He has moved ahead to negotiate with one of the boatmen. 'Coming?' he calls, and she realises he's already standing in one of the small wooden boats known as a *sampan*, holding his hand out to help her on board.

They cruise down the canal and chat to the vendors who pull up beside them, buying bags of ripe mango and papaya, eating dinner from skewers and banana leaves. All around, people call and clamour, sing and eat, cook and barter, argue and laugh. Noah has his arm around her. Alice has never felt more alive.

Then Noah leans in and whispers, 'I think I'm falling in love with you, Alice.'

She takes in his words, and her heart skips a few beats.

Noah watches her face, looking nervous and exposed. The hubbub, the lights and the people all disappear. They are alone, together.

And he's waiting.

Alice is desperate. She wants to tell him that she feels the same, but this is all wrong. Because how can he love her – truly – when she is still keeping parts of herself hidden?

Noah is beginning to turn pale. She senses his hurt, his worry that he might have misread the situation, and it overrides her fears. She takes his face in her hands, kissing him slowly and gently, savouring the feel of his lips on hers.

She moves back a fraction as she says, 'I feel the same.' Her voice is full of emotion. 'I really don't want you to go.'

He pulls her into a tight embrace. When Alice eventually opens her eyes, a few people are watching them curiously, sensing the gravity of the moment.

'I don't know how this is going to work,' Noah whispers, kissing her hair. 'But we're going to figure this out and be together. I can feel it.'

She nods. She wants to believe that too. But first they need to talk.

'We should find a bar somewhere,' he continues, looking around. 'Make a toast to our future.' He gets the attention of the boatman, and gestures towards the water's edge.

'Noah, wait...'

His hopeful expression falters. 'What's wrong?'

'I just – I need to talk to you. Can we find somewhere quiet, please?'

'Of course.'

Once they have disembarked, they head towards the first place they see, a little restaurant selling noodles. Once inside, it takes them a while to settle as the owner arrives to fuss over them with drinks and menus. Noah keeps glancing at Alice, and as soon as they are alone, asks, 'What is it? Are you okay?'

She takes a deep breath. 'There are some things I want to tell you, and I don't know how to start this conversation when you're flying thousands of kilometres away in the morning. It's nothing to do with how I feel about you, but it explains some of who I am... and why I'm here.' She stops, thinking of her dad. She sees him in her mind's eye, encouraging her. But where should she start?

In the end, she just blurts out, 'My dad is in prison.'

She waits as a mixture of emotions pass across Noah's face. Some, like shock, are clear. Others are harder to read. But now she has come this far, she will have to try to explain.

How much should she say right now? If she tells Noah the whole story it will dominate their night, and it will be the last thing she leaves him with, before they go their separate ways tomorrow. And yet, to explain means thinking about the worst night of her life. And whenever she does so, she gets a suffocating pressure in her chest, a trapped roar of distress that she doesn't know how to release.

'Can I tell you a bit about him?' she asks, struggling to keep her voice steady.

Noah takes her hand and strokes it in encouragement. 'Okay.'

'Right,' Alice begins, after a sip of her beer, 'well, my dad was an accountant for over twenty years, but that's just how he earned his money. His real passion – apart from me – was working in the nature reserve near our home. He spent countless hours there as a volunteer, caring for the plants, conducting surveys, weeding, cataloguing everything he saw. He worked so hard to keep that one piece of bushland pristine, when so much of the land around our town was getting neglected or flattened for building projects.'

She pauses, remembering all the time she had spent in the nature reserve as a young girl, following his careful instructions, stripping back the overgrowth with secateurs, cataloguing the wildflowers and the sightings of small marsupials. She'd gradually stopped going when it became more interesting to hang out with her friends, but it had remained a special place for them.

'One night during the summer – seven years ago now – a group of schoolies went down to the beach for a bit of fun, and managed to set the surrounding bush alight. The fire ripped through two-thirds of the protected area that my dad managed. They destroyed a lot of his work. Dad was devastated, and I was mortified, because the people who did it went to my school.'

The fire had made the local and state news. She could remember her father coming home the day after it happened, his hair and clothes scented with a peculiar mix of wood fire and eucalypts. He had collapsed into a chair and hunched over, his face hidden in his hands. She'd held him as he sobbed. Every shake of his shoulders had scooped out a little more of her until she felt utterly hollow.

She comes back to the present to find Noah's anxious eyes on her. 'At first I wasn't sure who the culprits were, but in the weeks that followed I began to hear rumours. A couple of the guys who had left school, but who had younger brothers in my year, began boasting to friends about getting away with it. Their brothers came to school and told their mates, like it was something to be proud of. To them it was a joke, and I was sickened by that. I was scared too, because these guys weren't nice to be around, and I knew they came from families you shouldn't mess with, but every time I looked at Dad, I felt so guilty that I was protecting the perpetrators rather than speaking up.'

Noah's grip tightens around hers. She stares at their intertwined fingers as she talks.

'So eventually, I broke down and told Dad. And of course, he immediately went to the police.' Her eyes meet Noah's, and she wonders if he can read the distress in them – the fervent wish that she could go back and reverse that one fateful decision.

'We had no idea what we had got ourselves into. We only found out afterwards that the families were associated with one of the local bikie groups. The two ringleaders who had caused the bushfire both got six months' prison time and community service, but the only plans they made on release were how to torment us. For the next couple of years they continually waged war on us. As soon as they were out of prison, I was cornered on the way home from school, right in the middle of my Year Twelve exams.'

She only has to close her eyes to see it again. Jason Reidy and Dean Morris advancing on her, backing her up against a tree and telling her what they would like to do to her. She couldn't think about it without a bolt of terror, an echo of how she'd felt that day.

She takes a deep breath. 'They put a dead rat in our mailbox. Slashed my dad's tyres. Poisoned more of the plants in the reserve. That's just a few examples of the constant crap we put up with. Then it began to get even more personal. They went to Dad's office, pretended to be clients to get in, and poured hot coffee over his laptop. It died immediately, along with weeks' worth of his work. We were considering a restraining order when the first things went missing from our house. My phone. A couple of my T-shirts. A small penguin toy I'd got from a roadtrip with Dad when I was a kid. Nothing really valuable – they were too clever for that. Sometimes things would come back. My T-shirts were hidden in a kitchen drawer. My phone turned up in the toilet.'

'That's terrible,' Noah cuts in. 'Couldn't the police do anything?'

'They were sympathetic. They advised changing the locks and pushing for a restraining order. But then I went off to uni, and Dean Morris reoffended and got put back in prison. I hated thinking of Dad dealing with it alone, but things seemed to calm down a bit that first year. However, when I was home for Christmas, Jason Reidy came back.' She can't contain the tremble in her voice.

Noah's fingers tighten around hers.

'Out of nowhere, one night he appeared in our lounge. I was reading by lamplight and Dad was already in bed, so perhaps he thought the house was empty... we found out later that he'd jimmied a window and climbed in. But when he saw me...'

She stops, remembering his initial surprise, before his expression warped into a sneering, snarling smile.

'He looked agitated, ready for a fight – there was a glint in his eyes, like he was high on something. I ran for the kitchen door, but he was too quick. He caught me and shoved me against the wall, then he noticed the knife block nearby. He grabbed one of the largest ones and began threatening me with it.' Her chest burns with the old fear and she focuses on the table as she talks. 'He wanted to hurt me, I have no doubt about that. He was laughing so loudly that he didn't even hear Dad come in.'

She recalls her father's stunned face, and braces herself for what comes next.

'Dad saw what was happening, and tried to get Reidy off me.' She swallows hard, her finger rubbing at a blemish on the tablecloth. 'Then Reidy turned on him, and Dad grabbed another knife in self-defence.' It's a struggle to get the words out because the memories still sicken her. 'The blade hit an artery. Reidy died on our floor.'

Finally, she dares to glance up at Noah. He's staring at her, horrified.

'We thought the police would see it as simple self-defence, but the investigators, Reidy's family, everyone seemed suspicious that Dad was out for revenge. He'd been overheard threatening Reidy the day before, and he didn't just stab Reidy once, but a few times. So Dad was accused of manslaughter.' She pauses to take a slow, shaky breath before continuing. 'Once my dad was arrested, he was tortured by the thought that Reidy's family might come after me for revenge, and this time he wouldn't be there to protect me. I'm not sure how much of his fear was justified, but then again we'd already been targeted just for putting Reidy in jail, and now Dad had killed him. The Reidy family made their fury known through the press, and after that, Dad was adamant that I should leave the country.

'I didn't want to at first. I moved to Sydney and stayed in a share house, eventually dropped out of uni and trained to teach English as a second language. But I was always looking over my shoulder, imagining there were people following me, or waiting for me in my room. The only escape I had back then was climbing. It saved me time after time.'

'So what made you finally come away?'

'Dad's sentencing. He got five years – he's served nearly three of them now. There was no trial as he pleaded guilty. His lawyer wanted to contest it, but Dad didn't want to go through the ordeal. I think he was determined to speed the process up and get it over with. He kept begging me to leave. When I told him I was coming to Thailand, he was so relieved. He doesn't want me to go back.'

She has to stop there or the memory will overwhelm her.

Noah takes her hand, squeezing it over and over. 'Oh, Alice... I don't know what to say.'

'Neither do I. I don't talk about this with anyone – but I wanted you to know.'

Noah exhales slowly. 'I'm glad you told me. And I'm really sorry, Alice.' He hesitates, his eyes not leaving hers. 'So has it helped, being away from home?'

'I think so. I miss Dad. My friends too, but everyone has their own lives now – and I got fed up of being the gloomy one.'

Noah's frown is sympathetic. 'And what about when it was all happening? Did you have people around to look after you then?'

Alice frowns. 'Kind of. Although never the ones we thought. Some good friends faded out fast, while some really unlikely people went out of their way to help us. Even so, there were plenty of times when I felt incredibly alone, particularly after Dad was sentenced. It was unbearable, feeling so stuck and scared while I watched everyone else moving on with their lives. That's partly why I came here.'

Noah leans forward, his face full of concern. 'And how are you doing now?'

She shrugs. 'I'm okay. I keep to myself most of the time.' She gives him a tentative smile. 'But somehow you caught me off guard.'

He doesn't smile back. 'So you're not sure if you'll come back to Australia?'

She glances at the table. Then into his eyes. Then back at the table again. 'No. I don't know if I can feel safe there anymore.' She falls silent, unable to explain any further. The effort of this conversation is exhausting.

'So what were your plans... before you met me?'

'There's no master plan, Noah. I'm winging it. Taking it one day at a time, while I try to figure things out. You don't fancy joining me, do you?'

His face falls. 'Oh Alice – you don't know how much I want to say yes. But—'

'Your family,' she interjects. 'And the inquest. And your whole life. Don't worry, I get it.'

Noah runs his hands over his face. 'This is a nightmare.' His eyes plead with her to understand. And she does. Right now, he needs to be there just as much as she needs to be here. She takes his hand. 'We'll find a way to make this work, Noah. I don't know how yet, but we will.'

He squeezes her fingers, and she replies in kind, but she can't meet his eyes. He knows more about her than almost anyone else. But still, it's not quite everything. Not yet.

11

By the time they reach the apartment, there are only hours left together. Noah is shaken by Alice's story. He needs a way to remind her that in his absence there should be no doubts between them. There is little sleep to come – only their entwined bodies on the mattress, the floor, in the shower, as though this might sustain them. It isn't the ecstatic connection of those first few days anymore – they are anchoring themselves to each other, ensuring that nothing can tear them apart.

Noah has no doubt. He cannot live without her now.

His flight is at eleven am. The alarm trills at seven and they surface reluctantly from sleep, bleary-eyed. His bags are all packed, ready to go. There is still so much left to say, but they are out of time. Beyond words, they hold one another until the last possible moment, when the taxi pulls up outside.

'I love you, Alice,' Noah says, his voice ragged as he cups her face for one last kiss. 'This hurts like hell.'

'I know – but you have to go,' she replies, holding tight to him, dreading the thought of letting him leave. 'We can do this, Noah. Your family needs you right now.' She brushes his cheek with her fingertips. 'I'll miss you like crazy, but we'll work everything out, because I love you too.'

Foreheads touching. Eyes closed.

'See you soon, okay?'

'Okay.'

His lips brush hers. He picks up his suitcase and bag. And then he is gone.

On the ride to the airport, Noah stares out of the window, his eyes on the blurry streets of Thailand, his mind back in Alice's apartment. He has the unnerving sensation that the last few days are unspooling, like those cine films his grandparents had shown him when he was a kid, when they would wind them back after viewing, until the tape fell off the machine with a sharp click, and the memories were packed away.

No one at home will understand. They will see this as a holiday fling. The idea of Alice squeezed into two-dimensional memory is unbearable. He will not let her become the near-miss he looks back on with a rueful smile and the nagging thought, *If only I'd been braver...*

Stop panicking, he tells himself, needing to dispel these continual prickles of unease. *Why are you so frightened?*

He sees Alice's pinched face last night at the bar. Her father is locked up for manslaughter. Her mother committed suicide. Alice avoids hospital when she's hurt, climbs rocks without safety gear. She'd stood in front of an elephant and let it charge her. Either she doesn't notice danger, or she doesn't care.

As much as he loves her, he knows there's more, still unspoken, between them. After all, he hasn't shared everything. Perhaps she hasn't either.

He leans forward, opening his mouth to tell the driver to go back. He's desperate to pull Alice close and feel how snugly she fits inside his arms. He wants to reassure her that everything between them is real. He needs to remind her, one more time, of how much she means to him.

But then, overhead, he sees the first green sign for the airport.

He sits back and lets his shoulders sag. Prolonging things now won't make this parting any easier, because he has to go home. There are things he needs to deal with before his life can move on. Memories that must be shared; details he's never spoken of aloud.

All visions of Alice are briefly overlaid by Lizzie. Her stricken face a question. Her expectation clear.

His head spins. He sits back, and closes his eyes.

It's time to face Tom.

12

Alice curls up in bed, wrung out, casting around for evidence of Noah – something he might have forgotten, an excuse to go after him. There's nothing.

It's like he was never here.

She feels nauseous, calls in sick, sleeps for a while, and wakes to find the air conditioner has gone off and she is soaked in sweat. She gets up to shower, leaving the water cold, and realises that even this little cubicle is crowded with memories – beautiful memories that threaten to turn painful, now they are marked with an absence she doesn't know how to bear.

She dresses quickly and heads to a small roadside café that serves banana pancakes. It's her usual comfort food, but today the batter sticks in her throat and she can't finish them.

What now?

She's neglected her chores lately. There is school prep and marking and a pile of washing waiting for her. However, she hasn't emailed her dad for nearly a fortnight. That's got to be top of her list.

The thought of him in prison is a continual waking nightmare. To begin with she had been a regular visitor, baulking at the sight of him in prison scrubs. The chairs they sat on were bolted to the floor, likewise the table, which kept them a discrete distance from one another. 'Stops them throwing the furniture around – or passing drugs so easily,' her dad had said wearily, the reflections of the harsh strip-lights overhead beginning to flicker in his eyes.

After his life of hard work, those furniture-throwers and drug dealers were her dad's cellmates. The torment overwhelmed her at first. During her visits he had seen it, and reminded her of her dreams to explore the world. As the first couple of years passed, her distress grew, and her choices narrowed, until it was either leave the country, or climb rocks without harnesses and spend nights paralytic in low-lit bars. Finally she had saved herself, if only because she'd promised him she would.

He cannot emerge from this unchanged, and she aches at the thought of him slowly disappearing. He had always tried so hard to be dad *and* mum to her – fumbling her hairstyles with awkward, stubby fingers; leaving her books about the human body when he hadn't words to explain; dancing and clapping awkwardly to the chart-toppers she liked to listen to after school. Even when the demands of his job increased, and he was always on his laptop, feigning interest and murmuring platitudes while he examined rows of figures, she'd understood he was doing his best.

She longs for the moment she can hug him freely again, without being watched. She needs him out of prison. His freedom is the only thing that can release them both. There's two years left to go, and she's counting the days.

Back in her apartment, she opens her laptop, fingers hovering over the keys as she searches for the right words. It seems wrong to tell him about her adventures when he's stuck staring at the same four walls every day. Nor can she fully confide, when his emails are printed and presented to him via the prison mail, obviously read by others. The thought of strangers' eyes on her words always stilts the flow of them.

I've met someone, she begins. *His name's Noah.*

Her fingers pause. She can't hope to explain the intensity of everything that's happened. She tells him about their trip to Khao Yai, all except for the free-climbing rock rescue. She doesn't try to explain how Noah has turned her inside-out. She suspects her dad will recognise that this man is important to her, just from the fact she has mentioned him. *Let me know how you are*, she finishes, understanding that his reply will take weeks, since he can only use snail mail to communicate with her. *I love you. I'll write again soon.*

Once finished, she checks the time and realises that Noah's plane will have taken off by now, carrying him further and further away. She rereads her email, but the words are swimming.

She pictures her dad taking her hands and saying, 'If you really want to be together, he'll have to know everything.'

No, actually. The old Dad would have said that. Now, surely, he would tell her to say nothing. Now they both know that some secrets should be starved of oxygen.

Emotions rise, wave upon wave. She quickly sends the email, then flicks over to Google and types in: '*Lizzie.*'

Adds, '*Missing. Sydney.*'

Clicks search.

A second later there's a list of results. She knows instantly that she has found the right girl.

Lizzie Burdett. Age seventeen. A close-up photo of a beautiful young face smiling for the camera. Fully present in that moment, no inkling of how this photo would be used.

The sight of Lizzie is jarring. Alice begins to wind strands of her hair through her fingers as she clicks on the tab for more images. The same photo replicates itself numerous times, sometimes inset into a 'Missing' poster, and interspersed with algorithm oddities, random photos of people and places that appear to have nothing to do with Lizzie. Alice selects the image of a family holding one of the posters, knowing instinctively that these people are Lizzie's parents and sisters. Her mum and dad sit on dining room chairs, stiff-backed and sombre, while the sisters stand behind them in a macabre family portrait, the middle child reduced to a piece of paper. The mother has tried to cover her grief with makeup. The sisters are ashen-faced teens, leaning in, shoulders touching, as though propping each another up. The article had been written not long after Lizzie disappeared and the quotes are all from Lizzie's father. *'We're in a waking nightmare,'* Miles had told the reporter. *'We just want Lizzie home.'*

He'd uttered those words twelve years ago, and Lizzie still isn't home.

Alice's heart goes out to them. She knows something about living with an empty place at the table, an imaginary presence so close that it can make you whip around, expecting to find someone there. Her mum had always been a shadow in the background of life – her absence continually revealed in the times other mothers flocked to their daughters: the school pick-ups and end-of-term shows, the elaborate hairstyles and carefully chosen outfits. Alice understands that even when you have lost a person, and you know in your heart they are never coming back, part of you never stops looking, or wishing.

She turns her focus back to the internet. To Lizzie. She scans the photos again, clicking at random. There are numerous articles, most containing only brief snatches of information, things Noah has already told her. The last sighting of Lizzie. The argument with Tom.

One article shows Miles Burdett again, still holding the same photo of his daughter. His hair has receded and gone grey at the sides, while Lizzie hasn't changed, trapped in time like an insect in tree sap. FAMILY OF MISSING GIRL HOPE INQUEST WILL REIGNITE THEIR SEARCH FOR ANSWERS.

Alice searches Miles Burdett's eyes for a sign he might be hiding something, but he just appears sad, slightly dazed, and exhausted.

He looks like my dad.

And that's not the only unnerving similarity. She studies Lizzie's photo again in Miles's hands – the long hair, that wide smile. Alice is stunned. Now she understands Noah's intense stare on the boat. He had mentioned nothing of Alice's hair, but it's unmissable – a shining cascade of wavy red tresses.

Just like mine.

13

Noah is almost back in Australia, but his heart is lagging behind somewhere, lost in the clouds. All day, it's been hard to settle to anything. To begin with, at Suvarnabhumi Airport, he had anxiously debated each minute away, telling himself he could still get a taxi back to Alice's place, say to hell with the rest of his life. But while he had agonised through check-in and customs and onto the plane, an aggravating sense of obligation had driven him forward. Once the plane took off, deliberation became pointless.

There'd been a short flight to Singapore, then a few hours' wait to pick up his Sydney connection. On board the second plane, he spends a while trying to find a good movie, avoiding glimpses of the blue and white crosshatch beyond the windows. How does anyone settle while thousands of feet in the air? He chooses a horror film, plugs himself in, and watches as unconscionable monsters terrorise an innocent family. Sometime during that he remembers Rachel's podcast.

When the movie ends, he finds his phone and scrolls to the latest episode. No more excuses, he thinks, as he downs his mini can of beer in almost one gulp. It's time to reacquaint himself with Tom and Josh.

Once listening, he realises he's heard a lot of the story before. He grimaces as Josh insists that Lizzie had feelings for him. '... *it was only a matter of time before she realised we were a better fit. We laughed so hard together. We under stood each other.'*

'But weren't you going out with Lizzie's best friend?' Rachel cuts in.

'Oh, things with Gemma had run their course.'

'Did Gemma know that?'

Silence.

When Tom comes on, he repeatedly denies his involvement. His voice is measured, only cracking once, when he insists, *'I loved her.'* It's a shade lower than Noah remembers, but there's enough familiarity in the baritone to make Noah's stomach clench, as though braced for a phantom jab. He replays the sentence, wondering why the break in Tom's voice had occurred at that moment. Was it pure sadness, or the briefest note of guilt?

Then Lizzie's sister Kate begins to talk. *'Lizzie was really troubled by Josh. He was Tom's close mate, and was supposed to be dating Lizzie's best friend, but he kept coming on to her. She found it really awkward. She didn't want to be mean, but she was only interested in Tom. However, I think... look, she knew that Josh's attention was making Tom jealous. She wanted Tom to notice, because it made him more attentive, but she didn't realise she was playing with fire.'*

Kate's words are firm. Decisive.

Noah shudders. *She thinks Tom did something to Lizzie. And she's not the only one.*

He pulls out his earbuds, just as a voice says, 'Ladies and gentlemen, this is your captain speaking. We have begun our descent into Sydney. Please return to your seats and fasten your seatbelts.'

Noah's belt is already tightly fastened. As they descend, he peers out and sees the sunrise casting its pastel palette over the familiar harbour, the perfect arc of the iron-boned bridge beside its showy little sister, those iconic white sails jutting towards the water. He has a moment of horror that Alice is now so far away. It's disorientating when he can close his eyes and still feel the press of her damp skin against his.

He craves her naked beneath him. He wants her teasing him with that mischievous look on her face. He hopes she understands why he's had to leave. Nevertheless, it feels like he's let her down. He's desperate to have her back in his arms, to pull her close until there's no space for the doubts to sneak in and fester.

There's a short, sharp bump as they land, and, simultaneously, Noah senses the shift in him. Which version of him has returned? Is it the conscientious son, too busy with the family business to give any time to a decent relationship? Or the exhilarated man who has been abseiling down a waterfall and found love where he least expected it? It's hard to reconcile those two versions of himself, never mind determine how they might work together.

It's time to find out. As soon as the plane stops taxiing, he jumps up to collect his bag.

He isn't expecting anyone to meet him, but spots his mum straight away. His heart sinks as she waves, those familiar rows of bangles along her wrist jangling and winking in the light. His mother always stands out in a crowd, partly thanks to the heavy jewellery she wears. Today a bright stone necklace is paired with earrings so long they almost skim her shoulders, and she appears to have dyed her short-cropped hair an even lighter shade of platinum while he's been gone. Even in the airport concourse she's wearing the kind of sunglasses that make her look like an Audrey Hepburn devotee. Which she is – she's told him a thousand times that her favourite movie is *Breakfast at Tiffany's*.

Noah suspects his mother imagines herself as some kind of forgotten movie star. When she visits the restaurant she drifts beside tables, stopping to chat to everyone, bestowing free drinks or desserts if she discovers they are dining out for a special occasion. More than once, Noah's father had threatened to ration her visits, for fear of losing too much money.

Noah returns her wave and tries to smile with equal enthusiasm, but the sight of her brings home just how much he has enjoyed his weeks of escape. The idea of sitting with his parents tonight over dinner and drinks, listening to their rundown of every tiny development and hiccup at the restaurant, leaves him instantly jetlagged.

'The prodigal son returns,' Cathy cries as he reaches her. She cups his face as she kisses him, two sets of immaculately manicured nails digging into his cheeks. 'Well, whatever you've been up to, you're looking very well on it, thank god. Your father was beginning to wonder if you'd got caught up in some kind of drug scene over there. Come on, the car is this way.'

He trails her up lifts and across walkways until they reach the LandCruiser. Once they are inside, his mother puts the ticket for the barrier between her teeth, so she can't talk until they are out in the open. Then come the questions that Noah's expecting.

'Okay, spill the beans. What on earth possessed you to stay there for so long? You had us worried, and it's been a nightmare trying to manage on our own. I hadn't realised how much your father is struggling. He can't handle the long hours, and I'm sure he's taken to drinking more since you left. I think he's had a shock realising how much you do for us nowadays.'

'Well, I wish he would stop pushing himself so hard.' Noah stares at the scenery as he talks, trying to quell his frustration. 'He must know I'm capable of running the restaurant by now. Just think, if he slowed down you could have more time together, maybe do some travelling of your own.'

Cathy snorts. 'Yeah, I can just see your dad sipping cocktails in a Hawaiian shirt. Seriously, Noah, you've got to understand that he's fought so hard for that place for so damn long that it's become part of him. He doesn't know who he is when he's away from Carruso's. Anyway, tell me, how was your trip? What did you enjoy the most?'

Noah reddens, and hesitates. He doesn't find it easy to talk to his mother about women. Ever since Lizzie, in fact. He still cringes recalling some of their conversations back when he was a teen, his hormones raging. She'd always meant well, but had been a death hex on his self-esteem. He could remember her sitting at the breakfast bar, asking Noah and Tom if they had enough condoms – and Tom, two years older and dating Lizzie, had jumped at the chance to stick the knife in. 'I'm fine, Mum, thanks,' he'd said, 'and I don't think Noah has any use for them.' And he'd messed up Noah's hair and laughed as Noah shoved him away. Noah hadn't spoken to his mother for a few days after that, and she'd seemed to get the message. At least, she'd never asked him that question again.

'So, go on then, tell me about Thailand,' Cathy prods.

Still he hesitates. He's never brought girls home. There's been nothing serious for years, and he'd thought perhaps he was too much of an idealist – or scared of commitment. However, in the last few weeks a different answer has surfaced. He has simply been waiting for Alice.

'Noah?' Cathy says loudly. 'Talk to me!'

'Sorry, what were you saying?'

'I was asking about Thailand. Why did you stay there on your own for so long?'

He exhales. 'I met someone.'

The car lurches momentarily to the left as his mother's gaze swings towards him. 'You met someone? You mean a girl?'

He laughs. 'No, a Martian. Yes, Mum, a girl.'

'I knew it. And was it a holiday fling or is this a special someone?'

'I think she might be a very special someone.'

His mum purses her lips. 'I see. So go on then, tell me about her.'

'Her name is Alice. She teaches English in Bangkok.'

'Where did you meet her? It wasn't at one of those full moon parties, was it?'

Noah laughs out loud. 'Seriously? What makes you think I went to a full moon party? And how do *you* know about them?'

'I know stuff, Noah, I might be old but I'm not dead yet. I thought that's why all you young things went to Thailand.'

'I'm twenty-seven, Mum, not seventeen. And I went to Bangkok, not the islands. So no, I didn't meet her at a rave. I met her at a Buddhist temple.'

'What the hell were you doing there?' his mum cries, as though this was worse than the rave.

'What do you think? I was sightseeing.'

'I see, well, at least you weren't joining the monastery, I suppose!' She swings the steering wheel to the right to avoid a bicycle and Noah grabs the dashboard. He's lost in thoughts of Alice again, wondering if she's ever been to a full moon party – whether she has danced drunkenly with her arms in the air, a beer or cocktail spilling from her hand. He pictures her in that white playsuit she wore on their first proper date, her lithe pale limbs, those beautiful full lips. His groin begins to tingle. Just the thought of Alice's naked body sends an ache through him, and he despairs at the unknown number of weeks ahead, months even, where he will only imagine her curves and contours, those soft, open places where his hands and mouth have travelled, the feel of his hips against the insides of her thighs.

'What are you grinning about now?'

'Nothing.' He's glad his mother can't read his thoughts – or maybe she can, because she gives him a very strange look.

'So when do we get to meet her?'

'I don't know.'

'It isn't serious, then?'

'It's not that. She's teaching over there, she has a contract. So it might be a while.'

'Well, that's probably for the best, considering what we've got on our plate right now.'

Instantly Noah's on the alert. 'Have you spoken to Tom?'

'Yesterday.'

The thought is surreal. He knows his mum has had sporadic email contact with Tom over the years, but as far as he's aware, Tom has refused to speak to her – or to any of them – before now. For a long time, Cathy hasn't been able to say Tom's name without her eyes glistening.

His tone softens. 'What was that like?'

Cathy sighs. 'Strange. He sounds different – well, I could still tell it was him, but he sounds – I don't know – more grown up, maybe.'

'I've heard his voice. You know he's on a podcast, talking about Lizzie?'

'Yes, I've been told, but I haven't been able to bring myself to listen to it. I'm glad you have, you can fill me in. Is there anything on there that we should know?'

Noah thinks back. 'Not really. Tom and Josh both deny they would ever hurt Lizzie. It's all very dramatic, but that's the point, isn't it? Rachel wants people to keep tuning in, even though she's not really saying anything new.' He hesitates. 'So when are we likely to see Tom?'

'He's not planning to come back until just before the inquest. And he's going to stay in a hotel – says he doesn't want to bring unwanted attention to the house. He thinks he might get hassled by the press or the police or whoever.'

Noah's glad to hear that, although he doubts his brother's motives. More likely Tom doesn't want to face them for any length of time.

'Which hotel?'

'He didn't tell me.'

'And the inquest still starts in a fortnight?'

'Two weeks today, yes.'

She keeps her eyes on the road, indicating left, and swings the car round the corner sharply. 'Now, your dad wants me to talk you through the requests from the Bensons for their wedding reception. We only have a day left to make sure everything goes smoothly.'

Noah can hear the rebuke in her tone. He tries to concentrate as she begins a monologue about orders and place settings and how difficult it's been to source the right shade of blue for the napkins, but as hard as he tries, he keeps tuning out. Right now, he couldn't give a shit about the Bensons' nuptials.

His lethargy is troubling. Things are changing. So far he has fulfilled everything his parents have ever wanted of him, learning the ropes of the restaurant, eager to prove his own worth, to help shape the business and propel it to greater heights. He'd been determined to make up for his older brother's failings, because every time Tom's name came up, Noah watched his father bristle at the mention of his eldest son: the person who had let them all down. With Tom gone, Raf had set about grooming Noah to continue the family legacy. It was billed as his destiny, a foregone conclusion, and he'd accepted it.

Until now. Until Alice.

In the last few weeks he's realised how apathetic he's been about his life. He's followed the path laid out for him, because there's never been reason to change direction. But Alice has opened his eyes, forcing him to question everything. There's no going back. How long has it been since he's felt such exhilaration, such fear? He's finally found the scaffolding that bridges his past to his future, and he's tiptoeing along it, wavering as he tries to balance, but heading for somewhere new.

There's the inquest to get through first, but other than that, his whole focus is on reuniting with Alice, and seeing if they can carry on where they left off. He'll have to talk to her soon. They need a plan.

He takes a sidewards glance at his mother, who is concentrating on the road. All along he'd thought he was helping his parents by cushioning them in false security, accepting his lot. But now, unless he can find his way back to that, it could be Noah rather than Tom who will finally crush their dreams, and break their hearts.

14

Alice is awake before dawn. She flicks on lights, picks up her book, then sets it down when the words keep blurring. Grabs her iPad and browses Netflix. Finds nothing of interest.

She checks the time. He should be home now. She consults her phone and her Skype call log. Nothing.

She should get organised. There are lessons to plan, food to buy, washing to be done. If only she could find her mojo. Tonight she's only capable of sitting and staring at the wall.

She wastes another half-hour staring into space, and then remembers the podcast. She jumps up and finds her phone, intending to set about tidying the house as she listens. But as soon as she hears the first line – '*I did not kill Lizzie Burdett*' – she sits down heavily in her chair again.

Tom's voice is deep and has a lazy drawl to it. There's nothing about it that reminds her of Noah. The overhyped tension of those initial minutes – the dramatic music cutting in and out – leaves Alice with an immediate distaste for Rachel Lawrence's style, but she doesn't turn it off. Much easier to let Rachel tell her everything than to quiz Noah, when it's obviously so painful for him.

She settles back to listen.

'*Lizzie lived with her mum, her dad and her two sisters on the outskirts of Belhaven,*' says Rachel. '*The Burdetts were well off, both parents were doctors, although since having children, Lizzie's mother had worked part time. To the outside world they were a happy, wellfunctioning family, but at the time Lizzie disappeared, Miles had been suffering from stress-related fatigue, having lost a considerable portion of his savings in a bad investment up in Queensland. Lizzie had spoken occasionally to Gemma about her father's stress and anger in the weeks before she went missing.'*

'I've known Miles since kindy,' says a different voice – it's Gemma, Lizzie's best friend – *'and he was definitely struggling before Lizzie disappeared. But I never believed the rumours he could have hurt her. He loved his kids too much – it was obvious in the way he looked at them, or whenever he spoke about them. I think he was just gutted because he'd lost a heap of money that was meant for their future.*

'And you know –' Gemma's voice wavers, *'– out of everyone, he's never given up on Lizzie. He's still searching for her, poor bloke.'*

Alice pictures Miles carrying around the rumpled poster of Lizzie, his entire life dictated by the tiniest chink of hope. It's heart-wrenching.

She really should get on with her chores.

Instead, she presses play on episode two.

The next twenty minutes prove highly unsatisfying. What has Rachel really uncovered, Alice wonders, once she has listened to Tom's and Josh's versions of events. Two teenage friends who fell for the same girl – that's not uncommon. There doesn't seem much basis for suspecting them of murder. The whole episode is salacious: street gossip dressed up as media savvy. Alice swallows a surge of discomfort. She knows all about that. Her father's name had been in the papers too, and she hadn't found the man she knew in any of those stories. *'The reason we fought that night was because I loved her,'* Tom tells Rachel, his voice breaking. *'It was a silly, jealous fight, and every day I wish it had never happened. Lizzie and I were meant for each other.'*

Josh's words are spookily similar. *'Part of me will always love her, because I never had the chance to get over her. When she disappeared, I thought we were at the start of something. That last night, at the party, she told me she might call things off with Tom. She'd finally realised how controlling he was. I was so happy. I really thought she might be the love of my life.'*

Alice chews on her thumbnail as she listens. These men seem like two sides of the same coin. They weren't even adults when all this occurred, but the upfront way they both talk about that final evening, and about Lizzie, is disquieting. If one of them is lying, they must be psychopathic. How else could they fool everyone around them for so many years? It's unlikely, but there were cases, weren't there? Occasionally, people were arrested decades later for crimes they had lived with and consistently denied.

She shudders. Why is she dwelling on this? It isn't good for her, when she knows firsthand that after trauma, nothing returns to the way it was. The shockwaves go so deep that everything shifts, and the newly exposed edges of life begin wearing away at one another, to eventually settle, or explode again. She wishes her dad had told her that every choice a person made would only reveal itself fully in retrospect, through a never-ending chain of consequences. Then she wouldn't have told him about Jason Reidy setting the fire, and thereby sealed his fate.

And what about Lizzie? Was she doomed when Miles's investment failed? Or when she chose Tom instead of Josh? Or perhaps when she assumed it was safe to walk home alone in the dark?

And what about me? Where am I heading now?

The questions surge and multiply, until Alice grows lightheaded. Since coming to Thailand, she had pretended her life could settle down, directionless but benign. Now her time here feels more like a stint in a waiting room. Everything changed the moment Noah offered to fix her broken lens. Sooner or later she will need to make a decision: tell him her secret and risk everything; or safeguard it, and accept that part of her will always be alone.

15

Noah can tell his father is home, as Raf's wheelchair is in the entrance hall, and there's cricket commentary coming from the TV in the lounge. He follows the sound, entering the room to see the balding dome of his father's head peeking over the back of the sofa.

'Hello, Dad.' Noah pats him on the shoulder.

'You're back then,' Raf replies, eyes still on the screen.

'I am. You're up early.'

'Wanted to see this, and I couldn't stay awake last night. So how was it?'

Noah moves around to take a seat opposite. 'Really good.'

Raf's eyes flick away from the TV to scrutinise his son. 'Well, you look relaxed. Pity it won't last for long now you've got so much to do.'

Noah isn't sure how to respond. He's come to expect this kind of antagonism, but for once it's easy to ignore, because he's studying his dad in shock. Raf is pale, the hollows under his eyes coloured with dark smears. The furrows in his brow have carved deep lines across his forehead, so he looks like he's permanently frowning. The anger at being left in the lurch is radiating from him, and he appears to have aged a year in the last couple of weeks. Or has their separation just highlighted what Noah had failed to notice each day?

Cathy's worries in the car suddenly seem real. Raf is

shrinking before their eyes. Noah glances at the old photos of his dad on the wall, and can hardly believe this is the same person. The father he'd known in his early childhood was always active, playing rugby and AFL and cricket with his boys, wrestling them and hoisting them upside down, their heels resting on his square-set shoulders. At school drop-off and pick-up the other fathers had flocked to Raf, while the mothers flirted with him. He'd been the star of summer barbecues, reliving his career highlights to a rapt audience while lazing in the pool, or pouring more wine for the women, who fluttered their eyelashes and seemed to hold on to the glass for a few seconds more than they needed to.

Then his footy career finished – with too many injuries and not enough goals. Raf began working at the restaurant, and a different man emerged: short-tempered, self-centred, and permanently in a rush. For the first few years Raf had worked alongside his father, and Noah could well recall the formidable Stefano Carruso, who ran the place like an army camp, and had no time for slackers. Noah's grandfather had helped to design and build the restaurant himself, slowly adding extensions and tinkering with the *à la carte* menus until, by the nineties, Carruso's was regularly feted as one of the North Shore's top restaurants.

However, with success came a different struggle, as both Raf and his father became obsessed with their standing in the community: '*Reputation is everything*,' Stefano would repeat to young and old at every family dinner, where Carruso's always dominated the conversation. '*Takes years to build but seconds to blow up. We've always got to watch our step.*' But when Stefano had a heart attack, soon after the millennium, it quickly became clear that Raf didn't have the same business acumen as his father. Rather, he enjoyed charming the customers and inviting local sportsmen in for meals on the house. Noah had witnessed the dark circles under his parents' eyes, as profit margins began to fall and staff were laid off. During family visits to the hospital,

Stefano barked orders from his bed, and seemed perpetually disappointed with his son's struggle to maintain his strict standards. When he passed away in 2003 he left Raf an inheritance with a caveat: he could only use the money on the restaurant's upkeep.

The funds had saved Carruso's for a while, but the windfall couldn't last forever. In the years after Lizzie disappeared, as Noah began his apprenticeship, the profits nosedived again. Raf had fought day and night to hold everything together, as his hair receded and his frown lines deepened. '*Don't be like your selfish brother*,' he would slur at Noah, on the occasions he found solace in a line-up of shot glasses. '*Don't you run away from your responsibilities too.*'

Once again, the family had managed to hang on to the business. And then, in 2009, Raf fell off Carruso's roof. The house was re-mortgaged to keep everything afloat during his rehab, and Noah began to work longer hours. The survival of the restaurant became all that mattered.

Through sheer grit and toil they'd done it: Carruso's had not only been saved but had thrived in recent years. And yet, Noah knew it had come at considerable cost to his family.

The workload and the last decade of struggle had taken its toll on all of them, but most of all on Raf.

Raf's eyes cloud as he surveys Noah's face, as though he can sense these thoughts, and Noah quickly hunts for a safe topic. 'You heading in to work today?'

'I'll see – maybe later. What about you?'

'I need a sleep first. I'll take the day to get myself sorted and head over in the morning. Mum's told me where you're up to with the wedding reception. I'll get on to it first thing.'

'It'll be a rush to get it done now.' Raf's eyes are back on the cricket. 'But I'm sure we'll manage.' There's a bitter edge to his tone. 'We always do.'

Noah heads back to the hallway to grab his luggage and takes it upstairs, leaving it in a corner. Then he lies down on his bed, grateful finally to have a comfy place to sleep.

Noah doesn't wake until late afternoon, and as soon as he's up, he Skypes Alice. She answers straight away, her hair in the plaits she often wears for work. Her bright pink strappy top shows just a hint of cleavage, and he wishes he was there to undress her. Just the thought of what they had been up to the last time they were together is making him wild. He needs to make a plan, he realises. He has to know when he's going to see her again, and it needs to be sooner rather than later.

'This is horrible, seeing you on a screen, knowing I can't touch you,' he says. 'Christ, I just want to come back, Alice.'

'I know.' She bites her lip. 'I wish you were here too.'

'So tell me, what have you been doing since I left?'

'Aside from missing you? It's just been the usual day – teaching sentence structure to my students at school. What about you? What was the flight like?'

'Long.' He pauses, and when the silence lingers he searches quickly for another subject, hating that he can't fill the gaps in their conversation with a cuddle. Then Alice cuts in.

'I found some information about Lizzie online.'

'Oh, yeah?' A nervous charge flashes through him.

'She looks a bit like me, don't you think?'

He hesitates. Tries to swallow his discomfort. 'A little bit – I thought that too the first time I saw you. It's just the hair though, really – you're taller than she was. And very different in many ways. So what else did you find?'

'Just stuff about her family. It's terrible, I feel so bad for them.'

'Me too.' He pauses. 'I think about them a lot at the moment. It's going to be awful watching everything get raked up again.'

He recalls the appeal in the first days after Lizzie's disappearance. The horror of watching Miles and Sylvie Burdett sobbing on screen, publicly begging for Lizzie's safe return, for their daughter's life, their own lives, a futile plea that things might one day return to normal. They had asked people who knew anything to come forward, but they had spoken to Lizzie too. *'Please, Lizzie, if you are somewhere and want to come home, please don't think you'll be in trouble. All we want is to know that you're safe.'* Even now, the memory tears at his heart.

He focuses back on Alice, who's still talking.

'How are your mum and dad? Did they forgive you for staying longer?'

'Honestly, I'm not sure yet. I'm going to have to work my arse off in the restaurant to make it up to them.'

Alice laughs. 'I've got to go in a sec. I'm meeting a teacher from the language school – she wanted some help with lesson plans so I offered. I figured I should keep myself busy – less time to miss you.'

'Okay.' He smiles. 'Remember to miss me a little bit.'

She blows him a kiss. 'That won't be hard. Talk tomorrow?'

'Sure. I–' He stops. Changes his mind. 'Have a good night.'

After hanging up, Noah stares at the empty screen and says softly, 'I love you, Alice. I wish you were here.'

The next day Noah wakes early. Knowing Alice will probably be sleeping, he sends her a text: *Dreamt of you all night. Missing you like crazy. Talk later. Nx*

Once that's done, he reluctantly turns his attention to his first day back at work. It's a short drive along the coast from his house to the restaurant. He's done it a thousand times, but today it takes focus to keep going. Jetlag is making him drowsy, and with each kilometre he's moving towards a different reality, while Alice recedes further and further away from him.

He greets the staff with as much enthusiasm as he can muster, then heads for his office. Even though he's expecting the paperwork that has piled up on his desk, his heart sinks when he sees it. He can't be bothered to have awkward conversations with contractors, double-check complicated invoices, or deal with the minutiae of the Bensons' wedding plans. He's not missed the neck pain that comes from doing admin all day.

He can't believe how much his dad has let things mount up. Noah had started out as his father's sidekick, slowly drawn into every aspect of the business while his dad strategically tightened and loosened the reins. It had taken time to grow used to Raf's unanticipated demands, to find himself dealing with angry contractors or irate customers, or getting home only to be called straight back again to help if they were short-staffed in the kitchen. But Raf had constantly reminded him how lucky he was to have a successful business waiting for him. And in the early days it had seemed so, as his friends counted their change during uni then took their time getting jobs. There had been plenty of rewards to begin with too: unexpected days off, being wined and dined by suppliers, plus the occasional cash bonus as Raf's thank you for his hard work. But these had tailed off over the years, as Raf's health declined and there was less time for non-essentials. Noah isn't being groomed for the business anymore – he's in charge in everything but name.

Once seated, he immediately sees they are behind in paying key invoices, while some of their orders have slipped, meaning they have been crossing things off the menu. The head chef, Frank, hands over a list of problems and complaints as soon as he realises Noah is there, and Noah diligently works on everything all morning, grabbing food from the kitchen and taking it to his desk. At one time he would have found this satisfying – would feel an absolute buzz after another five-star review on Zomato. Today he's apathetic at best. He can see what a mess they're in, and it alarms him how little he had cared about the restaurant's upkeep while he was in Thailand.

However, perhaps this heavy workload is a blessing. It will keep him busy and out of sight, avoiding the gossip that the inquest will inevitably stir up. And it will stop him pining for Alice.

There's another reason he's glad to be occupied, too – one he has tried not to think about until now.

She finds him as he's loading rubbish into one of the bins out the back. She knows he doesn't want her to visit him in the office – he's always been keen to keep them separate from work. She comes up behind him and pinches his bum. 'Hey, you. Good to have you home.'

He swings around. 'Hey, Soph – you startled me.'

As soon as she sees his face she takes a step back and her expression falters. 'You have a good time in Thailand?'

'Yeah – yeah – it was amazing.' He tries not to picture Alice. Perhaps he should have confessed about Sophie, but he'd been scared she would see it as betrayal. It isn't like that, at least not for him. Sophie is five years older with a little boy at home that Noah has never met. The arrangement for the past six months has been to wait until Ash is asleep, sneak into her bed for an hour, then sneak out again.

'So... do you want to come over tomorrow night?'

He hesitates. He doesn't want to have this conversation at the restaurant, but nor does he want to string Sophie along for one second more than he has to. She doesn't deserve that. 'Listen...'

'It's okay, I get it.' She takes another step away. 'Doing some thinking in Thailand, were you?'

'I'm sorry, Soph, but we agreed, didn't we, that this was just fun – you said that you didn't want a relationship or a long-term thing...'

She studies the floor, then looks up again with a smile fixed to her face. 'Yes, I did, didn't I? So I guess it had to end at some point.'

It had begun as a joke one night, when they were clearing tables together after a big event. She'd asked Noah if he was seeing anyone, and he'd laughed and said the restaurant was his lover, keeping him so busy there was no time for anyone else. Then he'd asked her the same question. He knew her husband had left a few years ago, because they tried to give her as many shifts as they could, particularly during school hours. However, he wasn't sure she would still be single. She had long dark hair and a vivacious nature that the regulars loved, and he'd seen her turn down requests for a date on more than one occasion. However, that night she had shrugged at the question, admitting it was hard to meet anyone when you were either working or caring for a kid.

They had both fallen silent. When they'd finished clearing the tables Noah had asked her if she wanted to stay for a drink. They both knew the idea was circulating, but needed Dutch courage. Noah didn't want to press it, since it might be construed as harassment. He didn't know if Sophie would dare.

However, after a glass of white wine, she'd said, 'You can always come to mine if you want a bit of no-strings fun.' Her hand had flown to her mouth. 'Did I just say that aloud?'

He'd grinned. 'I think you did.'

'So?'

He'd looked around. 'You mean now?'

'Ash is staying at his dad's tonight.'

It had taken them fifteen minutes to get back to her flat. Another five to get naked. That first night she'd told him he could stay, but he hadn't thought it was a good idea. Raf had warned him about mixing business and pleasure.

She had texted him the next day. *I hope I didn't overstep the mark...*

I've been thinking the same thing, he'd replied.

No strings, came the response. *Don't worry.*

Are you sure?

Yes.

And so they'd fallen into a pattern. He had to take her at face value, because she'd repeated the phrase 'No strings' numerous times. But was it really the same on both sides or had she hoped it would lead to something more? She'd made sure he never met her child, though, and he knew that once he told her about Alice, she would step back and let him go.

Yet he's still uncomfortable. Perhaps it's just the natural awkwardness of ending things. He isn't sure.

'I met someone,' he confesses. 'While I was away.'

She seems to see his genuine discomfort, and her expression softens. 'Well, she's a lucky girl, Noah. I hope she knows it. I'll miss our time together.'

'Are you okay?'

'Course I am. We're fuck buddies, Noah, we're not in love. I'll just miss your arse, that's all.' She pats his bum again. 'I will literally miss your arse.'

If she's hurt, she's hiding it well. He breathes an inward sigh of relief. He'd love her friendship, she certainly makes work a brighter place to be.

'So,' she says, 'I met your brother while you were away.'

It's like she's punched him. He steps back and puts a hand out to lean against the wall. Tries to act normal. 'What? Where?'

Sophie clocks his reaction and looks confused. 'He was here.'

Noah reels. In front of him, Sophie's expression is changing rapidly to concern, but he can't speak.

'Noah... are you okay?'

He tries to focus. He hasn't talked about Tom with Sophie and he's unsure what she does or doesn't know from elsewhere. 'Sure, yep... it's just a shock, thinking of him being here. I haven't seen him for a long time. So, what – did you guys have a proper conversation or was it just a quick hello?'

'Your mum introduced us. It was pretty quick. Then they went into the office.'

'My office?'

'Yes.' She laughs awkwardly. 'There's only one office here, as far as I know!'

'And how long were they in there?'

'I don't know. I didn't see them again – I was busy with the lunch trade.'

'Right.'

She steps forward and gently touches his arm. 'You look like you've seen a ghost. Are you okay?'

Noah stalls. How can he possibly be okay while his brother is circling his life again. He can feel the distance between them narrowing. Any day now, they will have to face one another.

'Sure,' he manages. 'Look, Soph, I'd better go and do some work. Let's chat later, yeah?' And he hurries away before she can ask more.

Back in the office, Noah casts around as though he might find some evidence of Tom. He picks up papers and wonders if Tom was left alone in here. Whether he might have snooped around the place. What he'd made of the chaos. Trust him to come here while they were in a mess. If it's the same old Tom, he'll have something to say about that. He's hardly back in town for a minute, and yet he's overstepping boundaries already.

Noah bangs a fist on the desk. After all the time he's spent imagining meeting his brother again, how can he still feel so under-prepared? He growls in frustration, muffling the noise with his hands.

He's about to call his mother and ask for more details of Tom's visit, when his phone buzzes with a message from Alice. *Are you home yet?*

It's like she's opened a window – the air clears and he can breathe. He types a reply. *Not likely to get home any time soon. Can we Skype while you're there?*

He calls her straight away, heart skipping as her smiling face comes up on the screen. Her long hair is swept back into a neat bun, and she looks more businesslike than he's used to, with a crisp white shirt, pink cheeks and glossy red lips. In fact, she looks so hot it hurts.

'You're back from work early?'

'It was a short timetable today,' she replies. 'So now I'm

free as a bird. I think I might go and have a walk down to the river later.'

He feels another pang. 'Sounds great. God, I wish I was there.'

'Me too,' she says, blowing him a kiss. 'So how's work?'

He holds up a pile of paperwork. 'Somehow this isn't taking my mind off you.' He leans closer, and says in a whisper, 'You look so sexy in that shirt, I just want to rip it right off.'

'Want me to show you what you're missing?' She begins to unbutton the blouse, pulling the camera back so he can see more of her.

'Oh god, stop,' he groans, unable to wipe the smile from his face. 'You can't do that to me.' He leans closer. Whispers, 'Or maybe you can when I'm home later.'

'Ha,' she says, her face filling the screen again. 'Maybe, if you're lucky.'

There's a cough from the doorway. He looks up to find his father sitting in his wheelchair, watching.

Noah grits his teeth. 'There's someone here. Enjoy your walk. I'll call you later, okay?'

'Okay,' she beams, blowing him a kiss goodbye.

Raf manoeuvres into the space in front of the desk. 'Your new lady friend, I presume?'

'Yes. Mum told you then?'

'She did. Which explains a lot. I hope she was worth it, because it was a bloody awful time to be away, Noah. You can see what a backlog we've got now.'

Noah tries and fails to stop his hackles from rising. 'She was definitely worth it, Dad. And if you want me to continue running this place, you're going to have to let me hire some staff to cover for me properly so I can have a break now and again.'

Raf grunts as he picks up some of the invoices. 'How's it going?'

'Slow but steady.' Noah gestures to the mountain of papers. 'We should've got someone in to help, not left this to pile up.'

'I don't trust anyone else with this stuff,' Raf snaps. 'The day you let other people manage your money is the day it all starts going wrong.'

Stefano Carruso has been dead for fifteen years, but Noah can still hear echoes of him in those words. His grandfather had been as formidable and implacable as Raf. Of course the restaurant came first! Of course the Carruso legacy must be nurtured! The only time Noah had ever seen Raf unsure was around his own father, who could demand a detailed breakdown of the business at any moment, even from his hospital bed. He wonders how his dad had felt when he'd first been ensconced in the restaurant, whether he'd ever wanted something different – although it had provided a natural solution after his pro-football career had finished. Perhaps he'd been thankful for that. Some of his friends hadn't been so lucky and had ended up labouring or out of work.

However, Noah suspects his dad isn't grateful for much nowadays. Raf is always frowning as he watches everyone scurrying around, while he sits in a corner and painstakingly tackles the paperwork, often with a tumbler from the bar beside him. Long gone are the days of his booming voice helping the staff or joking with customers as he pulled out chairs for them. Now he speaks to everyone in short, sharp sentences, as though conserving his energy just to get through the day.

And at home, whenever Raf needs help, particularly for intimate things like getting dressed, Noah avoids his eyes. Sympathy drives Raf crazy, and usually ends in a petty argument. Despite all the support he has, no one can give Raf what he really wants. They can't restore his pride.

'Noah, will you concentrate! I'm asking what you're going to do first.'

Raf's outburst brings him back to the present, and Noah shrugs off the uneasy mix of sympathy and frustration. He tries to focus. 'Don't worry, leave it with me. I'm doing my best to get through everything, but it'll take me a while.'

'Why don't you eat here?' Raf suggests. 'I'll call your mum and we'll join you, then we can help you tackle it.'

Noah's morale plummets at the thought of the three of them toiling and bickering into the night. Then his father adds, 'If you're taking time off for the inquest as well, we should get on top of things now.'

It's the first time his dad has directly mentioned the inquest. Noah frowns. 'I'm sure they'll manage without us for a few days.'

'No, no,' Raf says sharply. 'I'll have to stay here and supervise things, but I can't manage all the paperwork as well.'

'You don't want us all to go – to support Tom?'

Raf's features tighten. 'He hasn't supported us much over the last ten years, has he? Your mother will be there. You'll be there. You don't need me or my wheelchair slowing you down. And besides, we've still got a business to run.'

Noah studies his dad, and finds he isn't surprised by the decision. Raf has always struggled with his eldest son. 'Sophie mentioned that Tom was here. Did you see him?'

'No, I wasn't well that day so your mum showed him round. She says he's planning on heading back in another week or so. I'm sure we'll see him then.' Raf's voice dips as he continues, 'Also, you need to be on alert here, Noah. Someone might be tipping the media off. Since Tom came, I think we've had journalists in.'

Noah tenses. 'What makes you say that?'

'The waitresses have been asked questions about Tom.'

'Really? What kind of questions?'

'Just things like have they seen him? Do they know if he's coming back? The bastards are still digging away, hoping to find something.'

Noah puts his head in his hands and massages his temples. This is all they need. Why did they have to work in a place that allowed the public in all day, every day?

'Do you have descriptions of them?'

'No. I think one of them was a woman though – maybe

that Rachel Lawrence. Do you know her? Your mum seems to think so. Perhaps you can at least get her off our backs.'

Noah lets out a bark of laughter. 'I doubt she'll listen to me, Dad.' He hesitates. 'You know... if it gets too much, we could close up for a little while. Until this is all over.'

His father's eyes narrow. 'You want us to give in to the bullies? After all these years, when we've come this far? I thought more of you than that, Noah.'

Oh, get stuffed, Dad. He stifles his anger. 'All right, forget I said that,' he snaps, 'but right now, this backlog isn't going away on its own. I should get on.'

Raf begins to reverse out the door, and Noah can see by the tic in his father's cheek that he isn't happy. 'Fine. I'll check how they're going in the kitchens.'

Once Raf has gone, Noah grabs the first invoice he sees and tries to focus. He should get this done as quickly as he can, in case Tom's return causes chaos. The situation might be tense now, but he suspects things are only going to get worse.

16

By the weekend, Alice is bereft. Everywhere she looks there are memories of Noah. Or things she wishes she could show him.

She can't face Niran's next house party. Instead, on Friday evening, she takes a minibus out of town, heading for Nam Pha Pa Yai – a climbers' camp she's visited once before, hoping a day on the rock will lift her spirits. When her father was arrested, climbing had been the only thing that seemed to help: there was no space for emotions when you were clinging to a cliff-face, or when someone was relying on you to belay them.

The next morning, she zip-lines across the river, throwing her head back so her face is tilted to the sun, remembering what it felt like last week, halfway up the waterfall, its deluge powering past her, flinging spray into her face, daring her on. Once you knew the thrill of hanging off a ledge by your fingertips – with only your own strength and savvy keeping you alive – it was hard to go back.

However, free climbing is forbidden here, so she buddies up with a very fit Thai woman called Khun Mae. They climb a mid-level route together with their belts full of clips, their ropes secure and their fingers well chalked. It is focused and fun, but something is missing. Back at camp, she watches the thousands of moths flitting around the bulbs of the low-lit room, and daydreams about what Noah might be doing right now.

There's no mobile reception. She packs her things and takes the night bus back to Bangkok. They travel in a storm, rain cascading down the windows, the darkened highway daubed with smears of light. Alice leans against the cold glass and listens to Rachel Lawrence's dulcet tones in the third episode, as she lists known sex offenders and killers who might have snatched Lizzie. There's rapist Fred Baines, who had lured fifteen-year-old Rosie Daniels into his car at a beachside bus stop, and left her body hidden in a patch of bushland forty kilometres away. David Hutchins, a local loner who had raped a tourist in a park the year before Lizzie disappeared. And Simon Shepperton, who had worked as a barman in the area, plying girls with Rohypnol, promising to get them home safely, then sexually assaulting them in their own beds.

Alice recoils, yanking the headphones from her ears. Her stomach heaves and she dry retches. She fumbles with her phone and stops the podcast, pulling her coat tighter around her.

The young guy behind her leans forward. 'Are you okay?'

'Fine, I'm just travel sick.' Her stare is so fierce that he immediately sits back.

She shrinks into her seat, closing her eyes. It hurts to think of the world like this: full of threat and pain. That monster Shepperton had taken the one place those girls felt safest and ripped it away. She knows exactly how that feels. She understands the bone-chill of a malicious leer; the horror of an intruder intent on their craving. The dread realisation that they don't intend to stop.

She closes her eyes, trying to block out the nightmares. For a moment, Lizzie's story – all these stories – feel way too close to home.

17

When Noah wakes from fitful dreams it takes him a second to realise he isn't at home: he's folded into himself on the sofa in his dad's office, fresh light glinting through the closed blinds.

This has only happened a handful of times before, but on each occasion he's regretted it. It might seem a good idea to blitz the paperwork and thoroughly check the prep and set-up before a big event, to promise himself a quick snooze after a few beers, but now there's tons to do for the day ahead and he needs to go home, shower, change, and be back before any of the staff.

He heaves himself upright, grabs his jacket and heads for the entrance. He's intending to hurry – but then he catches sight of the tables in the main restaurant, cutlery gleaming, napkins fanned on plates, wine glasses sparkling in the streaks of sunshine that stream through the long windows. And there, beyond it all, is the ocean view, tipped with gold at this hour, its rippled movement impossible to see from here, rendering the scene as still as an oil painting.

This is when he loves Carruso's the most. The irony's not lost on him that it's the emptiness – a suggestion of people rather than their actual presence – that fulfils him. As soon as paying customers arrive, all this promise becomes a parade of practicalities: apologising for an overcooked lobster or an undercooked steak, consoling a harried waitress, or attending to a blocked toilet. His father had always seemed to delight in the busyness – coming alive as he attended to customers, organised the wait staff, and pitched in with the fervent activity in the kitchen. As hard as Noah tries, he can't feel the same excitement about all that, but he's grown ever more proficient at pretending.

Once he's been home to shower and shave, the hours flash by as he runs between restaurant and kitchen and office, checking staff, supplies, bar stocks and staff temperaments – there's often a blow-up over wedding preparations, since no one wants to ruin a couple's big day. Ray is prepping another plate of hors d'oeuvres, while Kevin is overseeing the orders and Stan is coordinating the mains. He watches plates filling up, and wonders how many guests consider the hours of preparation it takes for them to enjoy those few delicious moments of pleasure.

Whenever he has a few spare seconds he texts Alice, who fills him in on her latest climbing adventure. He pictures her again on the side of the waterfall. Recalls the invigorating rush of adrenalin, and realises it's been missing ever since he got home.

So what are you doing today? he asks.

Staying in bed for as long as I can.

Perfect. Wish I could join you.

Me too – and I'm completely naked. When are you coming?

Stop torturing me! The bride's arriving. Got to go. xx

He waits with the staff to welcome Mr and Mrs Benson inside. 'You look beautiful, Mrs Benson,' Noah says, and Amelia Benson, nee Rogers, flutters her thickly mascaraed eyelashes at him and beams, her face flushed with joy. He shows the couple through to the central area, where the tables have been rearranged to fit around a small disco later on.

'As soon as you give me the word, I'll start bringing out the hors d'oeuvres,' he tells Ted Rogers, father of the bride, who is paying for the whole shebang.

Noah's focus sharpens as more guests arrive: he collects

coats, directs people to tables and bathrooms, and overhears muttered comments about how parched everyone is, because the photos took forever.

Then he sees a familiar lanky figure hobbling through the doors on crutches.

'Jez, mate, what are you doing here?'

'Thought I'd gatecrash!' Jez chuckles. 'No, seriously, I play soccer with Sammy. I've known him for years.'

'No way,' Noah says. 'I thought I knew all your mates. So why didn't you tell me you were coming?'

'You've been busy,' Jez replies cheerfully. 'So how's it going? I haven't seen any photos of your trip yet – or did you not want to make me jealous?'

Noah laughs. 'No, I just haven't had the chance.'

'So are you missing your new girlfriend?'

'Yeah, actually, I really am.'

'Any idea when we get to meet her?'

'I wish I knew. She's still working in Bangkok.'

'Excuse me,' interrupts an elderly man with a handlebar moustache, 'is there anyone on bar duty here?'

Here we go, Noah thinks, as Jez raises an eyebrow. 'I'd better get back to it,' he says. 'I'll talk to you later.'

He doesn't get another opportunity for a good few hours, as they go through dinner and speeches and move the guests outside so the band can set up. It's a beautiful mild autumn evening, and raucous laughter echoes from the terrace as Noah helps clear and move tables.

Jez pauses on his way to the bar. 'Everything all right?'

'I think so.'

'I've been watching you, Noah. You don't stop, do you? It looks like a hell of a lot of hard work.'

'Yeah, it is.'

'But you love it?' Jez prompts, eyeing Noah carefully.

'Jez... let's not go there tonight.'

'Okay, I won't.' Jez holds his hands up and looks over

towards the kitchens. 'So how are your mum and dad holding up with the inquest coming soon?'

'Oh, you know. Doing their best.'

'You only have to shout if you need a friend there, you know. I don't want to intrude, but I'll be there if you need me.'

Noah musters a smile. 'Thanks, mate, I appreciate that.'

Jez nods. 'Have you seen Tom yet?'

'Nope. But I listened to the podcast. I can't believe he did that. It's weird – the Tom I knew wouldn't have gone anywhere near something like that.'

Jez narrows his eyes. 'Maybe he's changed.'

Noah pulls a face. 'We can only hope. Look, I've got heaps to do. I'll catch you later, okay?'

He leaves Jez at the bar, and another couple of hours pass in a flash as he ensures the drinks are flowing, and organises taxis for those older family members who are keen to depart early. He's cleaning one of the toilets when a couple of blokes come in and stand at the urinals.

'So,' one of them says good-naturedly, 'that's the last we'll see of Sammy.'

'Probably, but she already had him well under the thumb.'

'Yeah, Nash was telling me she's been a nightmare about this place, ever since she found out the owners are the parents of that guy who offed his girlfriend. You know, the one who's been in the papers again lately. Apparently Amelia was really upset that it might bring them bad luck, and begged to change the venue, but her dad insisted they honoured the booking. Must have got a discount or something.'

They laugh as they stroll out, but Noah stays frozen in the dimly lit toilet cubicle until he's sure they've gone.

He needs some air. He heads for the car park, wishing for the first time that he could join the small circle of smokers and give his unsteady hands something to do. Instead he stands on the cold footpath in the dark, hands in pockets, watching the silhouettes moving behind the restaurant windows. Observing the warm lights, the bobbing heads; hearing happy chatter and raucous laughter.

He's never felt more alone.

Could I leave this behind?

Since he got back from Thailand, the idea won't stop nagging. This place is swallowing the best years of his life. He's almost twenty-seven, and some of his friends have already had weddings like these, and now they have babies and jobs with six-figure salaries. Noah's wage is decent enough, but there's no time to spend it.

A friendly face appears in the doorway, interrupting his brooding. It's Sophie, looking for someone, her expression relaxing as she sees him.

As he returns her wave, an idea springs to mind. Sophie is reliable, desperate for more work, and knows the restaurant inside out. They don't need to sell the place, they just need an independent manager – or a team of people – who are able to run it without too much supervision. The Carrusos will still own it, and the business will remain in the family.

Best of all, Noah will be free.

Why have I never thought of this before, he wonders, as Sophie hurries towards him. Perhaps he'd needed the holiday to help him see it. He'd finally stepped away and met someone wildly exciting, who offered him a tantalising glimpse of a different future. It won't be easy to convince Raf – his father can't handle letting go of the reins even now, when he should be taking it easy. But at least it's a compromise – something he can offer his family, other than outright rejection. He'll talk to them after the inquest, when things have calmed down.

Sophie reaches him. 'The happy couple are about to have their first dance,' she says hastily, 'and the band are having a problem with the lighting in the corner. Can you come inside?'

'Of course.'

They head back in, and he runs another extension cable for the DJ, then watches from the sidelines and remembers what he'd overheard in the toilets. Amelia's arms are around her husband as they dance to Bruno Mars, their expressions blissful, noses almost touching as they gaze at one another. Noah isn't angry with her. He understands why she wouldn't want her day tarnished. After all, he's spent years trying to escape the gossip. He wonders if there will ever be a day like this somewhere in his future. He thinks of Alice. Sends her a quick text: *Missing you. Just saying hello.*

The wedding guests fill the floor, whooping and hollering as the groomsmen put on an impromptu dance performance to a Black Eyed Peas medley. Everyone's happy. Everything is under control. Relieved, Noah retreats to the office.

There's a new voicemail on his mobile. He calls his message bank, hoping it's from Alice.

'Noah.'

He freezes. Goosebumps on his arms. A chill down his spine. It's one thing hearing that voice on the podcast. Another to have its gravelly drawl directed at him for the first time in over a decade.

'I think we should talk. Before I come down for the inquest. Call me.'

His brother sounds so arrogant and assured. Exactly like the Tom of old – fully expecting Noah to do his bidding.

Go to hell, Tom.

Noah presses delete.

18

Alice jogs up the steps to the language school, skirting around students playing on phones and eating hasty breakfasts of fruit and sticky rice. She hurries inside the airless building, aware she's cutting it fine for her first class, and is halfway down the corridor when Niran approaches.

'Alice – please, come with me.' He motions her towards his office.

She follows, hoping she isn't about to be reprimanded. Is he cross she's running a little late? Could the students have complained about her being so distracted lately?

Once inside Niran's office, she stops in surprise. There's a stranger waiting for them, a middle-aged man wearing suit trousers and a shirt and tie.

'This is Alice Pryce,' Niran says, and then he gives a little bow and closes the door, leaving them alone.

The man extends a hand. 'Harry Petrowski. I'm from the Australian Consulate. Won't you sit down, please, Alice?' He gestures to a chair, and, heart thumping, she sits.

He has a kindly face but his eyes are sombre. 'I'm sorry to be the bearer of bad news. We've been trying to locate you for a couple of days. It's about your father...'

Her hands start to tingle. *No, please, not this*.

'There's been an incident at Brentwood Correctional Centre.' Harry's brow is riven with lines. 'And your father suffered a severe head trauma. He's on life support in hospital. I'm afraid you need to get back to Australia as quickly as possible.'

Alice's skin turns cold. 'What do you mean, a head trauma?' Her voice is shaky, not quite her own. 'What happened?'

'I'm afraid I don't know any more than that right now.'

Alice stands up abruptly, and the room swims. Harry jumps forward to catch her as she staggers, and guides her back to the chair.

'Please, Alice, take your time.' He marches across to the door and calls to reception, 'Could we get some water in here, please?' Then he's back, crouching in front of her. 'I understand you're on your own? I can help with arrangements.'

Alice nods, head in her hands. Her breath is shallow, her lungs are locked and her head is swimming. He's talking about her *dad*. The only family she has.

'I have a car outside,' Harry continues. He's holding a glass of water that has materialised from nowhere, and pushes it into her hands. 'If you want, I can drive you back to your apartment, and I'll ask my secretary to look at flights for you.'

Alice lifts the glass to her lips, and finds she's trembling. Water trickles down her chin and she wipes it away. Her vision blurs as she lets Harry help her up and guide her out of the building. She senses people watching, but she is trapped in a bubble of fear, floating towards the door. She goes blank as she gets into Harry's car and comes to in her apartment, alone. On her phone there's a text message from Harry with details of an evening flight, along with a taxi booking, and instructions to pack.

As she gathers her belongings, her buzzer goes. Downstairs she finds Bussaba at the security gate, clutching a plate of food, offering it with a little bow.

It takes all Alice's strength to remain composed in the face of such kindness. 'Thank you, Bussaba, you're so thoughtful.'

'*Chok dee*, Alice. We'll see you soon, yes? You will come back soon?'

'I – I hope so.'

Bussaba waves, and turns away. Alice heads back upstairs with a lump in her throat.

She finishes packing then mechanically eats Bussaba's red curry, watching the clock, counting down the minutes until the taxi arrives. She studies the ceiling fan until its relentless rotation becomes a hazy white circle.

She has been in Thailand for three months, but there is hardly anyone to farewell. On paper it has been exactly what she wanted: a time of very few connections.

With one exception.

As though he's telepathic, her phone pings.

How's your day going?

She begins to reply, then stops, deletes her half-written message and puts the phone down. She desperately wants to confide, but knows he'll want to drop everything and come to her. How can she ask him to do that when his family need him right now? Besides, she has to stay strong, and his sympathy and kindness might break her. She should get home first, and find out exactly what's going on. Then she can tell Noah.

She lets out a choked sob. *Please hang on, Dad. Please wait until I'm there.*

The last time she'd seen her father, he had taken her hand the moment she sat down. Held it until she had to leave. He'd been quieter than usual, fingers squeezing hers as he asked about her flight plans, where she would be staying, the classes she'd teach. He nodded as she answered, storing each fact away. His eyes lingered on hers, his look conveying all the things he couldn't say. When they got up he had embraced her and turned to leave. She'd watched him go, wishing she was a little girl again and could run into his arms without a thought.

Finally, she'd turned away.

'Alice...' His voice had cracked as he'd called her name. She'd turned back. He was standing a few metres away, and his gaze was fierce. Unequivocal.

'Go and live your life, Alice. *Live*. Let *me* find *you*. Don't come back.'

He wanted her safe. That was all he'd ever wanted.

At the airport, she checks the monitors. The Sydney flight leaves in two hours. She's supposed to go to the Qantas counter and collect her ticket, but instead she scans the other destinations. Singapore. Siem Reap. Hong Kong. Mumbai.

Don't come back.

It's as though her dad's there beside her, whispering in her ear.

Should she listen, and keep running? Or defy him, and go home?

19

As Noah wades into the ocean, the icy water is a shock. Lately he's grown used to a quick swim in a heated pool, rather than a long front crawl through chilly early-morning breakers that toss him around and occasionally try to swallow him.

He looks to the shore. Misses the dog. Dives in and swims hard against the current until he begins to dwell on the notorious rips at this beach, which occasionally claim lives around here. Then he imagines sharks circling, closing in, until he's stroking hard back to the beach, certain he's being stalked from below. The waves spit him out and he lies on the sand, utterly spent, while his breathing recovers.

He finds his towel and sits on the beach, shivering, watching the water rolling in and out, froth foaming at his feet. The skin around his rashie is stinging from an attack of sea lice. He'd thought this swim would refresh him, but he shouldn't have come.

Tom's message loops in his mind. He quickly checks his phone: no voicemails, thank god.

But no other messages either.

Alice has gone silent on him.

He's sent half a dozen messages to her without receiving a reply. He's tried Skype, but there's no answer. What the hell has happened? One minute they'd been chatting back and forth; the next, nothing. She wouldn't change her mind about him that abruptly, surely? His last message had been so benign: *How's your day going?* Before that she'd sent a hasty hello: *Running late for work again – arrgh. Talk later. Love xx*

Had she retreated back into that fierce independence he'd sensed from her? Had he made a mistake leaving her in Thailand?

Did he know her as well as he thought?

The sting on his skin is easing, but the needling fear of rejection is only getting worse. He tries to stay calm, but no matter what he tells himself, his pulse keeps quickening.

He stares at the ocean. *Breathe*. But another memory surfaces, unwanted and unbidden.

Lizzie in his kitchen, watching as Noah worked at the bench.

She'd seen him frowning at a maths book. 'Need a hand?'

He'd thrown his pencil onto the page, sat back and rubbed his eyes. 'Yes. I can't tell you how much I hate algebra.'

She'd sat on the stool next to him, her hair brushing across the back of his arm as she leaned forward to look at his work. She was good at maths. She'd helped him before.

'Where's Tom?' he'd asked.

'Your mum had to borrow him for half an hour. They need to move some furniture at the restaurant. Your dad asked for him.'

'You've been upstairs?' Damn, he could have been chatting to her instead of doing his homework.

'You want me to talk you through it?' She'd nodded at the book, those piercing green eyes meeting his.

He'd felt himself redden, and turned away. 'Er, not really, but I guess I have to learn it somehow.'

She'd laughed, picked up the pencil, pulled the book towards her and begun to scribble. Then she'd pushed it back to him. 'There you go, you're done.'

He'd stared at the perfect page of problem solving. 'Wow, thanks. I'll rub it out and rewrite it, because my handwriting isn't that neat – but thanks!'

'So...' She'd put an elbow on the countertop and rested

her chin on her fist, her face inches from his. 'What are you going to do now?'

Her eyes had sparkled. Her lips were a deep pink. The question seemed suggestive, somehow. Sexy. Lizzie was so sexy.

Before Noah could think, he'd leaned in and kissed her.

For an instant he'd felt her soft mouth against his, but then there was only cold air between them, and the rough scrape of her stool as she jumped backwards. His brow creased in shock as he saw that her cheeks were a deep red, and her fingers strayed to pat her lips, as though soothing the spot where his mouth had been.

'Noah.' Her tone wasn't cold but it was clipped. 'You can't *ever* do that again, okay?'

'I'm sorry.' His shoulders slumped. His face was on fire. 'It's just – I like you.'

'I know, but it's *never* going to happen.' She frowned, and bit her lip. 'Don't ever let that happen again. I'll wait for Tom upstairs.'

'Please don't tell him,' Noah had called desperately as she hurried from the room. She hadn't replied. Once she'd gone he'd torn the page out of his maths book, scrunched it up, and hurled it across the room.

Noah shakes off the memory, jumping to his feet. He grabs his towel and strides towards the car park, his face burning. He's worried about *Alice*, for Christ's sakes. Why the hell has he ended up thinking about Lizzie?

He goes home, showers, and drives to the restaurant, pitching in with the clean-up, collecting the linen to be taken away and washed. He counts down to nine am in Thailand, the number for the English school at hand. He rings and asks for Alice Pryce, and a hesitant woman on the other end informs him in faltering English that Alice is gone. They don't know when she'll be back.

He ends the call, shuts the office door, sits down again, and covers his face with his hands. His tries not to panic, but his thoughts are swirling. He calls her number twice more, but both times it goes straight to voicemail. He doesn't leave a message. As he hangs up, his head begins to throb. He can't believe this is happening.

She's gone.

There's a knock on the door. He rubs his eyes, and calls out, 'Give me a minute...'

'It's Stan – I need to talk to you about the menus for lunch.'

'Okay, I'll come to the kitchen in a sec.'

The shadow behind the frosted glass disappears.

Noah steadies himself. *Don't panic. Trust Alice. Trust what you have.* Still, his legs are leaden as he goes to speak to Stan, and is immediately caught up in a drama about an order of prime beef that hasn't been delivered. He spends an hour on the phone to the supplier, willing his mobile to flash up a message, but when it's all been sorted there's still nothing. Noah needs time to think, but the rest of the staff are coming in, the bar needs replenishing, and before they know it the doors are being opened and the first customers are being shown to their tables.

When it's quiet, Noah grabs some food from the kitchen and takes it to the office. Checks his phone.

Nothing.

Please, Alice, he urges her, as though with enough concentrated effort she might sense his despair. He looks around, at the overflowing filing trays, the noticeboards full of papers. This life has swallowed him already. Alice seems more dreamlike every day they are apart. How soon until she's just a phantom?

He can't bear this. He picks up his phone and dials the language school again, this time asking for Niran.

'*Sawatdee-krap*,' Niran says moments later.

'Hi, I don't know if you remember me – my name is Noah, I came to your house a couple of weeks ago, with Alice Pryce.'

'Hello, Noah,' Niran says. 'Yes, I remember you. How can I help?'

'I'm looking for Alice. I can't get in touch with her and I'm worried.'

'Ah, I think Alice has gone home. Something happened in her family.'

'Home?' Noah can't hide his surprise. 'Do you mean Australia? What happened?'

'I think you need to ask Alice about that.'

'Okay.' Noah frowns. 'Thanks anyway.'

'You are welcome, Noah.'

Noah ends the call, and sits back in shock. Could it be possible that Alice is here, in Australia? If so, why hasn't she been in touch?

Another knock interrupts his thoughts, and Sophie's head appears around the door.

'There's a woman here asking for you.'

Noah's hopes soar. He leaps up and rushes through to the restaurant, a huge smile on his face.

Which vanishes when he sees Rachel Lawrence sitting at a table, waiting.

'Oh.' He stops short.

'Well, I'm obviously not the person you were hoping for,' Rachel trills.

'No.'

Rachel pats the vacant seat next to her. 'Can I have a minute of your time, Noah?'

He looks around at the other diners. The last thing he wants is a scene. 'I suppose so.' He sits down.

Sophie appears next to them, pad in hand. 'What can I get you?'

Noah waves her away. 'She's not staying.'

Sophie's eyes widen and she drifts backwards.

'That's a bit harsh, Noah.' Rachel smiles sweetly. 'I haven't been here before but I've heard great things.'

'Just tell me what you want.'

'Okay, apology first. I'm sorry about what happened last

year. I shouldn't have done it but I wanted information on Tom, and back then you were the easiest way to get it.'

Noah frowns. 'Well, I don't understand why you're here now, because you obviously got Tom to talk. What do you need me for?'

'Come on, Noah. Have you listened to my podcasts?'

Noah hesitates. He doesn't want to say yes and give her the satisfaction. 'Not all of them.'

'Well, if you've heard any of them, you should know exactly why I'm here.'

'Weren't you looking into serial killers and rapists?'

'Oh, that's just padding. Those lunatics weren't involved, there are too many holes in the theories, and none of them feel right.'

'Is that how you conduct your investigative journalism? On feelings and hunches?'

Rachel tilts her head as though considering this. 'Sometimes, yes. People discount the sixth sense way too much. It's fine to have a hunch, as long as you look at the evidence to back it up, and turn it into something more substantial.'

'Right... and your point is...'

'My point is, Noah, that when I talked to you at that bar, I just wanted to get into your house and snoop around a bit. But, do you know, I've talked to a lot of people connected with crimes over the years, and they fall into different categories. Psychopaths and swindlers, for example, are both pretty good at pulling the wool over people's eyes. However, there's another group – the "innocents", I call them – who get caught up in things beyond their control. They're not looking to be part of a cover-up, in fact, they hate it, but for various reasons they feel the need to conceal information. And these guys have certain tells...'

Noah becomes aware of every part of his body: his narrowed eyes, his pursed mouth, the tilt of his head.

'When we were in the bar that night, Noah, talking about Tom and Lizzie, you had a lot of those tells.'

Noah folds his arms. Leans back in his chair. 'Really? Okay then, what did I do?'

Rachel's laughter is like rain spattering on tin. 'I'm not going to tell you my trade secrets, Noah. But I can tell you that you're doing at least one of them right now.'

Noah stands up. 'I think you should leave.'

His voice is louder than he intended. A few diners turn to look.

Rachel puts her business card on the table. 'I think you know something, Noah. It could be big or small, but there's something you're not saying. And I would love to talk to you about it, if you can get control of that temper of yours. Do both the Carruso brothers have the same problem, I wonder?'

Noah grits his teeth, realising that he's giving Rachel exactly what she wants. He's trying to steady himself when a voice beside him asks, 'Noah Carruso?'

There's a tall man at his elbow, dressed in shirt and tie.

'Yes?'

The man offers him an envelope. 'You have been served with a subpoena to appear at the Coroner's Court on the twenty-first of May. Please could you sign here.' He holds out an iPad and a stylus.

In a daze, Noah tucks the envelope under his arm and signs his name in the blank space. The man disappears without another word. This day can't possibly get worse. Alice has gone, and now holding the summons feels like poison is entering his pores and creeping up his arms. He wants to get rid of it, but Rachel is watching everything, and she cannot hide her delight.

'Looks like I'm not the only one who thinks you've got a story worth telling.' She picks up her water and finishes it, eyeing Noah all the time, somehow managing to smirk as she drinks. 'I hope you'll be in touch, Noah. I'd love to hear what you've got to say.' She sets the glass down and heads for the door.

Noah stares at the envelope, his pulse hammering in his ears.

He looks at Rachel's glass, and it takes all his self-control not to pick it up and hurl it against the wall. As though reading his mind, Sophie ducks past him and collects it, scurrying away.

'You all right, mate?' a man at a nearby table enquires.

'Fine, thanks. Sorry about that. Your desserts are on me.'

He stalks back to his office, stewing about Rachel. He hates her for pushing and probing and having the gall to say he knows more than he's telling.

But most of all, he can't stand her because she is right.

20

Her father is so white that for a moment Alice is sure he has died already and no one has told her. She casts around wildly and sees the monitors flashing numbers. There's his heart rate, flickering between 68 and 69, proof he's still in there somewhere. A thick bandage obscures most of his hair. His stubble is peppered with grey. A breathing tube, taped in place, protrudes from his mouth.

She can barely remember getting here, along the highway from Sydney airport then through the streets of Blacktown. Thank god she'd come. Whatever her dad would say about her decision, she needs to be here. Each moment of the long journey had been agony, wondering what she might find.

She takes his hand, intertwining her fingers with his. 'I'm so sorry, Dad,' she whispers, biting back tears.

She turns to the doctor and the prison guard who stand beside her. 'How long has he been like this?'

'Forty-eight hours,' the doctor replies, her greying hair pulled back in a limp ponytail. 'We've had to place him into an induced coma while we operated and removed a clot, and there's still a lot of swelling on his brain. The coma sounds dramatic, but it allows his brain function to slow, and gives it more chance to heal.'

'And what happens now?'

'Well, he's had a severe traumatic brain injury, so progress will be slow and very carefully monitored. As soon as I get the latest test results, I'll update you properly.'

As the doctor leaves the room, the prison guard brings over another hard red plastic chair.

'Thank you.' Alice sits heavily. 'I still can't believe this.'

'I know, me neither. Your dad's a nice guy. Not your average con.'

'Have you been here all the time?'

'We're here in shifts.' He holds out a sweaty hand for her to shake. 'I'm Gary. I wish I could go and get you a drink or some food, but I have to stay here with your dad.'

'So what happened?'

'Well, I didn't see it myself. There was a brawl in the rec room. Apparently your dad was trying to break it up. Got himself in front of a punch, and his head hit the concrete.'

She tries to picture it, but the scene jars.

'You've come all the way from Thailand, eh?' Gary says. 'Never been myself. What's it like?'

She stares at him, confused and exhausted. This whole place feels surreal. *Surely he doesn't expect us to make small talk? Shit, is he going to be here all the time?*

'I – it was good. Different... Look, I didn't sleep on the flight and my brain is fried.'

Gary smiles. 'Don't worry. Here.' He gets up and pushes the chairs together, laying his jacket on them. 'I'll get a couple more of these from the nurse, then you can have a lie down.'

'Thanks.' She waits, letting him sort this for her, then lies gratefully on the narrow makeshift bed, trying to ignore the hard plastic edges jutting into her ribs and thighs. She tries to sleep, but each time her mind drifts, her body jolts her awake. There's too much noise and strangeness around for her to settle. And too much awareness of her father lying comatose just metres away.

Eventually, she stands up and stretches, taking in the room. There's a print of a beach on one wall, and a clock ticks steadily on another. Equipment surrounds them – machines on wheels, plastic pipes, a catheter bag and an IV line. A cupboard door hangs open showing dressings and sterile gloves inside, and by the door there's a bottle of hand sanitiser in a basket hung at chest height. She squirts a little gel onto her palm and rubs it in. Sits back down. Watches. Waits.

Her dad's chest rises and falls to the sound of the ventilator. There are tubes in his arms, and disappearing up his nose. These machines compel him to keep living, overriding his broken body, while the Bobby she knows and needs is somewhere else.

As she watches, her heart pines for any sign of him. The flicker of a smile. The twitch of a finger or eyelid. But the only signs of life are mechanical beeps and whirs.

She moves her chair closer to him, and looks for something to do. Gary is playing on his phone, but her battery has died, and the idea of locating her charger amongst her bags is exhausting. Her eyes drift to his discarded newspaper and she gestures to it. 'May I?'

He looks up. 'Sure.' Passes it across.

The front page is a close-up of a sportsman's tear-stained face, above the headline, CHEATER! and the subtitle, CHESHOLM COMES CLEAN. Alice couldn't care less. She begins to flick through, idly skimming articles, trying to find something of interest.

She stops abruptly on page 5.

BURDETT INQUEST TO GO AHEAD, the headline reads.

Her mouth goes dry.

The high profile case of missing teen Elizabeth Burdett will be re-examined during a coroner's inquest beginning in two weeks. Witnesses will include Detective Glass, who led the investigation at the time, and Tom Carruso, the missing woman's boyfriend and the police's prime suspect in her disappearance.

The article goes on to outline the mystery of Lizzie's disappearance, and the family's ongoing search for answers.

There's a little paragraph inset into the bigger story too, entitled: LOCAL JOURNALIST'S PODCAST BEGINS TO TREND.

Sydney-based journalist Rachel Lawrence has turned sleuth in the runup to the Lizzie Burdett inquest, talking to family and witnesses on her popular podcast. Interviews include Lizzie's boyfriend and prime suspect Tom Carruso, who denies any involvement in Lizzie's disappearance. Lawrence also explores questions around known offenders, including rapists and serial killers, another avenue that police continue to explore in their hunt for answers.

Alice's hands are unsteady. The words wobble in front of her. She sets the paper down.

She gets it now. This isn't just a story, to be discussed at the dinner table then set aside with the dishes. This is real, and hideous. A sleeping giant is stirring into life, thanks to this inquest.

She stares across at her dad.

Noah is caught up in something huge. And my life's a mess. What does that mean for us? How can I tell him about this, when he has so much to cope with already?

She's still reeling from the question when there's a soft knocking, and a familiar voice says, 'Alice?'

Alice turns and her spirits soar. 'Toni! I didn't expect you to come!' She jumps up and rushes across to the middle-aged woman with short curly hair who hovers at the door. Toni opens her arms and wraps Alice in a hug.

Toni was the only person Alice had called when she landed in Sydney. Many of Alice's and Bobby's friendships had wilted over the last few years, people dropping from their lives like petals from dying flowers, as the Pryce situation became too much to handle. The few good friends Alice still had were, according to Instagram, all busy with study and work and travel. Their posts were carefree and content, and she hadn't seen or spoken to them for months, so it felt wrong to drag them into this latest crisis. She already hated that most of her friendships had become more like counselling sessions, the worry writ large on their faces.

Fortunately, Toni was more like a friend than a caseworker. Alice had found her in those first bewildering weeks after her dad's arrest, when the Community Support Centre, which assisted families of prisoners, had felt safer than the police-appointed counsellor, who clutched a clipboard and made notes and couldn't look her in the eye. Toni had listened, offered tissues, helped with umpteen practicalities, and held Alice's hand as Bobby pleaded guilty and was sentenced. She had understood when Alice kept breaking down during those first long years without her dad. She'd kept Alice going: supporting her when she'd dropped out of uni, encouraging her to make visits to the prison, to research jobs in Thailand, and follow her dreams. Time and again, when Alice couldn't bear the struggle, Toni had pulled her back from the edge, and showed her how to keep going. And now here she is again, releasing Alice and regarding her with concern.

'I'm so sorry about Bobby.' Toni's eyes flicker towards the bed, then back to Alice. 'How are you going? You must be exhausted if you've had a long flight.'

'Yep, I'm knackered, to be honest.'

'And where are you staying?'

Alice stares at her. 'I – I haven't even thought about it. Here, to start with.'

'You can't sleep on hospital chairs for long. Have you at least asked if they have a camp bed? Or do you want me to look into some places for you? There might be hostels nearby?'

Alice glances across to Bobby. 'No, not yet. I've come all this way... I want to be here if – *when* he wakes up.' She gives Toni a sad smile.

'All right, well, just take it day by day, eh? Remember you need to look after yourself, that's what Bobby would want most, so resting and eating are priorities, okay? Starting now. If you tell me what you'd like, I'll go and find some food and bring it here.'

'It's all right, there's a café in the next building. I'll stock up there.'

'Come on then.' Toni waves her forward. 'Let's do it together.'

'Oh... okay.' Alice looks at her dad again, then across to Gary. 'We're going to the café, won't be long. Want anything?'

'I'd love a coffee,' he says, shifting his weight to one side as he sits, searching for coins in his pocket.

Toni holds up a hand. 'Don't worry, it's on me.'

As they set off down the chilly corridor, Alice wraps her arms around herself. 'How are *you*, Toni? I'm sorry I didn't keep in better touch while I was away.'

'I don't mind that a bit – but I hope it's because you were having too much fun.'

'It was great.' Alice tucks a few loose strands of hair behind her ears. 'Thanks for encouraging me to do it. I'm glad I went... even though...' She waves a hand back towards the room.

'You couldn't have changed this, Alice, no matter where you were. So tell me about Thailand.'

'Well, I met some lovely people and...' She pauses, but in the end, the need to share overwhelms her. 'And I met a guy, actually. He was on holiday and we really hit it off.'

Toni laughs. 'Now that does sound like fun!' Then she notices Alice's smile fading. 'So what's wrong?'

Alice sighs. 'He has a lot going on at home. And, as you know, life here is complicated.'

They arrive at the café and join the queue to be served. Toni turns her back on the line so they can continue talking. 'You sound like you've given up before you've tried. Is this fella – what's his name?'

'Noah.'

'Is Noah worth a bit of worry and discomfort?'

'Yes, of course. It's just—' She stops.

It's just he instinctively knows me, and that's so good it's frightening. When I'm with him I forget all the sadness and everything feels new. But how on earth will that work here, in hospital limbo? I'm scared it won't be the same.

Toni's eyes are searching Alice's face, waiting for her to speak.

Would you understand if I explained, Toni? Or does it sound crazy when we've spent less than a fortnight together? Does it sound healthy and romantic, or desperate and screwed up?

They edge forward in the line. 'So where is Noah now?' Toni asks.

'Oh, he's back home – he lives near Manly, he works at his family restaurant.'

'Well, that's not far away at all. So is he coming to see you here?'

They reach the front of the queue, and are distracted choosing food and drinks. When they move to one side to wait for their order, Alice says, 'I haven't told him about Dad. He doesn't know I'm here.'

Toni frowns. 'Why not? If he's a wonderful guy he might be a great source of support for you?'

'Yes.' Alice hesitates. 'But it's a really bad time for him... I—' She struggles to find the words. 'I don't want to drag him into this.'

Toni tilts her head, thinking. 'Have you told him about what happened to you and your dad? The trauma you both went through?'

'I tried.' Alice shuffles her feet, studies the floor, then throws a quick look behind her, as though someone might be watching.

Toni says nothing. The barista calls their number and hands them their hot drinks and sandwiches. Alice turns to go.

'Alice, let's sit over here.' Toni gestures to a table tucked discreetly in one corner of the café. When they are seated, Toni leans forward so she can talk quietly. 'Remember, Alice. Jason Reidy is dead. He can't hurt you anymore. Dean Morris is back in prison. There's no one else you need worry about.'

Alice takes a long sip of her tea, then dares to catch Toni's eye. The woman's brows are raised, inviting agreement.

'I know,' Alice says, opening the takeaway lid so she can stir in more milk. 'Most of the time, I'm fine. It's just sometimes...'

'Those "sometimes" are perfectly understandable, Alice. You went through a very traumatic experience. But you need to keep telling yourself that you are safe now. You don't want to shut people out, thinking you're doing them a favour.'

'But in Thailand, things were different,' Alice says, jumping as her first sip of tea scalds her top lip. She sets the cup down. 'Over there, I didn't have to shut Noah out, because I could be the person I wanted to be. But here, I'm being sucked back into old nightmares. I want to move forward and travel more, but I can't expect Noah to follow me and leave everything behind.'

And I have to keep moving, because life can shatter in an instant. Look at us now.

She'd been thinking of her dad as she spoke, but has a brief flash of Lizzie Burdett walking along that dark road, unaware of whatever was coming towards her.

'And what about the Reidy family?' she continues. 'Or even Dean Morris's family? What if they start on us? They might know Dad is in hospital; they might think it's easier to get at us here.'

She knows she sounds paranoid, but it's so hard to stop looking over her shoulder. Bobby had warned Alice over and over to be wary, taking the public statements from the Reidy family as direct threats to their safety. He'd been haunted by one sentence in particular, spoken by Reidy's father outside the courthouse after sentencing: 'Bobby Pryce'd better pray that he'll never know what it's like to lose a child.'

Alice has a sudden memory of Jason Reidy wheezing and gurgling as he took his final breaths, his eyes fixed in horror. She closes her eyes, allowing the panic and nausea to wash over her. She's learned the memories only get worse if she fights them.

Toni is talking, her calm voice returning Alice from her nightmares. 'You've made it through the last three years, Alice. If the family wanted to harm you they would have tried something by now. If they hear your dad is badly hurt, then that will feel like justice to them. And really, what's the point of retribution if he isn't around to see it? That's a terrible thing to say, but it's the way these people think.' Toni reaches across and squeezes Alice's hand. 'Don't be afraid, Alice. Call Noah. Let him in, and see what happens.'

The doctor visits Alice as promised that evening, as the hospital lowers its lights for the night shift, and nurses begin speaking in hushed tones. They sit together and run through the latest test results and everything else about Bobby's condition. Alice learns of the craniotomy they'd performed to release two blood clots, after the initial trauma. The importance of the induced coma to facilitate healing. The intubation tube to aid breathing and prevent damage to the lungs. There is so much to take in that, halfway through, Alice wishes she'd been writing it all down.

When the doctor leaves, she leans against the wall, using her backpack as a pillow, and spends a few hours in fitful slumber. When she finally moves, her neck protests with spikes of pain, and she finds a different guard sitting near her. He nods curtly and then ignores her. She's deeply uneasy at the thought of people moving around in the room while she's semi-conscious, and she misses Gary's friendly face.

She unplugs her phone from the charger and finds two missed calls and a string of messages from Noah.

Alice, where are you?

Can you let me know you're okay?

I'm worried, Alice, please get in touch.

Can't stop thinking about you.

There's a recent voice message too. '*Where are you? Call me when you get this, Alice. I'm worried about you. I miss you.*'

His concern floods her heart, and she can't put him off any longer. She texts back quickly.

Dad's in ICU. Traumatic brain injury. I'm with him now in Blacktown. I might need a few days to get my head around this, so please be patient with me. I miss you too.

As soon as she sends it she half-wishes she'd called, but the sound of his sympathetic voice right now might be too much to bear.

Her phone pings seconds later. *Alice, that's terrible. I understand. I'm here when you're ready. Stay strong xx*

As Alice keeps vigil at her father's bedside, the days and nights become a blur. She researches everything she can, learning more than she ever wanted to know about traumatic brain injury. Some details help; others produce squalls of anxiety. She stares for hours at her dad, waiting for a sign – something, anything she can work with. But in all the time she's been here, he hasn't moved a muscle.

Noah texts often. He encourages her to send updates, however small, and seems to sense that she's struggling, urging her to rest. The staff have found her a camp bed, but it's scarcely more comfortable than the chairs. By the time Toni visits again, Alice is exhausted.

'Have you been out of this hospital at all in the past four days?' Toni asks, half scolding, half concerned.

'No,' Alice replies, struggling to keep her eyes open.

'You need a break, honey.'

'What if he wakes up while I'm gone? I can't leave.'

Toni frowns. 'What's the latest news from the docs?'

'Judging by the swelling, he'll be in the coma for at least another few days. Quite possibly longer.'

'So there you go. Nothing's likely to change here.' Toni pauses. 'Would it help if I sat with him for a bit while you're not here?'

That gets her attention. 'Would you do that?'

'Sure, I can bring a book and keep him company... If it helps you, I will.'

'Oh, thank you, Toni.' Relief washes over Alice. She begins to hunt for her phone, texting Noah as soon as she finds it.

Dad's condition hasn't changed. I need a break. Can I come to you?

21

Noah waits on the station concourse, shifting from foot to foot. In a few moments Alice will be in his arms again.

Finally, his anticipation turns to elation as he spots that waterfall of red hair. She's wearing jeans and a grey T-shirt, glancing around, looking vulnerable, pale and tired. He hurries towards her, calling her name.

She hears his voice, and her face breaks into a huge grin. She drops her bags, runs at him, jumps up and wraps her arms around him. Noah laughs in surprise as he stumbles backwards, trying to hold her, and a grey-haired businessman has to steady them to stop them from falling. They apologise, but the man cheerfully waves them away.

'Young love is wonderful,' he says. 'Enjoy it.'

'Oh god, that was embarrassing.' Alice's face is flushed. 'I was just so happy to see you.'

Noah strokes her hair. 'Do you know how much I've missed you? I can't believe you're here, but I hate the reason. Do you feel okay being away from the hospital? I'll drive you back whenever you want. I'll understand.'

Alice runs her fingers through her hair. 'Thanks, but I'm under strict instructions from my friend Toni to get a break and a proper sleep. I think things are going to be in limbo for a while, until the swelling goes down. She'll call me with any updates.'

Now he's this close to her, Noah can see the strain on her face. He puts her large backpack on his shoulder while Alice collects the smaller one, and they walk through the concourse hand in hand.

When they reach the car park, Alice does a double-take as Noah unlocks a gleaming black LandCruiser.

'Wow, Noah, this car is fancy. Is there something you're not telling me?'

He laughs. 'Nice, isn't it. It was a gift from the restaurant. Check out the signage.' He points to the Carruso's logo on the driver's door. 'I think the idea is that if the restaurant has a car this swanky, just imagine what the food will taste like!'

'So what else do you own?' Alice asks as they climb in. 'A little place in Saint-Tropez?' She runs her hands down the smooth leather seats and across the polished walnut interior of the car. 'Seriously, I don't think I've ever been in a car like this before.'

An uneasy silence follows her words, apprehension hovering between them. Their relationship has a new setting now.

'Will I meet your parents today?' she asks as Noah starts to drive.

'No, they've gone to a wine event in the Hunter Valley. It's a perk of the job, being wined and dined. They usually stay over as Dad finds the travelling tiring, so they won't be back till morning. Nice timing for us,' he says, grinning and squeezing her knee, 'but good for them to get a break too. The inquest is next week, and the strain is already showing. They're tired and grouchy. We all are.'

'Have you seen your brother?'

'No, he hasn't turned up yet.' Noah doesn't mention the message because he can't bring himself to call Tom back. He wants to tell her about the subpoena too, but he doesn't want to dwell on what he might be asked. He's already talked to Peter Bowles, his father's lawyer, who thought his summons was probably just a formality. 'You were one of the last people to see Lizzie alive,' Peter had reminded him. 'They'll want to hear what you witnessed in case it helps determine Lizzie's state of mind.' This should have reassured him, but he's still terrified.

Unaware of Noah's turmoil, Alice begins to tell him about her dad's injuries. He listens until she pauses as they turn into a wide driveway with a large double gate, which he opens with a remote.

'Far out, Noah, do you live in a mansion?'

Noah smiles. 'It's plenty big enough, that's for sure – although it's one of the smallest on this road.'

As they pull up on the drive, he follows Alice's gaze and notes everything she's seeing: the fountain and manicured garden at the front; the rows of double-storey windows. He collects her bags, then lets them in and leads her to the gleaming steel and granite kitchen.

'Wow.' She spins around to take it all in and then walks over to the long windows at the back of the house, through which they can see the sparkling twelve-metre pool. 'This is incredible!'

Noah relaxes. She isn't judging him; she's enjoying this. Bolstered by her enthusiasm, he lets her check out every room of the house, saving his till last, finally leading her upstairs to the top annex, to his suite of bathroom, lounge and bedroom.

Alice puts her small bag down on his bedside table, and Noah loves seeing it there, her belongings in his space. Her phone pings and she scrambles for it. They both hold their breath as she reads.

'It's okay, there's no change,' she says.

His heart goes out to her. Her eyes are so tired, and so sad.

'Hey,' he says, hugging her, 'how about you have a sleep for a while?' He points to the bed.

'Really? You wouldn't mind?'

'Of course not. You look exhausted. While you rest, I'll organise some food.'

'Of course you will.' She's smiling, already pulling her

shoes off, lying down and closing her eyes. 'Thank you, Noah,' she whispers, and closes her eyes.

He goes downstairs and searches through the wellstocked fridge. One advantage of the restaurant is that they are rarely short of meals. Once he has everything ready, he heads upstairs again.

She is asleep on her back, her hair fanned out around her. She looks thin and frail, like she hasn't eaten properly for days. He lies next to her, puts his arms around her, and dozes too, holding her close.

He wakes as it's going dark, to find Alice on her phone.

'Everything okay?' he asks, propping himself up on his elbow.

'Fine. Toni's messaged me: there's no change with Dad.'

'Are you hungry?'

'Yes.' She rubs her stomach. 'Actually, I am, but I'd love a shower first.'

'There are towels in the cupboard in the bathroom. Go ahead, and I'll get the food.'

When he returns she is in fresh clothes and her hair is wet. She leans on his window ledge, staring out at the trees that shade the pool at the back of the house.

'It's so beautiful here,' she says. 'When you said you lived at home, I didn't imagine it like this. This is your own little apartment, isn't it?'

'It's part of the deal. They had it converted to lure me into staying. It would be easy to miss each other for days, if Dad didn't need my help.'

Alice looks longingly at the huge tray of salads. 'Are you sure you've got enough food there?'

'You can thank the restaurant for that. Want a drink?' He goes over to his fridge. 'I have beer and water up here or I can get you something else downstairs.'

'Beer is good.' She stares wistfully out the window again. 'Your pool looks very inviting too.'

'We could go in later, have a night swim,' Noah suggests. 'It's solar heated, so it should be warm enough.'

'You really do live in paradise, don't you?'

He has never once thought of this place as paradise. 'Maybe.' His voice takes on a teasing tone. 'It's paradise now you're here.'

She pretends to be sick into a bowl of salad, and he laughs.

After eating, they sit on the bed for a while, chatting and drinking their beer. The strain on Alice's face has lessened and, to Noah's joy, this all feels as comfortable as it had in Thailand.

Alice begins to wander around the room, looking at Noah's books and photos.

'Who's this?'

She's pointing to a picture of a man with chestnut skin, his arm around a younger Noah, two beers held aloft in their free hands as they grin. 'That's my mate Jez and me on my twenty-first. I've known him forever. He's the one who was meant to come to Thailand.'

'And this one?'

The image is of a young man with thick black wavy hair, wearing AFL shorts and a singlet, caked in dirt, his mouth-guard visible as he stares off to the side as though waiting for a pass.

'That's Dad when he was playing pro football.' Noah relives the usual mix of pride and sadness as he stares at it. 'He looks pretty different nowadays.'

'Well, I'm impressed – what a great photo.' She holds up a small silver frame. 'But I think I like this one the best.'

It's Noah and Pepper at the beach, a close-up of their faces pressed together. Pepper's mouth is hanging open so it looks like he's smiling.

'Me too. I miss that hound. I got him a few years after Tom left – my parents weren't keen but I saw him on a rescue ad and fell in love. So I persuaded them he'd be a good guard dog while we were out, although in actual fact he was terrible. Hardly ever barked. He'd sleep up here with me every night, unless I was swamped at the restaurant, in which case he'd go on mini break to Jez's place. Jez loved him so much that I had trouble getting him back at times. He was such a great buddy.' He sighs, as he watches the sun beginning to set beyond the window. 'So, are you ready for a swim?'

'Sure.' There's a mischievous glint to Alice's eye. 'But are you certain your parents won't be back, because I didn't bring a swimming costume?' She pulls off her T-shirt, unhooks her bra, and puts her hands on her hips, waiting for an answer.

Noah laughs and jumps off the bed, desire pulsing through him at the sight of her. 'You want to skinny dip?'

'The neighbours won't see, will they?'

'I don't think so, but even if they do, let them watch.' He moves closer, pushing a lock of hair from her shoulder and leaning in to kiss her. His hands float towards her breasts but she guides them away.

'Swim first,' she insists. 'And then you never know...'

He throws his arms up in mock frustration. 'Seriously? You're going to torment me like this?'

She nods, grinning.

'Okay then, I'll get some towels.'

'Don't worry, I'll use this one.' She slips off her jeans and underwear and wraps herself in the towel from her shower. 'Ready?'

Noah leads her through the house and out the sliding doors into the back garden. It isn't completely dark yet, but it's quiet save for a few parrots still gossiping in the tall trees behind the house. There are half a dozen steps leading down to the pool area, and once there, Alice drops her towel, steps into the ink-blue water and begins to swim. The lights at either end of the pool illuminate her perfect silhouette.

Noah runs back to the house to grab a bottle of wine and two glasses. He sets them at the edge of the pool, strips off and dives in. He wants to show off his strength, and powers through the water to where he thinks she is, but when he comes up she has already swum to the other end.

She laughs. 'You'll have to do better than that to catch me.'

'Oh, is that a challenge?'

'Absolutely.'

She's a good swimmer, but Noah has spent years getting strong in this pool and in the sea. She evades him for a minute, but then she's back in his arms.

'I brought wine,' he says. 'Want some?'

'Yes, please.'

Noah fills their glasses and they sit on the lower steps of the pool, submerged to their chests. Alice sets her glass down and leans against Noah. Water laps at them as they gaze up at the stars.

'The sky's beautiful tonight,' Alice murmurs.

'Mmm.' Noah nuzzles her neck. Her hair smells of chlorine and shampoo.

'The night sky is so comforting, isn't it,' she continues. 'What's that about, do you think? Because they're just random pricks of light, and the sky is a false canvas. Really we're looking at a picture that doesn't exist.'

Her words send a prickle down Noah's spine, as though he's close to some kind of realisation, but it ducks away before he gets the measure of it. He kisses a path along her shoulderblade. 'You're like no one else I've ever met,' he whispers into her ear.

'That's good – I think.' She rolls over so she's facing him, ducks her head underwater and comes up again, smiling. He pulls her onto his lap, and she wraps her legs around him. His lips trace light patterns across her breasts, and she arches towards him and moans softly, as his grip around her tightens.

He is lost in the softness of her when she goes stiff in his arms.

'Noah,' she hisses, pushing him back, her eyes wild, 'there's someone in your house.'

22

Alice watches, horrified, as the patio door slides open and a man steps out. He is tall and clean-shaven with a receding hairline, wearing a navy T-shirt, his hands in the pockets of his tan shorts.

She still has her arms around Noah, but as he turns to look in the same direction, his whole body goes rigid. He grabs a towel close by and stands, ignoring his own nakedness as he quickly holds it up for Alice, shielding her from view so she can wrap herself securely inside it.

The intruder is already coming down the garden steps. He's close enough for them to see the huge grin on his face. Alice's heart begins to race. It's clear he's taking pleasure in their discomfort.

'Entertaining the neighbours, are you, Noah?'

Noah grabs his own towel and wraps it around his waist. He steps in front of Alice. 'Hello, Tom.'

Of course. Alice gapes at Noah's older brother as the two men stare coldly at one another. For a moment, neither of them seems aware she is there. She has the strongest urge to run, and looks behind her, but there's only the dark shadows of the trees. To get back into the house, she'll have to go round Tom.

Then Tom breaks the stare to give her an assessing look along with a strange, lascivious smile, as though conveying exactly how much he has just seen.

'You must be Noah's girlfriend?' He offers his hand.

Noah doesn't give her the chance to answer, taking a few steps towards his brother. 'What are you doing here? How did you get in?'

Tom turns back to Noah and rolls his eyes. 'Mum still likes to keep a spare key in the watering can. She hasn't changed.'

'So what do you want?'

Alice baulks at Noah's tone. His voice is unusually low, stripped of everything but hostility.

'For Christ's sake, Noah – there's an inquest coming up, isn't there, so I thought I'd come and get reacquainted with you beforehand, since you won't return my calls.' Tom oozes aggression as he flicks at the towel around Noah's waist. 'You've filled out a bit, haven't you – not such a skinny runt anymore, eh?'

Alice strokes Noah's back protectively, as Tom extends a hand towards her again.

'Nice to meet you,' he says. 'Apologies for the intrusion, didn't mean to disturb.' He's still smirking. 'I'm Tom – Noah's older brother, black sheep of the family.'

'Alice,' she replies, one hand pushing the towel against her chest as she reluctantly extends the other to meet Tom's. As his grip tightens around hers, he gives her arm a little tug as though he might pull her forward. She snatches her hand away, and steps closer to Noah.

Tom turns back to his brother. 'Guess you hoped you'd never see me again, eh, little bro?' He puts an arm around Noah's neck and roughs up his hair. Noah pushes him away and Alice sees the glint in Tom's eye harden.

The brothers square up to one another. No one speaks. Alice grabs Noah's hand and squeezes it, letting him know she is with him, willing him not to lash out. Despite all she's heard, she isn't prepared for this. Everything about Tom is taut. Surely it wouldn't take much to make him snap. *Do something, Noah*. She feels light-headed and nauseous. And so vulnerable, in just a towel.

'The next time you want to come round, maybe check you're invited first,' Noah growls.

'All right, pull your head in.' Tom throws the key at Noah's feet. 'I thought it'd be a nice surprise. It's good to see you're still living with the olds.'

When Noah speaks, he sounds disgusted. 'And do you know why that is? Have you seen Dad?'

'Not yet, but I gather he's pretty much a cripple now.'

Alice winces at the description, and sees Noah bristle.

'Yes, because he was scrabbling about on Carruso's roof trying to fix it himself and save money, while everyone was boycotting the restaurant and sending him bankrupt.'

Tom glares at Noah. 'And that's my fault too, I suppose. And what about Mum? She's put on a heap of weight, hasn't she – was that from comfort eating because I've caused her so much grief?' Tom laughs, and the sound makes Alice's skin prickle. 'Christ, Noah, you always were such a serious little shit. Just look at your face. Well, don't worry,' he puts his hands around his very slight pot-belly and jiggles it, 'where Mum's concerned I'm not one to judge.' He eyes Noah up and down again. 'Never thought you'd be fitter than me, Noah, but then nothing works out quite the way you think, does it?'

Noah rubs his forehead in agitation. 'Just tell me what you want, Tom, and then go.'

'Look, we need to talk.' Tom squares his shoulders. 'I want to sort out our issues, without Mum or anyone else getting involved.'

Noah snorts. 'Bit late for us to bond now, isn't it?'

Tom folds his arms and leans towards Noah. 'So you're saying that's not possible, are you?'

'You really want us to be mates? Perhaps you'd better focus on the inquest first, and then we'll see what happens after that – if you're still around.'

Tom raises an eyebrow, and puts a hand on Noah's upper arm. Despite the fact Noah is obviously fitter than his brother, he's still a few inches shorter, so Tom can peer down menacingly at him. 'Don't worry, we don't need to be friends – we'll always be brothers. You can't change that, even if you do think I'm a murderer.'

Then he slaps Noah's shoulder hard and jogs briskly back up the steps, disappearing into the house.

For a moment, Noah remains frozen, except for the rapid rise and fall of his chest as he stares after his brother. Then he turns to see Alice standing there, shivering, wearing nothing but a wet towel.

'Shit, are you okay?' He hurries across and wraps his arms around her. 'You're shaking.'

His caress locks out the cold, and she clings to him. 'Your brother is unbelievable,' she murmurs, trying to stop herself from trembling.

'That's an understatement.' Noah's words are muffled in her hair as he holds her close. 'I thought he might have changed by now, but apparently not. I should go in – check he's actually gone and isn't making himself at home.'

Alice stares at the door to the house, which stands ajar.

'I think he already got exactly what he came for,' she says.

23

The driveway is dark and empty. Noah closes the door and slides the bolt across. *Try getting past a deadbolt, you arsehole*.

Adrenalin floods through him. With Tom in front of him, he'd had to remind himself of childhood strategies long forgotten: *Don't let him see he's getting to you. Let it wash over you. Pretend you're immune*. He'd forgotten how much energy it took to push away Tom's provocations. It had been hard not to charge after him, beat the crap out of him, show him that, for all the name-calling and aggravation, he can't always win anymore.

There'd been a lot of the old Tom in that visit, but something hadn't been quite right. Perhaps it's the lines on his forehead, or the weathered tan. Tom might look older, but after that encounter, Noah knows he hasn't mellowed. He's still one sarcastic comment away from a fight.

Alice is upstairs, getting changed. Noah had seen the defiant lift of her chin as she spoke to Tom, but he'd also felt her trembling in his arms. This was the last thing they needed tonight.

He goes to find her. She's already dressed, and stares at him as he appears.

'What the hell just happened?'

'You met Tom.' Noah grabs his jeans, pulling them on. The evening suddenly seems cold.

'He is... well, I don't know what he is, but he's absolutely nothing like you.'

Noah strides over to wrap her in his arms, taking strength from the warmth of her. 'That's the nicest thing anyone has ever said to me.'

It breaks the tension and she smiles. 'Should we go downstairs?' she asks, scraping her hair into a ponytail. 'We can have a hot drink of some sort, sober up a bit, and you can tell me about him.'

Noah raises his eyebrows. 'It's a long story.'

'I've got time.'

They make cups of tea, and Alice curls up on the enormous lounge. Noah feels exhaustion lurking. Not only is he coming down from the adrenalin rush of seeing Tom, he's also disappointed. The memory of Alice's wet naked body, an unfulfilled promise, is distracting him. But now she's waiting for him to talk.

'So where does that huge chip on your brother's shoulder come from?' she asks.

He rallies at her words. If there's anything positive he can take from tonight, it's that Alice appears to see Tom for exactly who he is.

He sits next to her and sets his tea down. 'Who knows. We've never got on. Mum always said that Tom's toddler jealousy never left him, but she thought that was enough of an explanation – when really I could have done with some practical help to stop him messing with my life. I look at Jez, and he's practically best mates with his brother. They're always having a laugh, whereas all I've ever had is mind games and showdowns.'

'Your parents never intervened?'

'Not really. By the time we were teenagers, they were so busy with the restaurant that either they didn't notice what went on, or they kept their heads down and hoped we'd work it out. Carruso's was a nightmare in those days, leaking the profits while my Nonno – my grandfather – tried to shore it up with wads of cash. So we had to fend for ourselves quite a bit, and Tom seemed to spend most of his waking hours thinking of ways to provoke me.'

'That's awful.'

Noah tries to laugh, but the memories are too painful. 'It was.' He takes a sip of his tea. 'When he first got together with Lizzie, I had a bit of a crush on her.' His face heats up as he speaks. 'And I couldn't understand why she was interested in my arrogant brother. I'd have to watch them all over each other, and whenever Lizzie came to the house, I didn't have the first idea what to say to her. I'd go red and stammer, and, of course, Tom loved it. One time he called me a "lovesick puppy" in front of her. I was mortified but Lizzie got really angry with him, told him he was a dickhead, and stormed out. From then on, he didn't openly humiliate me, but he was always watching. If he saw me looking, he'd pretend to touch her breasts or grab her bottom. One time he kissed her with his eyes open, watching me over her shoulder. He was an absolute dick. Afterwards, if he got the chance he'd whisper in my ear, "Why are you blushing, Noah?"' He grimaces. 'I hated him for all of it, but although he was a shit to me, I could tell he really liked Lizzie. And, honestly, I felt like I had finally spotted a weakness in him that I could use to my advantage. Sometimes I'd hang around them just because I knew it annoyed the crap out of him. I wanted him to explode so that Lizzie would see through him. The tension was terrible. Looking back, he was forever goading me, and I was slowly losing it. One of us was bound to snap.'

He can remember the day it all came to a head so clearly. Tom with his mates in the lounge; Noah hiding in his room, wishing they'd leave. Eventually hunger had driven him through to the kitchen to make a sandwich, and of course Tom spotted him. 'Hey there, monkey boy,' he'd called, adding sotto voce to his friends, 'You should see all the hair under his pits now, and on his chest – he's sprouting more every hour.' There'd been a cacophony of ape noises in response, then Lizzie's irritated voice rose above them all: 'Why are you always so horrible to him?'

It was the sign Noah had been waiting for. Her words twisted his inner rage into defiance, and he'd grabbed his hastily made sandwich and headed for the balcony.

Noah hesitates, knowing what comes next. His stomach lurches at the memory. Alice watches him, waiting for him to continue.

'At our old house, there was a balcony directly above the pool,' he says. 'And for years, Tom had been daring me to jump.'

He rubs his thigh, and Alice notices the gesture.

'I think I see where this is going,' she says.

Noah nods. 'One day, the summer before Lizzie disappeared, he invited all his mates around, and they pooled their money and offered it to me if I'd do it.'

He doesn't go into the details. That Tom's friend Phil had opened the sliding door to the balcony, stolen Noah's sandwich, and announced the dare as he ate it, proffering the money with a sadistic smirk. That when Noah looked beyond Phil, Tom had been settled back comfortably on the long sofa, legs spread wide, arm hooked around Lizzie. That all the boys began a long, slow clap. That Lizzie looked really worried and had mouthed the word *Don't*.

At that moment, he'd hated Lizzie for pretending to care about him while she sat there keeping Tom happy. She must be pretty dumb, he'd decided, if she couldn't see past Tom's buff exterior into his rotten soul.

Now he meets Alice's sympathetic gaze. 'I remember glancing down at the water in the pool, trying to decide if it was worth it. There wasn't a ripple, it was just one clear sheet of blue. Tom and his friends were slow-clapping, and I knew they thought I'd bail. They were like a pack of hyenas, just waiting to rip into me.' He lets out a bitter laugh. 'To be honest, the pool seemed like the easier option.'

He could still remember the feeling as he'd climbed over

the railing and his heels began to tilt, the flash of panic as he committed to the fall. His thumbs remained hooked around the top of the rail for a second as his body pushed forward, and he'd heard Lizzie shouting his name, but he'd thought, *Screw you*. Either he would fall and land in the pool, heroic and richer. Or he would fall and die – and they could live with the guilt. He'd show Tom. Or he'd punish Tom. In that crazy moment, both options had felt fine.

'Lizzie told me later that when I bent my knees to jump, Tom flew off the couch so fast that she thought he'd get to me in time. She assumed he was coming to save me, but I knew him better than that. He was only coming to watch.'

Alice lets out a long breath. 'That's horrible, Noah.'

'I know. It's a blur after that. I remember a burning sensation in my chest as I fell. By all accounts, I dropped like a rock. Straight into the pool.'

'You did the biggest belly flop I've ever seen,' Tom had cackled days later, when Noah finally came home from hospital. 'I was actually impressed. The water sprayed up like a bloody whale had just crash-landed in the pool. You completely disappeared, but me and Phil had the money ready – we were going to throw it over the balcony for you, until you came up face down and we saw the blood. So then we had to come and drag you out, didn't we. I don't even know what happened to the fifty bucks – maybe you'll find it in the garden somewhere.'

'My face hit the water so hard that I had two black eyes,' he tells Alice. 'But my leg was worse. I'd often jumped in the pool while the little robotic pool cleaner was at the bottom, so I'd thought nothing of it. But when they pulled me out, part of the cleaner came with me, embedded into my thigh.'

'So *that's* the scar on your leg?'

'That's the scar on my leg.'

Alice looks horrified. The silence stretches into the night, and across Noah's memories. Because that was just one story; there's so much he hasn't told anyone. How could he ever explain what it felt like to be tormented daily, when there were rarely wounds to show for it, only the scars in his mind?

He thinks of Tom earlier, watching them in the pool, and fumes with a rage that only his brother is capable of inducing. He had forgotten that feeling – the toxic mix of anger and shame that Tom can so easily manipulate him into.

'My brother,' he says eventually, 'has always seemed to want to punish me for existing.'

Alice frowns. 'But was he just like that with you? Tonight... he said you think he's a murderer. Is that true?'

Noah sits back and stares at the ceiling. 'That question has driven me insane for the past twelve years. What I do know is that Tom came home in a very dark mood that night, and Lizzie turned up on our doorstep five minutes later, in a complete state and drenched from the rain. As soon as he opened the door, she began yelling at him. She told him he was insecure and jealous. She said she loved him but she couldn't cope with his moods anymore. I think she was hoping he'd see sense and comfort her, but instead he was furious: told her she was a pricktease, and asked how many of his friends she'd slept with. She seemed, well... gobsmacked is the best word I can think of. When he'd finished she ran off sobbing and Tom slammed the door so hard I swear the whole house shook.'

How can he convey to Alice the horror of what he'd witnessed? The way Lizzie had cowered and cried as his brother screamed obscenities and towered over her. And all the while, Noah standing silently on the stairs in the semi-dark. Terrified. Watching.

'And you saw all this?'

'Yep. When he turned and spotted me, I was petrified, but I was too frightened to move. I thought he might come after me, but he kicked out at the wall instead and then stormed off towards the kitchen. I took my chance and ran to my room, but a few minutes later the front door slammed again. When I looked out the window I saw Tom hurrying down the driveway, hunched over in the rain, presumably going after her. I thought that even Tom, stubborn as he was, would be regretting what he'd said. I remember hoping she wouldn't accept his apology. I thought she deserved better. When he came back, I pretended to be asleep, and he's always said he never found her.'

'But you don't believe him?'

'I wish I knew. He was a complete arsehole to Lizzie that night – and I was the only one who saw it. I was frightened just watching them, because Tom was vicious. It must have been much worse for Lizzie.'

Noah hesitates. Should he tell her the other things that happened that night? Things he'd locked away for over a decade? No, it wouldn't be fair. The portion of the story that he'd told her was all on public record. The remainder was his guilty secret, and he doesn't want her to carry it for him. He won't tell her more until he's decided how much to say in court.

Alice sips at her tea, lost in thought. 'So where were your parents during all this?'

'Still at work. They often worked late in the restaurant. We still do. Sometimes we even end up sleeping there. That night they didn't get home until about midnight, an hour or so after the fight. I heard them coming in and debated telling them what had happened, but I was too scared I'd run into Tom.' He rubs his stomach gently as though to ease away knots, feeling the taut muscle beneath his hand. He has a flash of memory: Tom breaking down at home after the first police interview. Watching from a distance, as his brother alternately stomped through the house or sat shaking and sobbing in his bedroom, Noah had wondered if Tom was just frightened for Lizzie, who by then had been missing for over forty-eight hours. Or was he scared for himself?

One thing was clear: Noah would never be his brother's confidant. He seemed to hate Noah more in the days after Lizzie vanished, scowling as soon as he saw him, as though he somehow held Noah responsible. Meanwhile, Noah's fresh animosity towards Tom had simmered away too. They'd barked and growled at each other until one evening a couple of weeks later, when Noah's outrage reached its peak. He'd been glaring at Tom throughout dinner until Tom had raised his hands as if to say, '*What?*' And Noah had mouthed three words to him: *Tell the truth*.

Tom had found him upstairs that night and pounded him in the stomach and ribcage while Noah hollered and curled up on his bedroom floor, trying to fend off the blows. Moments before their parents arrived, Tom had whispered in his ear: 'Whatever you think you know, keep your mouth shut, or I'll make sure you suffer, you little snitch.'

After that, their parents kept them apart. Cathy had stayed by Tom's side, while Raf made sure Noah got to school, so there was suddenly more one-on-one father–son time than Noah could ever remember before. Raf refused to even look at Tom, and began taking Noah to the restaurant. He'd do his homework in the office, then help his dad with whatever was needed. His parents had moved through those dark days robotically, quietly getting essential tasks done, then heading to bed earlier and earlier. The house felt like it was filling up with toxic fumes and one wrong move would cause an explosion.

Noah realises he's been lost in his memories and Alice is waiting expectantly. 'After Lizzie vanished,' he continues, 'it was chaos to begin with. I overheard a lot of gossip and didn't know what to think. Tom was a mess – crying in his room or yelling at everyone.' He registers Alice's stunned, pale face and remembers what she's going through. 'Shit – look, I shouldn't be burdening you with this.'

'It's okay.' She leans forward and squeezes his hand. 'Now I've met Tom I can see why you were worried. He's so aggressive towards you.'

'I know,' Noah concedes. 'After those first few weeks we spoke less and less about Lizzie, but of course she was constantly on everyone's mind.'

He can well remember the daily speculation at school. Lizzie's disappearance had been a defining moment for the kids of Belhaven College. Until then, the horrors of the world had been second-hand stories, but here was a girl they knew: there one day, vanished the next. Feared taken. Feared killed. Perhaps even by someone they knew. In the days after Lizzie disappeared, the kids had found their freedoms instantly curtailed. It's no wonder, Noah thinks, that Lizzie's name still crops up in late-night conversations, synonymous with danger.

His thoughts have drifted again, and Alice is waiting. 'Eventually,' he says, 'Tom dropped out of school under a cloud of disgrace. Dad refused to let him work at the restaurant, saying he was unreliable and bad for business. He seemed to treat Tom with contempt, constantly pushing him to get a job even though he knew most of the town wouldn't go near him. Once when Tom dared to answer back, Dad lost his rag and threw a glass at him – it missed Tom by inches and shattered against the wall. I dreaded them being in the same room together.'

Noah hesitates as he catches Lizzie's eye. 'Of course, we couldn't go on like that forever, and one night Tom paid me a visit.'

Tom had come to his room and watched him lifting weights. Noah had decided to get fit, to ensure he could stand up for himself with Tom or anyone else who wanted to take him on. 'You're getting strong, little brother,' Tom had said, arms folded as he leaned against the doorway. Then he'd stepped closer. 'Tell me, do you think this place would be better off without me?'

Noah hadn't even hesitated. 'Probably,' he'd replied as his arms pumped up and down. He'd grown too used to their bitter arguments to think of this as anything but one more unwelcome conversation.

In response, Tom had come closer to Noah, picked up the

weights that were making him puff and pant and put them down like they were nothing.

'Then he asked me outright,' Noah tells Alice. 'He said, "You think I killed Lizzie, don't you?"'

Alice's eyes widen. 'And what did you say?'

'Nothing at first. We just stared at one another for a long time. Our faces were almost touching, like we were trying to force each other to back down. Eventually I said, "I don't know, Tom. Did you?"'

'And?' Alice whispers, her whole body tense with anticipation.

Noah shakes his head. 'He kept on eyeballing me, and I could tell he was on the verge of saying something. I was so bloody tense. I thought he might confess right there – either that or attack me – but then he shook his head and left my room. And that was the last time I saw him. Until tonight.'

24

They head upstairs in the early hours, in a strange fug of exhaustion. Alice climbs into bed quickly, but Noah stays up for a while, moving around the house. She's almost asleep by the time he joins her, his hand coming around her waist and slipping under her strappy top. She doesn't move, letting him caress her slowly, his fingers gliding down, circling the inside of her thighs, until she's pushing against his touch as he brings her to climax. Physically it's satisfying, but there's another kind of yearning in the aching pulse he leaves behind.

When Alice wakes around seven, Noah entices her into the shower, and they replay some of their favourite scenes from Thailand, gasping and giggling together under the pounding water. Eventually, Alice dries herself and stands naked in front of the washbasin. Noah comes up behind her, a towel around his waist. He kisses her neck, burying his face in her hair.

'You're so beautiful, Alice,' he murmurs, his hands running over her breasts, caressing her as she watches. 'I love having you here with me. I wish we could stop time right here, and make the rest of the world wait until we're ready to join in again.'

His eyes meet hers in the mirror as he strokes her hips, his fingers inching forward.

She leans in to his touch. 'I'm not sure we'd ever be ready,' she replies, closing her eyes.

Midmorning, they reluctantly get dressed and drive to the restaurant. As they pull into the little clifftop car park, Alice gets her first glimpse of Carruso's.

'I feel like I'm about to meet an important member of your family,' she says to Noah.

He laughs. 'You're not wrong. This place is the matriarch!'

The path up to the door has oblong ponds either side of it, containing a few goldfish in hot pursuit of one another. Pots of bright pink flowers are set by the entranceway, so wonderfully in bloom that Alice has to restrain herself from digging her fingernails into the petals, to see if they're real.

The main doors open automatically, and they walk straight into a large, airy room with floor-to-ceiling glass on one side and a huge double-framed mirror with gilt edging on the opposite wall. The space is filled with rows of silver chairs tucked in to white-linened tables, and all the places are set ready for the lunch trade.

'This is beautiful, Noah!'

He smiles. 'Come into the kitchen and meet everyone.' He grabs her hand, and they head down a short, narrow corridor, past a number of black and white photos.

Alice pauses at one. 'Is that Kylie Minogue?'

'It sure is. That photo's pretty old now, I was still in primary school then. It's a Carruso's claim to fame, but I was spewing when I realised she'd been here while I was tucked up in bed. Apparently she booked in under a false name, so I had to forgive them for not telling me.' He pushes open a pair of white double doors. 'And here's the hub of the action.'

Inside, three middle-aged men in chef's uniforms are all busy with preparatory work, their faces ruddy as they move between steaming pans and piles of chopped veg.

'Ray, Stan, Kevin, meet Alice.'

There's a chorus of hellos, and the man closest to them shakes Alice's hand. His grip is soggy but his smile is welcoming. 'Pleasure to meet you, although I don't know why you've chosen to hang around with this idiot.'

'Thanks, Ray.' Noah bats him on the shoulder. 'Ray has been our head chef for nearly seven years. Ray and Dad created everything on the menu. Now, come on, I've got a surprise for you.'

He pulls her back through the restaurant and they head through another set of doors, emerging onto a spacious terrace, with a dozen tables running along the side of a railing. The view is pure ocean, the gunmetal water speckled with a few sailboats. All except one of the tables are empty: the table with the clearest view has been laid for two.

'The restaurant doesn't open for another hour,' Noah tells her, 'but I thought you might like a private dining experience.'

'This is amazing, Noah,' she says, as he pulls out a chair for her to sit down. She tries to look over the railing to see how high they are, but one of the clear plastic blinds has been rolled down to keep the breeze at bay. On the other side, something white moves in one of the trees. She stares after it, trying to see what it might be.

'Could be a cockatoo,' Noah says, his gaze following hers. 'Years ago we used to feed them to entertain the guests. Then they became a bloody nuisance – our fault, of course – raucous little buggers kept landing on tables and throwing punk-rocker tanties, flicking their little crests up and down if no one fed them. So now we discourage them –' he points to a subtle layer of netting overhead '– and we've learned they don't like the colour white, so this area gets a regular paint job.' He hands her a menu. 'Now, what would you like to eat?'

She studies the little booklet. 'The pumpkin and fetta salad, I think.'

'And to drink?'

'Water's fine.'

'Okay, I'll be back in a sec.'

Alice waits, enjoying the view. This time with Noah has been amazing – except for Tom's appearance last night. She hasn't met anyone so intense and threatening, since...

No, don't even think his name. Don't let him invade this space.

She shivers, watching a few white triangles of yacht sails moving across the ocean as she waits for Noah. She's scared for both of them. She wants an unwritten future, not a blighted one. *Can we do that?* she wonders. *Will we get that chance?*

She recalls their first night at Niran's house, and their date at the restaurant – the irresistible surges of attraction to each other, their easy banter before they'd even begun their confessions.

We are strong together, she reassures herself. *There's a lot more to us than tragedy.*

As Noah reappears, her nervous heart settles at the sight of his gentle face.

'This is such a lovely place, Noah,' she says as he sits down. 'I can see why your family are so invested in it.'

Noah's eyes follow hers around the verandah. 'Yes, it's three generations of investment and hard slog. Sometimes it's good to see it through someone else's eyes, to remember how special it is.'

He stops talking, his gaze drifting over her shoulder.

'What is it?' Alice turns to look.

A middle-aged woman in a brightly coloured kaftan is holding the double doors open for a man in a wheelchair. Alice's composure scatters as she realises who they must be.

The woman's eyes seem to widen at the sight of her and her lips move quickly. The man frowns, his mouth dropping open, while his fingers pause on the wheelchair controls. They both stare at Alice, and then the woman seems to shake off whatever has halted her, and hurries forward.

'You must be Alice. I'm Cathy.'

Alice stands up and is swept into an embrace, as though

they were dear friends. When Noah's mother finally steps back, his dad holds out a visibly shaky hand. 'Raf.'

'Do you mind if we join you?' Cathy asks as she kisses Noah on the cheek. 'What did you order, Alice?'

'The pumpkin and fetta salad.'

'Ooh, that's delicious – but you must try some of our other dishes too. I'll pop to the kitchen and see if they can do a mini tasting plate for you,' she says, hurrying away.

'Stan's going to love that.' Raf grimaces. 'Listen, we won't intrude. I'll get her to leave you alone.'

He looks at a spot between them as he speaks, as though his thoughts are elsewhere. Alice can see the strong Carruso genes running between Raf and Tom: thick dark eyebrows twinned with deep-set brown eyes. Noah's eyes are dark too, but his face is less contoured and narrower, more like Cathy's.

'No, no,' she says quickly. 'Please join us.'

Raf smiles politely then turns to Noah. 'Have you been into the office yet? I left a few statements for you.'

'No, Dad.' Alice can hear the strain in Noah's voice. 'I brought Alice in to show her around – I'll do that later.'

'All right, well, don't let it build up. We've had enough of a backlog lately,' Raf says, picking up a knife and beginning to polish it with a napkin. 'So, tell me a bit about yourself Alice.'

Alice finds herself unexpectedly tongue-tied, and Noah comes to her rescue. 'Alice is a brilliant rock climber.'

'Is that right?' Raf's expression is unreadable. He looks towards the doors where Cathy has just reappeared, hurrying back towards them.

'I took Noah climbing in Thailand, actually,' Alice says quickly to fill the awkward silence.

Raf raises his eyebrows at Noah. 'Really? Well, that's a surprise.'

'What Alice isn't telling you is that I was stuck there for a few minutes, completely paralysed by fear,' Noah adds. 'In fact, if Alice hadn't climbed back up with her bare hands like a monkey and talked me down, I might still be there now.'

'Have you climbed in the Blue Mountains before?' Cathy asks, overhearing the conversation as she rejoins them.

'Yes, but not for a while.'

'We have a little place there.' Cathy opens a napkin and sets it on her lap. 'Noah will have to take you now you're here. Are you back for good?'

'I don't know. My dad is sick... I've come home to see him.'

Cathy gasps. 'Oh no, what's wrong?'

'He fell and hit his head. He's got a brain injury. In fact, I should get back to him soon.' Alice looks to Noah for help, unwilling to elaborate.

'Let's go as soon as we've eaten,' Noah says, squeezing her hand. 'I'll drive you.'

Raf frowns as he watches Noah. 'What about the lunch trade?'

Cathy tuts. 'We can cope with that for one day, can't we, Raf?'

Raf doesn't reply but his annoyance is obvious. He refuses to look at any of them and Cathy fills the silence with a story about the disappointing hotel they'd stayed at the previous night, where the walls were too thin and the cistern in the bathroom wouldn't stop running.

Fortunately, the food arrives in minutes. As they eat, most of the conversation revolves around the restaurant, with Raf occasionally chipping in, sullenly reminding Noah of everything he needs to do, and Cathy smiling reassuringly at them all as she fidgets with her bangles. There's plenty of unspoken tension round the table. Alice can see why Noah finds his father such a challenge.

'Oh, Noah,' Cathy says, setting her knife and fork down, 'I need you home for dinner tonight.' There's a brief pause, before she adds, 'Tom is coming.'

Noah briefly closes his eyes. 'Really? Are you sure you want me there?'

As Alice watches, Cathy's expression flashes from friendly to fierce. She glares at him, her lips tight. 'Yes, of course we want you there, because we're a family. Who knows how long Tom will be in town for – and it's been eleven years since he's been home. *Eleven years* that he's refused to see us. I'm just relieved he wanted to come at all – *please* do not ruin this before we've even tried.'

Alice waits for Noah to mention something about Tom's appearance at the house, but he just stabs his fork into his salad and continues to eat. She finds she has lost her appetite, despite the platter of delicacies in front of her. Noah senses her anxiousness and makes murmurs about leaving. In response, Cathy rushes back off to the kitchen again to get their food wrapped for the journey. As they say their goodbyes, Raf is still thinking up things he needs Noah to do.

Alice waits, watching as Noah listens and nods, placating his father wherever he can. She's beginning to wonder how Noah has coped with this for so long. *He's trapped*, she realises in dismay. So how much does he want to escape? Because it looks like his parents have no intention of making it easy for him.

25

Alice doesn't say much on the drive back to the hospital. Noah lets her rest, understanding she needs to gather her energy. Even so, he wants to apologise for the way his family have gate-crashed on the last twenty-four hours. He's mortified by the tension they'd brought with them. And although he doesn't want to admit it, he suspects it might often be like this if he and Alice try to bring their lives together here.

The thought is appalling. He wants a chance to live with his attention fully on Alice, not for her to be the person he fights to get home to, beyond a million other distractions.

'I can come and get you any time you need a break,' he tells her as they near the hospital. 'You don't have to come to my place, we can do anything, go anywhere you like.' He bites his tongue, hoping he doesn't sound as desperate as he feels.

'Thanks, Noah.' Alice briefly strokes his arm. 'But don't get distracted from work or the inquest because of me. I can see why your family need you.'

His spirits sink. *I don't want to be needed by them. I want to be with you, and to recreate what we had in Thailand, because for those few days everything felt right.*

At the hospital he gets out of the car to hug her tight. 'I hope it goes well up there. Tell your dad I'm looking forward to meeting him. Tell him I think his daughter's amazing.'

She leans in to kiss him, triggering a familiar ache of

longing. He doesn't want to let her go, but she is stepping back, collecting her bag, and moving away.

'Talk tonight?' he calls after her.

She turns and nods, blows him a kiss, then disappears through the sliding doors.

It takes all his willpower to get back in the car, gun the engine, and drive out of the hospital grounds alone. He's had to leave her twice in two weeks now, and it doesn't get any easier. Still, at least she's only an hour away this time.

He arrives back at the restaurant mid-afternoon, to find the usual list of problems that need his instant attention. He works diligently, letting the clock drift past six and then seven. He watches the evening trade roll in, and checks they are being well looked after. Only when his mother calls his mobile for the fourth time, after leaving two messages on the restaurant's answering machine, does he pick up.

'You're being ridiculous,' she says without preamble. 'Can you get yourself home? Tom's been here for an hour already.'

'Oh, has he? I lost track of time.'

'Hmm... well, just come now. Your dad's already gone to bed with a migraine. He didn't cope well at all with the long day at the restaurant.'

Noah hears the unspoken reprimand and experiences a twinge of guilt, but he doesn't have time to dwell on it, because Cathy adds, 'And be prepared for a surprise.'

She hangs up quickly, while Noah is still saying, 'What do you mean? Tell me?' It's a ploy to get him to come, of course. He grabs his jacket and heads for the door.

He gives himself a talking-to while he's manoeuvring out of the car park. *Don't let him piss you off. Don't let him get under your skin. Say as little as possible. Get out as soon as you can.* He's expecting traffic, but green lights and clear roads greet him all the way home. He sits outside for a moment, noting the unfamiliar black car in the driveway – a nice-looking Hyundai. Takes a few long, deep breaths.

Showtime.

As soon as he lets himself in, he can hear the murmur of voices. He strides down the hallway to the kitchen, but there's no one there. Incredible. They are eating in the dining room – a place practically reserved for royalty. Since when did Tom get such special treatment?

He appears in the doorway to see his mum on one side of the table, her back to him and an empty space beside her. Beyond her, facing Noah, is Tom. And next to Tom is a woman Noah has never seen before.

'Ah, little brother finally makes an appearance,' Tom says, holding a large bowl and serving salad onto his plate.

'Hope you knocked this time,' Noah retorts.

Cathy twists in her chair to regard him quizzically, and too late he realises what he's let himself in for.

'Oh yeah, I forgot to tell you I came the other night, and found Noah here skinny-dipping with his lady friend. The one with red hair – always had a thing for redheads, haven't you, Noah? They were putting on quite a show for the neighbours.'

Noah squeezes his fists hard, nails digging into his palms, as Tom flicks his eyes up to his brother and away again. Noah watches Cathy inhale, and waits for an exhale that never comes. This only means one thing: she's close to losing it.

The mystery woman digs Tom in the ribs with her elbow, but she's smiling. 'Okay, okay,' Tom says, holding up his hands in mock surrender. 'I'm sorry, Noah. No harm intended. I'll stop teasing, promise.'

Noah ignores him, instead catching the eye of the woman, and leaning across to offer his hand.

'Hi there, I'm Noah.'

'Nadia,' she replies, and pushes her chair back awkwardly to rise and shake his hand. It seems to take her a lot of effort, but as soon as she's on her feet Noah sees why. Her belly protrudes as a huge, round bump.

Tom chuckles at his expression. 'Noah, meet Tom Junior,' he says.

Nadia laughs. 'Or Thomasina.'

The accent is unmistakable. 'You're Italian?'

'*Si.*' She beams at Noah. 'But I've lived here for five years now.'

'I brought her back from Italy,' Tom says proudly. 'Best souvenir ever.'

Nadia squeezes his arm affectionately.

Completely flummoxed, Noah sits next to his mum, grabs a bowl of rice and begins to serve himself, the pile heaping up while he digests this information. He wants to ask if this can possibly be real – perhaps Nadia is some kind of hired performer?

What the hell? Why does Tom always make me feel insane?

When he looks up again, Tom and Nadia are watching him, as though waiting for him to say something.

'So when did you go to Italy?' he asks, avoiding all eyes.

'I went with a mate back in 2010 – we followed the Grand Prix around Europe for a few months.'

'Sounds expensive.'

Tom smiles. 'When you work in the mines for a few years, your savings pile up nicely.'

Up to this point, Noah has not much cared what Tom got up to after he left town. Or rather, he'd assumed his brother would be his usual miserable, resentful self, moaning about everything and drinking too much. He hadn't considered that Tom might go gallivanting around the world, while Noah was left taking care of their parents and the business. Tom had found freedom, and now he has a partner and a child on the way. All this time, Noah had thought his life was better than his brother's, but where Tom's concerned, he's a loser. As usual.

He stabs his fork into his vegies, listening to Cathy bombarding the happy couple with questions. She's the doyenne of small talk, her skills cultivated at the restaurant. They learn that Tom and Nadia live by the water in Broome. Tom's given up working in the mines now the baby is on the way, and in the last six months has taken various casual work, as a labourer, a deckhand on a scuba-diving boat, a bus driver... and eventually he's hoping to go into tourism. Nadia has worked in a clothes shop for years, but will give it up to be a mum. They sound happy. Focused. Confident in themselves and their plans. They smile at each other while they talk. As Noah watches them, he is mesmerised by this different, warmer side of Tom. He's only seen it once before, he realises uncomfortably. It was over a decade ago, back when Tom was dating Lizzie.

'So how long are you staying in town?' Noah asks them.

'Just for the inquest,' Tom answers.

'And what then?'

Tom frowns. 'Then we go home and get on with our lives.'

Noah has a brief flash of Nadia alone with a baby while Tom sits in prison, and Tom appears to read his mind. 'Whatever happens in this inquest, it's not going to affect me.' He sits back and folds his arms, his eyes daring Noah to challenge him.

'Why do you say that?'

'Well – perhaps because I'm *innocent*.'

The word hangs in the air. Tom picks up his napkin and wipes his hands. When he lays it down again, Noah sees Nadia put her hand over his, and give his fingers a squeeze. The air is thick with everything unspoken.

Even so, Noah can't resist probing further. 'So what do *you* think happened?'

Tom sits back and sighs. 'I don't know. But why is no one talking more about Josh? He left the party soon after Lizzie. What if he followed her? He said he went home, but the only person backing up that story is his mother, and of course she would. You know what I think? I reckon he followed Lizzie to our place, saw us argue, and hid somewhere when I went after her. Perhaps he'd already confronted her and that's why I couldn't find her. I'm telling you,' Tom mutters, speaking through a mouthful of pastry, 'he's been let off the hook way too easily. I just wish Lizzie had told me about him harassing her – I would have warned him off. It didn't look one-sided to me, but then I was just a jealous kid.'

Noah considers all this, disconcerted by how plausible it sounds. 'So is that why you did the podcast?' he asks. 'I was surprised about that.'

'Yeah, it's not really my thing,' Tom agrees. 'But Nadia thought it was a good idea. She said, "What's the harm in speaking if you've got nothing to hide?"'

Nadia gives them all a tentative smile, but Noah can't help himself. 'And you're absolutely certain you've got nothing to hide, then?'

Tom glares at him, but before he can answer, Cathy gets up. 'Noah, can you help me with the dessert trays?' she trills in her faux hostess voice.

Noah follows her into the kitchen.

'Will you stop baiting him?' she hisses. 'Why can't you have some faith?'

'Perhaps because he's always so sure of himself and his theories,' Noah whispers back. 'Sitting there all loved-up with his girlfriend, when the last one is still missing, and he's barely bothered checking in with us for over a decade...'

'Sshh, keep your voice down... and Nadia is his fiancée.'

'Whatever. I just don't want him to think we're welcoming him back with open arms, and he can do or say whatever he likes. Because he'll end up causing us trouble again, I guarantee it.'

'And what about me, Noah?' Cathy cries. 'Have you thought about what I need? That's my long-lost son and his girlfriend in there. My grandchild. Some happiness in my future. You're barely back together for a night, and already you want me to choose between you.' She throws her dishcloth down and storms away.

Noah watches her go. Her words have struck him, and he collects the desserts and turns towards the dining room with renewed determination to be polite. He watches Nadia rub her belly, and tells himself to keep calm.

'How are you feeling about the inquest, Tom?' he asks as he sets the desserts down.

'Not my idea of a fun week,' Tom replies, taking an empty bowl and handing it to Nadia. 'I'll be glad when it's over.'

'Won't we all,' Cathy mutters from the doorway, as she returns with a tissue in her hand.

'Any problems at the restaurant because of it?' Tom asks as Cathy takes her seat.

'Not yet – except for a few nosy journalists, a bit of gossip from people trying to liven up their dull lives,' Cathy replies. 'It's set your dad on edge though. You know what it was like for business the last time.'

Noah doesn't want to dwell on Carruso's, since his relationship with the restaurant feels more fractious by the day. 'So, do you have any other theories about what might have happened?' Noah presses, his gaze fixed on Tom.

Tom looks up from helping himself to a slice of citrus tart. 'Not really. Miles is unlikely, isn't he, but I guess it could have been some random serial killer stalking the woods. Rachel's podcast certainly brought up a few interesting things I didn't know.'

Noah can't take his eyes off his brother. Tom's speaking so calmly. Is he really this unruffled, or has he been practising for the inquest, learning his lines?

'Anyway, it was all a long time ago, and I have a different life now. A *better* life.' Tom grins at Nadia, and she beams back at him and rests her head on his arm. They are obviously in love, and Noah knows he should try to be happy for them – but then he thinks of Lizzie, and the future she never had.

He grits his teeth. Until he's certain his brother wasn't responsible for that, he'll never join in this charade.

26

'We want you to be prepared. This could be the beginning of a long road.'

Toni grabs Alice's hand as soon as the doctor starts talking. The new guard, Trent, sits in the background, listening too.

It's hard to take everything in, but Alice gets the gist of it. The swelling in her dad's brain isn't subsiding as quickly as they'd hoped. On the scans, they can see substantial damage. They'll keep him in the coma for another week, and then try to bring him round. Meanwhile, as his next of kin, Alice will need to make decisions about long-term care and different treatment options. And in the worst-case scenario, she may have to decide whether to switch off the equipment and end her father's life.

All because a few idiots couldn't control their temper.

As Alice listens, she closes her eyes and sees her father lying on the cold prison floor, a circle of inmates staring at his lifeless body. It takes all her strength to stay in her chair and not throw things around the room. Perhaps they should nail the hospital furniture down too.

In contrast, Bobby lies before them like a tombstone effigy. Is he listening to this, she wonders, or has the best part of him already moved on?

Come on, Dad, she silently pleads. *You need to fight like hell, and wake the fuck up.*

'Alice?'

The doctor is staring at her. She must have missed something.

'Sorry, what?'

'Do you have any questions?' Dr Green is a patient woman, her manner kind, but her eyes are beginning to flicker towards the door. Alice wonders how many of these speeches she has given already today.

'I don't think so.'

Toni pipes up instead. 'Will you keep him here, when he's out of the coma, or will he be moved?'

The doctor pauses, considering. 'That's an ongoing question. We certainly won't be moving him yet, and we'll give you as much warning as we can if we need to.' She turns back to Alice. 'My advice is to get prepared now. Find out what funds and support mechanisms you have at your disposal. It'll make your decisions easier, when the time comes. But keep rested too. As soon as he comes round, he's going to be needing you a lot more than he does now, and you don't want to start off exhausted. I see too many relatives run themselves into the ground. You must look after yourself, or you're no good to him.'

'I hear you,' Alice says. 'I'll do my best.'

'Well, I'll leave you to it, then.' The doctor gets up. 'See you tomorrow, Alice.'

Once she's gone, Toni shifts in her chair, letting out a groan. 'Well, chairs at hospital bedsides are definitely not designed for long-term comfort. So it sounds like you need to make some plans, honey, and I'm here to help. Do you know where you'd like to start?'

'I...' Alice hesitates. 'I think perhaps I need to go back to the house.'

'You mean your dad's house – your old house?' Toni's brow creases in concern. 'Are you sure that's a good idea?'

'I'm going to have to face it sometime, and it sounds like I need to suss out our assets.'

'Hmm. Well, why don't you sleep on it? I've got some

good news for you, actually. I've managed to snaffle a bit of money from the support centre, and I can get you a bed in a local hotel tonight. It's nothing snazzy, but it's close by. How does that sound?'

'That's great, Toni. Thank you.' The thought of a decent bed makes her instantly weary. Her sleep is jittery at best at the hospital. The number of strangers around means she's constantly on guard.

Toni smiles but her eyes are still full of concern. 'I'll give you a lift over there when you're ready to go. And if you do still want to go to the house tomorrow, I'll juggle things round and come with you.'

They stay a while longer, playing cards until a nurse comes in to close the blinds and switch on soft bedside lights. As they gather their things, Alice goes across to the bed. 'See you tomorrow, Dad. Once I've been to the house.'

She waits, giving him a moment to wake up and object to the plan, certain he wouldn't want her going back there. But there's not even the flicker of an eyelid. His hand is limp in hers.

He's not there. Her whole body clenches at the thought. *Oh god, Dad, I wish I could talk to you.*

She kisses his cheek. 'Love you.' Then she turns and follows Toni down the long corridors to the car park. She's so glad for the guards now. She'd hate to leave her father entirely alone, even if it meant months of sleeping on hospital chairs.

As they drive away from the hospital, she's flooded with anxiety. 'I don't like leaving him. I always worry something will happen when I'm not there.'

'I know it's hard, but the doctor's right, you need a break sometimes,' Toni replies, her eyes on the dark road. 'You can't be there twenty-four seven – it's a life of absolute limbo. And just imagine, after months of it, you could still find yourself stuck on the toilet the moment he decides to wake up!'

They both begin to chuckle.

'Oh dear, hysteria is setting in,' Toni says, wiping her eyes. 'Tell me some good news – how are things with Noah?'

Alice taps her phone automatically, checking for messages, but there's nothing. 'Okay. Kind of.' She twists a tendril of hair around her fingers as she talks. 'It's just the worst possible timing. It was great to see him, but it's obvious his family have a lot going on too.'

'Well,' Toni purses her lips, 'if there's one thing I've learned in my life, it's that there is no right time. If you really like him, keep trying to push through and make it work. Hiding away will hurt more in the long run. You might as well live your life, make mistakes, fix them, and see what happens. We're all travellers in this world, honey. None of us get to sit still.'

The hotel has patches of peeling paint and a garish doona cover, but there's also a proper mattress and an en suite, both luxuries for Alice of late. Toni leaves with a promise to call first thing, and Alice settles in, then finds her phone.

She texts Noah: *No change with Dad. Doctor scared me today with worstcase scenarios. Toni found me a hotel near the hospital for the night. How are you?*

Three little dots instantly appear beneath her message. She waits for his reply.

Want a visitor?

The words set her heart racing. *Are you serious?*

You're only an hour away. I can't stop thinking about you. I could be there by ten.

I love that idea.

I'm on my way.

She replies with directions, then lies on the bed and stares at the ceiling, her mind struggling to settle, flitting between the doctor's solemn speech and the anticipation of seeing Noah. Finally, at ten, her phone pings again.

I'm downstairs.

She hurries to meet him, and he strides across and gathers

her in his arms. 'This is becoming our thing – meeting in hotel lobbies,' he whispers into her ear. He smells so good, a mix of soap and spice. His hair is tousled, his cheeks stubbled. It reminds her of those heady days in Thailand, and she wants to get him upstairs as quickly as possible.

Once in her room, they come together in a frenzy, shedding clothes, falling onto the bed in a tangle of limbs, as though they've been starved of each other for months. When they finally come apart, Alice is surprised to find her eyes are glistening.

Noah moves back to look at her, sensing the change of mood. 'Are you okay?'

'Yes. I just can't believe you came all this way.' She runs a finger along his bare chest, tracing circles across his skin.

'It's not that far,' he says. 'I'd travel a hell of a lot further to get to you.' He gently kisses her forehead. 'So tell me what's been happening.'

'Well...' She takes a big breath, the words catching in her throat. 'I'm not sure Dad is going to wake up, and even if he does I don't think he'll ever be the same again.'

Noah doesn't speak, just pulls her close.

'And now I'm going to have to go back to the house, to see if there are any valuables or insurance policies that might help pay for his care.'

She feels Noah tense. 'You mean your old house, where your dad...?'

She sits up. 'Yes, and I should have sorted it out before now. Dad wanted me to sell it, but I couldn't find the strength, so it's just sat there, with the neighbours keeping an eye on it. But now I've got no choice – I've got to do something.'

'Won't the prison authority have to help with hospital costs, since this happened on their watch?'

'Maybe, but red tape takes time. And anyway, I need to know where we stand.' She jumps up and goes across to the bar fridge. 'I wonder if there's anything in here...' She pulls out two bottles of beer. 'Bingo! Want one?'

'Sure.' Noah grabs the bottle she offers, and twists the cap off it. 'So how do you feel about going back?'

She bites her lip. 'It isn't going to be easy, I've not been there for ages, and I've not slept there since the night Reidy came in.'

'Do you want me to go with you?'

She climbs back onto the bed. 'Thanks, but doesn't the inquest start tomorrow?'

'Yes, but I'm not on the stand until Friday.'

'Stay with your family, they'll need you. Anyway, Toni said she'll take me.'

'Toni sounds great.'

'She is.' Alice pauses for another sip of beer. 'I suppose she's been a bit like a mother figure to me. It's bittersweet, really. Makes me think about what I lost all those years ago.'

They fall silent, then Noah asks, 'Do you know much about your mum?' His tone is soft. Cautious.

Alice shakes her head. 'Not a lot. Building a picture of her is like having a jigsaw with lots of missing pieces. Dad didn't bring photos or memorabilia from England. He said he didn't want us to be sad all the time, and I think it hurt him to be reminded of her. He never spoke about her unless I asked, which didn't bother me when I was younger, because I didn't think I could miss what I'd never had. But I do miss her, somehow – or at least the idea of her – because how can I miss her when I never even knew her?'

Noah sets his bottle on the bedside table and turns back to her. 'Do you know why she ended her life like that?'

'No. Until I was fourteen I didn't even know she'd died that way – I was just told she'd been sick. Dad was forced to tell me when his sister came to stay and I overheard a conversation between them. She asked when he was going to tell me the truth, and she mentioned how much I looked like her. And I'll never forget my dad's reply. He said, "How do you think it feels to live with her every day, when she's almost too painful to look at?"'

'Shit, that's horrible.'

'I know,' she says, putting her drink down. She can still picture herself at that moment, reeling backwards, cheeks burning, shrinking, turning into a ghost on the stairs. She'd needed to ground herself, and had run upstairs to look in the mirror, stroking her cheeks, trying to absorb the new tangible connection with her mother. 'He felt terrible when he realised I'd overheard, but there was no pretending after that. He had to tell me everything.' She picks at the edge of a nail as she talks – a habit she'd developed around that time. 'Sometimes,' she says, 'I have vague memories of being held close by someone soft and loving, who wasn't Dad – but I think it's probably just my mind playing cruel tricks on me. I wasn't even two when she died.'

A flash of pain runs through her. When Alice grappled with her darkest moments, she always had to face down the notion she might succumb to some terrible genetic link. *'Any history of mental illness?'* more than one doctor had asked. No, she always answered, unwilling to be ensnared in someone else's dreadful decision. Nevertheless, her mother's suicide had lined up a stack of consequences that kept falling like never-ending dominos. There was no escaping that.

Noah seems to sense her turmoil. He kisses her forehead, pulling her closer. 'And your dad never found anyone else?'

'No – occasionally there would be a woman around for a while, and I liked most of them, but the ones I grew closest to seemed to disappear faster than the others. After we'd been through that a few times, I stopped longing for a mother figure, and just wanted Dad. Once I was a teenager he seemed to lose interest in dating, and threw himself into his work and outdoor projects. Sometimes he could be a bit mopey, but we had some great adventures together, camping, four-wheel driving –'

She stops, the memories overwhelming her. Her shoulders heave and she buries her head in Noah's chest. 'Oh god, what am I going to do if he doesn't get better?' she asks, taking long, shaky breaths, refusing to let her tears fall. There's a whole dam of them, threatening to burst, but she's not ready yet.

Pull it together, Alice, she tells herself, as Noah silently strokes her hair. She can feel the fear closing in, descending like a thick, grey fog. She needs to keep fighting it off.

'I'm here, Alice,' Noah murmurs, kissing her as he holds her close. 'How about I come after the inquest on Friday, and we drive over to my family's house in the mountains? It's less than an hour from here, and I can bring you back first thing on Saturday.'

Alice thinks quickly. If it's just for a night she can still be with her father all day. The doctors say he won't be out of the coma for at least a week. She imagines the renewing fresh air of the mountains and the panoramic views. 'Okay, sounds good.'

'Great.' Noah gives her a squeeze. 'So what else can I do for you? What do you need?'

What does she need? She needs a diversion, to escape her troubled thoughts. Of course there's an easy way for him to help.

'Distract me,' she says, and kisses him with all the intensity she can muster. 'Help me forget everything for a while.'

He strokes her face, his eyes never leaving hers. Then slowly his hand begins to circle down, every movement steady and gentle. He takes his time, as though understanding how fragile she is tonight. Showing her through his touch that he will not let her break.

27

'Where the hell are you, Noah?'

'I'm nearly home, Mum, nearly home.'

In fact, despite setting off at dawn, Noah is sitting in a rush-hour crawl, cursing the traffic. It would be far easier if he could head straight to the courthouse, but his mother had insisted they all go together, to put on a united front for Tom.

'What are you playing at, staying out all night before something as important as this?'

He resists the urge to snap back, to remind her that he isn't a child and he can do whatever he bloody well wants. He knows how wound up she'll be today. 'Don't worry, I'll be there.'

'I'm heading out the door no later than eight thirty,' she says.

'Dad definitely isn't coming?'

'No – he's staying at the restaurant.' Cathy sounds cross. 'I'm not happy about it, but he's worried about the wheelchair drawing attention to us and slowing us down. He has a point, I suppose. So I'm relying on you now, Noah,' she snaps, and hangs up.

Noah focuses on the traffic, as though if he concentrates hard enough he might force the line to move. He grabs his phone and prays there are no police around as he quickly checks the map and asks Google to revise his route. He tries not to panic as the cars continually slow to a crawl.

He thinks of Alice in bed this morning; her pale, peaceful face as she slept beside him. He misses her already.

The screen of his mobile flashes. He surreptitiously checks it, hoping it's Alice, but it's a Rachel Lawrence update, the title scrolling across his screen: 'NEW THEORIES EMERGE AS THE INQUEST BEGINS'. No doubt she's building up tension for her listeners, regurgitating morsels of speculation to shove down their greedy gullets, a mother bird feeding her gossipstarved chicks. *She's repulsive*, he thinks viciously, thumping the wheel.

And yet he wants to know these new theories. *Fuck*. He can't help himself. He presses play.

Rachel's dulcet tones begin to outline the inquest procedure: the key witnesses, the evidence to be reconsidered and reweighed. He almost switches it off, but then she says something that makes him pause.

'The roll call of witnesses suggests it isn't only those close to Lizzie who'll be questioned. A detective from Queensland will take the stand, to provide information about Simon Shepperton. Sources tell me that the serial date-rapist is under suspicion for a number of unsolved interstate crimes going back over two decades. And an unusual number of these involve girls who had long, red hair.'

A horn blares, and Noah realises the queue has begun to move without him noticing. He puts his foot down to catch up with the traffic, as Rachel's speculation swirls around the car. He wonders what kind of sicko would target girls because of their hair colour. He thinks of Lizzie, and Alice. Swallows hard.

What would Lizzie make of all this conjecture? She's the one person who could cut straight to the heart of this, who could deliver the truth with a pointed stare. Where would she turn her accusing eyes? Would it only be to the person who'd done her harm, or to all the people who'd let her down? The latter includes Tom, for sure. Others, too.

And Noah? What would she say to him, if she had a chance? *Coward.*

After a stressful drive around the winding suburban streets of the Northern Beaches, Noah makes it back home with twenty minutes to spare. He can hear voices in the kitchen but there's no time for apologies. He dashes upstairs and grabs his suit, spraying himself with deodorant and trying to flatten his hair into something approaching respectable. He's downstairs at eight twenty-nine.

Cathy waits by the door, bejewelled to the max with cascading, looping earrings, and rows of multicoloured bangles. Her makeup is even heavier than usual.

'All right then, let's go,' Noah says, leading the way. 'Do you want me to drive?'

'No, I'm perfectly capable, thank you,' she snaps.

They set off in silence and Noah stares at the familiar streets. He's been dreading this day for such a long time that it's almost a relief to find it's here. A new countdown can begin. Four days, sliced in half by the weekend. By this time next week it will all be over.

He frowns as his mother takes an unexpected turn away from the highway. 'Which way are we going?'

'We're collecting Tom.' There's a challenging note in her voice.

Noah stays quiet. The car grows stuffy. He loosens his tie a little and gets out his phone, flicking through apps and reading newsflashes, anything to keep his mind off their destination.

At the hotel, Tom is waiting on the footpath alone. Noah is struck by how respectable he looks, smart and freshly shaven, in a tailored dark suit and silver tie.

'Where's Nadia?' he asks as Tom climbs into the back seat.

'She's staying here. I don't want her put through this.'

Tom turns to pull out his seatbelt strap. 'She can support me by taking care of herself and our baby.'

Noah bites back his surprise. He'd thought Tom would take full advantage of his new role as supportive partner and father-to-be, and present himself to the court in a mature and loving light. Is he really only concerned for Nadia's welfare, or is Noah missing something?

'How are you doing today, Tom?' his mother asks without turning around.

'Oh, you know.' Tom pauses. 'Is Dad not coming?'

'No – he thought it would be difficult with the wheelchair, and that we'd avoid the journalists better without him. I'm sure he'll keep himself busy at the restaurant.'

No one says anything for a while, but Noah's aware of Tom's gaze scorching the back of his neck. He's glad he's in the front, because it's still painful to recall the car trips of his childhood, the whispered insults, stealth assaults and sly gobbets of spit. He continues to fiddle with his phone, fighting off the desire to engage, until the weighted silence becomes too much and he twists round in his seat.

'You ready for today?'

'Ready as I'll ever be. Thanks for asking.' Tom smirks. 'How about you? How's your girlfriend? She's a stunner, isn't she? How on earth did you manage to pull a chick like that?'

Next to Noah, Cathy blows out a long breath of frustration.

'I'm just pulling his leg,' Tom says with a chuckle. 'My little brother's a man now, isn't he? I saw as much the other night.'

Noah rolls his eyes. 'Shouldn't you be thinking about Lizzie today? Leave the brother-baiting for another time.'

'I *was* thinking about Lizzie.' There's a gleam in Tom's eye, and Noah realises too late that the trap is falling. 'And then I thought of your girlfriend. Funny that, eh?' And he sits back and turns towards the window.

Noah seethes. There might be no Chinese burns or dead legs on this trip, but Tom is still way too close for comfort. He wants to tell him to get fucked, but he's all too aware of their agitated mother, and her fervent desire for a united front. He'll play along for now, but when he takes the witness stand and swears on the Bible to tell the whole truth, he plans to do just that. No more ignoring things for the family's sake. He'll lay out everything that's niggled away at him for twelve years, and the coroner can decide what it means.

The car park is a few hundred metres from the coronial building. As they walk to the entrance, Cathy is flanked by her sons. No one says a word. When they round the final corner, Noah sees the small crush of photographers and journalists. He holds his breath, walking steadily, eyes fixed on a point beyond them.

They are quickly spotted, and the herd of hungry strangers presses forward, recording equipment all directed towards Tom.

'What are you planning to say in there, Tom?'

'Do you have anything to admit to?'

'Did you tell the truth back then, Tom?'

'Did you kill Lizzie, Tom?'

Noah tries to focus elsewhere, but at the last question he can't help but look at his brother. The words are so stark, so confronting. Tom stares into the middle distance as he walks, his face stony, giving nothing away.

Once inside the court foyer, they are wrapped in the civility of the law, and everything becomes calmer. Their bags are checked by security, and Raf's friend Peter Bowles, family lawyer and regular visitor to Carruso's restaurant, moves forward to greet them and ushers them down a long corridor to the courtroom.

For Noah it's like stepping into a bizarre waking nightmare, where all the people he most dreads seeing are gathered together in the same place. He spots the Burdett family first, only a few strides away and clustered around officials. He's seen Miles in the news now and again, but the stooped, hollowed-out gait of him is doubly shocking in person. Sylvie's swollen eyes suggest she has sobbed daily for years, while Lizzie's sisters are even more of a surprise: two women now, not gangly teenagers, both taller than their parents, straight-backed and pale. They stand protectively either side of their mum and dad, a hand straying to one of them now and again. Sylvie and Miles are holding hands, he realises – something he's not seen his parents do in a long time. He thinks of Alice, and wishes she were here.

Noah has stared a moment too long. He catches the eye of the taller sister, Rebecca, who'd once been the only girl to play the trumpet in the school band. Noah had played the clarinet, sitting opposite the brass section, his attention drawn to Rebecca's enthusiasm and the way her face gradually reddened as she puffed out each note.

Rebecca doesn't immediately register who she's locked eyes with. Only when she glances to the people either side of Noah does her gaze turn baleful, scorching Noah for a few seconds before she turns away. He disgusts her, Noah realises, immediately nauseous. She can't stand the sight of him, because he's a Carruso.

This is unbearable. Noah looks at the doorway they just came through, contemplating whether to make a break for it. But even as he's thinking this, an official begins closing the heavy double doors, trapping them all inside. And there is Rachel Lawrence, sneaking in, just in time, and glancing around, assessing them all. Noah catches her eye and she smiles. He doesn't return it, but looks at a group of people to the right of her.

And there's Josh.

Josh is the biggest surprise of all. He's barely recognisable. A keen athlete at school, he had once been as lean as a long-distance runner, but it appears he's spent the last ten years drinking protein shakes and bulking up. Whereas Tom looks like the stress has slowly chiselled away at him, Josh has piled on pounds of pure muscle. He's holding his suit jacket, and beneath his rolled-up shirt-sleeves his forearms are heavily tattooed. Alongside him are his parents, Neil and Noelle, once good friends of Raf and Cathy's, but who had disappeared from their lives in the fallout. Neil whispers to his son, while Noelle examines her hands, the court decor and the etchings on the ceiling, anywhere there are no eyes to catch or glares to wither under.

A door opens on the far side of the room and the State Coroner, Sandra Nowak, a middle-aged woman in a suit and heels, approaches her desk on the raised platform at the front. She bows briefly and everyone returns the gesture. Then she sits down and shuffles her papers.

The counsel assisting the coroner, a young man with a stocky build and thick-framed glasses, stands up and begins to talk directly to the coroner, his back to the onlookers.

'Your Honour, we are here because we hope to determine whether Elizabeth Grace Burdett is now deceased, and if so, the possible circumstances of her death. During these proceedings, we will be considering the following, which may or may not explain her absence. Elizabeth may have chosen to disappear and be discreetly living elsewhere. Or she may have chosen to leave and is being actively hidden by others. She may have set off on an innocent adventure and died a natural death, for example from cardiac arrest, and her body has not been located. Or she could have met an accidental death in the same circumstances, for example from a fall. Elizabeth may have chosen to intentionally end her life. Or she may have been the victim of an accident, where her death was caused by another and then concealed – for example, a motor accident. Finally, we will consider whether Elizabeth may have died at the hands of another.' He looks at his papers for a long moment, as though checking he has covered everything.

The coroner nods, adjusting her glasses and peering down at everyone in the courtroom. 'I understand that this is a very distressing time for family and friends of Miss Burdett. There will be regular breaks, and you may leave the room at any time should you need to. During these proceedings, I ask that you conduct yourselves in a manner befitting the court and restrain yourself from improper conduct.' She sends a sympathetic glance towards the family.

After this, there are a surprising amount of introductions to be made. Different lawyers represent the coronial court, the Burdetts, the Carrusos, Josh Arnold and the police. Then the counsel assisting the coroner reads out a list of documents that have been submitted as evidence. It's a while before the first witness of the day is called to the stand.

Noah watches as Detective Philip Glass walks purposefully to the front. His job has obviously taken a physical toll on him – even the short walk has him out of breath, and his expansive belly hangs over his suit trousers, straining the lower shirt buttons.

After he has taken the oath, the coroner's counsel dives straight in. 'Detective Glass, you were the lead detective on the Elizabeth Burdett case, am I correct?'

'Yes, sir.'

'Could you please read your prepared statement to the court.'

'Of course.' Glass peers at the sheaf of paper in his hand. 'We were first called to the family home of Elizabeth Grace Burdett at eight am on the first of July 2006, by Elizabeth's father, Miles. The family were very worried by that stage, having expected their daughter home from a party around midnight. They had last seen her when she was collected by her boyfriend, Thomas Carruso, at about eight pm. Because Elizabeth was almost eighteen, the family no longer issued curfews, but they did ask her when she thought she would be back so they could look out for her.'

The detective pauses, glancing around the room as he clears his throat, as though to check everyone is listening. His gaze lingers on some people for a little longer than others. Then he turns back to his notes and continues.

'Elizabeth's parents had not waited up as they were used to Elizabeth coming and going late. However, when Miles got up around half past five to go to the bathroom, he noticed

Elizabeth's bedroom door was not shut, which was unusual if she was in there. He checked her room, realised she was missing, and at that point searched the house then woke the others. Sylvie began to make phone calls to Elizabeth's friends, while Miles drove out to look for her, visiting the houses of Thomas Carruso, Beatrice Dalton – who had hosted the party – and Gemma Mackleford, who was Elizabeth's best friend. No one had seen her, although Thomas Carruso confirmed they'd had a fight and Elizabeth had been on his front step at around eleven o'clock, where they had another argument and she left his house. At that stage, this was the last time anyone had seen her. When Miles got in, and Sylvie's calls had failed to locate their daughter, the family called the police.'

Noah pictures the scene in the Burdett household that morning. Their initial frustration with Lizzie turning into outright panic, as they realised they couldn't find her. The mundane tasks of the day overtaken by a dawning, dreadful realisation that, overnight, something had gone terribly wrong.

The detective is still talking. 'Our initial search focused on the triangular area between the houses of Thomas Carruso, Elizabeth Burdett and Beatrice Dalton, as indicated in the police report, these being the last places Elizabeth was seen. Later, we widened the search to include the house of Joshua Arnold, when we discovered that Elizabeth had been involved in a heavy discussion with Joshua on the night she disappeared.'

The detective clears his throat and peruses his notes.

'This has been a very unusual case,' he continues, 'because we have always had very little physical evidence to go on. The last direct contact Elizabeth had with another soul, as far as we could ascertain, was her emotional confrontation with Thomas Carruso, where they discussed their relationship on the doorstep of his home. Therefore, she would probably have been upset as she left the house. We had two male witnesses come forward the next evening, after a radio and television appeal, to say they thought they may have seen Elizabeth walking home at around a quarter past eleven, not far from the Carruso family home. This is the last known sighting of her.'

The detective adjusts his glasses then carries on. 'When we initiated the search, the weather was tricky to begin with, and heavy rain hampered proceedings. We brought in tracking dogs to see if they could pick up a scent from the Carruso house. One dog was unable to track her. The other took us to a small wooded area two hundred metres from the Carruso house, and lay down in leaf litter a few metres from the road. We searched that area extensively but were unable to find anything. We also searched a ten-kilometre radius from the last place we believe she was seen. All in all, the SES logged over one thousand hours of searching.'

Detective Glass delivers this last sentence with fervour, as though reassuring those in the room that the emergency services really had done their best. Then he continues, 'With no sign of Elizabeth in the days that followed, we began interviewing everyone who might possibly have information. We checked taxi records but didn't find anything. We also received various tip-offs, but none that led anywhere. Our investigation naturally focused on Thomas Carruso as the last person to see Elizabeth, and because their last conversation had been, by various accounts, a heated argument. Thomas Carruso was always willing to be interviewed, and we found no incriminating evidence to suggest he had anything to do with Elizabeth's disappearance.'

Cathy snakes her hand into Noah's and squeezes, as though trying to reassure him that this is in fact true. Noah casts a sideways glance towards the Burdetts, but they all stare straight ahead.

'We also looked at violent repeat offenders who may have been in the area at this time, but again we have been unable to come up with any conclusive links between them and Elizabeth's disappearance. At the present time, we have no new leads in the case.'

The coroner's counsel nods as Detective Glass concludes

his statement. 'Okay, thank you, detective. Could I ask if you have reached any conclusions as to Elizabeth's wellbeing throughout the course of your investigation?'

Detective Glass hesitates, as though even after twelve years he's still considering the question. 'We have to consider options other than foul play, of course. Knowing that Elizabeth was highly emotional as she left the Carruso house, we did look into the possibility of suicide. However, there was no indication that Elizabeth was either depressed or suicidal in the run-up to that night. She had some problems in her life, particularly regarding relationships, but she was addressing them in a conscientious manner. There were dates in her diary that she was looking forward to and talking about right up until that night. Her sister informed us that they were due to go to a Snow Patrol concert in Sydney a few weeks after Elizabeth disappeared, and that the day before she vanished they'd been excited about that, making plans to get there and deciding what to wear.'

Noah jumps as there's a loud sob from the other side of the room. It is so unexpected, so visceral and raw, that he physically recoils from it. *This* – the raw emotion that threatens to burst forth every second – is what he's been dreading.

Detective Glass, however, continues as though he hadn't heard a thing. 'There are a number of stories like this, conversations that Elizabeth had in her last known days, that very quickly led us to believe she was mentally well. However, this doesn't rule out the rush of desperation she may have felt on ending her relationship with Thomas Carruso that night. Nevertheless, other than walking into the woods, there were not many places for Elizabeth to go. We believe that had she committed suicide, the body would have been located by now. The same reasoning applies to natural causes. If something fatal had occurred spontaneously, her body most likely would have been discovered. Therefore, we still strongly suspect foul play was involved in her disappearance.'

After the statement is read, the coroner's counsel spends

over an hour quizzing the detective on what seems, to Noah, to be the smallest, most inconsequential details of police procedure in relation to this case. There follows a short break, before the Burdetts' lawyer, a tall man with long, thinning, tied-back hair, who looks more like a grungy guitar player than a legal expert, stands up and begins to ask the detective more questions about the investigation.

'Why did it take you so long to consider previously known persons of interest?'

'Why did it take you so long to bring in Thomas Carruso for questioning?'

'Why did your extensive searches not go further into the national park?'

The detective stays calm, registering no surprise at the barrage. He deflects each sortie patiently, until at last the coroner thanks him, and lets him return to his seat.

The coroner checks her watch. 'May I suggest we break for lunch here before we call our next witness,' she says.

Once the coroner has left the room, Noah looks nervously towards his family. Cathy is pale, her fingers fretting across her bangles. Tom is straight-backed, staring ahead, the only sign of nerves a slight sheen of sweat on his forehead. Noah doesn't imagine any of them will be eating much.

People begin to move. The Burdetts are talking in a huddle with their lawyer, and Peter Bowles comes over to have a quiet word with Tom. Both families head for the doors at the same time, and stop in a silent, stony-faced standoff, before the Burdetts file past, eyes averted now, shoulders turned away.

'I can't believe they hate us so much,' Cathy whispers to Noah, her voice soft and tremulous. 'How can they be so sure Tom is to blame?'

Noah doesn't have an answer. He follows his family through the double doors. Thankfully, the Burdetts have already been led away. 'So what now?' Tom asks Peter. 'Is there somewhere we can eat?'

'Well, we can go outside,' Peter replies, 'but you'll have

to get past the journalists. Or there's a little café on the ground floor.'

'That's fine – as long as Miles Burdett doesn't turn up,' Tom mutters.

They head towards the lift, only to find Josh and his parents are already waiting there. No one speaks. The tension is excruciating, and Noah stares at the little flashing number above the lift doors, willing it to move. Finally, the doors open, and the Arnolds step inside. Josh's father holds the door for them, but Tom shakes his head. 'We'll take the next one,' he announces. The doors begin to close. 'Hope you're planning on telling the truth, Josh,' Tom calls after them.

Josh sticks a hand out and blocks the moving doors before they meet. 'What the fuck did you just say?' he growls.

Noah sees his brother straighten. He exchanges a quick worried glance with Cathy. *Please don't let them start brawling here.*

Tom folds his arms and firms his stance. 'You heard me.'

'You always were a smug prick,' Josh snarls. 'But you're not pinning this on me. When I get on the stand, I'll—'

'Josh!' his mother cries out, stepping forward and tugging at his arm, her face frantic. 'Stop!'

Josh turns towards her, then looks back at Tom. He shakes his head in disgust, then steps away to let the doors close.

Noah lets out a sigh of relief, but he doesn't relax until they reach the ground floor café and there's no sign of the Arnolds. However, to his dismay, Rachel Lawrence is already there, tapping away on an iPad. She senses them staring, looks up, and her mouth twitches at the corners.

'Let's sit over there,' Noah says, pointing to a spot as far as possible from Rachel.

Tom grabs them some menus, but just as they're sitting down, Noah's phone rings.

'It's Dad,' he announces to no one in particular as he answers. 'Hi, Dad, you okay?'

'You need to come now, Noah. The restaurant is being

evacuated, we've had a call mentioning an explosive device in the toilet. It'll probably be a prank but we have to follow procedure.'

'Oh, for fuck's sake,' Noah says grimly. 'Here we go again.'

The others frown at him, and he sees Rachel watching, eyes narrowed. He gets up and goes across to a far corner where he can talk discreetly. 'When did this happen?'

'About half an hour ago. Sophie took the call, and some bastard told her there was a device in one of the bathrooms, and this was our first warning.'

'I'm not sure I can leave.'

'I need you, Noah,' Raf insists, sounding flustered, his tone shaky. 'It's chaos. Find out and get here as soon as you can. The police are on their way.'

Noah strides back over to the table. 'Peter, can I have a word?' He looks again at Rachel, who is still openly staring at them, head cocked to one side.

'What's going on?' Cathy asks.

Noah realises it's pointless trying to keep this latest drama from them. He sits down and says in an urgent whisper, 'Keep your voices down. Let's not give Rachel her next story too easily, hey? Dad says someone has threatened the restaurant – Sophie took a call about an explosive device in the toilets.'

'It'll be another prank,' Cathy replies immediately.

'I know,' Noah agrees, 'but we still need to follow procedure.'

Peter Bowles cuts in, alarmed. 'What do you mean, a prank? How are you so sure?'

Cathy sighs. 'It happened the last time, back when Lizzie first went missing. We had all sorts – fake bookings, threatening messages – we even think someone released mice in the kitchen. Yobbos with nothing better to do.'

'I think they're called trolls nowadays,' Tom says.

Cathy glares at him. 'I can think of plenty of other names for them.'

Noah frowns. They're getting off track. He leans closer. 'Dad sounds panicked – he wants me to go—'

'You won't be called today, Noah,' Peter assures him. 'If you want to go, you can.'

Noah grabs his jacket and squeezes his mother's shoulder. 'Keep me in touch with what's going on here,' he says, trying not to show how glad he is to be leaving. 'I'll be back as soon as I can.'

He can feel Rachel's curious stare burning into him as he hurries away.

28

Alice's head begins to throb as Toni drives them along the narrow back roads that lead to the small town of Brighton Bay. It's already past lunchtime, but she can't eat until this is done. The only thing she's managed are sips of cold water and her body is objecting to the lack of nourishment.

She's grateful for Toni, who knows more about what's happened to Alice than anyone in the world – more than Noah even. But how she wishes Noah were here now. He makes her feel so safe, with his spontaneous gestures of comfort – his hand squeezing hers or his lips pressing against her forehead. He has a sixth sense with her, always anticipating what she needs. He'd know exactly how to soothe her nerves.

She peers through the car window as they travel into town, watching the ghosts of her former self pass by. There she is walking to school, hunched over from the weight of her books. There's the corner where she once stepped off the kerb and straight onto the gelatinous hide of a dead rabbit, its accusing eye staring reproachfully. There's the track where her father taught her how to ride a bike and her friends played bulldog. And there's the cluster of trees where Jason Reidy ripped off her backpack and tipped its contents onto the wet grass.

She turns away. She hasn't got time for these memories.

Her old house will be coming up soon, and she needs to psych herself up just to see it.

A minute later, Toni brings the car to a stop and turns to Alice. 'You ready, then?'

Alice doesn't reply. The red brick of the modest two-storey is achingly familiar, but tired and dated too. There's her old bedroom window, and she can picture the room behind it, wallpapered with *National Geographic* photos. As a teen she'd spent hours studying the manipulation of light, the tricks of composition, fervently hoping she might match the artists' skills one day. Back when dreaming was an easy thing to do.

She gets out of the car, moving past the old cypress tree at the front, which had once held a rope for her to swing on. She glides down the driveway as though in a trance, heading for the peeling blue front door. She automatically twists the silver handle – which used to turn without a key being needed, back in childhood – but it doesn't budge. She finds the key in her bag, but before trying the lock, she moves to the window and shades her eyes so she can peer in. Sees the little lounge area she had used for homework, when she wanted peace from her father's talkback radio programs in the kitchen. There's the wooden table, and the black swivel chair neatly pushed into it. There's the bookcase, filled with coffee table nature books and a smattering of her dad's favourite Lee Child novels.

The glass is a portal to another time, and she steps back, disorientated. When a hand touches her shoulder she half expects to turn around and see her father, to look down and find herself back in school uniform.

'Are you ready to go in?' Toni seems unusually flustered as she waves at the key in Alice's hand.

'Yes.' Alice moves to unlock the door.

It opens to reveal the dark, familiar hallway. She takes a step forward. There's a musty odour she doesn't recognise, but the faint scent of pinewood, too, which brings her home.

Then, without warning, there's a sharp metallic taste in her mouth. Her throat tightens and she clutches at her neck, trying to loosen the invisible hands that are choking her. She reels backwards and Toni catches her. 'Okay, take it steady, Alice, there's no rush. You're safe, remember. No one can hurt you now.'

It doesn't help. Alice is frozen. She knows what waits for her inside. There's a skinny man on the kitchen floor, staring at the white ceiling while the blood slowly spreads beneath him, painting him a pair of scarlet wings. Her father's ashen face is in front of hers, one of his hands crimson. A knife lies on the table.

Seeing that once is enough for a lifetime.

She can't go in.

She turns away from the innards of the house, hands reaching out to the door frame to steady herself. She gulps in fresh air, as though she's been drowning for years and has just kicked and clawed her way back to the surface.

'Alice?' Toni's face looms in front of her. 'Oh, Alice, it's okay, we don't have to do this.'

'Yes, I do.' Alice's voice sounds strange even to herself, her low tone undercut with a defiant, feline growl. 'Jason Reidy took my home and my dad.' She spits every word through gritted teeth. 'He took *everything*. And I'm meant to feel sad that he's dead... when he kept coming into this house and terrorising us, again and again.'

'You have nothing to be ashamed of, Alice.' Toni's voice is hoarse. 'Nothing. You don't have to mourn a man who made your life a misery.'

'So I can be glad he's gone? It doesn't make me a monster?' She swallows a surge of sickness.

'Yes, you can. And no, it does not.'

Her breath begins to settle.

'Come on,' Toni's arm is around her, 'let me help you to the car.'

'No!' She steps back inside the house. 'I'm here for Dad.

I need to stay.' She turns and heads down the corridor before there's any more time to think.

The next few hours are a flurry of frantic searching. The only way Alice can do this is if she doesn't stop. They empty the contents of her father's filing cabinet into boxes to take a look at later. She rifles through cupboards and drawers, pulling out anything that might be useful.

Even in her bedroom there's no time for nostalgia. Some of her stuff had already gone with her to uni, and is stored in a friend's loft. She takes a few photo albums, ornaments, books and clothes – finding surprisingly few things that really matter. She grabs bits and pieces from her dad's room – a watch, cufflinks, a photo of his parents. Toni works steadfastly beside her, packing the things Alice finds. In a few hours the car is loaded up, ready to leave.

'Dad always wanted me to sell this place,' Alice says, strapping herself in as Toni guns the engine. 'At first I couldn't bring myself to do it, but now I can't wait to see it gone.'

'I'm so proud of you.' Toni pats her knee. 'I can rally people to help clear the other bits and pieces. We'll figure it out so you don't have to go there again.'

Alice doesn't look back. Despite the heavy box on her lap, she feels lighter. She puts her hand inside and it falls on the top item. Her dad's passport.

Sometimes she'd imagined him at the airport in Thailand, the long reunion hug they'd enjoy with no one tasked to monitor it. He'd love the national parks. She might even have gotten him down that waterfall. She pictures introducing him to Noah, and how excited he would be for them both. Now she stares at his solemn face in the little square next to his name, and reaffirms the only promise he's ever asked for. *Whatever it takes, Dad, I'll get through this. I'll fight for the future I want – and I'll fight for your future too.*

Her thoughts of Reidy are receding. He's still on the floor

back there; no longer prowling the edges of her life. A wave of calm washes over her.

You tried to take everything from me, she tells him. *But I will not let you win.*

Toni drops Alice at the hospital and drives away to store the boxes at her place. Before going inside, Alice walks around the car park to a spare patch of grass. Sitting in the shade of a scribbly gum, she texts Noah.

How's it all going? Are you okay? Can you talk?

Her phone rings a few seconds later.

'I thought you'd be in court?' she asks, surprised.

'Me too. Instead I'm watching the police and the bomb squad hunt through the restaurant. We had a call about an explosive device. So far, they've found nothing, but of course Carruso's will be back in the news again – and all of it connected to Tom and Lizzie, just as we feared.'

'So did you not go to court at all?'

'I went this morning and listened to the detective. There wasn't much we didn't know already – and apparently there's been more of it this afternoon, mostly technical details of the search. So how did you get on? Did you go to the house?'

'I did – I collected what I needed.'

'That can't have been easy. I'm really proud of you.'

It's exactly what her dad would have said, she realises with a pang. 'Thanks.'

'And how are things at the hospital?'

'Nothing's changed. I'm about to go and sit with him. So what happens now? Will you keep the restaurant closed?'

'I'd love to, but Dad's insisting we reopen tomorrow. Says he won't be bullied.' Noah pauses. 'I've got a bad feeling about this, Alice. I just want to get through the next week unscathed.' There's a pause, then he lowers his voice. 'I loved our night at the hotel.'

A thrill shoots through Alice at the memory of them naked, limbs wrapped around each other. 'Me too.'

'I can't wait for tomorrow.'

'Likewise.' She smiles then grows serious. 'Good luck at court, I hope it goes well. Stay away from Tom if you need to.'

'Don't worry, I will,' he replies, but his tone belies his words and she can hear his nervousness. 'It's nice to have you looking out for me,' he adds, his voice softening.

When they hang up, Alice watches the golden glow of early evening fading from buildings and trees as darkness edges closer. She loves the easy intimacy between her and Noah, but there's still her dad, and the inquest. So much is beyond their control. The more she's drawn to Noah, the faster the questions circle. It's as though they are teetering on the edge of something, and she doesn't know if they'll fall or hold on. She wants him so much that she's searching desperately for ways to make it work, but the more she looks, the more the obstacles seem to multiply. What if they can't overcome them?

She shivers. The freedom, the victory she'd briefly tasted earlier, has all but gone.

29

'I, Thomas Rafael Carruso, do solemnly and sincerely and truthfully affirm that the evidence I give will be the truth, the whole truth, and nothing but the truth.'

It's a new day, as evidenced by outfit changes, but apart from that, the scene in the coroner's court is virtually identical to yesterday. The journalists are already scribbling. Noah had seen a few reports last night, most of them perfunctory. The details of the case are nothing new. *This* is the day they've been waiting for.

As Tom speaks, there's a complete hush. Noah has one hand on his phone, which he's set to vibrate, in case anyone from the restaurant calls. However, the only contact so far this morning has been a text from Alice: *Good luck today. I'm thinking of you xx*

Yesterday, by the time Noah had reached Carruso's, all the customers and most of the staff were already gone. Raf hadn't said much at all, but his face was haggard and his eyes bloated as they assisted the police with enquiries. As soon as they'd got home, he had disappeared upstairs, and this morning he hadn't been able to get out of bed. Cathy had explained it away as exhaustion, but Noah had noticed the empty wine bottles in the recycle bin.

Whatever the reason, it means Noah's beginning the day exhausted. He's been at Carruso's since dawn, checking everything's okay for them to open. As they suspected, the police had found nothing sinister, but the prank has still cost them a few thousand dollars in lost customers and wasted food. And that's not counting the days to come, since the threat had made the news and has already been connected to the inquest.

Last night, the podcast app on his phone had announced another new episode from Rachel Lawrence, the first of her daily specials to cover the inquest. He'd begrudgingly listened to her recap of the day's events and winced as she gleefully mentioned the simultaneous bomb scare at Carruso's. He was now all too aware that today it would be Tom, and perhaps himself, who would be the unwitting stars of Rachel's show.

'Thank you, Mr Carruso,' the coroner's counsel says, bringing Noah back to his surroundings, to the long-anticipated sight of his brother on the witness stand. 'Now please could you read your witness statement to the court.'

Tom looks down at the pieces of paper in his hands. Noah sees that they are trembling slightly. He hadn't expected nerves from his brother. Does it make him look human, or more like he has something to hide?

'I was in a relationship with Lizzie for seven months, from Christmas 2005 until the day she disappeared.'

As Tom begins to speak, Noah glances around the courtroom, realising that anyone with access to the podcast will know a lot about Tom and Lizzie already. Rachel catches his eye and smirks at him, unabashed. Noah frowns and quickly turns his focus back to Tom.

'In the weeks before Lizzie vanished, I'd noticed her getting closer to my good friend Josh Arnold. I was upset and worried that she might end our relationship. We had a few fights about it, including on the night she disappeared. We had been at a party at Beatrice Dalton's house, and I found her with Josh. Josh's arm was around her, and I was devastated, so I left the party and walked home. Lizzie came after me, and we had a big argument on my doorstep. Lizzie was very upset and accused me of making a lot of assumptions and of being jealous. I was tired and angry as I felt she might be playing me and Josh off against each other. I ranted at her and told her to leave.'

Tom glances at the coroner, and Noah sees his brother's shoulders shaking slightly. Is he upset? Noah can't quite tell from here, but the whole room is silent, poised for what comes next.

'I was supposed to be taking her home in my car, as I'd collected her from her house earlier that night, and it was at least half an hour away by foot. But I didn't offer to do that, even though it was raining. I just shut the door on her because I was still angry. About five minutes later, when I'd calmed down, I went out looking for her. I wanted to apologise, but I couldn't find her. I never saw her again.'

Tom bows his head, breathing heavily. Noah leans forward, studying every centimetre of his brother. What would they see if Tom looked up? Pain? Remorse? Or guilt?

Noah casts a sideways glance at his mother. She seems spellbound by her eldest son, her brightly painted nails scratching nervously at her leg.

Tom looks up, hands clasped in front of him as he composes himself. 'The first I knew that Lizzie was missing,' he continues, 'was when Miles Burdett woke us at about six forty-five am, banging on our door.'

Noah doesn't need Tom to describe this. He can still remember how incredibly white Miles's face was, blanched by worry and tiredness as he spoke much faster than normal, desperation accelerating his words.

'He'd tried to phone me but I hadn't heard the call.' Tom's eyes flicker across the room then back to the coroner. 'He told us he'd woken early and that Lizzie wasn't home. He'd driven to us via her normal walking route, and there was no sign of her.' Tom pauses. 'He asked why I hadn't dropped her off. I told him we'd had a fight, and Miles was furious with me.' Tom stares straight ahead, refusing to look in Miles's direction. 'Understandably so.'

Noah recalls the way Tom had shifted from one foot to the other as he'd answered Miles's questions that morning, as though the floor was scalding his feet. Tom had reeled off names, and Miles told him that Sylvie had already tried those people. Then Miles had lurched at Tom, demanding to know why he'd let this happen. 'You might look like a man but you certainly don't behave like one. You took her out, mate. When you take a girl out, you're supposed to get her safely home.'

Tom's face had gone bright red. Then Cathy appeared, dishevelled and worried. On hearing the news, she'd immediately called Raf, who was already at the restaurant for early deliveries, enlisting him in the search. Then Tom said he'd caught Lizzie with Josh at the party – and that's why he'd come home. He'd looked Miles right in the eye and said, 'Perhaps you should go to Josh's house and check his bed.'

As Tom relays this comment to the court, Noah can feel the mood darken. 'Miles looked like he wanted to punch me. He pushed his face into mine and said, "Perhaps she just needed some love and affection, you little shit," and then stormed out. And that was the last contact I had with him.'

Tom's recollection is exactly as Noah remembers it. But Miles hadn't witnessed the next part, when Noah and Cathy stared in shock at Tom until he shouted at them: 'She wasn't looking for love and affection, she was just trying to make me jealous.' He'd sounded like a petulant child.

'My family arranged to join in the search,' Tom continues. 'My brother stayed home, and Mum and I went out in the car, along different routes Lizzie might have taken. Dad took time off from work to help too. I remember it was still raining on and off, so we stayed in the car and shouted her name through the open windows. By lunchtime, when Mum called Sylvie and there was still no sign of Lizzie, I began to get scared. At first I really thought she'd just gone to a friend's. I was annoyed with her for getting me in trouble. But as time went by, I knew she wouldn't completely disappear like that.'

To Noah's surprise, Tom begins to cry.

'Crocodile tears,' a male voice barks loudly from somewhere amongst the seated rows of press and curious onlookers.

Tom quickly wipes his eyes and straightens his stance.

'Silence,' the coroner snaps. 'May I remind you all that Tom Carruso is not on trial here and has not been charged with a crime.'

As Noah watches Tom he realises he still can't get a handle on his brother. Had Tom truly loved Lizzie? Was that why he'd been so jealous? Or was Lizzie more of a status symbol for him, a beautiful girl to show off to his friends?

Sometimes Noah wonders what would have happened if Lizzie hadn't gone. Would she and Tom have made up? Still be together? Would Lizzie be his sister-in-law? Noah had never thought they were a good match, but part of that stemmed from jealousy. When Lizzie looked at Tom, she definitely saw something in him that Noah couldn't. She'd been distraught as she defended herself and sobbed on the doorstep that fateful night.

The coroner's counsel is talking to Tom again. 'You are aware of the two witnesses who saw Lizzie walking along the road, not far from your house, sometime after 11.15 pm?'

'Yes, I am.'

'So when comparing your statements, does it seem strange that you didn't come across Lizzie? She was travelling in the direction of her home, on the main route you'd take to get there, and you followed her after only five minutes?'

'Yes, I thought I'd find her quite easily.'

'But there was no sign of her?'

'No.'

'Could you indicate your route on this map?' The counsel hands Tom a pen and a piece of printed paper. 'Just draw it on here, please.' Tom does so and the counsel collects it. 'Thank you for that.' He puts the paper on top of his folders. 'So, how long did you spend trying to find her?'

'I jogged for ten or fifteen minutes.'

'To your knowledge, would she have taken any other route home?'

'No.'

'Do you have any other explanation as to why you didn't find her?'

He shrugs. 'She must have gone a different way.'

'But the men who spotted her soon after she left your house saw her along this route.' The counsel holds up the map.

Tom frowns. 'Well, maybe she hid from me.'

'Why would she do that?'

'Perhaps she was sick of us fighting.'

More likely she was scared of you, Noah thinks, remembering how intimidating Tom had been that night. He watches every movement his brother makes. Does his hand tighten on the rail? Does he blink faster than before?

'That's all I have, no more questions.' The coroner's counsel sits down.

The coroner leans back and pauses, eyes running over her notes. 'Mr Elwood, do you have anything to ask?'

The Burdetts' lawyer stands. 'Did Elizabeth humiliate you that night, Tom?'

Tom stares at the man, stony-faced. 'Yes, she did.'

'Had you felt that way before?'

'As I said, the thing with Josh had been building for a while.' Tom glances Josh's way as he answers.

'Did you always get jealous when you saw Elizabeth flirting with other men?'

Tom shakes his head. 'We were both mad with one another at times, for all sorts of reasons, but we were crazy about each other too. We were just kids, still getting to grips with how relationships worked. I wish I could change what happened that night, but I thought she'd be okay walking home – she'd done it before, she wasn't particularly drunk, and it would give her time to cool off.' He glances imploringly around the room. 'I loved Lizzie, and yes, sometimes I was frightened of losing her, but I never imagined this. I was devastated when she disappeared. Even after I left the state, to get away from the accusations, I spent a lot of time trying to figure out what happened. I want the truth as much as everybody else, but I also have the right to live my life freely, because I'm an innocent man and I'm sick of the suspicion. I know I let Lizzie down that night, but I am *not* a murderer.'

Noah is barely able to breathe. Tom maintains eye contact with the Burdetts' lawyer, and then turns his pleading eyes to the coroner. His statement is full of passion.

Noah catches sight of Josh, who is watching Tom intently, his arms folded across his chest. If Josh hadn't been trying to steal Lizzie from Tom, perhaps none of this would have happened. He imagines how he'd react if Jez set his sights on Alice, and the answer is a toxic mix of jealousy, anger and betrayal. For the first time in a long time, Noah has a stab of doubt. Had he really thought that his brother was a killer all these years when Tom is innocent and still trying to prove it? Or has Tom just become a more convincing liar in the twelve years that have passed?

Noah looks across to the Burdetts. Miles looks murderous. He doesn't seem to be hearing Tom's protestations of innocence. Noah suspects he can only see the person who should have protected Lizzie and got her safely home that night, but didn't.

The counsel for the Burdetts springs to life again. 'Mr Carruso, you mention that you went out looking for Lizzie, but couldn't find her. Did it not occur to you to inform her parents that she was walking home? Either by phone, or by driving to her house and letting them know?'

Tom hangs his head. 'No, it didn't. And I'm truly sorry for that. I really thought she would be okay.'

'Seriously? A young girl walking alone at night? Come on, Mr Carruso, you must read the papers like everyone else. Admit it, you were furious and didn't care what happened to her.'

The coroner cuts in. 'Mr Elwood, I need to remind you in the strongest terms that Mr Carruso is not on trial here.'

'Yes, I understand that,' the lawyer says, not appearing at all remorseful.

The coroner glares around the room. 'There may be people whose action, or lack of it, influenced the outcome of events that night, but this inquest is not the place for those judgements. We are here to see if we can move any closer to determining what happened to Elizabeth, and whether she is now, as we fear, deceased.'

There is silence in the courtroom. 'Does anyone else have any questions for Mr Carruso?' the coroner asks.

Silence.

'I'd like to thank you for your testimony today,' the coroner says to Tom. 'We'll take our break now.' She stands up and leaves the room.

Noah begins sweating, knowing he's next on the list. Peter Bowles comes to talk to him, but he needs a moment alone to psych himself up. 'I have to use the bathroom,' he tells Peter.

Peter nods. 'All right. You've got about fifteen minutes.'

Noah heads quickly from the courtroom and down the long corridor, trying to find a bathroom where he won't be disturbed. He locks himself inside a cubicle, leans against the door and wipes the sheen of sweat from his brow, trying to induce calm. But his thoughts are like battering rams. Just when he thinks he can do this, they strike again.

He texts Alice. *Tom's finished. I'm next.*

She replies straight away. *Good luck. You can do this. It'll be over soon, and I can't wait to see you later.*

Her encouragement, and the thought of seeing her in a few hours, temporarily quells his roiling stomach, until his phone pings with Peter's message. *Time to head back.*

Noah heads out of the cubicle and splashes his face with water. Stares at himself in the mirror.

This is it.

He takes his time, his legs dragging as though gripped by invisible weights. Inside the courtroom, most people are already seated. Noah is heading for his chair when he hears his name.

He turns in surprise. 'What are you doing here?' he asks, as Jez comes forward, looking slightly sheepish. He's wearing jeans and a hoodie, and stands out in the smartly dressed room.

Jez shrugs. 'It felt wrong not to come and support you.'

Noah tries to look grateful, though in truth he wishes his friend had stayed away. So much of his life is caught up in this nightmare that it's nice to have some places to escape. However, Jez isn't really disconnected from all this, is he? His older brother had sometimes hung around with Lizzie, Tom, Josh and Gemma, and Ellis was at Beatrice's party on the night Lizzie disappeared. Jez had been home when the police came round the following day; he'd hidden and listened to Ellis recount the evening, and told Noah everything he heard.

'Thanks,' he tells Jez. 'I'm next up. Tom finished his statement before the break.'

'Want me to take you for a drink afterwards, if you've got time?'

Noah hesitates. 'Maybe. I might have to get back to work. Did you hear about the bomb scare?'

Jez nods, but before he can reply there's a flurry of movement at the front. Everyone stands and bows as the coroner re-enters the courtroom.

'Good luck,' Jez whispers, patting his shoulder before he moves to take a seat by the exit.

The proceedings begin, and Noah stands when he hears his name, smoothing down his shirtfront, keeping his hand pressed against his squalling stomach as he makes his way to the front.

After he's sworn in, the coroner's counsel doesn't hesitate. 'Mr Carruso, can you confirm you were the only other person at the family home on the evening of the thirtieth June, 2006, when your brother Thomas and Elizabeth Burdett had an altercation on the doorstep?'

'That's right.'

'Could you tell us what you saw?'

I saw the way he loomed over her, and how she cowered. I heard the fury in Tom's voice, and the fear in Lizzie's. I jumped when he slammed the door. I ran from the rage in his eyes.

He takes a slow, steadying breath. 'I was woken by the sound of arguing,' he begins, wondering if they can all hear the tremor in his voice. 'I went to find out what was going on, and stopped halfway down the stairs. Tom and Lizzie were shouting at each other by the front door. They were emotional, and very angry.'

'Could you hear what was being said?'

'Most of it.'

'Can you relay that conversation to us please?'

'I can't remember all of it word for word. I know Lizzie told Tom he was moody and possessive and jealous and an arsehole. Tom was furious that Lizzie had "betrayed" him – he definitely used the word "betray". He told her that if she'd been cheating on him he'd make sure she paid for it, because she'd made a fool out of him in front of all their friends. And Lizzie kept saying she hadn't, that he'd got it wrong, but he wouldn't listen. Then she ran off.'

'And what would you say Lizzie's mood was like when she left the house?'

'Upset.' He hesitates. 'Devastated, I'd say.'

His glance flickers across to the Burdett family. Lizzie's sisters' pale faces are twisted in pain, and Sylvie clutches a tissue to her mouth. But Miles is expressionless. Noah has no doubt there's a pent-up storm of emotions raging inside Lizzie's father as he listens – but he's hiding it well.

The coroner's counsel looks briefly at his notes then back to Noah. 'How long did their conversation last, do you think?'

'I'm not sure, but less than five minutes.'

'And what happened after Lizzie had gone?'

'Tom paced around the house for a while, then he went after her.'

'What did you see, exactly?'

'He hurried down the drive.'

'And where were you standing at this point?'

'By my bedroom window.'

'What made you think he was going after Lizzie?'

'Well... I presumed he was.'

'Why did you presume this?'

'Because he was upset. Because I knew how much they cared about one another.'

From the corner of his eye, to Noah's irritation, Tom is nodding in agreement. *Don't get distracted*, he tells himself. *Don't react. Focus on the questions.*

'And how long was he gone, do you think?'

'Not too long – less than half an hour.'

'And then what happened?'

'He came back inside.'

The coroner's counsel shuffles his papers, as though checking something. Noah waits, aware they have arrived at the critical moment. He has to decide exactly what to say next, in front of his brother, his mother, the Burdetts, everyone, and even though he has thought about this for a long time, he's still not completely sure what he'll say. He looks at Jez, who is leaning forward, elbows on his knees, listening intently. As their eyes meet, Jez gives him an encouraging smile.

'You saw him come back?' the coroner's counsel asks.

'Yes, I watched through my bedroom window.'

'And did you witness anything else after that?'

The counsel is looking at his notes as he asks the question. It's clear he's expecting to hear a *No*. As far as he's concerned this witness is almost done and dusted.

'He came into my bedroom,' Noah blurts out.

The counsel's head snaps up. He looks uncertain. Noah can see him trying to equate this with what he knows about the case, running through the facts in his head.

'Right,' the counsel says. 'And what happened then?'

'I pretended to be asleep.'

'Why?'

Noah's mind moves away from the courtroom, back almost twelve years. Why had it felt so important to feign sleep at that moment?

Then he remembers how his whole body had throbbed with fear as Tom came close enough to lean over him. He could smell alcohol on his brother, and he'd waited for a body blow of some sort, but for once it hadn't come.

'I was scared,' he tells the court.

A few murmurs ripple through the room.

'So what did he do?'

'He leaned over me – it felt like he was checking to see if I was asleep.'

'What did you think Tom would do if you were awake?'

'I...' Noah looks at his shoes. 'I don't know.' *This is stupid.* For a second he's fifteen again: a paranoid adolescent wasting the grown-ups' time.

There's a long pause. Noah looks up to find the counsel staring at him, frowning, as though trying to figure out what's going on.

'So then what happened?'

'He left my room. A couple of minutes later I heard his car start. I ran to my window and he was driving away.'

Gasps echo around the room. The legal teams and the journalists look up sharply.

The coroner's counsel pauses, looks down at his notes, then up again. His face is a study of professional blankness, but Noah can see a hint of excitement in his eyes. 'You're saying your brother Tom Carruso went out in his car on the evening of the thirtieth June 2006?'

'Yes.'

'And this isn't in your original statement, Noah?'

'No.'

'Why is that?'

Keep your mouth shut.

'I didn't see it as important at the time.'

Someone groans, and Noah flinches.

'You think it's significant now?'

Noah hesitates. 'I don't know.'

He glances across the room. Cathy looks astonished, and Tom's mouth has fallen open. The murmurs from those watching are growing, but there's no going back now.

'Do you know how long Tom was out for?'

'Not exactly. I'd say between fifteen minutes and half an hour.'

'Did you see him come back?'

'Yes.'

'Can you describe what you saw?'

'I saw his car pulling up on the drive. He ran inside.'

'Was that the last time you saw him?'

'Yes – but soon after that I heard him being sick.'

Someone gasps. There's a buzz of conversation now.

'Quiet please,' the coroner interjects.

'Just to be clear,' the counsel says. 'You haven't mentioned this to anyone before? Nothing about the car trip or Tom being sick?'

'No.'

'You never once thought to tell the police?'

'Not in the beginning.'

The counsel bites his lip. 'Mr Carruso, did your brother ever ask you to keep quiet about anything you saw that night?'

Noah looks directly at Tom, who stares back at him, arms folded, eyes two pinpoints of darkness. *You can't intimidate me anymore, big brother. The death stare doesn't work.* 'Yes. He told me to keep my mouth shut.'

The ripples of chatter become intense waves of frantic conversation. Reporters reach for notepads. Miles Burdett stands up and glares across at Tom as though he has just heard a confession. Cathy's face is ashen, while Jez is staring at

Noah in astonishment. Rachel Lawrence's face is a picture of open-mouthed delight.

'Everyone, quiet, please,' the coroner intervenes sternly. 'Mr Elwood, do you have any questions?'

The Burdetts' lawyer jumps up, followed by the police counsel. Each of them asks Noah to retell the events of the night Lizzie disappeared, probing for different angles on the things he'd seen. Noah feels like he's just run a marathon as he answers: he can't catch his breath and his legs are shaking. He can tell he's frustrating them as he provides the same answers, over and over. He's given them the scent of blood, and now they want the kill.

When everyone has finished, the coroner turns to Noah.

'I have a couple more questions, Mr Carruso,' she says politely.

Noah waits.

'How would you describe the relationship you have with your brother?'

Noah baulks. He hadn't expected this one. His eyes shoot to Tom, who sits with his arms folded, eyebrows raised. He has the stillness of a predator eyeing his prey.

'It's... strained,' Noah says. 'We weren't close growing up, and he hasn't been around for quite a long time.'

'And on the night Lizzie disappeared – do you remember how you felt about your brother at that particular time?'

Noah frowns. 'In general, or while they were arguing?'

'Both.'

'In general, I tried to keep away from Tom because he liked baiting me. And that night, when I watched him fighting with Lizzie, I hated the way he spoke to her. I was disgusted with him.'

The coroner nods. 'Thank you for your testimony, Mr Carruso, you are free to go.'

Noah can't look at anyone, especially not his brother. Or his mum. He's only thankful his father isn't here to witness this too. But whatever happens now, it's done. He's told the court everything.

As he begins to move, the doors at the back of the room open, and Detective Glass enters, looking distinctly flustered. He glowers as his gaze falls on Tom. *No way*, Noah thinks, his heart beginning to gallop. *They can't just arrest Tom like this, can they – based on what I've just said?* He hadn't even noticed the detective was missing until now. Detective Glass surely won't even have heard this testimony yet, unless he's got someone in court relaying the proceedings to him.

The detective has moved to whisper to the officer of the court. Now he pushes a limp strand of hair from his forehead as he hurries over to the counsel assisting the coroner and whispers in the man's ear. The lawyer's eyes widen, and he immediately raises a hand.

'Your Honour, may we approach the bench?'

The coroner frowns. 'Yes, of course.'

The other lawyers hurry forward to join in a whispered discussion. Noah remains at the front. He looks down at his hands, then across the room at Tom. They hold each other's gaze as they wait.

Noah refuses to break the stare. *Screw you, Tom. Maybe now you'll have to tell the truth.*

An agreement is reached in hushed tones and each lawyer returns to their clients.

'In light of new evidence, we need to adjourn this inquest immediately,' the coroner announces, her words clipped and her expression grim. 'We will consider new dates for proceedings when we have further clarification of recent events.' She is quickly out of her chair and away. Noah watches nervously as Detective Glass heads towards Tom, but then, to his astonishment, Glass moves past Tom and disappears out the door.

The lawyer for the Burdetts is already ushering them out of court as though he can't get them away fast enough. Harsh, curious whispers are filling the room.

Peter Bowles is hurrying across to him. 'Noah, come with me.' He leads Noah to Tom and Cathy. 'We need to get into a briefing room fast,' he tells them all. 'Please follow me.'

As they leave, Noah looks around for Jez, suddenly desperate to see a reassuring, friendly face, but there's no sign of him. Noah's mother gives him a bewildered look as they are quickly guided into a small side room. Peter looks pale as he goes to close the door. Before it can shut completely, they hear a distraught scream.

'I think you might want to sit down,' Peter says.

Without a word, they all take a seat around a small table.

'There's been a tip-off from a prisoner, who was once the cellmate of a convicted rapist called David Hutchins.' Peter's expression is grave. 'When this man saw the inquest on the news, he told police that Hutchins once said he'd buried a woman in the Garigal National Park. They went to the site first thing this morning, and have found evidence of human remains.'

For a moment, no one moves.

Then Tom casts around wildly, grabs a rubbish bin, and heaves up his breakfast in front of them all.

30

Alice is in the hospital canteen buying a dismal-looking plastic-wrapped salad, when there's a newsflash on the TV on the wall.

'Breaking news in the Lizzie Burdett inquest –' says the ticker tape. *'Body found in woodland.'*

Unfortunately there's no sound. Alice watches the fresh-faced female reporter solemnly deliver the news, but has no idea what's being said. There follows a few seconds' footage of the Burdetts' lawyer making a statement, the family standing miserably behind him, microphones shoved in their faces.

Alice turns sharply, thoughts whirling. The assistant at the till has to call after her to pass over her change. She runs back along the corridors to her dad's room. Picks up her phone and goes straight to the news.

'Police are at the scene in the Garigal National Park, after human remains were discovered this morning. The development comes after a tipoff in connection to the Lizzie Burdett inquest, which had been in progress at the Coroner's Court of New South Wales. The inquest has now been adjourned.'

Alice gasps, and Gary, who is on first shift today, looks up sharply.

'You okay?'

'Yes, fine,' she says, still focused on the article. As she

scrolls down, her screen fills with a photo of Lizzie for a moment, before the text continues.

'Miles Burdett has stayed prominently in the news for the past decade as the family have searched tirelessly for their missing daughter. Detective Philip Glass, lead investigator on Lizzie's case, spoke briefly to reporters, asking them to give the family space during this distressing time. He refused to speculate further on whether the remains are those of Lizzie Burdett, saying only that a press conference will be scheduled as soon as there is more to say.'

Alice finds her earbuds and replays Rachel Lawrence's podcast, scrolling through to the part about Hutchins. Originally, Alice had thought Rachel was clutching at straws, highlighting every possible suspect just to heighten tension and prolong the series. Now, each revelation about Hutchins leaves Alice cold. He sounds evil and opportunistic. However, he has already passed away. Which means that if these remains are Lizzie's, the Burdetts will have no justice, no one to target their anger towards. Just a lifetime of dealing with bitterness, sorrow and regret.

She switches her phone off, pulls out the earbuds, and looks at her dad. *Life can be so bloody unfair.*

Gary is watching her curiously. 'You look like you've had a shock?'

Alice nods. 'Have you heard about the Lizzie Burdett inquest? They've just found a body in the woods that might be her.'

'Ah yes, I saw that too. Horrible business. I had a friend who worked with Hutchins. Said he was ice cold – a real Hannibal Lecter. There were always rumours he'd done more than he'd been charged with. When he attacked that poor girl in the caravan park... well, I heard some sickening details. You don't become that evil all of a sudden. It takes practice.'

Alice doesn't need to imagine the disorienting panic of an ambush, she knows it all too well. She thinks of Hutchins lurking, watching his victims, and recoils as though she's trapped in the scene, her eyes instinctively darting around the room, immediately aware of the empty space behind her.

'Are you okay, Alice?' Gary sounds concerned.

'Yes, I'm fine.' She avoids his eyes as she moves her chair against the wall, then turns back to her phone, just as a text flashes up from Noah.

Have you seen the news?

She taps a quick reply. *Just now. Are you okay?*

Can you talk?

I'll call you in five.

Alice makes her way outside, finding a spot away from the entrance where she won't be disturbed. Noah answers her call immediately.

'Oh god, Noah, this must be so traumatic for you and your family – are you okay?'

'I don't know. Everyone's still in shock.'

'Where are you now?'

'I'm just in a corridor in the courthouse. We're waiting for our lawyer to find out what's going on.'

'So do you know how long it'll be before they can say if it's Lizzie?'

'Peter says we're probably looking at days, maybe weeks, depending on how difficult it is to identify her...'

'I just listened to the podcast again. Hutchins sounds like a monster.'

There's a pause. 'I know,' Noah says. 'It's hard to take this in.'

'We don't have to go tonight if you need to stay with your family.'

'No, I need to get out of here or I'll lose my mind. I'll be there about six, if that's still okay?'

'It's fine. See you soon.'

She's about to hang up when Noah says, 'Don't go yet, Alice.'

His voice has gone husky, as though he's close to tears.

'What is it?' she asks with a prickle of alarm.

'In court today – I... I threw Tom under the bus.'

'What? What do you mean?'

'On the night Lizzie disappeared, I didn't just see him run after her. I saw him go out later in the car too. He was gone for a while, and when he came home, he threw up.' Noah clears his throat. 'When Tom realised what I'd seen, he told me to keep my mouth shut, and I'm ashamed to say I did. At first I was frightened of him, then later I got angry, but I never told anyone. It's haunted me for years, and I knew I had to say something at the inquest.'

Alice hesitates, shocked, searching for the right words.

'Please, say something.' Noah sounds desperate.

'Noah, I – I don't know what to say.'

'Do you... do you think I'm an arsehole?'

'No – no, I think you were a frightened kid. I've met Tom, remember. I've seen how intimidating he can be.'

'Thanks,' Noah says eventually. 'But I'll always feel ashamed that I covered for him. He didn't deserve it, that's for sure.'

Alice looks at the clouds scudding across the sky as she thinks about what he's saying. 'Are you sure you would've kept quiet if you really believed he was guilty? After today's developments, perhaps you've saved him from years in jail for something he didn't do.'

There's a long pause. 'Maybe.' Noah sounds hesitant. 'But then why was he so stressed at the time? He definitely didn't want me to talk. Even now, I still think he's hiding something.'

'Well then, you did the right thing at the inquest. Now he'll have to explain. You can't do more than that.'

'You're right,' Noah says, 'and after I'd finished speaking in court I did feel the weight lift for a moment. But now,' he pauses, then his tone darkens, 'if this body is Lizzie's it changes everything. For years I've thought my brother might be a killer. It's torn our family apart. Oh god, Alice, what if I was wrong all along?'

31

Noah returns to the private room in the courthouse, where his mother and brother wait on cold, hard plastic chairs. Neither looks up as he joins them, and another half an hour passes without Peter reappearing. The stench of vomit wafts around them, but no one speaks. Cold confusion is still emanating from Cathy and Tom, and their silent question hovers: *Why would you do that to us?*

Noah feels ill.

Raf calls, and Cathy takes her phone to the far side of the room, murmuring out of earshot. Noah tries to picture his father's face as he learns about the events in court. His skin prickles.

Finally, Peter comes back in. 'There's a ton of journos out the front,' he informs them. 'I'll go and collect your car if you like. I can bring it to the side entrance, past the gate.'

Noah envisions the scrummage outside. He nods agreement, seeing the others do the same. Still, no one says a word as they gather up their things, head for the side entrance and get into the car.

'Do you want us to drop you at your hotel?' Cathy asks Tom as they travel away from the court.

'No, I'll come home with you,' Tom says. 'I'd like to have a chat with Noah.'

His words are laced with quiet menace. Noah recoils, his muscles on fire, flexing and contracting, readying for a fight.

'Right,' Cathy says as she drives, in a tone that brooks no argument. 'I want you two to take it easy on each other. Understand? Which means there will be no fighting. *Do you understand?*'

Silence.

'You've both been under enormous strain in different ways. What's done is done. So give each other a break, okay? If you can't get along, just leave each other alone. And hopefully this body will be identified sooner rather than later and we can finally get on with our lives.'

Another pause. Then Tom says, 'It sounds like you hope Lizzie has been killed by a sadistic rapist, Mum?'

Cathy throws both hands up from the wheel in exasperation, and Noah winces, hoping she'll remember she's driving.

'For Christ's sake, Tom. I'm not even dignifying that with a response.'

The car falls quiet. Noah's thoughts are swinging between Tom's fury and Lizzie's fate. He tries not to imagine the body in the bush. Whatever they've found, it's only bones. They can't lay their hands on her joy, her wonder, her mercy, or her fury. There's so much of her beyond reach. Beyond desecration.

That's a comfort in some ways. In others, it's devastating.

His relief at finally drawing closer to their house is swiftly curtailed when they see there are already two media vans there.

'What the hell?' Cathy cries as they near. 'Why do they want to talk to us? What have we got to do with this latest discovery?'

'Perhaps they think I'm in league with Hutchins now,' Tom says.

Cathy yanks the wheel to make a sharp left turn up a nearby street. 'Well, I'm not going back there to be held hostage in my own home. Noah, text your dad, tell him what's happened and check where he is.'

Noah sends the message, and seconds later his phone beeps. He skims the text. 'Dad already took a taxi to the restaurant. He says there are journos there too.'

'Oh, for god's sake,' Cathy snaps. 'Perhaps we should head to the mountains for the weekend. Get right away.'

Noah stiffens. 'I'm going there later, remember?' He stops. He doesn't want to remind Tom of Alice right now.

'Oh yes, I forgot about that.' Cathy sounds irritated. 'Well, don't worry, I'm sure your dad won't leave the bloody restaurant anyway.'

'Let's head for my hotel in Manly,' Tom suggests. 'I'm staying at the Ambassador – and so far no one knows I'm there.'

Cathy swings the car around and they head south.

Noah's phone trills again with a message from Jez. *Just saw the news. Can't believe it. What do you know?*

The question takes Noah by surprise. He imagines Ellis looking over Jez's shoulder, probing for insider info for the newspaper. He quickly replies: *Nothing more. Call me if you hear anything.*

Next, he texts Alice. *There's journalists everywhere. We're looking for somewhere to lie low. It's like we're on the run.*

She replies straight away. *Remember, if you can't come tonight, I understand.*

He wants to tell her that the only thing keeping him going today is the thought of her gorgeous face, her sound advice and her easy laugh. Everything's better when he's with her. She makes him feel like a man with a future worth fighting for.

But now's not the time – he can't phone her in the car, with the others listening. So he just writes, *I'm still coming.*

Then he puts his phone on his lap and stares out the window.

They head quickly through the lobby, the staff greeting them with courteous hellos. Noah wonders if they watch the news.

Whether they've seen Tom on there, being asked about murder, cameras flashing in his face.

Upstairs, at the door to the one-bedroom apartment, Nadia greets Tom with a hug. They disappear into the bedroom for a minute or two, whispering to one another. Noah looks around at the cosy little studio with its small lounge area, and waits awkwardly by the door.

When Nadia reappears she offers them all a drink. Cathy says yes, but before Noah can reply, Tom is by his side. 'Noah?'

Noah turns to his brother. 'Yep?'

Tom's face is a determined scowl. 'Let's go for a walk.'

Noah hesitates. Nods. He might as well get this over with. He catches his mother's eye and she stares back nervously. Then he turns away and follows Tom.

'Let's go over to the beach,' Tom suggests as they wait for the lift. They are both still in shirts and ties, but Noah nods. Neither of them says anything more. Outside, the sky is a bitter white and the sun is sinking, draining the colour from the day. A cooling wind stirs pockets of sand and sends a few lolly packets skittering in front of them.

Tom sits down on a low wall, watching the water. Noah reluctantly joins him.

'Do you remember when Dad used to bring us down to the beach when we were little kids?' Tom asks, his feet scuffing the sand as he talks. 'He'd try to play touch football with us, but I'd sulk because he'd help you, or you'd end up in tears. Then he'd get mad and threaten to drive home without us. We didn't make it easy for him, did we?'

Is that why he's brought me here? Noah wonders, caught off guard. *To reminisce about the shittier parts of our childhood?*

But then Tom leans closer and says, 'What the fuck were you trying to do to me today, Noah?' His voice is a soft, menacing hiss. 'That crap back there, the way you described me to the coroner. You hate me so much that you want me to go to prison for something I didn't do?'

'Don't give me that bullshit.' Noah stands up and takes a step back. 'You know, and I know, that you've never told the whole truth about that night. All I did today was tell the court what I saw. If you have an issue with that then it's your problem. I should've said something a long time ago, but then I'm sure you remember telling me to keep quiet? I'm afraid I'm not so easily intimidated nowadays.'

'What? I don't know why you keep saying that, little brother. I was just a frightened kid, fighting for my life back then. Can you blame me for not wanting to go to jail for something I didn't do? Look, I went out in the car, couldn't find her, and came back and threw up because of the drink and the stress. I was gutted because I knew she wouldn't forgive me and we were finished.' Tom pauses to rub the side of his neck, as though easing tension. 'When she disappeared I realised I'd be in the shit if I said I'd driven after her. And then those men saw her walking along the road and became the last people to see her, putting me in the clear.' He shrugs. 'So I chose to keep quiet. I had to look out for myself, since no one else seemed to care. And now you've turned the spotlight on me again, yet here I am, still trying to make my peace with you.' Tom shades his eyes as he looks up at Noah. 'Does any of that make me a terrible guy, Noah? Does it?'

Noah stifles a bitter laugh. 'You've never wanted peace before. What makes you think it's possible now?'

Tom's brow furrows. 'Isn't it obvious? There's a new baby on the way. What better reason than that for a new beginning? Mum would love it. Nadia's parents are dead, and she wants this baby to know his family.'

'His? Is it a boy?'

Tom's smile is tight. 'We don't know for sure, but I think it's a boy.'

Noah stares at the water for a while. Kicks at a few loose shells. 'You always took such pride in being horrible to me when we were kids. Why?'

Tom throws his hands up in exasperation. 'I don't know!

Jealousy? Mucking around? Whatever – you always gave as good as you got. You liked nothing better than winding me up.'

'Seriously? How d'you figure that out?'

'Oh, I don't know, perhaps because you'd snitch to Mum and Dad about every little thing I did wrong. Or act like you were having fun when we were messing around together, then dob me in at the first opportunity. Believe me, Noah, you were really bloody irritating, so don't make out like you're Jesus Christ and I'm the devil.'

Noah doesn't reply. He's thinking hard. Had he really done those things? It's strange to hear himself painted like this, but he can remember certain times when he'd run to his parents, relishing their praise, maybe even enjoying being the dobber and getting his brother into trouble. Could Tom have a point?

No. This is how Tom gets under his skin. He's a master of manipulation, so that Noah always ends up feeling in the wrong. He squares his shoulders and faces his brother.

'There can be no trust between us unless you tell me the truth,' he presses. 'What happened to Lizzie?'

'Oh, for fuck's sake.' Tom leaps up off the wall. 'Will you stop harping on about it? I didn't kill Lizzie, okay? I only told you to keep quiet because I didn't trust you – you were always out to make me look bad and I didn't know how far you'd go. Look, how can you still doubt me now? It sounds like Hutchins practically confessed and told his cellmate where he buried her. What's it going to take for you to believe me?'

'I don't know,' Noah says, turning to face his brother. 'Perhaps I still think that you're covering something up.'

They eyeball each other. 'And why do you think that?' Tom asks, his jaw tight.

'Because I know you. That's why you hate me, because I see through all your shit. And I saw it that night – I could tell how rattled you were then, and how scared you were in the days that followed. You weren't just scared for Lizzie, you were scared for yourself.'

'Well, yes, of course I was, I've just explained that, you fucking idiot,' Tom shouts, throwing his hands in the air.

A mother with two children who are busy with buckets and spades looks at them sharply. Tom holds a hand up in apology and continues under his breath, 'I knew I was the main suspect from the start. It's always the boyfriend or the father, isn't it? When Lizzie didn't come back I was shitting myself, imagining going to prison *forever*. I was only eighteen, Noah. You have no idea what that's like, but I can tell you it's bloody terrifying. And you – you insisted on looking at me like I was a *killer*. I knew we hadn't always seen eye to eye but I'd never imagined that from you. That's why I left, because I didn't want to see your suspicious bloody face every day, or anyone else's for that matter, accusing me of something I hadn't done.'

Noah stares at his brother. Either he's a brilliant liar, or Noah has got this all wrong. Which one is it? If his brother is telling the truth, then why do Noah's instincts arc up every time he begins to concede? Why is he so sure there's a missing piece of the puzzle from that night, something he's never been able to find? Something he's certain Tom has known all along.

'I hate saying it,' Tom continues, 'but I almost agree with Mum. When Peter said they'd found a body, I felt relief more than anything. Lizzie is dead, Noah, she's never coming back, and I thought I'd always be under suspicion. Now there's finally an opportunity to get on with our lives and put the past behind us. Please. For all our sakes.' And he holds out a hand for Noah to shake.

Noah stares at the proffered palm, considering everything Tom has said. Instinctively, he's wary, but he's tired of fighting too. Finally, he puts his hand out to meet his brother's, and Tom's warm grip tightens around his fingers. 'I'll try,' Noah says. But he knows it will take a long time to engender anything close to trust between them. And even in this moment, when Tom has worked so hard to make it happen, he grips Noah's hand a little longer than needed, a hint of mockery in his eyes, before he lets go.

32

I'm here.

As soon as Alice sees Noah's text, she gets up, grabs her bag and goes to her dad. 'I'll be back in the morning,' she says, squeezing his hand, lingering for a second, just in case his fingers tighten around hers.

Nothing. They're still stuck in this heartbreaking loop.

In the car park she spots the car straight away. She hurries over and climbs in, saying, 'Hi there,' and leaning over for a kiss, then stops short at the sight of Noah. His eyes are hollow and red-rimmed. His expression is anguished. He looks... broken.

'Oh, Noah, are you okay?'

'Better for seeing you.' He leans across to meet her kiss. 'It's been a shitty day. How's your dad?'

'The same. Are you sure you still want to do this?'

'God, yes – it's been the only thing that's kept me sane today.'

As he begins to drive, their attempts at small talk give way to silence. Alice stares out of the window, a hand on her forehead, as dusk descends rapidly outside. She trains her vision on the shadow of their car racing alongside them, a phantom outlined against the bushland. She thinks of everything they cannot leave behind.

Before long, night swallows them whole. They travel into the mountains, leaving the towns behind, seeing fewer and fewer houses. By the time they take an exit off the highway onto smaller, narrower roads, Alice is uncertain about where they are. All she can see are narrow strips of road in the headlights. Insects dance frantically in the twin beams of light.

She begins to doze, until Noah says, 'We're here.' She comes to and sees they have parked next to the dim outline of a modest single-storey building. 'I'll come back for our bags in a second,' Noah tells her, and shows her to the front door. She hears the scrape of the key and then they are inside. Noah flips a switch and light bursts into the room.

She'd been expecting an expanse of space, but this is different to the Carruso house in the suburbs. Cosier. Noah disappears to collect the bags, and the car trills in the distance as he returns, as though bidding them goodnight. He closes the door, pushing back the cold, and sets their luggage down by a sofa, taking a couple of carrier bags across to the adjoining kitchen.

Now Alice is noticing details, seeing Carruso touches here and there. The colourful throws on the sofas are distinctly Cathy, as are the photo frames on the coffee table. The sofas are soft leather, and the kitchen countertop, while small, looks to be granite. The wooden cupboards gleam, and the floor and ceiling beams are polished, reflecting the spotlights.

Noah is watching her. 'What are you thinking?'

'That your holiday home is about the same size as the home I grew up in.' She laughs. 'It's lovely, Noah.'

'Yeah, no one spends much time here anymore – not since Tom and I grew up, and Dad got injured. It's a shame, really, as we used to love it.' He holds out a hand. 'Come with me.' He leads her down a small passageway then up a short flight of wooden stairs. There are more exposed beams on the first floor – she suspects this place wouldn't last long in a bushfire.

'This was the room we slept in as kids...' Noah shows her into a small room with a double bed. 'It used to have bunk beds when we were little. But tonight, you and I are in the master bedroom.'

She follows him across the landing to a beautiful little room made up with cream sheets with a subtle floral pattern running along the edges. Noah puts his arms around her. 'I can't wait to show you the view in the morning. It's pretty special. I like to think of this as the proper Carruso family home. There's some good memories here. Tom and I – our best moments as brothers were all here.' He stares out of the window into the black void of night. 'I just wish I could forget about the inquest for a while. It's ironic, isn't it? Lizzie's been gone for such a long time, and yet she's still everywhere.'

'Even here?' Alice asks softly.

Noah steps away, sitting on the bed. 'Yes, she came a few weeks before she disappeared, when Mum and Dad let us bring friends for the weekend. Tom invited Lizzie, Gemma and Josh. They all camped outside, and spent the whole weekend lighting fires and trying to cook food. Me and Jez had the bunkbeds: we brought the Nintendo and avoided them. I'm wondering if it was the weekend Rachel mentions on the podcast. The one when Josh and Lizzie were growing closer.'

'That was *here*?'

'I think perhaps it was.'

Alice has a flash of Lizzie's face in the firelight, sitting with her closest friends, her skin soft and warm, unaware that in a few weeks' time her life as she knew it would be gone.

She shudders. So many of their conversations revolve around this dead girl. They should be focusing on themselves and their future, not this. She sits down next to Noah and takes his hand.

'Look, I think *you* have to decide whether Lizzie's disappearance is going to screw you up forever.'

He stares at her. Says nothing.

'Noah? Are you listening to me? You can't change the past, and it sounds like you didn't have much say about it in the first place. So why are you clinging to it so hard? I don't think this is all about Lizzie. What's your problem, Noah? Why can't you let it go?'

Noah sighs, rubs his eyes. 'I don't know.'

'Yes, you do,' Alice insists.

Noah seems lost for words.

'You do know,' she repeats. 'Tell me.'

'I wanted to look after her,' he says, his face crumpled in pain. 'All the time she was with Tom, I knew he'd end up hurting her somehow. I promised myself I'd protect her, step in when I was needed, and after that she'd see me differently. And then I was there, that night. Mum and Dad weren't around – it was down to me. And I let Tom torment her. I let her run off into the night while I hid in my room. I've never felt so ashamed.'

'You were fifteen, Noah.'

'Don't give me that. I was old enough to stand up for her. Sure, Tom might have killed us both, but I made a choice – and I was a coward.'

Alice bristles as she watches Noah persecute himself. How can she show him what she can plainly see: that he's a decent, beautiful soul who got caught up in a terrible situation? She has a flash of anger at the unfairness of it all; that other people's recklessness has left him in so much pain. 'And so the rest of your life is about apologising for yourself, is it?' she asks gently. 'Doing your parents' bidding at the restaurant, trying to prove to yourself that you're better than you fear you are?'

Noah looks shocked. Then horrified. 'Maybe.' He stares at her. 'Fuck.'

She holds his gaze. 'Four years ago, a man died in front of me, and my overwhelming emotion was relief. Jason Reidy had terrorised us for a couple of years...' She hesitates. 'And yet, the guilt of living with his death, and the never-ending questions about me and my dad that came up as a result, they tortured me for a long time too. But so much of these experiences – yours and mine – were beyond our control. You had no idea Lizzie would die. Your brother had always bullied you, and you just wanted to keep yourself safe. Who says that intervening would have changed anything? Tom might have flattened you, and Lizzie would still have run off into the night. Is self-protection such a terrible thing?'

Noah is silent for a while. 'It doesn't make me proud of myself,' he says eventually.

'No,' Alice agrees, taking his hand, 'me neither. But I think it makes us human.'

Noah doesn't reply. Nevertheless, Alice mentally replays her words with increasing conviction, and a calmness settles over her. She can imagine her dad saying something similar. It's a comforting thought.

They undress slowly and lie in silence with their arms around each another. Alice stares at a few small dots of starlight winking through the open blinds. Has fate brought them together to help them heal from these traumas and move on? Or is this an ill-fated joke from a universe in chaos?

She shifts to get comfortable, and Noah's embrace tightens, netting her, drawing her in. His lips brush her forehead and she thinks of blurting everything out in the darkness – all her thoughts and fears, her deepest shame – in this night of truths being laid bare.

'Are you okay?' he asks, as though reading her mind.

Tell him.

She hesitates, but then just nods. She isn't ready, and the moment passes.

She only realises she has drifted off to sleep when she wakes up to find the bed cold beside her. The room is almost completely dark, there's just a small light coming from the hallway. She gets up, wrapping the blanket around her, tiptoeing along the passageway, taking a few steps down the stairs.

At the bottom, Noah is sitting in his underwear on the floor, staring out the back windows into the gaping maw of darkness beyond.

She takes a couple more steps then stops, unsure whether to go on. He's lost in a trance, and it feels wrong to watch him while he doesn't know she's there. 'Noah?' she whispers eventually.

He whips around, and jumps up as he sees her. For a second he looks terrified, then the panic disappears and his shoulders relax.

'What are you doing? Are you okay?'

He comes closer and the light from upstairs reflects the sadness that pools in his eyes. He kisses her so tenderly that she thinks of the little market in Thailand, the gentle rock of the sampan as he'd first told her he loved her. She wraps her arms around him. This is the Noah she craves.

'I don't want to live in the past,' he whispers, a catch in his voice. 'I only want you.'

His words go spinning into the night, disintegrating one after another in the darkness. Alice shivers. She understands the depth of his passion and pain, because it matches hers. Nevertheless, as hard as she tries, each kiss has begun to feel less like hello, and more like goodbye.

33

Noah wakes to find the first tentative light of the day peeping through the blinds. He picks up the phone to check the time, but there's a message waiting. Three little words from his mum that send him lurching upright.

It isn't Lizzie.

Heart hammering, he glances at Alice, who's still sleeping, then gets quickly and quietly out of bed.

Downstairs, he uses his phone to search the net for information. He finds a segment about the latest developments on a local news page, and clicks to watch the video.

'Police have confirmed that the remains found in Garigal National Park yesterday are not those of Lizzie Burdett, the seventeen-year-old who went missing twelve years ago.' The reporter is on location, wearing a smart black jacket, standing in a car park Noah recognises. His family used to park there when the boys took their bikes along the Cascades. *'Details concerning the identification of the remains discovered yesterday have yet to be released. However, the inquest into Lizzie Burdett's disappearance and possible murder will continue on Monday.'*

He needs to know more. He calls his mum, and she answers immediately.

'What the hell, Mum? How do they know already?'

'It's the hair, apparently.' Cathy's voice is thick, quivering, as though she's been crying. 'It's the wrong hair.'

'Fuck.' Noah's mind is spinning, trying to absorb the implications.

'Yes. It's another poor girl. We've been up all night. First, some moron threw a brick through the restaurant window—'

'What?'

'– And then Nadia came here in a state, because she couldn't find Tom.'

'*What?* What the fuck is wrong with him now?' Every hair on Noah's body suddenly stands on end. 'Hang on, is he still missing?' He has a ridiculous urge to check the doors and window locks, just to be sure they're secure.

'Not anymore, it was a misunderstanding. He's called round since then. He picked her up and took her back to the hotel.'

Noah stops and flops into a chair. 'What was he like when you saw him?'

'Honestly? He's devastated. After what you said in court yesterday, he thinks it's only a matter of time before he's arrested.' Noah can still hear the tremble in his mother's voice. 'And he's not the only one struggling. Your father's convinced we'll go bankrupt and lose the house. He started ranting and raving while he drowned his sorrows overnight, saying that everything he's done has been for nothing. He won't be in a pretty state today. When are you coming back?'

Noah stalls. 'I'm not sure. Maybe this afternoon.'

Cathy sighs. 'Can you be a bit more specific? Your dad will need your help, you know, with sorting out the restaurant. We can't open again till the window is fixed.'

Noah resists the impulse to yell, and chooses his words carefully. 'Mum, I realise that, but I promised this day to Alice. She'll want to get back to her dad before too long, so I'll try to be back sometime this arvo.'

'Fine,' Cathy snaps, her voice rising. 'Remind me not to bother you again in a crisis.'

The line goes dead.

He's relieved she's gone, because he needs time to think.

It isn't Lizzie.

He finds he isn't surprised. It had all felt too neatly packaged, and it didn't match his hunches. He snorts in derision. Now he's thinking like Rachel Lawrence.

Even so – even with the investigation back to square one – this morning, Noah is aware of a small undercurrent of relief.

I took the stand. I faced them all. I told the truth.

I can let it go now. I can't do any more.

It's something.

And now I'm here. With Alice.

He gets up, makes himself a cup of tea and takes it out onto the verandah. Despite the many things that have changed in his life, this vista has not shifted since he was a child. Beyond the garden, the valley stretches away into the distance, clouds casting pockets of shadow across the immense blanket of forest-green treetops that obscure the sandstone rock in all but a few places. Close by, rising up from dirt and leaf litter, the wilderness begins with a tangle of trees, vines looping over everything like giant umbilical cords. The outstanding view he had promised Alice is here in all its familiar gloriousness.

He sets his tea on the table and sits down. Stares at the panorama. Thinks of the unidentified body they'd found in the woods.

Where are you, Lizzie?

Despite his fears, sometimes over the years he's allowed himself to daydream, because, after all, who really knows the mindset of another person? He's considered what else might have kept Lizzie away. Amnesia? A desire to leave home? Is there a woman in her late twenties somewhere, packing lunches and getting the kids ready for school, who used to be known as Elizabeth Burdett? Or is she in a brothel, passed out on meth and unaware there's an inquest and people still care. His favourite vision is the cabin in the mountains where Lizzie shuns the world, lives off the land and sleeps outside beneath the stars in the summer, needing no one. They are comforting delusions while no body has been found. But that's all they are.

Lizzie's never coming back.

Noah stops himself there. Here he goes again, dwelling on the past, when in the warm bed upstairs there is beautiful Alice, who will open her arms and her body to him, who knows him instinctively and loves him as much as he loves her. Each moment with Alice highlights his schoolboy crush as a two-dimensional adolescent fantasy. He didn't really know Lizzie, nor she him. She was kind at times, and he'd clung to that because it was a welcome change in his turbulent family life, but if she hadn't died she would be forgotten now, just like Jez had long ago ditched his crush on Beatrice Dalton. It was Lizzie's disappearance that had warped her place in his life. Her absence had, ironically, kept her present for way too long.

But there's only one woman who has ever truly stolen Noah's heart.

As though he's summoned her, he hears the door to the verandah open, and Alice emerges with her coat wrapped around her, a glass of water in her hands.

'Wow, this is incredible,' she says, looking across at the view. 'To think this was all hidden when we arrived last night, and I had no idea. I wish I'd brought my camera! You spent all that money replacing the lens, and since then I've hardly used it.'

He hesitates, about to show her the newsflash and fill her in on everything Cathy had said. He imagines her face growing instantly solemn as she sits down to listen.

No, don't tell her yet.

He jumps up and wraps his arms round her. 'Hopefully you'll get more time to practise soon. And you're right, the view here is quite something, isn't it. But you,' he kisses her, 'are a thousand times more spectacular.'

She laughs. 'How long have you been sitting here thinking up that corny line?'

'Too long.' His fingers slide up beneath her coat, his breath catching sharply when he realises she's naked beneath it.

'You want something?' she asks, the tease clear in her tone.

'Oh yes,' his voice is deep with longing, 'I definitely want something.'

He carries her inside to the sofa, pulls off the coat and begins to stroke the length of her body, searching out all the places that make her moan with pleasure. Alice licks her lips and arches against his touch, until they can't take it anymore. He picks her up and she wraps her legs around him as they head upstairs, half-kissing, half-laughing as he staggers on the steps. Alice helps pull off his clothes and then he's inside her, holding on to her for as long as he can, before they both collapse against each other, content in the afterglow of this constant, insatiable need.

'Are you hungry?' Noah asks after a while.

She snuggles into him. 'A little.'

'I'll go and make us something. Have you checked in with the hospital this morning?'

'Yes, Gary says nothing's changed, but I don't want to be away for too long.'

'We can head back whenever you're ready. Do you want a quick walk first? There's a path behind the house that leads to a lookout. It's not too far.'

'I'd love that.'

'Okay, then.' Noah jumps up and grabs his jeans and T-shirt.

'There'll be some great climbs near here, too,' she teases as she collects her clothes.

'Er, I'm not sure I'm ready to scale the Three Sisters just yet,' he says. 'I'll meet you downstairs.' He watches as she turns for the bathroom.

Twenty minutes later, after tea and toast, they set off on the trail that leads to the woods. It's cold on the track, and soon their faces are pink, their breath misting in the autumn air. Noah still hasn't told Alice about the restaurant, or Lizzie, and so far the morning has been much better for it. *Perhaps this is the way to do it*, he thinks, taking Alice's hand as they walk, seeing her smiling up at him. *Pretend our problems don't exist, and we won't have to face them.*

But even as he thinks it, he knows it won't work for long. Besides, today is a new start, and he won't hide from discomfort anymore. It's time to tell Alice exactly what's going on.

34

Alice can sense there's something on Noah's mind before he speaks. His hand has been tight around hers since they set off, and his mood is sombre.

'I spoke to my mum this morning,' he confides as they walk, 'about the body they found yesterday.'

His tone is ominous. She pulls her coat around herself, taking comfort in its warmth, waiting for him to go on.

He clears his throat. 'It's not Lizzie.'

'Really?' Alice stalls, taken aback, trying to absorb what this means. 'How do they know that already?'

'Apparently they could tell because of the hair.'

'Oh.' She shudders.

They fall into a melancholy silence, each lost in their own thoughts. Ahead of them, a dense patch of trees casts the path in heavy shadow.

After a while, Noah says, 'Even without a body, we all know she's dead. But it's not the same as having closure, or finding out what happened.' His gaze drifts across the valley. 'When I was trying to get to sleep last night, I kept having these terrible visions of her, all bones and matted hair, when she was alive once, right here, exactly like us. I thought of her lying in the forest for years... desecrated like that... and I couldn't get rid of this awful rage. I hate the way people say, "She's at peace now", all that stuff. That rubbish is for our comfort, not hers. We can take our flowers and candles and stand there as though we can make these horrors better with our puny little efforts, but it's such a load of crap...' He pauses and picks at a thread on the cuff of his jacket. 'Do you know what I think? I think she would be fuming. She was robbed of her chance to live a full life, and I don't want to light a candle or sing a song to get over it. I want whoever hurt her to pay for it. I just hope the inquest can give us some answers.'

'So the coroner will just carry on now?' Alice asks.

'Yes, the next session starts on Monday. I should imagine Tom will have more questions to answer, either in court or with the police. And Josh hasn't given evidence yet. Neither have the Burdetts.' He kicks at a pile of sticks and leaves. 'I'm not going back, though. I've had enough. I'd rather look after the restaurant and support Dad. Mum says he's been drinking again, and she's obviously struggling with him. She also told me that some shithead has thrown a brick through one of the restaurant's windows. So as soon as I'm back I'm going to go through the CCTV and find out exactly who it was, and let the police know.'

As he talks, the path widens out and the foliage on the left-hand side disappears, revealing a breathtaking view across the valley, another unbroken vista of pristine treetops. In the distance, the soft-curving silhouettes of the mountain range are outlined against the pale blue sky.

Alice knows that somewhere close by there will be climbers, helmets on and ropes ready, chalkbags and clips swinging from their belts as they tackle tempting sections of vertical rock. She experiences a brief, disconcerting pull to leave Noah here, to find them and pit herself against the elements. To forget everything else.

'Before I went overseas,' she says, 'I briefly considered moving here so I could climb more often. I can't imagine ever tiring of views like these.'

He pulls her close, wrapping his arms around her. 'Yep,

it's beautiful. Though I think I could live just about anywhere if you were nearby.'

'You'd leave the restaurant?' she asks tentatively.

He turns to look at her.

'Yes,' he says. 'I know it won't be easy – I'll want to ease the transition for Mum and Dad's sake if I can. But it's been at the back of my mind for a while. I just needed a push.' He pulls her closer. 'You've turned my world upside down,' he says, leaning in to kiss her.

His words and the look on his face set off that deep ache inside her again. She doesn't want to wander along this track anymore, she wants to be back at the house, naked beneath him.

She looks back at the distant mountains, but this time she doesn't think about escape. Instead, she wonders if there are more bodies hidden out there, waiting to be reclaimed. If Lizzie is among them. And what the future holds for Noah and his family if Lizzie is never found.

She shivers, and turns away.

Back at the cottage they don't linger, all too aware of the family crises that are once again pulling them away from one another. As they travel to Blackheath, their conversation slowly comes alive, turning back to Thailand and their happiest memories, the days in Khao Yai. The air between them begins to crackle with excitement and their smiles broaden. Alice can feel other conversations playing out beneath their words. *This is us. The* real *us. Our memories and our hopes and dreams are binding us together, not just our struggles. There's a future out there for us, beyond all this. It's wonderful, and it's waiting. So close we can almost touch it.*

Then the hospital comes into view, and their voices trail away.

When Noah stops the car, Alice hesitates.

'Are you okay?' he asks, stroking her hair.

She turns to him. 'Look... would you like to come and meet my dad?'

He switches the engine off. 'Yes, of course – as long as you're sure?'

Alice nods. 'This might be all we have,' she says quietly.

They hold hands as they walk through the corridors to her father's room. Toni is there, and stands as she sees Alice. Then she spots Noah, and her face lights up.

'I know exactly who *you* are,' she says, hugging him. 'It's good to meet you, Noah.' She kisses Alice on the cheek. 'Good decision,' she whispers with a wink. Then adds, 'Nothing's changed here. I'll be off now, give me a call later.'

Once she's gone they say hello to Trent the guard, then Alice leads Noah over to the bed. 'Dad,' she says, taking her father's hand in hers, 'I've brought Noah to meet you.'

'Hi, Bobby,' Noah says, hovering close by.

No one moves.

Alice turns to Noah with tears in her eyes. 'Okay, I'll admit it, I thought he might wake up just to kick your arse.' She tries to laugh, unable to hide the catch in her voice.

Noah leans forward. 'Bobby, I hope you can hear me. I want you to know that your daughter has changed my life, and I'll always be there for her, no matter what.'

Alice leans against him. 'Thank you.'

They sit down and she rests her head on Noah's shoulder. The moment feels surprisingly peaceful. *We're in the eye of the storm*, she thinks. *But there's more to come. The shadows are still circling.*

She doesn't want to move, but Noah's phone begins to ring. He takes it out of his pocket and frowns.

'Who is it?'

'It's Sophie. She works at the restaurant.'

Alice watches as he cuts off the call, but Sophie immediately calls back.

'Looks like she really wants to get hold of you.'

Noah jumps up, heading for the corridor. 'I'll call her back quickly. I won't be a sec.'

He's gone for much longer than she expects. She tries to keep focus on her dad, but her mind keeps wandering, wondering what Sophie wants, and where Noah has got to.

When he eventually strides back into the room, his expression is thunderous. 'I'm really sorry, Alice, I've got to go.' His voice is strange, as though something is lodged in his throat.

She jumps up and guides him away from her dad. 'What's happened?'

'Sophie saw the person who threw the brick at the restaurant. She's hiding at home now, terrified to go into work.'

'Why? What did she see?'

Noah's fists clench and his jaw tightens, a nerve pulsing in his cheek. He looks ready to explode.

'It was Tom.'

35

Approaching the restaurant, Noah can see the smashed window, the jagged edges of glass highlighted by the soft glow of the interior lights. It's Saturday evening – the place would usually be packed. Instead, his parents' car sits alone in the dark car park.

Alice is at the wheel. At the hospital she'd watched Noah shaking with anger, then she'd taken his keys and insisted she drive, telling Trent she'd be back soon. On the way they'd tried to think of all the reasons Tom might have done it. But Noah suspects it's just the Tom he's always known, full of jealousy and spite.

'Are you sure you're calm enough to go in there?' Alice asks as she pulls into a parking bay. 'What are you going to say?'

'I'm going to tell them exactly what Sophie told me – and I'll call her so they can verify it,' he replies through gritted teeth. 'Then perhaps they'll finally see how vindictive my brother is and we can give up the hypocrisy of supporting him. Come on.'

'I think I'll wait here, Noah. It doesn't feel right to be part of this.'

He turns to her. 'I'm not leaving you out here in the dark.'

'I've got my phone. Why don't you go in, see what they

have to say, then come back and we can go somewhere else while you cool off.'

'Okay.' He leans over and gives her a long kiss. 'Thank you.'

The light from the dashboard glistens in her eyes. She is so beautiful. *Forget all this*, an urgent voice insists. *Tell her to drive away*. He looks towards the restaurant. Thinks of his parents alone inside.

He strokes her face, running his fingers across her lips, then leans in for one more kiss. 'Wait for me, I won't be long.'

He gets out of the car and hurries up the entrance path without looking back.

Inside, the restaurant is gloomy, the main area lit only by a few side lamps and the lights at the back of the bar. He finds his father first. Raf is sitting at one of the empty tables, glass in hand, staring into the shadows. He looks up in surprise.

'Noah, I didn't realise you were here.' Raf's voice is croaky and his features haggard. He surveys his son and seems to register the tension in him. 'Is everything okay?'

'No – listen, I just spoke to Sophie about the window...'

'Noah, finally!' Cathy interrupts, entering the room with a cloth in her hand.

Noah doesn't look at his mother. He stares over her shoulder instead, at the person trailing behind her.

As their eyes meet, Tom frowns.

'Why are *you* here?' Noah spits each word at Tom.

'Why do you think? I'm helping out.'

'Where's Nadia?' Noah demands.

Tom looks perplexed at Noah's open aggression. 'She's resting at the hotel.'

'Hang on, how does Sophie know about the window?' Raf interjects. 'She called in sick this morning.'

Noah keeps his glare fixed on his brother. 'Why don't you ask *him*?' He sees a glimmer of uncertainty in Tom's eyes. 'Tom, could I have a word outside?'

'Noah.' Cathy's tone is a warning, but Noah ignores it.

Tom nods. 'All right.' He moves towards the verandah doors and Noah follows.

As soon as they're outside, Tom turns to Noah. 'What – ?'

Noah doesn't wait for another traitorous word. Deep inside him, a long-burning fuse reaches its limit, and he sends his fist flying into Tom's jaw.

Tom staggers backwards. 'What the fuck are you doing?' he roars as soon as he recovers, hand clutching his face. They glare at each other, both breathing hard, then Tom launches himself at Noah, driving his whole body into him.

There's an *oomph* as all the air is punched from Noah's stomach. He's pinned up against the railing, leaning over the cliff-edge drop. He tries to fight, panic rising as the air billows behind his back, but Tom has him pinned.

'Let him go!'

Cathy is there, trying to wrestle Tom away, but he pushes her off and keeps hold of Noah. All Noah can see in Tom's eyes is pure, unfettered rage. Any pretence between them has been obliterated in the last few moments, and Noah stares back in open disgust.

Finally, Tom loosens his grip, and Noah stumbles a few paces forward, away from the edge. He rights himself then spins around to face his brother.

'You can stop all the lies now, Tom,' he yells.

Cathy runs between them. 'Noah, calm down.' Her hands are unsteady against his chest as she tries to placate him. 'What the hell are you talking about?'

Raf has made it as far as the verandah doors and grips them for support. He says nothing, watching, but his eyes are wide with fear, his whole body trembling with the effort of propping himself up.

'He's full of lies, Mum!' Noah looks desperately from one parent to the other, inwardly begging them to see through this facade. 'Or has he told you that he put a brick through our window this morning?'

'What are you talking about, Noah?' Cathy is shouting now too. 'Tom, what is this?'

'Sophie saw him!' Noah interrupts before Tom can answer. 'She was too scared to call you in case you didn't believe her, so she called me.'

'Tom?' Cathy gasps. 'Is this true?'

Tom doesn't answer. He's staring at Noah, and Noah experiences a familiar frisson of fear. For an instant he's fifteen years old again, and his brother's scowl can silence him. But then he returns to his senses, because he's not a scared kid anymore, and this is a rare, important moment of having Tom ensnared in his own deceits.

'Yes, tell us, is it true, Tom?' he repeats.

He sees Tom's face redden as his chest heaves. 'For fuck's sake, Noah,' he cries. 'You should be thanking me, you little shit.'

'What? How do you make that out?'

'Because I'm doing you a bloody great favour, that's why. The quicker we kill this place, the better. Last night, I had to sit and listen to Dad going on and on about the problems at the restaurant, and how if it continues then perhaps he should sell it because he can't go on like this – and d'you know what, Dad,' Tom turns to Raf, who looks stunned, 'that's exactly what you should do. I thought I'd help it along a bit, kill the trade while the haters are all gunning for us anyway. This restaurant, it just takes and takes. It's like a whiny child that's forever demanding attention – and you won't stop jumping to its every need. It's why you guys were never there when we needed you. Me and Noah, we were your irritating second job. And don't –' Tom turns to Noah, 'don't you dare say you didn't feel that too.'

Noah is mortified by the pleading looks in his parents' eyes as they turn to him. And the devastation when they see the truth written on his face.

His fury rises tenfold. This has always been Tom's forte – manipulating the situation and deflecting the pain he causes onto others. Bringing people low so he can feel better about himself.

It has to stop now.

'How dare you come back into our lives and rip everything apart,' he yells at Tom. 'Do you realise it's taken us years to build up the business again? Is this all you're good at – causing pain? Why don't we talk about the real issue, Tom? What happened to Lizzie? *That's* why you're here. *You* were the last person to see her. *You* said those cruel things to her on our doorstep. *You* went out in the car and came back and vomited everywhere. It was all *you*. So *stop* lying to us all.'

Tom gazes heavenward as though searching for an answer. He breathes out slowly then looks back to Noah. Begins to walk towards him. 'And I have *told* you a thousand times, I don't know what happened.'

'I'll never believe that,' Noah says, standing his ground.

'I really don't care what you believe, Noah.' Tom is getting closer. He stops within touching distance of his brother. 'Because I'm *not* a murderer.'

There is a new, menacing edge to Tom's voice, as though something inside him has snapped, and long-held secrets are close to pouring out. Noah holds his breath. *Tell us*, he thinks. *Please tell us what happened, Tom. Put us out of our misery. Let this be done.*

'You found her when you went out in the car, didn't you?' Noah presses, knowing this is the moment, with his parents as witnesses, that he has to get his brother to confess.

'Yes, all right, I bloody did.'

Noah's initial surprise at this abrupt confession is followed by a buzz of anticipation. 'I *knew* it. Finally! I've been waiting for the truth to come out of your mouth for the last twelve years.'

'Just hear me out.' Tom glowers at Noah, scratching at the tufts of his short brown hair as he talks, his chest rising and falling rapidly. 'She was walking along the road, and I pulled up beside her. I was scared, because I knew I'd gone too far with everything I'd said at the house. I wanted to apologise, and make up with her, but she was furious. She said we were finished – and she was going to have sex with Josh at the first opportunity. She wouldn't listen to anything I had to say, and refused to let me drive her home. I argued, but eventually she walked away and I could tell there was no reasoning with her. The whole thing lasted maybe ten minutes, until I decided to give up and go home. I've regretted that decision every day since. Imagine if you made one mistake and it cost you the person you loved most in the world – forever.'

Noah's mind flashes to Alice waiting for him in the darkened car park, but he quickly discards the tiny shard of sympathy. He won't let Tom get away with twisting the truth any longer. 'So why didn't you just tell the police everything?'

'I didn't think they'd believe me.' Tom throws his hands up in frustration. 'An eighteen-year-old with a quick temper, fighting with his girlfriend moments before she disappeared? It's pretty suss, isn't it? That other sighting of her was the only thing keeping me out of the shit. All you had to do was stay quiet, but you wouldn't let it go, would you? You kept goading me, and doubting me. I knew we weren't best mates but that shocked me, Noah.' He circles closer as he talks. 'You were such an annoying little prick, do you know that? All the bloody time, but particularly that night. You just came out of your bedroom and watched. Like you always did. You were *always* there, weren't you, *watching* everything. Judging everything, as though you were so much better than me. Well, you're not, Noah. You're just another Carruso arsehole, and I knew that if I stayed, you'd never let it rest.'

A flood of outrage engulfs Noah's self-control. He charges at Tom again, head down, wanting nothing more than to pelt that smug look off his brother's face. Tom is pure evil, a liar and a manipulator. He's never going to stop denying that he did something to Lizzie, but it's taken twelve years to get this far. There must be more.

Tom sees him coming and veers backwards, trying to

escape, but Noah drives into his brother as he would once have attacked a rugby scrum at school. He pushes every last ounce of his fury at Tom, expecting to feel resistance as Tom fights back. But instead, he gets a violent kick in the guts as Tom wobbles and tips backwards over the railing.

And then Noah is leaning over nothing but darkness, as Tom falls with a yell, and Cathy begins to scream.

36

Alice's nerves are electrified by the sudden scream. She jumps out of the car, hoping she's misheard, but it happens again, a harrowing wail breaking the silence of the night. She stands for a moment by the open car door, unsure what to do, but then her instincts take over and she is running to the front doors of the restaurant.

Once inside, she trips over a chair leg in the low lighting, staggering for a moment before righting herself. That awful noise continues, and there's a stooped silhouette straight ahead of her. Raf is half-collapsed against the open door. She hurries towards him and he turns at the sound of her approach, clutching the door jamb as he sees her. His eyes are wild.

'What's happened?' she asks as she reaches him. He doesn't seem able to speak, and she looks past him, out onto the verandah, where Noah and Cathy are leaning over the railing, and Cathy is shrieking Tom's name.

She rushes across to them. 'Noah?' She puts a tentative hand on his arm.

He flinches at her touch, and when he turns, his expression is almost identical to Raf's. 'Tom's gone over the edge,' he tells her. 'I – I pushed him.'

Cathy's cries overlay his words, and Alice isn't sure she's heard correctly. 'You *pushed* him?'

'Yes... I didn't mean to... we were fighting. Oh god, Alice, oh god... what have I done?'

She moves to the railing and peers into the blackness below, as the others call Tom's name. When there's no reply she turns back to Noah. 'Is it far down there? Do you have a torch?' She grabs her phone from her pocket and shines it downwards, but the light doesn't reach far enough. 'Noah?'

He gapes at her, stupefied.

'Noah?' She wants to shake him. 'Noah!'

She understands his inertia. She'd once been trapped in a cataclysm like this, and she'd frozen too. But she can't let those memories hold her hostage, because the Carrusos need help.

'Find me a better torch, Cathy,' she says, re-pocketing her phone and tapping the older woman's arm. 'And Noah,' she turns to him, 'call an ambulance and then go to your dad. He looks like he's about to pass out.'

Her urgent voice spurs them both to action. Noah grabs his mobile while Cathy rushes into the restaurant, returning moments later with a huge torch. She hands it to Alice, who shines it down into the void.

As the light jumps around there's a flash of Tom crumpled and unmoving below them. It must be about ten metres down. Noah is speaking into his phone now, and Alice is shaken by a bolt of fear as she listens to him stating his name and address. It's bringing back all the horror, all the memories she wishes she could banish forever.

She needs to keep moving. She takes off her jacket and shoes, leaving them on the ground.

Noah is still speaking rapidly into his phone. She puts her left foot on the railing, feeling the metal cold beneath her skin.

'Alice, what are you doing?' Noah yells.

'I'm going down there. It's not far.'

Noah looks stunned. 'My girlfriend is going to try to climb down,' he says in a rush, obviously answering the operator's question. 'Stop, Alice. They say you're not to do that, you'll put yourself at risk.'

Alice glares at him. 'Tom might be dead by the time help gets here.' She thrusts the torch into Cathy's hands. 'You'll have to shine the torch for me so I can see the way.'

Cathy obeys immediately, the torch trembling in her grip. Alice is on the other side of the railing by the time Noah reaches her and grabs her arm.

'Alice, don't! Stop! Please!'

'It's fine,' she tells him firmly. 'I'm not doing this for Tom – I'm doing it for you.'

She takes her hand from Noah's and sits on the edge of the cliff face, twisting herself around and searching for the first toe hold. She knows Noah's eyes are fixed on her but she doesn't look up again. She needs to focus on what's below.

It looks straightforward, with plenty of wide footholds, but she's well aware that a climber's complacency can prove fatal. She makes her way down carefully, occasionally calling out to ask Cathy to keep the torch still, and within a few minutes she's at the bottom, scrambling across the rocky ground. 'Tom, Tom!' she cries as she reaches him, shining her phone torch into his face and tapping his cheek. She checks his pulse: he has a heartbeat and he's breathing. The right side of his face is streaked with blood. He moans at one point, but otherwise doesn't respond.

'He's alive,' she calls up the cliffside, and hears a cry of relief from the top.

'Tom!' She pats his face a few more times, trying to bring him round. He moans again, and then his head comes forward and he vomits over his chest, coughing and choking. She grabs him and hauls him onto his side, trying to keep him from inhaling anything, but he cries out as she moves him.

'My arm, my arm. Argh, fuck, my arm. Stop, please, stop.'

She looks closer and sees that his arm is twisted like a coat hanger between elbow and wrist. She almost retches, but tries to focus. Now he's come around, he's sweating, panting and cursing.

'Tom, help is on its way,' she tells him, gagging from the rancid fumes of vomit that hit her in waves. 'Try to stay calm. Don't move. We need to keep you as still as possible.'

'Argh, I can't, I can't! Please, help me.' His voice is shrill. Then he sees her face and in the dim light she watches his eyes become two dark discs of horror. 'Lizzie? Lizzie, why are you here? Am I dead?' He closes his eyes. 'No, no, no, no,' he pants. 'Please go away. I'm sorry, Lizzie, I'm sorry.'

Alice opens her mouth to tell him he's mistaken, but the words don't come. 'What are you are sorry for, Tom?' she asks instead, eyes averted as she checks his other limbs.

Tom is crying now, lying awkwardly on his side. 'Who hurt you, Lizzie? I wanted to find them and make them suffer. I'm sorry I never did.'

Alice stops moving, staring at Tom, who's still folded foetally into himself.

'Is he talking?' Cathy calls from above. 'What's he saying?'

Alice hardly registers the question. She doesn't reply. All her focus is on Tom.

'Please don't let me die,' Tom says between sobs. 'Everyone thinks I *killed* you, Lizzie. *Argh*.' Another spasm of pain hits him and he bounces onto his back, hitting his head on the rock as he does.

Enough, Alice thinks. She leans over him. 'Tom, stop,' she says, putting her hands on either side of his face to try to get him to focus on her. 'I'm not Lizzie. I'm Alice. Noah's girlfriend.'

Tom's movements slow. 'Alice?' he frowns. 'Alice?'

He doesn't seem to recognise her, and she doesn't remind him of the one time they'd met. She takes his hand and talks to him, saying the same things she's been telling her dad lately. That he'll be okay; he'll get through this. She's cold now, too, in the burgeoning wind with no jacket and shoes. 'Hurry 'up,' she intones to the emergency services, who must surely be on their way.

'What's happening, Alice?' Noah calls down.

Tom has gone quiet, his hand slackening in hers. She starts to panic. It's a substantial fall, who knows what other injuries he might have.

'We're okay – but I wish people would hurry up and get here,' she shouts back.

She leans closer to Tom. 'Help is on the way,' she whispers. 'Hang in there.'

The torchlight shining from above them suddenly disappears, leaving her and Tom in darkness. 'You okay up there?' she calls.

No answer.

A shiver runs through her, but she's stuck. There's nothing to do except wait.

37

'Did you hear that?' Noah whispers to his mother.

'Yes.'

They both stare at the restaurant, their torchlights dancing over the walls. A moment ago there'd been a bellow of pain from inside, but now there's only silence.

'Where's Dad?'

As Noah asks, he hears the sound of smashing glass, coming from inside.

'I don't know.' Cathy's voice quavers.

'Mum, stay here, keep calling to Alice, okay? I'll go and check.' He takes a few steps towards the darkened interior. There's another crash.

Cathy shrieks, 'Be careful!' as Noah grips the door handle. He takes one final glance at his mother's fearful, tear-stricken face before he steps inside.

A burst of wind whips in with him, sending paper napkins skittering across tabletops, unbalancing the delicate stems of wine glasses. Noah stops, trying to absorb what he's seeing.

'Dad?'

Raf is leaning against the counter of the bar, panting with exertion. Half a dozen broken bottles litter the floor of the restaurant and the place reeks of alcohol. As Noah watches, Raf grabs a bottle of gin and launches it across the room, already turning for the next one as it smashes.

Cold fear grips Noah by the throat. 'Dad?'

'Get out of here, Noah,' Raf roars, throwing a bottle his way. It lands at Noah's feet, splashing brandy over his shoes.

'Dad, stop!' Terror burns through Noah's lungs as he edges closer. 'It's okay. Alice is with Tom. The emergency services are on their way. I'm sorry about the fight –'

Raf pauses, then fumbles for another bottle, his fingers tightening around the neck of it. 'You know all this was for you, don't you?' Raf waves the bottle wildly at the room, then clutches the countertop for support. 'The *years* and *years* of work, it was to leave you something you could build on. But neither of you want it, do you? You'll sell it the first chance you get.'

'You're wrong.' Noah creeps slowly forward, hands aloft as though in surrender. 'I've always understood how hard you've worked for us. So of course I want it,' he tries desperately, hoping the words don't sound as hollow as they feel.

'Liar,' his father hisses, glaring at him, the whites of his eyes gleaming in the low light. 'We're a bunch of bloody liars.'

Noah stares into his father's baleful eyes. *Why the hell am I begging for something I don't want?*

And then it hits him.

Raf is a narcissist, just like Tom. And they've manipulated Noah his whole life.

His brother might have left, but the bigger bully has been here all along.

Fuck. This.

'You're right,' he growls, glaring at his father, adrenalin kicking in as he takes a few steps closer. 'I *am* a liar. I'm *sick* of this place. I *hate* the fact that I've put my life on hold to help you, and you have no fucking appreciation at all – you just want more. Have you ever thought about what I want? No, because it's all about you. And don't blame the accident, Dad – other people have bad things happen to them and they don't become self-centred arseholes.' He watches the shock spreading across Raf's face, sees the bottle trembling in his father's hand. Searches for signs of remorse, but finds nothing. 'Well, it's over, Dad. You can take this place and shove it.' Noah gestures to the chaos of glass and liquid on the floor. 'Trash it all, if you want. I'm done.'

Raf gapes at him, and Noah's anger finally falters, giving way to the pain that's been sequestered for so long. 'What the hell happened, Dad?' he asks, his voice breaking. 'Why are you like this?'

Raf's jaw drops slightly, but other than that he doesn't move. His silence reignites Noah's rage. *Don't wait for answers. Don't give him a second more of your life.*

He turns away, locking eyes with his mother, who waits beyond the doors. Distress has drained all the blood from her face. She looks like a ghost.

'Noah, stop.' It's a command, but there's a strange edge to Raf's voice.

Noah hesitates. *Keep going*, a voice inside him urges. *Leave now, or you'll never be free.*

Noah doesn't turn, but holds up a hand. 'No more, Dad. I've had enough.' But as he reaches the threshold, the next words pierce him like bullets in the darkness.

'I know what happened to Lizzie.'

Noah freezes. A yawning abyss is opening. A terrible truth waits to swallow him whole. He turns slowly to face his father. 'What – what do you mean?'

Raf's eyes are deep, dark holes. 'It was me.'

Noah goes rigid. A cold trickle of horror snakes down the nape of his neck. '*What?* What the hell are you talking about?'

Raf takes a long swig from the bottle of whisky and eyeballs Noah, his chest heaving as though he's just run a marathon. Noah waits, his body racked by a soundless, unrelenting wail, an alarm siren on red alert.

'I found her curled up on one of the verandah chairs.' Raf clutches the bottle to his chest as he talks. 'That night, I couldn't sleep, and I heard her cough when I went for a drink.'

Noah's heart is drumming so loudly in his ears that he

can hardly catch the words. He watches Raf's mouth moving, trying to make sense of what he's hearing.

'I woke her and she said she'd come back to find Tom, but once she'd seen our car she didn't dare knock.' Raf pauses to take a long, shuddering breath. 'So I told her I'd take her home. I thought I'd drop her off then sleep in the office, ready for the dawn deliveries.'

'Dad,' Noah interrupts, almost choking on the word, 'please, stop... I don't want to hear this.'

Raf's face goes bright red. 'You need to hear this,' he roars. 'It's the end of the road now, my son.' His eyes are wide and wild. He takes another long, shaky swig of whisky, closing his eyes for a moment before he speaks again. 'In the car, she started thanking me for being kind. She said Tom's problem was that he found it hard to live up to me – because of all the impressive things I'd done – with the footy and the restaurant.' Raf lets out a crazy whoop of laughter that sends a shudder through Noah. 'And there I was, gutted my footy career was over, and on my knees trying to keep this bloody place from sinking.' He stops for another drink, his arm shaking, liquid running down his chin and soaking his shirt. 'I loved her version of me. I wanted to keep driving, just so she'd keep talking – because all I felt from everyone else,' he splutters, waving the bottle accusingly at Noah, 'was bitter bloody disappointment.'

Every sinew in Noah's body is straining with the effort of staying put. He watches in horror as Raf straightens, wipes his mouth on his sleeve, and takes another gulp of whisky.

'We were halfway to her place when she asked me to pull over. She said she'd be back, and disappeared into the bush. I gave her a few minutes, then went to find her.' Raf starts to cough and pauses, patting his chest, seeming to struggle for breath. 'She was squatting, relieving herself, her skirt up round her waist. Then she stood up and in the moonlight she looked unreal... with her long hair... the way it flowed over her shoulders.' Raf coughs again and sways and clutches at the counter. Noah waits, frozen.

'When she saw me she just smiled... and the sight of her... the things she'd said, it tripped a switch in me. I rushed across and kissed her, pushed her up against a tree... and then we were on the ground... and I thought –'

Raf suddenly drops the bottle. It topples then rolls off the counter, bursting into shards of glass at his feet. He hunches over as though his stomach is cramping, and rests his forehead on the countertop.

'You thought... what?' Noah's voice is strange and high-pitched. His guts are heaving at the images his father is forcing at him. His skin crawls with revulsion, but now they've come this far, he has to know.

Raf slowly straightens, his anguished gaze on Noah. 'I thought she wanted something too.' He shudders. 'But when I stopped I saw the terror on her face.'

Time pauses as they stare at one another. The words become a sword, cleaving Noah in two, severing his old self from this new, unimaginable reality. There is no going back.

Raf turns so his face is half-hidden in the darkness. 'She screamed... tried to run... and I panicked and grabbed her. She wouldn't stop fighting, and we fell over, so I put my hand over her mouth, just to get her to stop screaming, and I said sorry – but she was wild and she bit me. I had to hold her tighter after that, with my hands round her throat to keep her still... But I must have... It must have been for longer than – I just wanted her to stop. She just... She went limp.'

Raf stops. The pause stretches. Noah waits, terrified, unable to move as his whole world capsizes and sinks beneath a murky sea of lies.

'I stopped...' Raf's low voice shatters the silence, 'but... but by then she wasn't breathing. I shook her over and over, but her eyes – they were empty.' Raf stares beyond Noah, as though he can see something there in the darkness. 'I couldn't wake her up, Noah. I couldn't undo it.'

Noah's thoughts are splintering. *This can't be happening*.

'This is a sick, sick joke, right?'

Raf won't look at him. He doesn't reply.

Noah trembles with white-hot rage. 'You let your own *son* take the blame for what you did.'

Raf's attention snaps towards him. 'No, no – I stayed quiet for him – and for you and your mum. We would have lost everything otherwise. I devoted myself to this place, so you wouldn't suffer for my mistake. I kept quiet to save you all.'

Mistake? Noah's knees buckle as he pictures Lizzie's lifeless eyes, and he clutches at the wall. He's spent years hating his brother for something Tom hadn't done, and now Tom's lying nearby, seriously injured, because of their father's betrayal. He's overcome with shame and revulsion, and charges forward, grabbing Raf's shirt. 'Don't you dare twist this. You're a fucking *murderer*.' He spits the words into his father's shocked, crumpled face. 'How dare you carry on for all these years. Do you not have a conscience? Do you have no fucking soul at all?'

'Get away from me,' Raf screams, trying to push him off.

Noah shoves his dad against the bar top. 'Don't worry. I never want to be near you again.' He turns and walks towards the doors.

'Noah?'

Raf's voice is small and strange. The eerie change in tone makes Noah spin around.

'I'm nothing but a curse to you now.' There's a tremor in Raf's hand as he holds up the little butane torch they use for cocktails. 'So here's your freedom.'

There's a small, decisive click, and everything slows as the flame appears. Raf touches it to his shirt and then drops it on the ground. In seconds, he's engulfed in a greedy ball of fire.

'No!' Noah charges back towards him. '*No!*' He grabs a tablecloth, but not before smaller fires have scuttled off in different directions, gorging on liquor trails, heading for a gas heater in the centre of the room.

He sees the danger too late, turning to run as the world explodes around him. Before he blacks out he thinks of only one person: the woman he'll love forever, her hair the colour of flames.

38

'What going on up there?' Alice shouts to the paramedic tending to Tom's injuries. The chopper hovers noisily above them, almost drowning out their voices, but she's sure she'd heard a bang a few minutes ago, and now she can smell fire.

'Let's get you both safe first and foremost,' he calls back, and they winch Tom up, and then Alice.

Tom is still unconscious. From the air ambulance, Alice watches, horrified, as flames leap into the night from Carruso's windows. She sees three fire engines racing to the scene from different directions, and a silent howl runs through her, knowing Noah is down there.

At the hospital, they whisk Tom away, and Alice is shown to a small, private room. She waits on another set of unforgiving plastic chairs, picking at her nails until the skin around them is red and sore. It seems she's destined to live within hospital walls.

She texts Trent while she waits. *Is Dad okay?*

No change here, he replies.

She drifts into a doze, and wakes with a start to find someone tapping her shoulder. A young female doctor stands in front of her, pushing her hands into deep white pockets.

'Hello there. Alice, isn't it? You came in with the Carrusos?'

'Yes.'

'Are you a relation?'

'I'm Noah's girlfriend.'

'I thought so. Okay, follow me.'

She jumps up and they hurry through the labyrinth of corridors.

'Don't be scared when you see him,' the doctor tells her as they go. 'It looks shocking at the moment, but most of the burns are superficial. He's got some second degree on his hands, arms and neck, and a nasty lump on his head where he's fallen and knocked himself out, but that's it, and thankfully he's escaped any damage to his lungs. It'll take some time, but he'll be okay.'

'And the others?' Alice asks.

The doctor looks away. 'I'm not sure – someone will be in to update you.'

Seeing Noah in the bed, Alice stifles a cry. His face is a strange grey pallor, and his neck, arms and hands are covered in bandages.

'He's been sedated while we treat him – he won't wake for a little while,' a nurse tells her, patting her shoulder.

Alice strokes the uncovered part of Noah's arm, trying to send strength to him, to let him know she's here. As nurses move carefully around her, checking his bandages, she gets glimpses of the red, raw, bubbling wounds on his hands and arms.

Minutes pass, ticking towards dawn, and Alice hears snatches of conversation. Murmurs that Noah might be a lot worse if his mother hadn't dragged him back from the fire. That Cathy is being treated somewhere else in the hospital for mild burns on her hands and severe shock. Tom is having surgery on his broken arm, but no one mentions Raf, and the nurses avoid her questions. She can't comprehend what's happened.

By the time there's a knock at the door, a weak, tentative light is changing the darkness to day. Two police officers enter the room: a middle-aged woman with a short blonde bob and a bald man with piercing blue eyes. They introduce themselves as Detective Sergeant Thorp and Detective Sergeant Davies, and begin to bombard her with questions. Most of them focus on Raf.

After a while, she asks if they can go to another room, nervous Noah might wake and overhear them. Once there, she tells them what she can. Raf was terse. Unwell. He seemed obsessed with the restaurant. They keep pushing her for more information, and her discomfort grows. She asks why they want to know all this, and they exchange glances, before telling her that Raf has passed away. They think he may have deliberately set himself alight.

Alice is dumbfounded, unable to make sense of what they're saying. They don't offer explanations, but continue to quiz her, until the doctor eventually saves her by poking her head round the door.

'Noah's awake – he's asking for you.'

She jumps up and rushes back down the corridor.

Noah is propped up in bed, and a nurse is helping him sip water through a straw. His eyes are pink and his cheeks are mottled red. As soon as he sees her, he gets tearful.

'Alice, thank god you're okay.' His voice is croaky.

She hurries to his side as the nurse exits discreetly. 'I'm fine. How are you feeling?'

'Pretty terrible. Where's Mum?'

'She's sedated. And Tom's had an operation on his arm. But Noah, the police are saying your dad –' She stops. Their theory is so absurd and cruel that she can't voice it.

'I know,' Noah murmurs, unable to look at her. 'I was there. Oh, Alice...' his voice wavers on each word, 'before he killed himself, he confessed to Lizzie's murder.'

'*What?*' Alice sinks into a nearby chair. There's a long, heavy silence, and tears roll down Noah's cheeks. Her heart breaks to see him like this.

'I was hoping it was just a terrible dream,' he sobs 'Dad... Tom... the restaurant...'

Alice stares at his bandaged hands, wishing she could hold them. 'I don't know what to say. I'm so sorry, Noah.'

Noah takes a few jerky breaths, and twists awkwardly in the bed to look at her. 'You've been incredible, but now I want you to go back to your dad.'

'I know, I will,' she answers, a catch in her throat as she stands up and strokes his hair. 'I just wanted to make sure you were okay...'

To her surprise, he moves away from her touch. 'Thanks – but there's only one thing you can do for me now.' His eyes are glistening, each word an obvious struggle. 'You have to look after yourself, okay? Which means you need to stay as far away from me and this horror show as you can.'

He turns towards the wall and closes his eyes.

39

For days, all Noah can think about is the smell of burning flesh, the searing pain in his hands, his mother's screams, and the burnt-out shell of the restaurant. And beneath all those things are the inescapable visions of Lizzie on the night she died.

People come to see him – Jez and Sophie, among others – their faces blanched with worry. He nods and shakes his head on cue as they talk, but it's like he's watching them from inside a bubble he doesn't know how to burst. The side of his neck feels like someone has held a boiling kettle against his ear. Sometimes he forgets his hands are injured and tries to pick something up, even though they are bandaged so heavily it looks like he's wearing a pair of white boxing gloves. But these things are temporary, and already beginning to heal. The turmoil in his mind, however, is only getting worse.

He hears that a few journalists have tried to get into his room, thwarted at the door. He begins to dread seeing a shadow across the entranceway. Once, as he dozes, he's sure he hears Rachel Lawrence's tinkling laugh.

Alice sends messages of love and support, asking if she can come and see him. Each time he thanks her, then asks her to stay away. He feels contaminated, as though his father's confession has infected him with something terminal. The only way he can protect her now is to keep her away.

Cathy comes on day three. Her face is bloated, and her arms and neck a pasty white, devoid of all jewellery. Her hands are bandaged like Noah's, and she bursts into tears when she sees him. 'I'm so sorry, Noah.'

'How are you feeling?' he asks as she sits down.

She shrugs. 'Hard to tell. Exhausted. Shaky. Confused. Mortified. I've been discharged, though I think I would have preferred to stay here.'

'Where are you going to stay? Have you gone home yet?'

'No, I can't face it alone. Ray's sister has offered me her holiday apartment for a few days. Most of the staff are being very kind, considering they haven't got jobs to go to.'

There's a long silence. 'I don't know how to begin to get through this,' Noah admits eventually.

'I don't either.' Tears stream down Cathy's cheeks. 'But we have to try. There's a new baby about to be born into this family, and it deserves a decent start.'

'I can't eat or sleep. I keep having nightmares.'

'Me too. I feel like the biggest fool. Utterly betrayed, and incredibly angry. We might not have had the most passionate marriage after the first few years, once you kids were born and we got so busy with work, but I thought that at least I knew who Raf was – and that we respected one another.'

'How much did you hear... the other night, when Dad... ?' He can't go on.

'Enough,' she says, her lips tightening. 'Enough to haunt me forever.'

After another weighty silence, Noah struggles to sit up. 'Have you seen Tom?'

'Yes – he's in a ward a couple of floors above. He seems to be over the concussion.' Cathy's eyes flicker towards the door, watching the nurses walking by. 'They say he was very lucky, after a fall from that height.' She glances down at her nails, then continues, 'So physically he's healing. But he's still in shock too. He's lived under this cloud for so long, and the person supposed to love and protect him has let him down in the worst way imaginable.'

'Can you tell him I'd like to see him?'

'I'll tell him.' She gets up. 'But give him some time, Noah, okay?'

There's a rock in Noah's stomach as he thinks of his brother. 'I've been terrible to him. I can't believe how much I've let him down.'

Cathy pauses at the foot of his bed. 'He hasn't been a great friend to you either. I just hope that now you both realise you don't have to be enemies forever.'

The police visit Noah often over the next few days, with more and more questions. It's exhausting, but he does his best to help. Through them and Cathy he hears of police searches on the old house, the new house, what's left of the restaurant, and finally the holiday home in the Blue Mountains, which is where they discover human remains under the decking.

When Sergeant Thorp solemnly informs him of this, Noah remembers sitting on the verandah with Alice, admiring the view. For the next few days he stops eating, and his fractured sleep is all nightmares. The nurses give him meds to help, and everyone seems to be watching him with the same intense concern. On day six, Cathy tells him that Tom has been discharged. Noah wonders if he'll visit, but Tom stays away.

After seven days, Noah is finally released from hospital with a wad of prescriptions. He can't face going home, and doesn't want to stay at Peter's, but Jez comes to his rescue, volunteering his spare room. Once there, Noah drifts through the days, sleeping much of the time, lost in the corners of his own life. His mind is a site of devastation, a burnt-out, smoking ruin. It's as though he's trapped in an invisible mesh that's slowly tightening, choking him. And the more he struggles, the tighter it gets.

He takes to wandering along the beach, letting the

monotonous shush of the sea lull him towards calm as he goes over and over everything that's happened. Each day he thinks of Alice, but she's stopped messaging as often, and he doesn't get in touch. She has enough to deal with. He won't cause her any more pain.

The days grow longer. And darker.

40

Alice's life is all about waiting. Waiting for her dad to wake up. Waiting for Noah to call. Trying to hold out hope for both, which gets harder every day, as the hours tick by and neither happens.

There'd been one attempt to bring Bobby round, but it hadn't worked. His heart rhythm had become erratic, and the doctors had immediately increased sedation while they stabilised him. She still has the leaflets for the Brain Injury Unit, given to her ten days ago, with the idea Bobby would soon be transferred there. But in the last week he's been tachycardic twice more, and no one talks about moving him now.

Meanwhile, Alice has steadily adjusted her expectations of each day, splitting her time between the hospital and a nearby hostel. If she can get some sleep, have a shower, help the nurses with menial tasks and keep her dad company for a few hours, then it's a productive day. Any other plans are impossible while her father's life is in limbo.

At least she's stopped worrying about the Reidy family. In the last month there's been no suggestion they want to toy with her life now she's home. She's beginning to believe that the threat died with Jason Reidy. Most of the time, she's not on high alert anymore.

She tries to keep in touch with Noah, but he doesn't always answer her messages, and when he does it's with only the minimum of detail. She grows exhausted from the effort, and decides to leave him alone for a while. Toni encourages her not to give up, but, really, any hope seems futile. Just as she feared, these unbearable circumstances have built a wall between them, and she doesn't know how to bring it down.

For a while, Lizzie Burdett is news. Alice hears via the media that Lizzie's body was eventually found at a house in the Blue Mountains. It turns her stomach to think she might have walked over Lizzie's unmarked grave.

Once the news reports die down, occasionally a podcast still pings up from Rachel Lawrence, announcing a new development or detail. It feels like the most distasteful kind of rubbernecking, but nevertheless, Alice always finds herself listening. When Rachel recaps the fire at Carruso's, Alice even gets a mention, as one of two women at the scene: *'One was treated for shock,'* Rachel reveals. *'The identity of the other woman is unknown.'*

Alice is grateful for that. She doesn't want Rachel getting so much as a sniff of her. The more she listens and hears, the more she grows frightened for Noah. He'd been deeply affected by Lizzie's disappearance, well before he knew the devastating truth. How will he ever recover from this?

Eventually, even Rachel has nothing left to say. *'With the investigation at a close,'* she announces on her final episode, *'my thoughts and prayers go out to the Burdett family, whose lives will forever be affected by the tragic and irreplaceable loss of Lizzie. I hope that now they have answers, they can find the strength to move on. This is Rachel Lawrence, and you have been listening to* The Disappearance of Lizzie Burdett.'

The signature music rises and then slowly fades out, leaving Alice listening to a few seconds of dead air. She's about to turn it off when Rachel's strident voice is back again. *'Are you ready for more Rachel Lawrence investigations? Coming in July, on season two: serial killer David Hutchins, and an unidentified body in the woods.'*

Alice shudders as she lays down her phone, glad to return

to the calm, controlled environment of the hospital. Do these fractured lives have any resonance for Rachel, she wonders, beyond the thrill of titillating her growing, voracious fanbase? Rachel might be moving on, but for Noah, Cathy, Tom, and the Burdett family, a new chapter of an old nightmare is only just beginning.

The wrap-up of Rachel's podcast seems to trigger a restlessness in Alice. Over the following days, she can't stop thinking of the conversation with Noah that she never had. She begins to dwell on it, weighing up whether she dare make herself more vulnerable, to help him feel less alone. His messages are so cursory now, giving her little to go on, but when she remembers how broken he had been in the hospital, she can't shake the feeling that she has to try.

She sends him a message: *I need to see you. Can I come?*
He responds a few hours later: *It's not a good time.*
It might never be the right time, she presses. *Where are you?*
There's another hour's delay before he writes back: *Jez's.*
Let me know the address, she replies straight away.

And to her relief, he does. She tells him she'll be there in the morning, and makes a hasty arrangement with Toni, to borrow her car while Toni takes over Bobby's bedside vigil.

The next day, once rush hour is over, Alice drives to North Curl Curl, to Jez's place. She marches up to the door and knocks, shifting her weight from one foot to the other as she waits.

Moments later there's a shadow behind the glass, and then Noah is standing in front of her. He's unshaven and gaunt, as though the pain has scooped him out and he's caving in from the inside. His hands are still bandaged, and his expression hovers between exhausted and wretched. He looks so much older than he had mere weeks ago.

'Hey Alice,' he says, and her heart twists at the gentle, familiar sound of his voice. God how she wants to jump into his arms, but he's so stiff that she hesitates.

'I need to talk to you,' she says. 'But not here. Can I drive you to the beach?'

'All right. I'll get my jacket.'

They hardly say anything until they're on the sand. It's quiet there, most people working on this mild winter's afternoon. They sit near the water, staring at the horizon. Noah draws his knees up and hugs them close, while Alice struggles to find the words to begin. He doesn't appear to register that she's nervous – in fact, he hardly seems aware that she's there.

'So,' she says eventually, 'your burns are healing.'

He looks curiously at his skin as though he hadn't noticed before, but doesn't reply.

'Please, Noah. How have you been? You can tell me the truth, you know. You don't need to hold back.'

'The truth?' he murmurs, his eyes drifting towards the sea again. 'The truth is I'm lost. I'm devastated. I'm ashamed. I'm constantly nauseous. I'm blundering through every day, not knowing what I'm doing.'

'It's understandable, after what you've been through.'

He turns and frowns at her, as though he hadn't expected that reaction. It seems to spur him on. 'Yeah. And you know what? Some people in the hospital thought I got these burns trying to save my dad. They praised me for it. But I wasn't trying to save him, I was trying to stop him. He was such a coward, dumping his deranged secrets on us and then bailing. I didn't want him to die, I wanted him to live so I could watch him suffer. So he'd have to face up to what he'd done.' His voice breaks as he talks. 'I wish he could see how he's left us – but then I doubt he'd care. He never noticed anyone else, did he? He made excuses and backed himself right to the end.' Noah lets out a growl of frustration. 'I have no idea how to start dealing with this. It's too much.'

She edges closer to him. 'Maybe start by doing what you have to do to survive. Day by day. Hour by hour. When you don't know what to do, just do something to keep going.'

As she speaks, the moment she's been dreading finally

arrives, hovering above them. If she doesn't do it now, it won't stay. She leans closer. 'Noah, I want to tell you something.'

Noah looks perplexed, but she has his full attention now. She digs her nails into her fists, bracing herself, willing herself on.

'I need to tell you properly about the night Jason Reidy died,' she whispers.

'Okay...' Noah still looks confused.

'Let me explain a few things first.' She takes a big breath. 'The day before it happened, Reidy turned up at Dad's work asking for money. It was shortly before Christmas, and I'd just got home for the holidays. Until then, we thought he'd got bored with harassing us – Dad hadn't seen him for weeks – but that day he was obviously on drugs, and blaming us for all his troubles. When Dad told him to get lost, Reidy asked how I was. Dad took this as provocation and threatened to kill him if he touched me. They were both shouting, so some of Dad's colleagues overheard and came to intervene, and as soon as he'd gone Dad got a lawyer to request the restraining order. But the next night, Reidy broke in.'

She pauses. It's painful to dredge up that evening yet again. If she closes her eyes she can see Reidy's malicious leer and dilated pupils. His drugged-up, distorted face.

'I could see the vicious gleam in his eyes straightaway. When I ran for the kitchen door, he caught up and shoved me against the countertop, grabbed a knife from the block and held it against my throat. His eyes were popping as he spat words into my face. "You think you can fuck with me?" he was saying. "You think you can tell me what I can or can't do? Where I can or can't go in my own fucking town?" He pressed the blade of the knife flat against my cheek, taunting me, the tip of it pointing at my eye... but then my Dad was charging down the stairs and flying across the room, shouting as he tried to pull Reidy away. They fell to the ground wrestling, and when Reidy's hand came up with the knife ready to strike, I saw Dad desperately trying to grab his arm, to push him away. Reidy slammed the knife down and it hit the floor, but he brought it back up again, and I thought Dad was about to get killed in front of me. I have never, ever felt so frightened.' She hesitates for a moment, trembling at the memory, bracing herself for what's yet to come. 'So I grabbed a kitchen knife.'

'Fuck, Alice!' Noah is obviously stunned. Through his astonishment she sees a glimpse of the old Noah – momentarily pulled from his own devastation into hers.

Bile rises in her throat as she remembers. 'I knew I only had seconds to do something. Dad was fighting hard, but Reidy was stronger, so I lunged at him and the knife went into the side of his neck, just above his shoulder.' Automatically, she rubs the same place on her own neck. 'It went in a long way, and came out with a horrible gush of blood. I screamed and dropped the knife, and Reidy jumped to his feet, clutching at his neck. He tried to come at me again, but the blood was already pouring out of him, and he staggered and fell to his knees... The blood... it was everywhere.' She stops and shivers. 'And then Dad grabbed the knife from the floor and stabbed him again.'

She stops talking. She can see Reidy on the floor, each exhalation a wet, rasping gurgle, the thick pool of blood spreading away from him. She'll never forget the accusation in his eyes as he looked up at them, while they stood over him, frozen with terror.

Noah is watching her with an expression of open horror. She steadies herself before she continues.

'He only thrashed for a moment, then he went silent and still. I kept screaming and Dad grabbed me and held me as my legs gave way. He moved me round so I couldn't see, even though it was way too late. He held my face to get my attention and said, "You didn't stab him, it was all me. He attacked you and I stabbed him – okay? Do you hear me?" He kept repeating himself, clutching at my face and my arms in a panic, trying to make sure I was listening to him. He kept on saying, "You didn't do this. Are you listening, Alice? It was only me." And I was nodding and crying and not really understanding why he was saying that, and weirdly I was so traumatised that I almost began to believe him, to think I'd imagined my part in it all. He said, "If you're not sure what to say when the police get here, tell them you don't remember. Let me explain what happened. He attacked you. So I stabbed him. Say it, Alice." And I began repeating, "You stabbed him, you stabbed him," crying my eyes out. Our neighbour charged in at that point, and that was the first thing he heard me saying. Soon after that, the police and ambulance were there and I was taken to hospital and treated for shock. I didn't see Dad again until the next day, when the police had finished questioning him.'

She lets out a long, shuddering sigh as she finishes the worst part of the story, but she knows she needs to keep going, to make sure Noah understands.

'At first it was seen as straightforward self-defence. But Reidy's family stirred up the media and the local police and they picked holes in Dad's story. The more questions they asked, the worse it sounded. Dad had been heard threatening to kill Reidy the day before. There were the two different stab wounds, and the prosecution went on about the angle of the second wound in his back – saying it was likely to have been inflicted while Reidy was on the floor – and therefore when he wasn't attacking us. We couldn't refute that, and they even cast doubt on whether he threatened me first, because both of the knives involved belonged to us, and only one of them was used on Reidy.' She pauses for a moment, staring towards the horizon.

'Eventually, Dad was charged with manslaughter. He was shaken when it got that far, but he always tried to put a positive spin on things when he spoke to me, and refused to change his story. He pleaded guilty, even though he could have fought it, and I'm sure he was trying to protect me then too. He knew I'd have to testify and lie again in court otherwise, and he felt the whole situation was his fault for prosecuting Reidy and Morris in the first place, and inviting their retribution into our lives. He said that if the worst happened, and he ended up in prison, then every day he would be able to cope by knowing I was out there, living my life, being free. He made me promise I'd always stick to the story, and never tell anyone my part in it. And I've kept that promise, until today. But it was me, Noah. The first wound was the fatal one.' She shudders and wraps her arms around herself, a sob catching in her throat. 'And it's been unbearable,' she adds, her voice finally breaking, 'living with the guilt of letting Dad take all the blame. I've asked myself a million times whether it was really the right thing – particularly now, after what's happened to him. But I can't go back and redo it.'

Noah is staring at her, speechless. She waits for him to react, but he seems lost for words. 'Say something,' she whispers eventually.

'Alice – that's... horrific. And I know why you're telling me this. I can see you're trying to help me. But my situation's not the same.'

'I know,' she says sadly. 'I realise there are lots of differences, but I've lived with secrets and trauma and guilt and shame, and I've wished I could turn back time. I don't want you to feel alone. I'm here, and I want to help you.'

'But Alice,' Noah's tone is mild but he won't look her in the eye. 'You did what you had to – to save yourselves – and then your dad put you first. He defended you and lied to set you free. But my dad was like Reidy, Alice. He was a monster. He trapped us with his lies and he didn't give a shit. That's what I'm descended from. That's the story I have to offer you. And now he's left me all his anger – that's his legacy – and every day I can feel it burning through me, leaving this dangerous dark hole in here.' He pats his chest. 'And the last time I lost my temper my brother nearly died. So while I'm like this I don't want you anywhere near me.' He jumps to his feet. 'Look, I'm sorry, I have to go.'

And he hurries away, leaving her crestfallen, alone on the sand.

41

The last day of June comes around: the anniversary of Lizzie's disappearance and death. In Sydney, the day will be marked by a big memorial service, followed by a private family ceremony finally laying Lizzie to rest. Most of the community will be in attendance, but not the Carrusos. They wouldn't be welcome, so they have made other plans.

Noah has been awake most of the night, dreading the day to come. Cathy arrives at Jez's at ten thirty, as agreed, waving to him from the driver's seat as he makes his way over to the car. In the back, Nadia smiles. Tom, however, just raises an eyebrow. It's the first time the brothers have seen each other since their fight, and Noah's not sure what to expect. Tom's left arm is still in a sling, and Noah spots it with a sharp stab of remorse.

He gets in beside his mother, and they set off. No one speaks, but it doesn't take long before they arrive in the car park beside the burned-out shell of Carruso's. The tension in the car is palpable.

Noah takes his time getting out, then follows his family through a small side gate into the outdoor area, where he and Tom had faced off a month ago. There's not much damage here, and the café blinds bang in the breeze. Noah resists the urge to retie them.

They stand together on the balcony, facing the ocean.

'Before we do this,' Noah says, 'Tom, I want to say how sorry I am. For everything.'

Tom gives him a long, hard look. Purses his lips and pats Noah on the shoulder. 'Thank you. I'm sorry too. Now let's get this done.'

Cathy walks forward. 'It was on this day twelve years ago,' she says to them, resting the urn on the railing for a moment, 'that I lost my husband and you both lost your dad. It just took us a very long time to find out.' She slowly tips the contents of the urn over the edge of the balcony and they watch silently as Raf's ashes float down towards the rocks, some of them catching in the breeze and heading straight out to sea.

As they troop back to the car, Noah takes one last look at Carruso's. It had been his as much as his dad's in the last few years. But not anymore. The place will be bulldozed, and the land sold off. He thinks of Sophie, Ray, Kevin and Stan, and the rest of their dedicated staff. Most have already found different jobs. Noah and Cathy will be honouring lost wages with whatever profit they get from the land sale.

'Bye,' he whispers to what's left of the steadfast guardian of the Carruso family fortunes, the silent witness to three generations of triumph, toil and heartbreak. He's not as emotional as he thought he'd be, but as he stares at the halfburned shell of the building, it's clear that the soul of the place has already departed. Its lifeblood had been the flow-through of staff and customers and family. Without them, there's little left to mourn.

Back in the car, Cathy drives them out of the city, heading west. The hardest part of the day is still to come, and no one talks much on the way. As they drive past Blacktown, Noah wonders what Alice is doing right now. And how her dad is. He'd sent her an apologetic text after her visit, explaining that he respected her honesty, but it had been too much to deal with. He wasn't himself at the moment, and he hoped she could forgive him.

She'd sent a short reply: *I understand. Take care of yourself, Noah.*

It had felt horribly like goodbye.

When they reach the mountains, they don't park at the house but at the start of a nearby track. They each collect bouquets of red and white roses from the boot of the car, and begin to walk along the path through the forest. Nadia and Tom have their arms around one another, and Noah thinks again of Alice, and how hopeful he'd been for them as they'd set off on their own walk near here a few weeks ago. Half of him stands firm in his decision to distance himself from her, but the other half harangues him daily, trying to change his mind.

When they reach the narrow dirt track that leads to the house, they go in single file. Noah braces himself before he looks up at their familiar holiday home. The building looks just as it always has, but police tape still flutters around the back yard, which isn't grassed anymore, but uneven piles of dirt.

Cathy begins to cry. 'Oh, I loved this place,' she wails. 'He didn't leave anything unspoiled for us, did he?'

Noah puts an arm around her as they stare at their home. Then Tom steps forward with the flowers in one hand.

'Lizzie,' he says, as though she is nearby, listening. And then he is racked with sobs and can't go on. Nadia goes across to comfort him.

Noah moves forward and lays his own wreath at a small tree towards the southern edge of the garden. 'Rest in peace, now, Lizzie,' he whispers. 'I'm so sorry this happened to you.'

The others step forward and do the same. Tom recovers himself and goes last, crouching on his haunches by the tree, speaking softly, while the others hang back waiting. When he turns around the tears are still streaming down his face.

Nadia wraps him in a hug. 'It's okay,' she says. 'You can let her go now.'

Noah catches Cathy's eye. She nods. One by one, they turn and walk away.

Back in Manly, they head to a small café near the beach, and Cathy goes to order drinks.

'So what are your plans now?' Noah asks Tom and Nadia.

'We'll go back to Broome in the morning,' Tom says. 'Mum seems keen to come and visit soon. Has she told you she's thinking of staying with us for a while and helping with the baby?'

Noah raises his eyebrows. 'No – but it sounds like her idea of heaven.'

Tom smiles. 'You're welcome too, you know – if you want? We could find out if I'm capable of being a decent big brother. Better late than never, hey. I'm gonna buy a boat, take the tourists out. You could come for a holiday. Might even be a business proposition there for you, if you're interested.'

For a moment, Noah just stares. Surely he's joking? Or does he really think that now Raf isn't around, Noah would be happy to work for Tom instead. 'The holiday sounds good,' he says eventually.

Cathy returns with the drinks, and the conversation moves on to other topics. Noah can't keep up, because he's deep in thought. It's tough to accept how much his family's expectations had bound him to a single path in life. Scary how much of his life had passed him by without him really thinking about it. He's not going to let that happen again. The others all seem to be making plans, and starting to move on. He can't live in his best friend's spare room forever, so where are Noah's dreams? How is he going to put himself back together, and decide what to do next?

He has a sudden urge to call Alice and talk it through, but he knows that it'll take time to repair his life and heal his wounds. As much as he misses her, he won't make her responsible for that.

'We'd better make tracks,' Tom says after a while, and everyone gets to their feet. Nadia embraces Noah. 'Remember you have a sister now too,' she says, smiling. 'And this baby will want to meet its uncle sooner rather than later.' She rubs her tummy lovingly, and Noah smiles back.

Tom offers Noah his uninjured hand to shake, then squeezes Noah's tender fingers hard. Noah winces. 'Oops. Sorry.' Tom grins. 'No hard feelings, okay? New start and all that.' Then he pulls his brother closer, speaking quietly, directly into his ear. 'And remember, Noah, you're free now.'

Noah steps back, surprised at Tom's fervent tone. For once he sees no guile in his brother's face, only concern. For a moment, Tom looks like someone Noah might want to get to know.

42

Bobby Pryce slips quietly from the world on a gloomy July morning, six weeks after the Carruso fire, and forty-eight hours after the doctors solemnly inform Alice that all brain activity has stopped. Alice holds his hand as they turn off the equipment, while Toni hovers close by.

Once Bobby has passed away, Toni and the medical staff leave the room. After months of bleeping, whirring machinery and footsteps in and out, after countless hours of the guards scraping back chairs or crackling food packaging, Alice and her father are surrounded by silence. Finally, dad and daughter are alone, and Alice can say everything she needs to.

She strokes his cool fingers as she talks, trying to etch his features into her memory. Without equipment taped onto him, or tubes snaking inside him, he looks peaceful. Much more like the dad she's always known. She tells him all the things she wishes they could have done differently, and how much she'll always love him. She thanks him for his love and protection, and promises to remember everything he's taught her. The dam that has built inside her for the past few months is finally broken. Her tears drip onto his arm.

Walking away from him, for the last time, is the hardest thing she's ever had to do.

* * *

Bobby's funeral takes place a few days later. There are more mourners than Alice expects, as old friends converge and re-emerge. Toni is a godsend, as usual, and Alice is grateful for the effort everyone puts in. Once it's over, she sleeps for the best part of a week.

She thinks of messaging Noah, but decides against it. If he's not ready to support her, it will only cause them more pain. Her heart hurts at the widening distance between them, but she understands it too. Noah's world has changed forever, and until he can find a way through his nightmares, there's nothing she can do.

She lies low for a few more weeks, tying up loose ends. Every day she secretly waits for Noah to get in touch, and is disappointed. When she realises what she's doing, she knows she can't put her life on hold anymore. As winter turns its final corner, heading for spring, she makes a decision.

Niran is delighted to hear from her. Yes, he says, there's still work at the school. They'd love her to come back. And also there's a letter waiting for her – it's been there for a while.

She asks him to open it. To take a photo of the contents and send it to her straight away.

When she sees the photo and reads what's written, she sobs until she's spent. But now she knows she's doing the right thing.

Two days later, she phones Noah, but he doesn't pick up. After the third try, she sends him a text instead.

'I wish things could have been different. It might have been the wrong time for us, but we made memories that will last forever. I'm leaving for Thailand tomorrow night. Please take care of yourself, Noah. I'll miss you. Love Alice x'

Over the next twenty-four hours, she checks her phone every few minutes as she packs. But Noah doesn't reply.

43

Noah fidgets nervously, unable to take his eyes off the double doors. He has been waiting by the gateway through to customs at Sydney Airport for nearly two hours. He's checked the flights to Thailand, and there is only one, but so far there's no sign of Alice. He prays he hasn't missed her somehow.

He's not here to stop her. He knows it's right that she's going and reclaiming her life. But he can't let her leave without saying goodbye.

He's getting desperate by the time he sees her, but he would recognise her anywhere: the slight figure and confident walk, her pale skin and sea-green eyes. She is moving quickly across the concourse, wearing a small backpack, her camera case slung over her shoulder. He calls out 'Alice!' so loudly that a few people look at him, staring curiously at the wounds on his neck and hands.

Alice turns.

Noah hesitates.

He had wondered if, when he saw her, his emotions would overwhelm him. He thought he might be tempted to do something stupid, like beg her to stay. But instead he experiences a welcome, unexpected peace.

She comes across and hugs him tight. She smells like flowers and fresh air.

'It's so good to see you. Are you all right?' she asks. 'I haven't got long. They're already calling my flight.'

'It's okay, I don't want to drag this out and make it painful, but I had to come. I want to thank you for trying to be there for me, and for your trust in everything you've told me. I'm sorry I can't... it's just...'

'It's okay.' She smiles sadly, her eyes glistening. 'I understand. It's not the right time.'

'My mind is all over the place, Alice, and until I'm sure I won't drag you down with me, I have nothing to give you. So, as much as it hurts, and believe me, it *hurts*' – his hand rubs his chest as though easing a pain – 'I have to let you go. You know, don't you, that the only reason I'll watch you walk through those doors is because I love you so much that I'll always protect you. Even from me.'

She brushes her tears away with her fingertips. 'And I love you for that. Thank you.' She gives him one last hug, and he makes himself let go. 'This won't get any easier, will it?' she says, her eyes still wet. She picks up her bag, and kisses his cheek. Bye, Noah.'

She begins to walk away.

'Alice,' he calls after her.

She turns back.

The look that passes between them only lasts a few seconds, but contains a thousand conversations: all their jokes and confessions, their struggles and their joy. All their hellos and goodbyes. She puts her fingers briefly against her lips as though blowing him a small kiss. *Bye*, she mouths. She smiles, and her gaze lingers on him for a second longer, then she turns again.

He watches her move out of sight, until she's gone.

He stares at the empty space. Breathing hard. Trying to see through tears. He flops onto a nearby chair, devastated he's let her go, but knowing he had to do it. He won't trap her in his misery. He needs to put himself back together first, to have any hope of being the person she deserves.

His phone pings, and he pulls it out of his pocket to see there's a message from Alice.

Look at this, she's written, beneath a photo attachment. *I only got it a few days ago.*

In the photo, there's a short letter stamped with an official prison logo that says 'Outgoing mail'. Noah begins to read.

> *Dear Alice,*
>
> *I just got your email, and thought I'd write back straight away, as I know this will take time to reach you. There's not too much to report here. I'm making good use of the library, doing my chores, keeping my head down, and counting the days.*
>
> *Thailand sounds terrific. I enjoyed your news – and there was a spark in your words, a new energy about you that is making me smile as I write this. Is it to do with your mention of Noah, I wonder? If so, then I look forward to shaking his hand.*
>
> *It does me good to know your heart is open. As long as you're loving and living life to the full, I have all I wish for, and I'm a happy man. I have no regrets, Alice, so don't ever look back. Remember, it's okay to be scared. Terrified, even. Just never let it stop you.*
>
> *I'll see you soon.*
> *Love always,*
> *Dad*

Just as Noah finishes reading, another message from Alice comes through.

One year from now. Kalymnos. I'll climb. You can swim. We'll both drink the raki.

Work through whatever you need to, because the world is waiting.

And so am I.

Alice x

Noah absorbs every word. Then he looks up, and smiles.

Acknowledgements

I'm incredibly fortunate to have the support of some stellar people, who make the hard parts of writing and publishing much easier, and who make the fun parts even more enjoyable. Roberta Ivers, thank you for digging in with me, for your honesty and insight, and for always pushing me further. I love the way we work together, and your support and encouragement over the past year has meant such a lot to me. Michelle Swainson, your editorial notes were brilliant and made all the difference to those final important tweaks, so thank you. Also thanks to Kylie Mason, whose astute comments really helped when reworking earlier drafts, and to Claire de Medici for the early insights into how to make the book better.

Tara Wynne – you are a diamond. Thank you for ten years of hard work and incredible support. You are a wonderful champion, and I'm grateful for everything you do.

Anna O'Grady, you are extremely talented and I love listening to you talk about books. Thank you for doing everything possible to get my novel out into the world. I'm so lucky that my work is in such safe hands with you.

To everyone at Simon & Schuster, I truly appreciate all your efforts. You make a very special publishing team, and I love being part of it all.

Natasha Lester and Dearbhla McTiernan, thank you so

much for all the support, for being prepared to look at drafts when your schedules are already packed, and for the incredible feedback, which never fails to make my writing better.

Shelley McEvoy, you are a gift to our family, and I'm so glad you came into my life. Thanks for all you do.

Mum, Ray, thank you for always being there to back me up and for your steadfast support. Likewise, to the Foster family, I love you all.

Matt, Hannah and Isabelle: you three are my world. Thanks for rallying around me when I'm on a deadline, and being patient when my head is in the clouds thinking about stories. Matt, thanks for reading umpteen drafts, listening to me waffle on about plot, coming up with ideas (and often letting me reject them!), and always managing to help me find the solution when I'm stuck – sometimes without even saying a word! Hannah – thank you for always being interested in what I'm writing, and for all your lovely little letters of support. Isabelle – I love that you ask so many questions about what I'm up to, and thanks for all the jewellery you make for me. And to both girls, it's great fun watching you get so excited when you see my books in the shops, especially when you try to coerce people into buying them! Thank you for being so proud of me – I'm incredibly proud of you too.

To all my family and friends, who always offer support in countless ways, I really appreciate it, and you all make a difference. Likewise, to the book buyers, booksellers, and book readers, thank you to every one of you for championing my books, whether you buy them, recommend them, or drop me a line. It literally keeps me going, and I'm grateful more than I can say.

Book Club Questions

1. What did you think had happened to Lizzie Burdett over the course of the story? How did the author play out the different tensions and possibilities?
2. Discuss Noah's role in the Carruso family. How sympathetic are you towards the situation he's in?
3. Alice could be seen as 'running away' from her problems. Do you think she was empowered by her decision to leave Australia?
4. How do you feel about the sibling relationship between Noah and Tom?
5. One of the strongest themes of the book is shame. Discuss how this plays out in the novel. How do the characters handle their feelings of shame? What might this mean for them in future?
6. The author chose to weave a podcast through the story. Why do you think she did this? Does it remind you of any true crime podcasts?
7. A lot of the criminal incidents are told in retrospect. Why do you think the author chose to tell the story this way? How does it affect the story?
8. What do you think Alice and Noah offer each other (or don't offer) in their relationship? How do you feel about them as a couple?
9. Noah didn't tell anyone about some of the events on the night Lizzie disappeared. Do you understand his reasons, or do you think he should have come forward? Likewise, do you understand Alice's reasons for keeping her own secrets?
10. What do you imagine the future holds for these characters?

If you enjoyed what you read,
don't keep it a secret.

Review the book online and tell
anyone who will listen.

Thanks for your support spreading
the word about Legend Press.

Follow us on Twitter
@legend_press

Follow us on Instagram
@legendpress